HAND of
ISIS

...nce, in a palace by the sea, there were three sisters born in
... the same year.

The eldest was born in the season of planting, when the
... Nile had receded once more and the land lay rich and fertile,
... muddy, and waiting for the sun to quicken everything to life.
... in one of the small rooms behind the Court of Birds, and her
... a servingwoman who cooked and cleaned, but who one day
... Ptolemy Auletes' eye. Her skin was honey, her eyes dark as the
... aters. Her name was Iras.

... and sister was born under the clear stars of winter, while the
... and grain ripened in the fields, when fig and peach trees
... in the starry night. She was born in a great bedchamber
... windows open to the sea, and five Greek physicians in attend-
... was the daughter of Ptolemy Auletes' queen, and her name
... ra.

... ngest sister was born as the earth died, as the stubble of the
... red in the fields beneath the scorching sun. She was born
... ntain in the Court of Birds, because her mother was a blond
... n Thrace, and that was where her pains took her. Water fell
... nd misted her upturned face. Her hair was the color of tar-
... e, and her eyes were blue as the endless Egyptian sky. Her
... armian.

... a palace by the sea, there were three sisters. All of the stories
begin so.

BY JO GRAHAM

Black Ships
Hand of Isis

HAND of ISIS

JO GRAHAM

www.orbitbooks.net

ORBIT

First published in Great Britain in 2009 by Orbit

A CIP catalogue record for this book
is available from the British Library.

ISBN 978-1-84149-700-6

Printed in the UK by CPI Mackays, Chatham, ME5 8TD

Papers used by Orbit are natural, renewable and recyclable
products sourced from well-managed forests and certified
in accordance with the rules of the Forest Stewardship Council.

Mixed Sources
Product group from well-managed
forests and other controlled sources
www.fsc.org   Cert no. SGS-COC-004081
© 1996 Forest Stewardship Council

Orbit
An imprint of
Little, Brown Book Group
100 Victoria Embankment
London EC4Y 0DY

An Hachette UK Company
www.hachette.co.uk

www.orbitbooks.net

For Amy

Rome
Ostia

MT. VESUVIUS
Neapolis

ITALY

SICILY

GREECE

Philippi

Pella

Aegean

Athens

Mediterranean

NUMIDIA

© 2008 Jeffrey L. Ward

Black Sea

Histria

Byzantium

Troy

Asia Minor

Ephesos
Miletus

Sea

Rhodes

Crete

Sea

Cyprus

Antioch

Syria

Berytus
Damascus

Middle
East

Jerusalem

Ashkelon

Gaza

Judea

Alexandria

Sais

Pelousion

Bubastis

Memphis

Egypt

Nile

to Abydos
and Thebes

THE HOUSE OF PTOLEMY

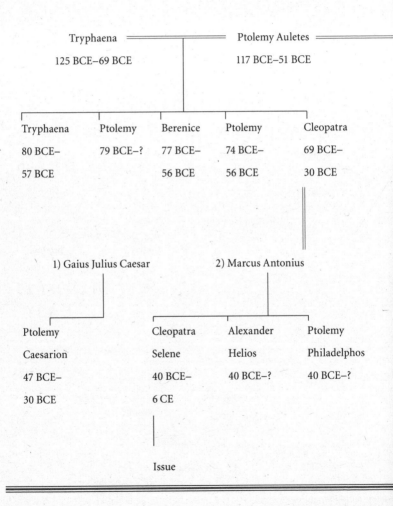

Tryphaena ═══════╤═══════ Ptolemy Auletes ═══════

125 BCE–69 BCE   117 BCE–51 BCE

Tryphaena	Ptolemy	Berenice	Ptolemy	Cleopatra
80 BCE–	79 BCE–?	77 BCE–	74 BCE–	69 BCE–
57 BCE		56 BCE	56 BCE	30 BCE

1) Gaius Julius Caesar   2) Marcus Antonius

Ptolemy	Cleopatra	Alexander	Ptolemy
Caesarion	Selene	Helios	Philadelphos
47 BCE–	40 BCE–	40 BCE–?	40 BCE–?
30 BCE	6 CE		

Issue

Cleopatra ══════ Phoebe the Thracian ══ Asetnefer

Arsinoe	Ptolemy	Ptolemy	Charmian		Iras
67 BCE–	Theodorus	60 BCE–	70 BCE–		69 BCE–
41 BCE	62 BCE–	44 BCE	30 BCE		30 BCE
	47 BCE				

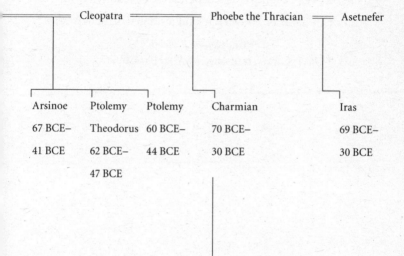

Demetria
47 BCE–?

Issue

The city of Alexandria is teacher, apex of Panhellenism
And in all fields of knowledge and all the arts the wisest.

— *The Glory of the Ptolemies,*
C. P. Cavafy, translated by Aliki Barnstone

◈ Amenti

In twilight I approached the doors, and in twilight they stood open for me. I was not surprised. I knew that I was dead.

I walked through the doors and through the hall beyond, pillars thick as the tallest trees carved round with symbols in red and gold, with stories of those who had walked this way before. Above the high capitals ornamented like lotus blossoms was not the star-painted ceiling one might expect, but the wide expanse of the night sky, blue-black and deep as eternity. I stood in the Halls of Amenti, the Uttermost West, and the sun did not come here. I walked in starlight.

Light glimmered at the end of the long hall. I walked among the pillars, my feet soundless on the stone floor. Shades make no noise, even in their sorrowing.

At last I came to the end of the hall, where the veil stretched between two pillars, and before it on a dais sat the thrones.

Serapis wore a robe of white. His gray hair was cut short and His eyes were as dark as the sky, an old man but hale, with a black hound sitting alert at His feet. Beside Him, Isis glimmered like the moon. Her gown was white as well, but Her dark hair was covered by a black veil, and beneath it Her face was pale and beautiful.

"Welcome to the Halls of Amenti, daughter," She said.

I knelt. "Gracious Ones," I said. To the side I saw the scales, Ma'at with a feather in Her hand, the golden balance waiting.

"You know what must be," He said, seeing where my gaze went.

I nodded, and moistened my lips. My heart should be measured against a feather to see whether the deeds of my life condemned or released me. I knew the formulas. Every child learns them. "Hear, Gracious Ones, how I have not offended. I have not done wrong. I have not robbed. I have not slain men. I have not spoken lies. I have not defrauded the gods...."

Isis raised Her hand, and it seemed for a moment that there was amusement in Her voice. "Well We can believe that you have memorized all of the words, Charmian. But when you stand before the Thrones of Amenti, it is not enough to have learned the words that should rest by your side on a sacred scroll. Your heart must be weighed on its own merits. You must be judged by your own deeds."

I looked at Ma'at, where She stood beside the scales with justice in Her hands, and I knew how heavy my heart must be. "Then condemn me now, Gracious Lady. I shall offer no defense." I felt the tears pricking behind my eyes, and all of the sorrow of these last days came rushing back. "I have no defense to offer, and readily accept whatever punishment you shall name."

"It is not that simple," Serapis said. "We are just, and do not condemn out of hand."

"Surely if the prisoner will offer no defense, the judge must convict," I said, and heard myself choke. Whatever should happen would be no greater than this pain that already was.

Her voice was calm. "In a human court, perhaps. But We are in no hurry. We shall wait for your testimony as long as it takes."

I bent my head and the tears overflowed my eyes. "I can give no defense, for I have failed in my charge. I have failed, and through my weakness have destroyed all those I love. I can make no excuses, now or ever."

Serapis put His hands together, like a philosopher in disputation. "I think perhaps you overestimate your own culpability. But We shall see, when your testimony is complete."

"I cannot do that, Gracious Lord," I said, and I could not even see His face through my tears, my hands pressed against the stone floor. "I beg You to condemn me. There is no punishment You could devise worse than what already is."

"We will wait," She said. "In time you will be ready to speak to Us."

I pressed my forehead to the floor, my hands in fists.

Above my head, I heard Him speak. "And yet while you are here, time runs true. Even the gods may not stop time. In the world, days and nights are passing."

"And what is that to me?" I asked bitterly. "There are none I love who still walk beneath the sun and moon."

"I do not think that is true," Isis said quietly. "Are there not those you love who have not yet crossed Death's threshold? In the world that is, time is passing for them, and things happen that cannot be amended."

"And what may I amend, dead as I am?" I asked. "There is nothing I can do for them, and You cannot persuade me that I am not really dead."

"No," She said. "You are dead. Even now your mummy lies in your tomb, preserved by the embalmer's art. Your life as Charmian has ended, and never again in that mask shall you walk under the sun. And yet your spirit endures."

"I should rather that it did not," I said. "When I have lost all, and when I can do nothing for those I have failed."

"You do not have the choice of that," Serapis said. I looked up at Him, and there was something in His face both familiar and serene, though a line of worry creased between His brows. "Your spirit is old, and you have endured much worse. But time runs true beneath the sun, and ships ply the seas homeward bound under the stars of heaven."

Ships… There had been something about ships, something in that last day… "The children," I whispered. "Oh, Gracious Lord, the children…"

"Even now they sail," Serapis said. "Horus and his brother, and the moon their sister. Even now, they are bound for Rome. And you sit here lamenting."

I knelt upon my knees, swaying before Their thrones. "Are You saying there is something I may yet do? Gracious Ones, if there is anything I may do at any cost…"

"There may be," She said. "But firstly your heart must be judged. You have come before the Thrones of Amenti, and what must be, must be. Speak true, and recall to yourself all that you have been, that We might test the weight of it."

"Then I shall begin, Gracious Lady," I said. And I stood up.

A CITY BY THE SEA

My mother was a Thracian slave girl who died when I was born, so I do not remember her. Doubtless I would have died too, as unwanted children will, had Iras' mother not intervened. Asetnefer was from Elephantine, where the Nile comes out of Nubia at the great gorges, and enters Egypt. Her own daughter was five months old when I was born, and she took me to her breast beside Iras, a pale scrap of a newborn beside my foster sister. She had attended at the birth, and took it hard when my mother died.

I do not know if they were exactly friends. I heard it said later that Pharaoh had often called for them together, liking the contrast between them, the beauty of my mother's golden hair against Asetnefer's ebony skin. Perhaps it was true, and perhaps not. Not every story told at court is true.

Whatever her reasons, Asetnefer nursed me as though I were a second child of her own, and she is the mother I remember, and Iras my twin. She had borne a son some years before Iras, but he had drowned when he was three years old, before my sister and I were born. It is this tragedy that colored our young lives more than anything else, I believe, though we did not mourn for him, having never known him. Asetnefer was careful with us. We should not play out of sight of people; we should not stray from her while she worked. She carried us both, one on each hip in a sling of cloth, Iras to the left and me to the right, until we grew too heavy and had to go on our feet like big children. She was freeborn, and there was doubtless some story of how she had come to be a slave in Alexandria by the sea, but I in my innocence never asked what it was.

And so the first thing I remember is this, the courtyards of the great palace at Alexandria, the slave quarters and the kitchens, the harbor and the market, and the Court of Birds where I was born. In the palace, as in all civilized places, the language of choice was Koine Greek, which educated people speak from one end of the world to the other, but in the slave quarters they spoke Egyptian. My eyes were the color of lapis, and my hair might glow bronze in the sun, but the amulet I wore about my neck was not that of Artemis, but a blue faience cat of Bastet.

In truth, that was not odd. There were golden-haired slaves from Epirus and the Black Sea, sharp Numidians and Sardinians, men from Greece fallen on hard times, mercenaries from Parthia and Italy. All the world met in Alexandria, and every language that is spoken was heard in her streets and in her slave quarters. A quarter of the people of the city were Jews, and it was said that there were more Jews in Alexandria than in Jerusalem. They had their own neighborhood, with shops and theaters and their own temples, but one could not even count the Jews who studied at the Museum and Library, or who taught there. A man might have a Greek name and blond hair, and yet keep the Jewish sabbath if it suited him. So it was of little importance that I looked Greek and acted Egyptian.

Iras, on the other hand, looked as Egyptian as possible and had the mind of a skeptic philosopher. From her earliest days she never ceased asking why. Why does the sea pile against the harbor mole? Why do the stars shine? What keeps us from flying off the ground? Her black hair lay smooth in the heavy braids that mine always escaped, and her skin was honey to my milk. We were as alike as night and day, parts of one thing, sides of the same coin.

The seas pile against the harbor mole because Isis set them to, and the stars are the distant fires of people camping in the sky. We could not fly because like young birds we had not learned yet, and when we did we should put off our bodies and our winged souls should cavort through the air, chasing and playing like swifts. The world was enchantment, and there should be no end to its magic, just as there was no end to the things that might hold Iras' curiosity. And that is who we were when we first met the Princess Cleopatra.

Knowing all that she became, it is often assumed that at that age she must have been willful and imperious. Nothing is further from the truth. To begin with, she was the fifth child and third daughter, and not reckoned of much account. Her mother was dead as well, and the new queen had already produced a fourth princess. There was little reason for anyone to take note of her, another Cleopatra in a dynasty full of them. I only noticed her because she was my age.

In fact, she was exactly between me and Iras in age, born under the stars of winter in the same year, and when I met her I did not know who she was.

IRAS AND I were five years old, and enjoying a rare moment of freedom. Someone had called Asetnefer away with some question or another, and Iras and I were left to play under the eyes of half the other slave women of the household in the Court of Birds. There was a fountain there, with worn mosaics of birds around the base, and we were playing a splashing game, in which one of us would leap in to throw water on the other, who would try to avoid being soaked, waiting her turn to splash the other. Running from a handful of cold water, I noticed a girl watching us with something of a wistful expression on her face. She had soft brown hair falling down her back, wide brown eyes that seemed almost round, smudged with sooty lashes. She was wearing a plain white chiton and girdle, and she was my height precisely. I smiled at her.

At that she came out from the shadow of the balcony above and asked if she could play.

"If you can run fast enough," Iras said.

"I can run," she said, her chin coming up. Faster than a snake, she dipped in a full handful of water and dashed it on Iras.

Iras squealed, and the game was off again, a three-way game of soaking with no rules.

It lasted until Asetnefer returned. She called us to task immediately, upbraiding us for having our clothes wet, and then she saw the other girl and her face changed.

"Princess," she said gravely, "you should not be here rather than in the Royal Nursery. They will be searching for you and worrying if you have come to harm."

Cleopatra shrugged. "They never notice if I'm gone," she said. "There is Arsinoe and the new baby, and no one cares what becomes of me." She met Asetnefer's eyes squarely, like a grown-up, and there was no self-pity in her voice. "Why can't I stay here and play? Nothing bad will happen to me here."

"Pharaoh your father will care if something happens to you," Asetnefer said. "Though it's true you are safe enough here." A frown came between her eyes, and she glanced from the princess to Iras, who stood taller by half a head, then to me with my head to the side.

A princess, I thought with some surprise. She doesn't seem like a goddess on earth. At least not like what I think a goddess should be.

"Has he not arranged for tutors for you?" Asetnefer asked. "You are too old for the nursery."

She shrugged again. "I guess he forgot," she said.

"Perhaps he will remember," Asetnefer said. "I will take you back to the nursery now, before anyone worries. Girls! Iras! Charmian! Put dry clothes on and behave until I get back."

SHE DID NOT RETURN until the afternoon had changed into the cool shades of evening, and the birds sang in the lemon trees. Night came by the time Iras and I curled up in our cubicle in one bed, the sharp smell of meat roasted with coriander drifting in through the curtain door. Iras went straight to sleep, as she often did, but I was restless. I untangled myself from Iras' sleepy weight, and went outside to sit with the women in the cool night air. Asetnefer sat alone by the fountain, her lovely head bent to the water as though something troubled her.

I came and stood beside her, saying nothing.

"You were born here," she said quietly, "on a night like this. A spring night, with the harvest coming in and all the land green, which is the gift of the Nile, the gift of Isis."

"I know," I said, having heard this story before, but not impatient with it.

"He is your father too," she said, and for a moment I did not know who she meant. "Ptolemy Auletes. Pharaoh. Just as he is Iras' father. You are sisters in blood and bone as well as milk sisters."

"I knew that too," I said, though I hadn't given much thought to my father. I had always known Iras was my real sister. To be told it as a great truth was no surprise.

"That makes her your sister too. Cleopatra. Born under the same stars, the scholars would say."

I digested this a minute. I supposed I didn't mind another sister. She had seemed like she could be as much fun as Iras, and if she was a goddess on earth, she was really a very small goddess.

"You will start lessons with her tomorrow," Asetnefer said. "You and Iras both. You will go to the palace library after breakfast." She looked at me sideways now, and I wondered what she saw. "Cleopatra is to have a tutor, and it is better if she has companions in her studies. She is too much alone, and her half-sister Arsinoe is barely two and much too young to begin reading and learning mathematics. You and Iras have been given to her to be her companions, to belong to her."

"Given by whom?" I asked.

"By your father," she said, "Pharaoh Ptolemy Auletes."

İf before I had learned what it was to be Egyptian, now I learned what it was to be a Ptolemy.

To be a Ptolemy was to be part of the longest and most successful ruling dynasty in the world. More than two hundred and fifty years before, Alexander the Great had died in Babylon, leaving the ashes of his empire to his generals and his unborn son. In the chaos that ensued, one Ptolemy son of Lagos had seized Egypt and held off all comers, crowned as Pharaoh by the old rites. Ruling from ancient Memphis and new Alexandria, queen of the seas, he built the greatest city in the world. It is true that Alexander himself set out the place for the city that bears his name, but he did not build it. Ptolemy did, and the men and women who came with him there from all over the world. It was he who set his stamp upon it, theaters and palaces, harbor and canals and sewers and docks and freshwater cisterns deep as three houses set into the earth, Egyptians and Macedonians and Jews and Nubians and all of the other peoples of the world in prosperity together under one king. Ptolemy son of Lagos was my grandfather's grandfather's grandfather's grandfather.

We learned that the first day, my sisters and I. We sat at the scrolls in the palace library around one table. Only Iras' feet touched the floor. On our three stools, our shoulders touched, Iras, Cleopatra, and me.

Apollodorus was a young man, with small children of his own, and came highly recommended from the Museum. He was also a well-rounded student of many arts in need of supplemental salary. The first scroll he laid before us was written by that same Ptolemy.

"This is his hand," Apollodorus said, unrolling it carefully. "Later we will work from a transcription, but you should see the original. This is what he wrote, and the paper he set his thoughts upon."

I looked at the writing, rendered spidery by two hundred years of fading. Or was his writing like that when he wrote it? He was an old man, eighty years old at the end of his life, when he wrote his memoirs.

Apollodorus took the ivory pointer, and showed us the words as he read. "'And it came to pass that Alexander saw a piece of fair land, between the sea and Lake Mareotis, where there was a village called Rhakotis. He turned to his architect, Dinocrates, and he said, "I shall build a city here and give it my name, for this harbor is unsurpassed and could hold a great many ships." And so it was done as Alexander decreed. But when the men came to lay the boundaries in chalk, there was no chalk remaining and none to be had, so they marked the boundaries out on the earth in grain. When this happened, a great flock of seabirds descended and the men hurried to lay out stakes and rope before the markings were obliterated. At this Callisthenes scowled, and said that it was an omen that the city would come to nothing. Alexander laughed, and said that rather it was an omen that men should flock here from all quarters of the earth. I leave it to my reader to determine whose prophecy was more accurate.'"

At this Cleopatra and Iras smiled and wanted words pointed out in the story. I was lost in the vision. I could see how it must have been, thousands of gulls descending and fighting, turning in the air, their wings beating together, and Alexander with his hat gone and his face red with sunburn, laughing. And Ptolemy impatient, ready to be gone, not knowing that this city would be his someday, that when Alexander was forty years in his grave he should write these spidery words on paper and remember.

Apollodorus looked at me. "Charmian? Can you point out words for me too?"

I hurried to do so. I wanted the word for birds.

APOLLODORUS WAS NOT A STRICT TEACHER, and I know now that he well understood how a young child's mind works, that there must be play and fascination rather than drudgery if there is to be real love of learning engendered. And if there was anything that was the birthright of a Ptolemy, it was learning.

When we were eight, and had learned to write ourselves, Apollodorus took us to the great Library. In that day it held more than seven hundred thousand scrolls, in five great buildings built to house them since the day that the second Ptolemy, Ptolemy Philadelphos, had decreed that the scholars of Alexandria should collect every book in the world that had ever been written, so that anyone who would study all mankind had ever achieved should find it in one place within these halls. The catalogs were nineteen hundred scrolls long. Separate buildings held different disciplines, different languages. All in all, Apollodorus told us, there were more than twenty written languages understood in the Library, and dozens more known where people had produced no books.

"What do they produce then?" Iras asked, her long black braids swinging against her neck as she looked up at the ranked rolls of scrolls that went nearly to the ceiling, daughter of a people that had produced books for three thousand years.

"Other things," Cleopatra said, standing free of us in the middle of the hall. "Grain and melons. Ships and tin and bronze and machines."

"You can't produce machines without books," Iras said.

"Stories," I said.

Apollodorus smiled. "Every people produces stories. And there are many stories written down here that are told by people who have never learned to write and have no symbols in their language. But they have told their stories to priests or scholars, and those stories are kept here too, because we never know when we may need their wisdom."

"You can produce machines without books," Cleopatra appealed to Apollodorus. "Can't you? An inclined plane is a machine, you said, and it doesn't take a book to see how that would work. Anyone with a brain can figure it out."

"An inclined plane is a simple machine," Apollodorus acknowledged. "Like a lever, a pulley, and a screw. And there are people who use simple machines without a written language. However, once you move beyond simple machines into something more mathematically complex like Archimedes' Screw, you need a symbolic language to perform calculations. So you are both right in a way. It's not books you need. It's math."

Which of course was another part of our study. By the time two years were past, I could do great columns of figures in my head, though Iras and Cleopatra were both faster and I did not enjoy it as they did. It was only interesting to me if it did something.

THE NEXT YEAR, Apollodorus deemed us old enough to take to the theater. We had seen scenes performed in the little palace theater, comic sketches put on for the court, and often acted in by amateurs who enjoyed that sort of thing, but at nine Apollodorus considered us old enough for Aeschylus. There was a production of *The Myrmidons* at the Theater of Ptolemy Soter, and so it was decided we should attend.

We left the palace fairly early in the morning, bringing with us our lunches, for we would eat in our seats at the inter-act.

There were seats in the front for the Royal Family, of course. Ptolemy Soter had built the theater, being a great patron of plays. It was said that Thettalos had played Alexandria in his last years, he who had been Alexander's player. I wondered if he had done the play we should see, and if whoever had the role now would be half as good.

We weren't sitting in the royal seats. One small legitimate daughter of Ptolemy, her handmaidens, and her tutor didn't rate the royal seats and the full pomp and ceremony Pharaoh did. Instead we spread our himations on the stone seats, which were still chilly from the morning air, halfway down the tiers facing the stage. Mine was green, Cleopatra's violet, and Iras' yellow. Cleopatra's was a finer material, but other than that you could not have told any difference. Apollodorus got out honey cakes, and we feasted under the clear blue sky of morning, chattering like little birds, and throwing the remains of our cakes to the finch that enterprisingly came to investigate us. He stood with his head to the side, his eyes evaluating, then hopped quickly toward me.

"He knows you've the softest touch," Cleopatra said.

"I am," I said, tossing him a crumb covered in sesame seeds.

As the theater began to fill, there was a rustle, and a boy descended the tiers above, jumping between people and leaping from seat to seat, like a bird himself. He landed beside Apollodorus, grinning. "Hello, Master Apollodorus," he said.

I looked up in surprise. He was a bit older than ourselves, eleven or twelve maybe, but still a boy, not a youth. His dark hair was neatly cut and trimmed, and his chiton was good, worked material with a border, but he somehow managed to look unkempt for all that.

"I saw you down here," he said, "and thought I'd see if anything interesting was happening."

"Hello, Dion," Apollodorus said mildly. "Run off from your tutor again?"

Dion winced. "Recitation," he said. "Nothing new. Just the same lines from the *Odyssey* until I could do them in my sleep. Thought I'd find something different to do with my day."

"I could tell your father, you know," Apollodorus said.

"You won't." The boy gave him a sideways smile. "Not when I'm the most brilliant mathematician you've ever seen."

"I never meant that for your hearing," Apollodorus said, but he smiled too. "Stand up straight now, and let me introduce the young ladies. Charmian, Iras, Cleopatra, this is Dion. He's the son of a friend of mine at the Museum, and a hopeless scapegrace."

"Hello," said Cleopatra politely. Iras and I said nothing, somewhat annoyed at this boy barging into our long-awaited special day.

"Hello," Dion said, and plopped down on the seats on the other side of Apollodorus. He leaned across him. "Have you seen the play before?"

"Not this one," Iras said quickly, forestalling my comment that I had never seen a play. She spoke strict truth, but gave him no room for superiority.

"They do the gods with the crane here," Dion said. "They don't do it in every theater. Lots of them use the god walk above the stage instead. But this one even has fire effects for evening shows. It's really impressive in *The Furies*. I saw that last spring. Lots of people get ripped apart on stage too, and there's a big sword fight and then the rain comes down and..."

He was prevented from giving us a complete description of the effects of every play he'd ever seen by the beginning of the play. I don't, frankly, remember what I thought of it. *The Myrmidons* is not one of my favorite plays, and I have seen it half a dozen times since. Or perhaps the thing that was most memorable was Dion.

He was never quiet. All through the play he kept up a running commentary on how this effect and that effect was achieved, critiquing with knowing eyes the workings of the crane and the sets, the thunder effect that announced the death of Patroclus. I got the brunt of it, as I was sitting next to him. I wanted to slap him.

As soon as the play ended, Cleopatra gathered her himation about her shoulders, though the day was warm. "It's been very nice," she said, sounding like the best possible imitation of Asetnefer. "But we had best be going now."

We made our way up the tiers and out of the theater into the busy street, Dion sticking to us like a burr. "Athena's my favorite," he said. "Though she never gets lowered out of the sky. It's usually Hermes. One time one of his lines snapped. They wear several, you know, so they won't fall. Anyway, one of them broke and he descended from the clouds almost upside down. Everybody laughed."

I was trying to visualize that when I heard a roaring sound. Around us, the crowd was scattering, people going one way and another, trying to dash back inside the theater portico, or into one of the shops on the opposite side of the street.

Up the main street came a huge mob, fighting and shouting, waving sticks and screaming for blood. One was waving something that might have been a man's arm, blood dripping down his chiton. They were screaming and yelling.

Apollodorus grabbed Iras' hand, as she was closest. "Hold hands!" he shouted. "Hold hands and get back!"

Iras grabbed Cleopatra's hand, and Cleopatra mine. Dion grabbed my other hand just as the mob broke over us like a wave, pushing us before them with shoppers, theatergoers, and anyone who happened to be in the streets, running to stay ahead of the crowd.

My new green himation fell from my shoulders. I saw it trampled underfoot as the crowd surged forward. Cleopatra screamed as someone shoved her hard, but she stayed upright, caught between Iras' hand and mine. And then we were all pushed together, the mob surging around a corner.

Dion was pressed up against my back so tightly I could feel his heart pounding. It gave me some comfort to know he was as frightened as I was.

"Hold hands!" Apollodorus shouted again. "Don't let go!" I couldn't see him in the press. Everyone else was bigger than me. If I fell, they would step on me.

"To their gates! Impious ones!" a man shouted almost in my ear. "Killers! Impious ones!"

I had no idea who had done what impiety. I wished we could push our way into one of the shops, but the shopkeepers who could had bolted their doors and closed their shutters. A vegetable seller who hadn't been able to stood pressed against his own door, shouting imprecations while his stock was trod underfoot, ripe melons sending up a heady fragrance into the air, mixed with the smell of fear and blood. As I watched, one of the rioters picked up a melon and threw it at him. "Oh, shut up," he yelled. "Roman lover!"

"What has happened?" I shouted to the world at large, Dion's elbows in my ribs.

"A Roman killed a cat." One of the rioters looked at me, no doubt an honest drover or workman. "He killed a cat for sport and then went and hid in their ambassador's house when he was caught. So we're going to burn him out."

"A cat?" I gaped. I couldn't imagine who could be so stupid as to kill a cat, thereby calling down Isis' wrath upon himself.

"We're going to break down the gates and light the Roman embassy on fire," he said, "if they won't turn him over to Pharaoh's justice. Romans think they can go anywhere and do anything, and that we'll all just roll over and kiss their pricks. Er..." He stopped, embarrassed no doubt to have used such rude language in front of a well-brought-up girl. Even with my hair falling from its pins, there was no mistaking my Koine or my dress.

The crowd shoved us apart, splitting where the Canopic Way divided and the crowd must take one of two smaller streets toward their goal.

Two large men shoved in opposite directions, half-crushing Cleopatra between them. My hand was numb in hers, and I heard her struggling to get her breath. The bones in my fingers ground together.

And then she was free, shooting out like a cork bobbing up in water, staggering against me and Dion. She and Iras had let go.

COMPANION'S OATH

Dazed, the three of us clung together in front of a potter's stall. Fragments of household pottery littered the street where vessels had been broken by the mob. Only the biggest pots were untouched, the tall ones half my size meant for storing lentils or beans. Above us, the red and white awning hung from its poles. The door to the shop behind us was closed.

Cleopatra tried it, and Dion joined her, shoving with his elbow, while the mob still pressed us tighter and tighter. Too many people were trying to fit into the square, or were carried there by the pressure of the crowd with nowhere to go. The door didn't open. The shopkeeper had barred it. It was only a matter of time, I thought, before we were separated, or crushed beneath the press of feet.

A woman shoved Dion, and he staggered back against one of the pots and nearly fell.

I seized his arm. He had filth all over his chiton from something someone was throwing. I had to shout for him to hear me. "Up!" I said, pointing at the awning.

The poles were only meant to hold cloth, and would never take the weight of a full-grown man, but we were three children. Above the awning was a second story, windows with the shutters closed, but there was a ladder to the roof. Doubtless the shopkeeper lived above his shop.

Dion followed my eyes, and I saw he took my meaning instantly. He grabbed Cleopatra. "I can boost you up!" he shouted.

She nodded, hitching up her skirts. Dion lifted her, and she got her belly over the pole. He gave her a shove, and she got one foot on the bar, reached up, and grabbed the awning where it fastened at the top. Luckily, it was good sturdy canvas. She hauled herself up, then looked about, judging the distance to the bottom of the ladder. The toe of one sandal found purchase, but the other didn't, and she kicked the sandal free. Without it, her toes wrapped around the bar, and she stood, stretching. It took a second to get the ladder, and she was up.

"Now you," Dion said.

Over the din of the crowd, we heard trumpets, and the wild whinnies of horses. Pharaoh had sent out troops to control the riot. They were fighting into the square, blue headdresses above the fray, laying about with the flats of their swords. People were screaming and trying to get out of the way, but there was nowhere to go.

I kicked off my sandals and put my foot in Dion's hands. He boosted me up. I clung to the bar, and I don't think I would have been able to get to my feet if my sister had not reached for me. "I've got you," she said, leaning down from the ladder that was fixed to the wall by the shuttered windows. "It's not far. Come on."

The cavalry was trying to sweep toward us. Of course they would protect Cleopatra with their lives if they knew who she was, but there was no chance to explain.

I seized her hand, and nearly fell. The skirt of my long chiton caught on a nail, and I heard it rip as Cleopatra pulled me as hard as she could. I grabbed the ladder.

"Climb!" Dion yelled. Nearby, a man went down beneath one of the plunging horses. We saw his blood on the stones of the street, the horse dancing to avoid stepping on him.

Cleopatra started climbing above me, and I hung three rungs below. Dion swung himself up onto the bar as nimbly as an acrobat, barefooted and sure. That was all I needed to see. I started climbing after my sister, thinking irrelevantly that she had one shoe on, and that Asetnefer would be furious at us for losing them. Our sandals were good leather and expensive.

We clambered onto the roof, and dropped over the low railing.

There were some floor mats up there and a few cushions. The shop-keeper's family must use this as a cool place to sit or sleep on hideously hot nights. Many people did that, because you could catch the ocean breeze. I lay on a faded red cushion, trying to get my breath back.

Dion clambered over the rail and skidded to a stop on a mat. His eyes were wide.

Cleopatra was sitting cross-legged, her arms behind her and her face to the sky, taking deep breaths.

"Everybody all right?" Dion asked.

I nodded. I wasn't sure I could talk yet.

Below there was clamor and screaming. We didn't look.

At last Cleopatra said, "What happened?"

"A Roman killed a cat," I answered. "That's what a man said to me."

"Who would kill a cat?" she asked. It was as much a rhetorical question for her as for me.

Dion looked solemn. "Someone who doesn't know. There are lots of people who don't, in other countries."

"If they come here, you'd think they'd learn," she said. "It's stupid to go somewhere and wander around offending their gods and people."

"He was Roman," I said.

Dion snorted. "Which means he didn't care." We looked at him, and he went on. "That's what my father says. He says the Romans don't care anything for the customs of other people, and that they don't even want other people to worship their own gods. That the worst thing that can happen to a people is to come under Roman rule."

"Why would you care who your subjects worship?" Cleopatra said practically. "As long as they pay their taxes and don't rebel? I mean, most people worship Isis and Serapis at least some, but if they don't it's not like there's anything bad that happens to them."

"Like the Jews," I said, thinking of the most prominent group that didn't worship Isis and Serapis. Jews had been in Alexandria forever, but there never had been any kind of problem with them.

Dion nodded. He looked very serious. "Since Rome annexed Judea four years ago, lots and lots more Jews have come to Alexandria. Haven't you noticed?"

I hadn't, but didn't say so. I didn't know a huge amount about Judea, truth to tell, though of course I knew about Queen Salome, who had only died seven years before and had been the most powerful queen in generations. Since her death, her country had fallen into all kinds of disarray.

"The Roman Pompeius Magnus even went into the Temple, into the Holy of Holies," Dion said. "It was his way of showing that he could do whatever he wanted."

That was serious, I thought. Almost all temples had an inner sanctum, where no one but priests were allowed. It was horribly blasphemous for anyone else to go in, and it certainly would never have occurred to Auletes to do it, even in the temples of our own gods. And it's always a bad idea to offend other people's gods. You never knew what might happen.

Cleopatra must have been thinking the same thing. "What happened?" she asked.

Dion shrugged. "Jews hate Pompeius. And lots and lots have come to Alexandria since then, bringing their money and their crafts."

"And so their economy is hurt and ours benefits," Cleopatra said with satisfaction, her question answered. "My father would never do any such thing, and people know it."

"They do," Dion said. He gave her a smile. "And neither would you, if you were queen."

"I wouldn't," she said seriously. "But I'm not going to be queen. I have two older sisters, and my father says that when the time comes I will be married to someone advantageous."

"Maybe even in Judea," Dion said. "Queen Salome's grandsons are in Rome and might be made kings—you never know. One of them would make a good husband for you."

Cleopatra considered, her head to the side. I did too. If she married a foreign prince, in Judea or wherever, we should go with her as her handmaidens, Iras and I. I didn't think I would mind Judea. Jerusalem or Ashkelon were not the ends of the earth.

"I wonder where Iras is," I said.

Cleopatra sat up straight, and Dion crawled over to the edge of the roof. "I don't know," he said.

"I couldn't hold on," my sister said. Her brow furrowed. "I'm sorry. I couldn't hold on even though Apollodorus told us to."

"He's probably with Iras," I said. "I thought they got pushed that way in the crowd, back toward the Palace Quarter."

"Apollodorus is a lot bigger than us, and he pushes better," Cleopatra said.

"Then they're probably fine," Dion said cheerfully. "Apollodorus could look after Iras. They're probably worried about you."

No doubt, I thought. Apollodorus was probably frantic. He had no way of knowing where we were, or if we were safe. Here we were on somebody's roof, with no shoes, and a riot between us and the palace. The last thing we wanted to do was wade back into that, especially with the troops out, and I said as much.

Dion nodded, looking at Cleopatra's white feet, one in a sandal, one bare. "We can't go too far," he said. "We could go to my house. It's not a long way, and my mother will know what to do. She might be able to send a slave to Apollodorus, or when my father comes home he could take you back to the palace."

That seemed reasonable to us. After all, Apollodorus had said that he knew Dion's father because he worked at the Museum, so he must be a trustworthy person.

Dion had told the truth that his house was not far away. Though I had never been in this part of the city before, I knew we were in the neighborhoods south and east of the Soma, because I could see the Soma's dome occasionally over the rooftops. The houses were fairly large, with courtyard gates on the street, and trees and vines just visible over the walls. Most of them didn't have shops on the ground floor, except on corners, where there might be a larger apartment building with rooms above. Even those looked nice, I thought, with communal courtyards and awnings on the balconies, a couch or two put out where people might catch the sea breezes.

Dion's house was one of the freestanding ones on a quiet street. There was an old slave watching by the courtyard door, doubtless because of the riot. He looked dismayed when he saw Dion. Or maybe it was the state of Dion's chiton, and the fact he was barefooted.

"Nothing to worry about, Eucherios," Dion said breezily as we limped past him. "Is my mother home? I've rescued some young ladies who are in need of refreshment." He didn't wait for an answer, just guided us past the slave and into the courtyard.

I looked about with satisfaction. It was nothing like the palace, of course, but the courtyard was almost completely shaded by two massive terebinth trees and a weeping almond. There were three couches arranged in a semicircle on the flagstones beneath them, a mosaic table with geometric patterns set by, and the tripod for a krater. On summer nights, it must be a lovely place for a dinner party. The garden was beautiful. Oddly enough, though, there were no statues.

"Mother!" Dion called, motioning us to follow after. "Mother? I was in a riot, but I'm fine!"

At this a woman came hurrying from the back of the house, dusting off her hands on her skirts. She was older than I expected, with gray streaking her dark hair, but the shape of her face and her laughing eyes were the same as Dion's. "You were what?"

"In a riot," Dion explained.

"Dion was very brave," Cleopatra said helpfully. "I'm sure we would have been killed if it weren't for him."

His mother seemed to be hiding a smile, something one did around Dion frequently, I thought. "Come and sit down, girls," she said. "I'm sure you'd like some water, and to get the filth of the streets off your feet." She gave Dion a look that said more clearly than words: I'll deal with you later, young man.

"And some more lunch," Dion supplied helpfully. His mother glared at him and he shrugged. "I would hate for the Princess Cleopatra to think our hospitality is lacking."

"The what?"

Now if looks could have killed, it would have been Cleopatra laying

Dion out. "I'm Cleopatra," she said. "Apollodorus' student. My father is Ptolemy Auletes. And this is my handmaiden Charmian." She gave Dion's mother her best smile. "Please don't distress yourself on my account. We are already beholden to your family for the great service Dion has done us."

Dion stood up a little straighter, as though anticipating that he'd gotten out of the caning he richly deserved for running off from his tutor.

His mother shook her head. "I'm sure Dion gave perfect satisfaction." She called for a slave to come wash our feet, and another to bring fruit and fresh bread and cheese.

I was hungrier than I thought, and sat beside my sister nibbling apricots on one of the seats in the public room overlooking the garden. It was nice and cool, though the day was getting quite warm, and the terebinth trees gave off a pleasant, resinous scent.

Dion chattered on about this and that, while Cleopatra nodded. My chiton was a mess. There was a long tear down the side where it had caught on the nail, and it was streaked with various stains. Asetnefer would be none too pleased either. I supposed mothers were like that. But for now, it was wonderful to have someone wash my torn feet with cool water, and to eat apricots somewhere safe.

Cleopatra looked at Dion seriously. "You did save my life, you know."

He stopped in mid-gesture.

"I want you to know," she said, "that you have the eternal gratitude of the House of Ptolemy. I shall never forget what you have done for me, and if ever I may repay you, I shall."

It was well spoken, and what a princess should say, but even I could see that it was incongruous from a nine-year-old girl to a boy in a dirty chiton. Still, Dion knelt before her like her true companion.

"Gracious Lady," he said, "I am at your service. Always."

IN AN HOUR OR SO, Dion's father came home. He was heavy-set and about fifty, with a gray beard and a very serious way about him. I should have been intimidated, had he not seemed to share his son's good humor. By now we had learned that Dion was the youngest child of parents long married, and that he had three older sisters and an older brother who had long since had children of his own. Dion was the only one still a child, since his next oldest sister was fourteen and had recently moved to her betrothed's house to live with him and his parents until the wedding was celebrated.

He glanced back and forth between me and Cleopatra. "So which of you is the princess?"

It hadn't occurred to me that it wasn't obvious; we were two girls the same age and same height, with the same look of the Ptolemies about us, and wearing equally disheveled clothes. My hair was lighter than hers, and my eyes were blue instead of brown, but unless one were looking carefully, one wouldn't know if one had never met the princess before.

"I am," Cleopatra said, getting to her feet.

"Apollodorus will be half-mad looking for you," he said. "I'll take you back myself. They're bringing the litter now."

"Thank you," she said.

"Do you teach at the Museum?" I asked.

He nodded. "Mathematics. I lecture in the applied sciences as well, mostly hydraulic engineering." Used to Dion, he assumed we quite understood what hydraulic engineering was. Something to do with irrigation, I thought.

"Would you teach me?" Cleopatra asked.

He blinked. "Hydraulic engineering?"

"Hebrew," she said. Cleopatra glanced at me, and I knew she was thinking of the princes of Judea we'd discussed on the roof. "After all, who knows whom I might marry, or where I might go?" It would be better for her if she spoke the language of her husband's people. Better for us too, if we were to accompany her. It would be very hard to manage her household in a country where neither Iras nor I spoke the language.

Dion's father blinked again. With his gray hair and beard, and white robe, he had the look of an overstuffed owl, I thought. A very nice overstuffed owl. "I'm not really a teacher of Hebrew," he said. "Nor do I think you need a rabbi, just to learn to converse. You could learn as well from anyone. And you should learn Aramaic, the language as it is spoken, not the Hebrew of the Law."

"I'll teach you," Dion volunteered, leaping off the couch.

Cleopatra gave him a measuring look. "You would do nicely."

Dion stood straighter. "See, Papa? My first student!"

His father laughed. "If it is agreeable to Apollodorus, I see no reason why you can't join the young ladies' lessons occasionally and teach them conversational Aramaic."

Dion's mother made a noise in her throat.

His father turned to her. "Can't do the boy any harm, can it, Mariamne, to have a taste of patronage at the palace?"

It certainly couldn't. One thing I had amply learned from Apollodorus was that the Library and all of the lectures and schools surrounding it ran on money granted from wealthy patrons, and the wealthiest and most generous funder of research was the House of Ptolemy. Some Pharaohs gave to music and the arts, some to the sciences, some to literature and drama in greatest measure, but all of them gave to the great Library, and their patronage was by far the most stable. Grant money from a princess could make a young man's career.

"Please?" Dion asked, appealing to his mother.

She shook her head. "I suppose." She gave him a raking glance that took him in from his lost shoes to his wild hair. "You're more trouble than the other four children put together."

⊙ UR RETURN TO the palace was anticlimactic. Apollodorus was still out looking for us, and nobody yet knew we were missing. We'd had our dinners before Dion's family slave found him, and he came back gray with anxiety. If something had happened to Cleopatra, no doubt he would have been killed in a gruesome way.

We sat in the bath, Cleopatra and I, telling Iras all that had transpired. All that had happened to her was that she had been dragged around town by Apollodorus all afternoon, getting increasingly frantic. She had a few tart words to say about Dion taking us where nobody would know to look for us. And a few more when Cleopatra told her about the Aramaic lessons.

"I don't see any need for it," Iras sniffed. "Not with that impossible boy. He's not a proper teacher. I'm going to find something else to study when he comes."

"What if I marry one of the Jewish princes?" Cleopatra asked. "And we all go to Jerusalem together?"

"There are plenty of people who speak Greek in Jerusalem," Iras said. "It's a perfectly civilized place."

"You don't have to if you don't want to," Cleopatra said, taking the sponge and running it over her legs. The three of us fit the bath perfectly, and never minded sharing. "The thing that's awful is that Apollodorus says I can't go out of the palace on foot ever again. He says that I can't go without a litter and guardsmen now, because something might happen to me."

"Ouch," I said, examining one of the alabaster jars of hair treatments on the ledge beside the bath. It smelled wonderfully of roses. I poured some into my palm. "No more plays? No more markets? No more just going about with Apollodorus and seeing interesting things?"

"I'll never see anything interesting again with a dozen guards hovering around me," Cleopatra said.

I scooped the roses into my hair and started scrubbing. "That's true," I said. Our legs looked alike in the water. Iras' were longer and her skin darker, but then she had brown eyes like Cleopatra.

An idea struck. I ducked my head to wash out the suds, then dashed the water out of my eyes. "What about me and Iras?" I asked.

"It doesn't matter about you and Iras," Cleopatra said despondently. "You can go and do whatever you like. It's only me that's stuck."

Iras caught my eye. "Are you thinking what I'm thinking?" she asked.

"I think so," I said. Sometimes we were so alike it was uncanny. "So as long as you stay here, we can go out."

"That's what I just said," Cleopatra said.

"Then as long as one of us stays here, the other two can go," Iras said. She leaned back against the tile wall of the bath. "Most of the guards don't know us well enough to tell us apart, especially if we wear our himations modestly over our heads."

"If you wear my clothes, and pretend to be me..."

"Or me," Iras said.

"...then you can go out," I finished triumphantly.

"We can take turns," Iras said.

"It will never work," she said. But it would. Oh, it would.

"We could try it," Iras said.

And that is how The Game was born.

IN THE HOUSE
OF PHARAOH

A setnefer had kept us close when we were children, but as we grew older, Iras and I had more freedom to come and go. Oh, the whole of the city was not ours, and we dared not run from Apollodorus and roam as Dion did, but when our studies were done we could go about the palace and the grounds, the park and the Royal Cemetery. We could even go down to the palace docks, where merchants with special licenses were allowed to bring goods for sale to the inhabitants of the Palace Quarter.

The palace was not the only thing in the Palace Quarter, not by far. Many nobles maintained houses there, some grand enough to have their own walls and gardens, their own orchards of sweet fruit, and little pavilions hidden among the trees where dinners and revels might be held. And of course there was the park and the tombs.

When the city was built, two hundred years ago, the cemetery had been outside of town, but the city had grown up around it. It was parkland, now, with trees and pleasant walks, fountains playing in the sun. White mausoleums and the entrances to tombs were scattered about, some with plain markers, and some with more grand ones. Beneath it all was the city of the dead. The catacombs stretched beneath the entire park, connecting some tombs and not others in a vast unmappable net.

Since the incident of the riot, Cleopatra had to stay in the palace unless escorted. Apollodorus was inflexible on this. No doubt he was simply green with fear at what might have happened, but we thought it wildly unfair.

Our world was remarkably safe. Yes, of course there was Pharaoh Ptolemy Auletes, our father and our master, but we saw him once every six months, and he did not enter our world. Our world, the world of the palace, was the world of women. Pharaoh might speak to his Major Domo about something, who would in turn speak to a eunuch, who might speak to the chief housekeeper, or to Asetnefer. They would then assign tasks, rewards, and blame. The authorities of our life were women, with the exception of put-upon Apollodorus. We did not know, yet, that there were sterner masters. Our greatest challenge lay in The Game.

The Game was this: The three of us should go together into Cleopatra's rooms, talking loudly and being seen, our himations about our shoulders. Then once we were alone, Cleopatra would change clothes with either Iras or me. We took turns. Dressed anew, two of us would take our leave of "Cleopatra," the same himations draped about our heads. The one who waited would settle down in Cleopatra's rooms to read. The other would explore the palace with her sister.

It was a wonder to us how easy it was. People see what they expect to see. We were three little girls of the same age, and there was a resemblance between us. Iras was taller, and we had to be careful lest that be marked, and my eyes were the wrong shade, but that should pass except for close inspection. Differences in skin color are difficult to see in semidarkness, and could to some extent be remedied with the cosmetics we experimented with lavishly.

Language was more difficult. The palace, like the city, relied upon Koine Greek for most public business, but outside of the corridors of power native Egyptian was still the language of the people. Proclamations and such were generally done in both languages.

Iras and I had learned both together from babyhood, as both were spoken in the slave quarters. At first it drove Cleopatra wild that Iras and I could converse in front of her in a tongue unintelligible to her, but that didn't last long. With the facility of a child, it was not long before she spoke the native language too, and could sound like me if she wished.

Thus the three of us had many innocent adventures, and thought ourselves daring as any hero of old.

I HAVE HEARD IT SAID that everyone longs for some lost paradise, some golden age, which is really no more than the state of things in infancy, a half-forgotten nursery where nothing ill ever happened. I have had that. My golden age was in the palace by the sea, with Aset-nefer and Apollodorus and my sisters. But of course that ended. We do not stay children forever.

I expect that in due course of time Cleopatra would have married. Perhaps it would have been one of the Jewish princes, as we had discussed, or perhaps some scion of the royal families of Numidia or Pontus. It would not have been one of her brothers, not with two sisters her elder. While the Ptolemies marry their kin in the Egyptian fashion, it's only Pharaoh who does so. The third daughter is for making alliances with, not for making queen. Even when the eldest of her brothers died, it was of little account in these plans. Her second brother should follow Ptolemy Auletes on the throne, matched with her eldest sister, Tryphaena, or with the second, Berenice.

If I have said little of these other sisters, it is because I knew them very little. Both had their own households before I joined Cleopatra's. Tryphaena was eleven years Cleopatra's senior, and Berenice eight, so they were great ladies of the court while we were in the schoolroom.

Arsinoe was the sister we knew. Three years younger than we were, she was the daughter of Ptolemy by his second queen, and had two little full brothers. The three of them had a separate nursery to themselves, with an extensive household staff, five tutors, a physician, a teacher of rhetoric from Athens, and a great deal else. But Ptolemy's second queen cared little enough for the children of his first, and least of all for a third daughter who was the heir to nothing. It was quite enough to allow Cleopatra to amuse herself with her studies until she could be married off to the advantage of the dynasty.

It had never occurred to us that if she were to marry elsewhere in the great wide world, she might go to a husband who did not think that wives should enjoy the freedom of women in Alexandria. We should have been shocked had we known that in Athens respectable women did not go about unveiled in public, and that in most places in the world there were no women who pled cases in courts of law, or who studied medicine in the Temple of Asclepius. Only in the Hellenized east were these things true, in the kingdoms of the Successors that followed after Alexander, of which Egypt was chief. We lived in the freest place the world had ever known, and we did not understand at all but took it entirely for granted.

All of that changed when we were eleven.

For more than a hundred years, the Ptolemies had held the island of Cyprus as part of the empire. Now it was lost to the Romans.

I understood little of the politics at the time, but we all understood the mobs in the streets, tearing their hair and casting their cloaks over their heads, wailing, "Cyprus is lost! We have lost Cyprus!" Worse was what they did not cry, but muttered together on corners. "Cyprus is lost, and Ptolemy Auletes did not lift a finger to save that land which belongs to us. See how our fleet sits in the harbor still? He would not send a single ship to defend Cyprus against the Romans!"

It angered me, for I had always thought of my father as a good ruler. Perhaps he looked nothing like the fine carvings of kings on the walls of the Serapeum, being instead fifty and somewhat stout, with round smooth-shaven baby cheeks and rather less hair than desirable, but looks are not the measure of a man. They are absolutely not the measure of a king. Ptolemy Auletes was no Alexander, but I had taken a certain pride that he was a good king, and a tolerably fair man, at least as fair as a ruler may be.

I decided to ask Asetnefer. It was true that she was not a scholar, but she heard a great deal as she went about her work, and knew everything worth knowing in the royal household. Moreover, she was not the least afraid of Pharaoh.

After Cleopatra had gone to bed, I waited until Iras was also asleep in the small chamber off the Court of Birds that we shared. Then I went in search of Asetnefer.

She was sitting with some other women around the fountain, enjoying the cool of the evening, and the end of the day's work. I came and stood beside her.

"Still awake, little cat?" she asked me, the pet name of my childhood. "Can't you sleep?"

"No," I said. "Will you talk to me?"

She came with me and we sat under the stars, listening to all of the insects of the night. "What's the matter?"

I lowered my voice. "Why did Pharaoh lose Cyprus?"

Perhaps she had expected some trouble of the heart, not politics, or the news that I had begun my woman's blood. I was eleven, after all, and Iras had bled first of us the month before.

"I know it's difficult," I said. "But I truly want to know."

"Mind you, I am no diplomat or soldier."

"I know," I said.

She lowered her voice. "We lost Cyprus because we could not keep it. If we had sent ships, they would have been defeated. The Romans had too many ships, and all we should have done was to provoke war with them." Asetnefer leaned back, and I could see her profile against the stars, elegant and fine. "These are not the ancient days, when the Black Land could stand against all of the kingdoms of the earth, or even the days of the first Ptolemies. No kingdom can stand against Rome, so Ptolemy Auletes tries to walk a careful course, being the friend and ally of Rome while maintaining our independence. If he had gone to war with Rome over Cyprus, we should lose, and Egypt would become one more province."

Her words were bitter in my ears. "Can it be that there is no way to win?"

Asetnefer shrugged. "Not without some second Alexander. And how often is one such born?"

"If he were born," I heard myself say, "why should he be born to the House of the Ptolemies? There is all the world to stretch beneath his feet, and there are more lands than this, which do not await him like a bride the bridegroom." The stars were very bright, Sothis rising in the darkness. "The Black Land knows her lover, and will welcome him as she did at Siwah."

"Sometimes you say the oddest things," Asetnefer said.

"I do," I said, but I was learning not to.

APOLLODORUS WAS VERY STERN about this—the mark of an educated person was a rational mind. In ages past, people believed that the Nile rose and fell by the will of the gods, that sickness came because of evil spirits, that everything that happened was blessing or curse. Now we knew better. The Nile rises and falls because of the rains in Africa, far to the south. Sickness comes because of filth or bad water, and things happen because science provides explanations. To believe in prophecy or the intervention of the divine was no more than sloppy thinking.

Once, when I told the other girls of some dream I had that came true, Apollodorus frowned. "If you say things like that, people will think you are no more than another silly superstitious woman. I am training you to be rulers, the three of you, royal Ptolemies conversant with philosophy and able to hold your own with any man in the world. If you believe in prophetic dreams and other nonsense, you are no better than the most ignorant old woman in the market."

I turned deep red, and felt a shame so acute that I shook. I had not told him the half of what I dreamed.

It was Cleopatra who came to my rescue. "But Apollodorus, why is it wrong to tell of dreams if they do come true? Charmian dreams true all the time, about small things. What harm can it do?"

Apollodorus was grave, and his eyes strayed to Iras. "There are many in the world who do not think that women or people who are not born Greek are capable of learning, who will look down on you because you are female, or because Iras' skin is too dark and Charmian's too fair, who will say that they are both barbarians. If you descend to silliness and womanly superstition, you lower the regard of all women and all people of your bloods. You merely confirm the worst prejudices—that women are stupider than men and more prone to error, and that barbarians cannot learn science and rational thought." His eyes fell on me again, concerned. "Do you not understand that when you talk of these things, Charmian, you harm all women?"

"No," I said very softly. I felt the tears starting behind my eyes. "I didn't know that."

"You would not want to do so, I know," he said kindly. "You are young, and some of these superstitions are entertaining. But you are an example. If, with your education, you are frivolous, you provide men with reasons why women should not attend lectures at the Museum, or should not publish books. You must do twice as well as a boy so that opportunities will not be denied to other girls because of your behavior."

"I will not speak of it again, Master Apollodorus," I promised, blinking back tears. I could not cry without piling further disgrace on my sex. So I did not.

Yet it did not escape me that Cleopatra still looked rebellious, though she said nothing.

After that, I did not dream so much, and they were not half so clear. Perhaps they had never meant anything at all.

THERE HAD BEEN RIOTS in the city when the news from Cyprus came, but now there were rumors and counter-rumors, stories that Ptolemy had been paid off by Pompeius Magnus not to intervene in Cyprus.

At our lessons, we could hear the shouts as a dull and distant roar beyond the wall that encircled the Palace Quarter. Apollodorus had slept in the palace the night before; he did not dare leave and try to walk through the streets to his house. All night the mobs had been camped before the gates.

"Don't worry, girls," he told us. "Pharaoh has soldiers on every gate, and people will get tired of shouting soon and go home."

They didn't. The next night there were fires in the city, and none of the slaves would leave the Palace Quarter on any business after a man who was sent on an errand was set upon and beaten. Our lessons were quiet and tense.

"It's because of the bad harvest," Cleopatra said. "The flood was low last year, and the harvest poor. If the flood is good, things will change."

Already the flood was late. Each year the Nile rises at the appointed time, in more or less accord with the heliacal rising of Sothis. It may be a few days more or less, but until the river begins to rise, everyone must wait. The flood comes pouring down the cataracts from the mountains far to the south of Nubia and Kush, bringing life-giving sediment to our fields. Alexandria is on the sea, and served by the canal to Lake Mareotis rather than the river, but the Nile is the blood of Egypt. We waited to see if the river would rise.

Because of the messengers, we knew one day before the people. The river was rising, but again the flood was short. Great stretches of fields escaped the Inundation, lying baked in the sun. Even with all of the floodgates open, even with each sluice and barrier wide, the flood was too little. It was the day the Queen and her children took ship to Rhodes. Everyone bustled about the palace, slaves and courtiers alike. On the afternoon tide the great ship sailed from the palace harbor, carrying the Queen, her two small boys, and Arsinoe away.

Iras and I looked at one another, watching the ship making for the breakwater, her mighty oars moving in unison. Another ship was being prepared by the docks.

"Do you suppose it is for us?" I asked.

"Not likely," Cleopatra said. "I expect it's for my older brother." Ptolemy would want to keep the heir to the throne safe.

Cleopatra should have been sent with the younger children, but the Queen did not want her, and we hardly expected Pharaoh to remember. After all, she was no more than a piece in the marriage game, a third daughter of little account.

"Will Tryphaena and Berenice go?" I wondered aloud.

"I doubt it," Iras said. "They will not want to." Which was true. They were twenty-two and nineteen, and had factions of their own at court. "Where does the ship go?"

"Rome," Cleopatra said, and I looked at her, startled.

She shrugged. "I know no more than you," she said. "But where else would it go? My father has risked the peace of his land to keep faith with Pompeius Magnus. Who else should he appeal to for aid?"

Iras looked glum. "We should not have to owe them anything."

"I know," Cleopatra said.

"Maybe we will go with him," I said. I was curious. I wanted to see this city across the sea that was the source of so much strife, much as a moth wants to see the flame of a lamp, not knowing what flame is.

It was Ptolemy who took ship with his heir, Pharaoh himself stealing away at night with portable valuables, bound for Rome and his ally. We did not know he was gone until morning, waiting in the half-deserted palace like an afterthought, left to the mob.

Cleopatra clenched her lips, and looked toward the window, toward the harbor where the ship's sails were fast disappearing around the breakwater toward Pharos.

I put my arm around her. I had not thought that Auletes loved me. "Are you very hurt?" I asked.

"I'm angry," she said. "That's all." Her shoulders were unyielding under my arm, and I moved it. "It doesn't hurt at all."

Iras, more wisely, said nothing, but she shared a look with me behind our sister's back.

"We won't leave," I said. "We'll never leave you."

Apollodorus burst in. "Are you ready?" He had a cloak about him, though the day was warm.

"Ready for what?" Cleopatra got to her feet, her long chiton pooling gracefully in a way mine never did.

The Jewish Quarter, I thought. If worst came to worst, Dion would hide us. We could go into the city unremarked as always. Dion would help us. We could wait until the fury of the mob was past.

"There is a ship to take you to Pelousion. Get your things."

"Tryphaena," Iras said. While I had been thinking of ways to survive, she was parsing out the politics of it. Tryphaena would declare herself queen. And what she might do with a younger sister she barely knew was an open question. House arrest, probably. But murder is tidy, and not unknown in the House of the Ptolemies.

"Pelousion?" Cleopatra said.

"Pelousion is fortified and loyal to Pharaoh. Come on!" Apollodorus urged. "Come, Cleopatra."

We sailed at sunset, under a leaden sky. Clouds had come in off the sea, and the variable winds hindered our passage. We beat out to sea on oars only, around the massive breakwaters. The sun slipped toward the sea, and Pharos kindled, bright flame flashing out over the waves, brighter than the dying sun, fire from heaven.

I stood beside the rail, Iras next to me, looking back. The waves lifted us and the ship swayed strongly in the currents around the islands, but it seemed a familiar kind of movement, more pleasant than frightening. I had only to look at Iras to know she was thinking the same thing.

My himation blew in the wind behind me. Something touched me, soft as a prayer, as the quiet part in the hymns to Isis when one waits, wondering if one imagined that one heard the music begin, or just anticipated it. The roofs of the city to the west were blue against the sunset, a haze of cooking smoke over the lands of people. A sadness took my heart.

"Do you think we will come back here?" I asked Iras.

"Of course we will," she said softly, not in her usual tones. "We will all come back here together. You'll see."

I had no certainty of my own, and this one time I was content to rest upon Iras'.

CATS AND SNAKES

e arrived in Pelousion at night, after an uneventful voyage of a few days, and we did not stay long. Pelousion stands at the easternmost point of the Delta, where the farthest branch of the Nile flows into the sea and the coast begins to curve northward toward Gaza. While it is not so large a city as Alexandria, the greatest city in the world, Pelousion is of fair size.

It was there that we heard that Tryphaena had been proclaimed Queen in Alexandria, and that a Seleucid prince was on his way from Syria to marry her. Auletes, it was said, had been tepidly received in Rome, and he had not been allowed to address the Senate.

It seemed that the governor of Pelousion was also interested in walking a fine line between Auletes and Tryphaena, and was eager to have the Princess Cleopatra off his hands. It was only a few weeks before he gravely informed Apollodorus that he could not guarantee her safety in Pelousion, given the uncertain times, and that he advised her to seek sanctuary in one of the temples of the Delta.

I don't know how Bubastis was decided upon. Perhaps Tryphaena cared little where this much younger sister went, as long as it was nowhere she could raise a faction. Perhaps she thought it wise to keep Cleopatra as a pawn, just in case. Or perhaps Tryphaena had nothing to do with it, and the estimable governor simply wanted us gone. In any case, it was decided that we should sail up the branch of the Nile that watered Pelousion, and go to the Temple of Bastet at Bubastis, there to stay for some indeterminate amount of time, perhaps forever. Should Tryphaena hold her throne and produce sons and daughters of her own, this sister would be well disposed of at the temple.

And so we came then to Bubastis, not knowing if we should ever leave.

Alexandria and Pelousion were Greek cities, modern cities laid out according to principles of geometry and urban planning, part of the great world that looked on the Middle Sea. Bubastis belonged to the Black Land.

Bubastis was old, older than it is almost possible to imagine. The first stones had been laid more than two thousand years before, and it had been the holy city of the Goddess Bastet for as long as anyone could remember.

Bubastis was also hot. It wasn't the sea-cooled heat of Alexandria, but the heat of the Delta, humid and thick. The river ran slowly there, with snags and bars, and it twisted about, joining and rejoining in many channels as it made its way to the sea, creating tiny islands of reeds and palms. Waterbirds called in the dawn, great white ibis standing solemnly to let our ships pass. Occasionally, a hippopotamus would rear its head. I had not thought there were any still living so close to the abodes of men, and perhaps there were not on the Saite branch of the Nile, near Alexandria. But we were far to the east, and much farther south.

Fishermen poled along in little woven boats, looking like the pictures on the walls of temples. In the dawn, the river steamed, clouds of vapor lifting in the morning air.

The ship left us, the captain making time upriver, and Apollodorus, Iras, Cleopatra, and I entered together. It was just the four of us. We had left Alexandria with few servants, and they had stayed in Pelousion. Now it was just us.

We waited in the outer courtyard of the temple, for we had arrived during the morning services, when the Adoratrice and her priests were busy with the rites of Bastet. I looked uneasily at Cleopatra.

She sat down on the base of one of the columns, her feet and sandals dusty from the street. Apollodorus shifted about. "This is what it is," she said, looking around. Above, the courtyard was open to the sky, the color shifting to the opal of another stifling hot day. Under the pylons that marked the Inner Court, a lean tomcat stretched and settled down to wash, watching us with green eyes. "We'd better get used to it."

The great columns were painted like trees, their capitals surmounted with palm fronds opening wide, their bases carved with stories. The massive pylons at the entrance to the Inner Court showed a Pharaoh in a starched linen skirt presenting gifts to Isis and Bastet, while Sekhmet stood behind him, her head that of a lioness.

Iras took a step toward it. She read hieroglyphics better than I.

"Who's the Pharaoh?" I asked.

"'Osorkon Usermaatre, Great is the Soul of Ra,'" she read. "Only eight hundred years ago." She pointed. "There's his cartouche, there. I think he rebuilt the temple after somebody damaged it in one of the wars then. There's a story all along here."

"Read it to me," I said, coming closer. I could get some words, but not all of it.

Iras looked up the wall. "It says that he dedicates this wall in the twenty-second year of his reign, he and his wife Karomama, may their souls endure forever. That he has restored the worship of the gods and that he has followed the way of Ma'at in all things. He has restored the temples in Memphis as well, and has brought the sacred archives to safety. Over here he's being presented to Bastet," Iras said. "And he's got the uraeus on his brow now, and he's blessed by cat and snake."

"By cat and snake?" I said.

"By cat and snake," said a voice behind me. I spun round to see an elderly lady standing beside Apollodorus. At least I thought she was elderly. Her face was wrinkled, but her hair was completely black, hanging in heavy plaits around her head, each plait tied with gold wire and ending in green malachite beads. "But then I should not expect a Greek princess to understand. I imagine you have interpreters for that sort of thing," she said in perfect Koine.

I flinched, half in surprise and half in confusion.

She was only a little taller than we were, but she seemed tall as the sky. "I am the Adoratrice. I understand that you seek sanctuary here."

I opened my mouth and then shut it. I was the fairest of the three, and had been talking to Iras. She had taken me for Cleopatra.

Apollodorus spoke before we needed to. "Gracious Lady," he said, "Pharaoh Ptolemy Auletes asks the Temple of Bastet for sanctuary for his daughter in this uncertain time."

The Adoratrice snorted, and continued in her perfect Greek: "Ptolemy Auletes is not here, and I doubt he asked any such thing. But it is just as well you ask in his name, rather than that of Queen Tryphaena, as she is dead."

Cleopatra gasped. Iras and I did not move.

The Adoratrice shot Cleopatra a dirty look. "Your handmaiden is unschooled, Princess," she said to me. "Such gulping is unseemly. Tryphaena is dead. Killed by Princess Berenice, it is said."

Spots of color showed on Cleopatra's cheekbones, and though her voice was cool, it shook. "It is true I am unschooled as a handmaiden," she said, "for I am Princess Cleopatra. Such strife between my sisters saddens me."

The Adoratrice transferred her gaze. Cleopatra looked less a princess at the moment, seeming younger and sallower. "It is unlikely there shall be further strife between your sisters, Princess, unless you have other sisters. Berenice has proclaimed herself Queen of Egypt, and Auletes waits in Rome for Pompeius Magnus to give him crumbs from his table. Why should you be welcome in Bubastis?"

Apollodorus moved to speak, but Cleopatra forestalled him. "I have no faction," she said. "And yet I may be of use to someone. Would you throw away out of hand a weapon that may prove useful, simply because you have no use for it at the moment?"

The Adoratrice looked at her keenly. "You are a very minor playing piece."

"But not entirely inconsequential," Cleopatra said, meeting her eyes.

"I shall not conceal your presence here from the Queen," the Adoratrice said, and I let out a breath I had not been aware I was holding.

"My sister Berenice and I are on the best of terms," Cleopatra said serenely.

OUR ROOMS FACED one of the smaller courts, with windows and doors only on the courtyard side. The rooms backed up to one of the chapels along the side wall of the Sanctuary of Bastet. There was a small chamber for Cleopatra with a good couch, table, and chest, and a somewhat heavy and sprung couch in the antechamber for Iras and me. Apollodorus must sleep elsewhere with the male priests.

One of the temple slaves brought in an armload of linens and put them on the outer couch.

"Aren't you going to make up the beds?" Cleopatra asked.

The girl blinked at her. "You have slaves of your own. It's their job to wait on you. You'll take your meals with the Adoratrice, but anything else you need, like your tiring and laundry, is up to them. That's what you have slaves for, isn't it?" She gave a very scanty bow and went out.

Iras and I looked at each other. Neither of us had made up a bed in our lives.

I picked up a handful of bed linens, my face scarlet. "Then we'd best get started." The largest piece must be the undersheet.

Cleopatra hesitated, then plucked at one sheet. "I suppose we can figure it out."

Iras snatched it from her. "We are not sunk so low as that! If it is necessity, let us make a pride of it. No one will touch your things except for us. Charmian and I can perfectly well learn to serve you as well as anyone. Better." She grabbed up a load of linens and started sorting them out.

I followed. The long thin ones must be the curtains for Cleopatra's window. I had seen the rod and clips in her room. By dragging the table over, I could stand on it and fix the curtains in the clips. I sweated and swore, balancing on the table, wishing I were taller, while Iras made up the bed.

Cleopatra hovered about, picking up one thing and then another. At last she said, a little sadly, "I have never thought of you as slaves."

Tears filled my eyes, and I came down off the table and threw my arms around her. She bent her face against my shoulder. "I want to go home," she whispered.

After a moment, Iras came and put her arms around us both, her long braided hair against my neck. "So do I," she said.

"We'll be the best handmaidens anyone has ever seen," I said, a tear running down my nose and splashing on my sister's shoulder. "There will never have been a princess in the world waited on like you. People will be amazed by us. You'll see."

THUS WE BEGAN a new life. Each day Cleopatra rose at dawn to begin the Morning Offices with the temple's acolytes. Male and female alike, they tended the statues in the sanctuaries, flinging wide the doors and sweetening the air with incense, bathing the statues of Bastet and all who shared Her temple, the statues of Nepthys and Horus in the side chapels, the old-fashioned statue of Isis Pelagia raised by Ramses III long ago in gratitude for his victory over the Sea People.

The morning hymns were sung. Iras and I were expected to join the others in the Inner Court and sing, and to join the temple servants in bringing the ritual meals to be blessed, that the gods might break their fast—bread and honey, melons dripping with moisture, fresh-drawn milk, fish or olives, and sometimes the flesh of a duck or a kid that had been dedicated for sacrifice. We carried them in all solemnity to the doors of the sanctuary or chapel, and handed them to the priests who waited within.

Since this was the Temple of Bastet, we were usually joined by a throng of Her sacred animals. Each morning, twenty or thirty cats would appear, ambling out of the shadows or flashing down from the rooftops, twining around our ankles adding their song to ours. Meowing, they leaped onto the altars. The milk and fish and duck did not last long, though they turned up their noses at the honey. Some of them, smaller kittens who could not yet jump up to the main altars, waited mewing on the floor while their mothers claimed a choice bit of duck entrails for them and dragged it down.

Needless to say, after the Morning Offices were completed, the next thing was to mop and clean the chapels entirely, getting the remains of the meal off the floor. Every last spot of blood and milk and honey must be scrubbed away by the temple servants, which in this case included Iras and me, while the Adoratrice, the priests, and Cleopatra retired to the dining room for their own breakfast, the Morning Offices having taken some two and a half hours after the sun rose. I hated this part of it, for the main statue of Bastet was not the common kind where she is shown as a smooth, sleek cat, but rather a seated queen with a cat's head, the pediment completely covered with incised carving, perfect for getting tiny bits into where they should have to be scrubbed out.

When the temple and chapels were sparkling, the dining hall was cleared of the priests' breakfast and the tables were laid again for ours. By this time the sun was high, and my stomach was invariably growling. The food was good and plain, fresh bread, honey, eggs, and milk and there was plenty of it. Still, breakfast was an ordeal for me.

From the first day, no one would sit beside me except Iras. The other girl servants all moved down to the far end of the table, whispering and speculating in native Egyptian.

Iras gave them a scornful look and sat beside me. "They don't think you understand," she said.

I shrugged. "Do you think I care if they talk to me or not? Or if they think my hair is too light and my skin looks like an unbaked pastry? I just don't understand why they hate me and not you." For it was true that as we went about our work, other girls were happy enough to talk to Iras.

Iras shifted on her bench, looking down at her dish. "It's because I look like them. Nothing more. We have the same father, you and I. But you look Greek."

"I'm Egyptian," I said. "We both are. We're Ptolemies."

Iras laid aside the piece of bread she had picked up and glanced sideways at me. "They don't count the Ptolemies as Egyptian, here. We may have been in Egypt nearly three hundred years, but that doesn't count for much in the Black Land. We're not real Egyptians. Or you're not. They asked who my mother was, who my people were, and when I told them my mother was from Elephantine, the daughter of a scribe sold into slavery to pay her father's debts when he died, they all understood that. Don't you see? I have a place and people here. You don't. Your mother was a foreigner from across the sea. And no matter what you believe or how you've been raised, your face says you don't belong."

I got up and ran outside, ignoring the derisive giggles that followed me. No doubt they thought Iras had put me in my place as well. Tears blinded me, and I dodged about the columns and courts without thinking. I heard Iras calling after me, but I didn't turn back. Left and right and left again.

If I went back to our rooms, Cleopatra would ask me what was wrong, and I didn't think I could bear to tell her. They must hate her too. Only they could not touch her because she was a princess.

I finally sat down in a sunbeam that came in through the sungate in the roof in the Chapel of Horus. If I sat between the statue and the wall, no one could see me from the door. At this hour the chapels were empty and quiet. I curled my knees up and hugged them to my chest.

Iras found me anyway. She came in and sat down cross-legged opposite me, her saffron chiton all Greek, not Egyptian. "It's stupid," she said. "I didn't say it was right. I just said that's how it is." I didn't say anything, and she went on. My chest hurt too much to talk.

"It doesn't matter in Alexandria," I said.

"It doesn't matter as much," Iras corrected. "Do you think there aren't places in Alexandria where people stare at me? They don't expect a native to speak such good Koine. Or that the scholars don't watch me closely when Apollodorus takes us to the Library?"

"But you're brilliant!" I said. "You're much better at mathematics than I am!"

"I'm an Egyptian, and I'm a girl."

"There are plenty of women scholars in Alexandria," I said stubbornly. "There's no reason you can't be one."

"But there aren't in Athens," she said. "Even Plato says that women are by nature inferior to men in intellect, and that true companionship and discourse are only possible with equals, not with women and barbarians."

"Who cares about Plato?" I said rudely, sitting up. "We aren't in Athens. And I don't see what Athens has on Alexandria, anyway. It's been generations since anything came out of Athens except posturing and hubris. Euclid and Archimedes, Herophilus and Pythagoras, they were Alexandrian, like us. They belonged to the freest, most interesting city in the world. We both belong there. In a place where it doesn't matter so much who your mother was, but what you can do. People may look at you funny, but they've never tried to stop you from learning, have they?"

"No," Iras said. She shook her head. "No. Not like they would in Athens. It just hurts sometimes, the things we read."

"They're stupid," I said.

"You can't call Plato stupid."

"I can," I said. "If the things he says are contradicted by the evidence of my senses and by my practical experience of life, it's only intellectually responsible to dismiss him."

Iras laughed. "You don't dismiss the gods so easily."

"Oh, that," I said, glancing up at the gilded statue of Horus that loomed above us. They called him Harpocrates in Alexandria, but he was the same person. "Isis is the Mother of the World. It's just that people can't see things as clearly as She can. Just because the Adoratrice isn't nice doesn't mean that Isis doesn't love me. After all, the Adoratrice is just a woman."

Iras put her arm around me, tanned skin against my cream. "Sometimes I'll never understand you, Charmian. But I love you anyway."

"I love you too, sister," I said.

Our lives settled into the long, slow rhythms of the life of the Black Land, harvest and fallow and inundation, season following season. My blood came in, and then Cleopatra's. We grew taller and our shapes changed, the curves of our bodies carrying us toward womanhood.

In the mirror we looked like variations on a theme. Cleopatra and I were the same height exactly, while she and Iras had the same eyes, warm brown and beautifully expressive. The sun lightened my hair with gold, while Iras' remained dark and Cleopatra's the same shade of medium brown as always. Yet our faces were alike. The shape of our noses and chins, the arch of our brows were identical.

Outside these walls, girls only a little older than us were courting and marrying, moving to the houses of husbands and mothers-in-law, bearing their first children. In Egypt, wives were not kept apart, as they are in some lands. They would be working at trades, brewing beer and making paper, tending animals and weaving cloth, selling goods in the markets and shopping too.

We were neither dedicants of Bastet who might look forward to a life spent in the temple precincts, nor servants who might come in to do work and then go away again. Nor were we the other girls, orphans or children of the temple who lived here until they were grown and married. Bastet loves children, and there were always orphans coming and going. Sometimes they stayed only a few nights until some relative from another city came to claim them and conduct their parents' funeral rites. Sometimes they stayed years, until they were grown, if there was nobody who wanted them.

We were not like them, learning proper trades by doing the work of the temple. I was not sure what we were.

Yet to my surprise, I found myself coming to love Bubastis. It was true that I no longer had lessons, and instead had hard work to do, but there was a piercing beauty to it. When I stood in the temple for the evening rites, seeing the first stars appearing above in their endless dance, I felt my heart fill with a sense of rightness. Here, there was love. Here was peace. Here it mattered to serve Isis and Bastet through service to Their people.

Iras missed lessons terribly, and I pretended that I did too, though in many ways I was relieved not to have them. I had always been the slowest of the three, the one who fell behind in mathematics and sciences. I did not know, then, that Apollodorus had pushed us far beyond our years, and the lessons I had been behind in were normally given to men of twenty, not girls of twelve. I merely thought myself much stupider than my sisters.

Here, other things mattered. I could remember every word of the offices and hymns after hearing them once or twice, every word of the long complicated litanies that the acolytes took years to learn.

"All hail Isis, Mother of the World. I am She who rises with Sothis. With My brother Osiris I made an end to the eating of men. I taught men to honor the gods. I break down the governments of tyrants. I make an end to murderers. I make the Right stronger than gold and silver. I ordained that the Truth should make men free."

Singing each of the litanies, my voice soaring up through the sun-gate, I knew that what I sang was true, and felt in each word the beauty and mystery of it sinking into my bones, timeless and real. Justice. Mercy. Freedom. Those were the things that mattered, the things that made people happy.

And the dreams came back.

At first they were no more than pale shadows, scenes of unfamiliar places or people, but as time passed they grew stronger. Often when I slept I dreamed that I walked in strange lands. I dreamed I sailed blue waters aboard a black ship with a leaping dolphin on her prow, or journeyed in high strange hills with a pacing cheetah at my side. I dreamed of battles that echoed with distant trumpets. Once I dreamed that I fought on horseback on the banks of the Nile, while darts rained down from archers mounted on elephants. I shouted aloud, a sword in my hand, rallying men who struggled in the mud, their horses terrified of the great beasts, while about my horse's legs I felt the tug of current, the river rising at last.

I woke with tears on my face and lay awake in the bed beside Iras, watching the curtains move in the faint breeze at the window. But I told no one of my dreams. I did not want them to think me foolish.

THE HANDS OF ISIS

leopatra turned thirteen, and then I did. Here, away from
Alexandria, we heard little news that wasn't months old.
We heard that Auletes had left Rome, then that he had gone
to Ephesos, that he was living in sanctuary at the Temple of Artemis. Then
we heard that while it was true he was in Ephesos, he was there to confer
with the new Roman governor of Syria, a man named Aulus Gabinius,
from whom he hoped to borrow troops. It meant little to us.

Berenice had married a man named Archelaus, a son of a great
general of Mithridates of Pontos, and it was reckoned that they would
hold the throne together. In time, perhaps, Berenice would send for
Cleopatra to make an advantageous marriage. Or she might simply
think that forgotten was best.

In the afternoons, Cleopatra had lessons with Apollodorus, though
Iras and I did not. We had clothes to wash and linens to hang and fold.
We had to help in the kitchens and with the ducks kept behind the
temple, clean the dishes Cleopatra would use at her evening meal, and
tend to anything she might need.

On the other hand, Iras and I had much more freedom than
Cleopatra now. When our work was done, we might leave the temple
and go about the city of Bubastis as we wished. Often we went down to
the market beside the river docks, not because we had money to spend,
as we did not, but for the pleasure of seeing all of the goods assembled,
and talking to the crews of the riverboats. We were, after all, thirteen

now, and more than one young sailor called after us when we walked along the river. We would pretend to ignore them, putting our heads together and laughing, cutting them glances out of the corners of our eyes. I liked the dark-skinned boys with long black hair, the ones who leaped from deck to dock without looking, surefooted and at ease.

Iras seemed to enjoy all of these games less than I did. She would hurry me along sometimes.

"Don't you like it?" I asked, looking back at one especially pretty young man who was watching us, his arms crossed on the rail of a fast scout ship.

Iras shrugged. "I don't like it when they make crude comments, like they're measuring our breasts and bottoms. I like men who have interesting minds. Most of these men can't even read! I don't understand what you could see in them. They're nothing but sweaty soldiers and fishermen, men who ought to be beneath your notice."

"You like men with minds." I was distinctly skeptical. Minds were all very well, but there was something to be said for an expanse of muscled chest, sculpted by rowing.

"Minds," Iras said firmly. "Men with interesting things to say. Intelligent men with daring thoughts."

"Like Dion," I said.

Iras snorted. "Dion thinks he's a philosopher when he's just a bratty boy. Besides, he's forgotten about us by now."

"Probably," I said. But it didn't escape my mind entirely that two years had passed since we left the city. If we were thirteen, Dion was sixteen, and a man already.

SOMETIMES Apollodorus made short trips up the Nile to Pelousion for news. Then Cleopatra was able to go with us, since her afternoons were free until an hour before sunset, when they began the evening offices.

I was delighted, and enjoyed every minute of showing her our discoveries, the shops with the cloth brought in from Parthia embroidered with leaves and berries, the shop that sold sticky pastries that weren't expensive at all, the lady from Palmyra with gorgeous patterns painted in henna on her hands.

The sun lowered in the sky, and we began walking back to the temple, past the fruit and vegetable sellers who were packing up. One poor farmer's children were helping him pick up the last of his melons, two boys and a little girl, the youngest five or so. Their eyes were swollen and red, flies continually landing on the little girl's face, crawling on her eyelids as she cried and batted them away.

Cleopatra stopped. "Why doesn't he get a doctor for that little girl?" she said. "She's got conjunctivitis. Any doctor can fix it with eyedrops."

Iras took her arm. "He probably can't afford it," she whispered.

"Oh," she said, and though she let us lead her away, the set of her jaw didn't change.

It didn't surprise me in the least that as soon as we got back to the temple she sent for the Greek doctor. Cleopatra received him in her inner room, with Iras and I standing behind her one chair, as handmaidens should, impassive and lovely, part of the trappings of royalty.

"I would like you to treat the three children of the vegetable seller at the south gate," she said without preamble. "They have conjunctivitis in their eyes, and I am given to understand that their father has no money to pay for the treatment." Her voice was cool, and I thought she did very well indeed, sounding as though she had a huge staff to do her bidding, not just me and Iras.

The doctor looked amused at her stern gravity. "I shall do so upon your command, Princess," he said. "But as you know my services require payment."

With greatest dignity, Cleopatra took one of the thin gold bangles from her arm, one of the ones we had brought from Alexandria. She handed it to Iras, who passed it to him. "Will this suffice to pay for their treatment and the eyedrops they will need?"

He took it with a bow. "Assuredly, my Princess. However"—he met her eyes as he straightened—"there are a great many children in Egypt. And I do not think you have so many bracelets."

After he had left, we sat together on Cleopatra's bed. Iras sat on the edge, and I sprawled across the pillows. Cleopatra sat cross-legged, playing with the three bangles still around her wrist. There had been six when we left Alexandria, but two had already gone to pay for various things. Needless to say, Queen Berenice was not sending her an allowance.

At last she burst out, "If Isis is the Mother of the World, why does She let Her children suffer? And don't tell me it's a Mystery and we're not supposed to understand."

Iras looked sad. "Maybe Isis doesn't have hands, up among the stars."

"Isis has hands," I said, sitting up. "Ours."

Iras looked surprised. "I suppose in the old days people believed Pharaoh was Horus, in some actual way. And that the Queen was Isis Herself."

"Her desires given flesh," I said. A shiver ran through me, like a cool hand at my back. "Her voice and Her hands."

"Her voice and Her hands," Cleopatra repeated, looking down at her wrists, at her slender, ordinary hands against her lap.

"Her avatar," I said. "Isn't that what you are, when you give your bracelet to the doctor to fix those children's eyes? You're a princess of Egypt, born to be the voice of Isis."

"You may not have enough bracelets now," Iras said. "But there's plenty of gold in the Royal Treasury in Alexandria."

"Not really," Cleopatra said. "That's the problem, isn't it? My father ran out of money. The wealth of the Black Land is in grain, and in our trade. We have to manage our trade as carefully as our farms if we want them to yield well now and every year. And we have to get the money out of Alexandria and into the countryside."

Iras frowned. "How?"

Cleopatra smiled at the back wall of the chapel that made up her bedroom. "Just like Osorkon did. You pay people to build things for the public good, canals and temples and dockyards. When they have money they spend it on food and cloth and household things, things that are made by other people. Then the merchants are happy and the craftsmen are happy, and so is the Royal Treasury, because the taxes enrich us. Then we spend that money again on things that we need."

"Like a fleet," I said. "So we never fear the Romans again."

"Like schools," Iras said. "So that we invent new things that make things better, like Archimedes' Screw makes it much easier to irrigate the fields."

"Like hospitals," I said, thinking of the one in Alexandria where the young doctors learned how to treat every disease, and would work on poor people for free for the practice.

"Like floodgates and cisterns," Iras said, "so that when the Nile doesn't rise enough we can still get enough water."

"The Royal Treasury isn't mine," Cleopatra said. She let her hands fall to her lap.

We all waited, while it hung in the air around us: treason.

The cool touch was at my back again, as though something huge turned on a fulcrum. I shrugged and said it. "It should be."

Iras looked at me, her face inscrutable. Then she nodded like a soldier facing his opponent in a practice bout. "You'd be a better queen than Berenice."

"You're the avatar of Isis," I said. "You're Her hands."

"I'm thirteen," Cleopatra said. "Berenice is twenty-one. She has a soldier husband and an army, a powerful faction of the nobles, and the city of Alexandria at her back. I have exactly two handmaidens and a tutor."

"You have Isis," I said.

Iras and Cleopatra both looked at me.

The absence of Apollodorus made me bold. "Well, what is the use of being the avatar of Isis if you don't ask Her for anything?" I said. "She has the power to make you queen. I don't see the harm in asking Her to do it."

"What, just ask?" Iras said.

"She's the Mother of the World," Cleopatra said thoughtfully, chewing on her lower lip. "What's the worst She will do? Say no, as a mother will, when you ask for something that's not good for you? Charmian's right. She won't punish us for asking."

" 'Us'?" I said.

Cleopatra gave me a penetrating look. "If we're going to do this together, all of us Her hands, then it's not going to be just me asking. You're both of the blood of the Ptolemies. Either one of you could be Her avatar. Either one of you could be Pharaoh, if you were boys. Auletes was the son of a woman of the harem. He had no more claim to the throne than you. If we're going to do it, then we're going to do it together."

Iras nodded solemnly. "Then we need to do it right, so it's respectful."

We all fell silent. None of us was quite certain how to do it.

"We could go in the chapel," I said. "There's no one in the Chapel of Isis at night. And they don't lock it up like the sanctuary of Bastet, because there's no Inner Room, just the votive statue under the sungate."

"We need some incense," Iras said. "And an offering. I can get some incense out of the storeroom when we reset the temple after the Morning Offices. But we need something to offer."

One of the birds was out, I thought. To start with, every cat in the temple would come around yowling, wanting to know why they were being fed at an unexpected time.

"Wine," Cleopatra said. "It won't make any noise. And we can get it in the kitchen."

The next evening, when everyone had gone to bed, we rose in the tenth hour of the night and slipped out of our rooms.

The Chapel of Isis was bathed in moonlight streaming in from the sungate overhead. Through the square we could see the night sky, the stars paled by the light of the full moon. It lit a lozenge on the stones in front of the statue.

Isis sat regally, infant Horus on Her lap, His lips against Her breast. Her face was serene, carved eight hundred years ago from black basalt. On the walls behind, Her face looked out at us over and over, from different stories. Enthroned beside Her husband Osiris, She presided over the judgment of the dead, Lady of the Halls of Amenti, with Her wise eyes. On a different panel She ruled the waves, Isis Pelagia, the Lady of the Sea, Queen of Love and Desire.

They were all Her, I thought, the chaste Widow with Her sorrows, the Sea Lady with Her breasts like shells, untamable and unknowable, and the Mother of the World with Her child, compassionate for us all. They were different sides of Her, different faces. No one would ever know all there was of Her. No one could ever embody it all.

There was the sudden scent of smoke and resin as Iras lit the incense on the brazier at the back of the chapel, stirring the coals to life. Cleopatra stood in the middle of the lozenge of light, the moonlight shining on her white linen gown as she waited, a cup of wine in her hands. She looked up, and the light limned her face, as though she were carved from white stone, counterpoint to the black.

"We could sing the welcome," Cleopatra said. We all knew the beginning of the Morning Office, and even though it was the middle of the night, it seemed like it might be a good idea. I came to stand beside her, and we began.

> *Morning Star, Lady of Morning,*
> *Queen of the Heavens bright*
> *You come before the sun to show us*
> *Hope of the coming dawn . . .*

She stepped out of the shadows made by the moonlight through the sungate. I thought that She was young and slender, Her red sheath ornamented with gold beads and Her hair worked in dozens of braids, Her high, small breasts half-covered by the straps of the dress. "What do you seek, daughters of Ptolemy?" She asked.

I clutched at Cleopatra's hand, wondering if she saw Her too. From the expression of utter terror on her face, I thought that she did. Iras looked disbelieving, as though of all things she had not really expected this to work. I looked at Cleopatra and she looked at me, each of us willing the other to say something.

Isis laughed, and Her voice was clear and soft. I thought, with some surprise, that She looked hardly older than us, a girl in the first flush of womanhood, serene and confident in Her own beauty, and exactly my height. "Are you so frightened, little sisters?"

"Yes," Cleopatra said, at exactly the same moment I said, "No." Iras said nothing.

She laughed again, and Her eyes fell on me, dark and warm and sparkling, as though I shared Her joke. "Why then do you call Me, daughters of Ptolemy?"

Cleopatra cleared her throat. "To ask You...to petition You...to make me Queen of Egypt."

Her eyes grew serious then, and She put Her head to the side like a questioning cat. "No questions about lovers? No pleas for beauty or love, as young women most often do? 'Make me Queen of Egypt'? Why should I do that?"

"Because she's the best heir there is," Iras said. "Because You love the Black Land, and Cleopatra will take the best care of it."

She stopped in the shadow of the statue, one hand tracing the smooth carving of the knee, dwarfed by its height and weight. "Is that true, Cleopatra?"

My sister raised her chin. "I don't know that I would be able to do everything, but I would try. I don't think the others will. Great Lady, I promise You that I will try!" She leaned forward, and I saw all of the passion and intensity in her face, all of the will that I knew she possessed.

Isis turned, only Her hand still in the stream of moonlight, pacing as Cleopatra did when she worried. "Three hundred years ago, Ptolemy Soter came to this land. In that day, the Black Land was without a king, the line broken and the heirs slain, with no Horus to come forward and lead the people. He came with Alexander, who swept through like a cleansing wind, scouring the shadows that had gathered. But it was not Alexander who was truly Pharaoh. To be Pharaoh, you must Come Forth by Day." She stopped, turning, and we heard Her voice out of the darkness. "The gods of Egypt offered a bargain to

Ptolemy. He should keep Our enemies from Our door, and We would aid him. We would grant to him all of the powers that should go to Horus by right, and he would be Pharaoh in truth, Horus returned. But with the powers came the responsibility. If he would be Pharaoh, if he would be Horus, then he must guard the Black Land with his very soul, and he must seek no other treasure." Her eyes lit on me, glittering. "And what do you think he did?"

I swallowed, but the answer was in my throat. I had known it forever.

Cleopatra said it before me. "I think he made that bargain gladly, Great Lady. And I think he fulfilled it all his life."

She nodded, and Her smile was like balm. "He did. And since that day, the House of Ptolemy has ruled as the rightful pharaohs of Egypt. Eleven times Horus has descended to the Gates of Amenti as Osiris, and reigned in the world beyond. Eleven times the heir has ascended into daylight, Pharaoh of Egypt." She raised a hand to forestall Iras' argument. "Not that the succession has always been smooth, or that the heirs of Ptolemy have loved one another with true affection. But the line has not broken, and neither has the sacred trust. Until now."

"With my father," Cleopatra said.

She nodded. "Pharaoh is in Rome, the puppet of rich men, while his children slay one another. He bargains with his throne, hardly knowing what he does. If he sells Egypt to the Romans, there will be no more Pharaohs, and no more of this sacred trust. It will be as it was before Alexander, when the Persians ruled, and all that has been achieved, all that might be, will wither away." She stepped forward again, and the moonlight lit Her, the lines of Her face graceful and young. Like us She had the long straight Ptolemy nose. "You are the children of Alexandria, born of Ptolemy's stolen fire, and you do not know how rare the peace and freedoms you enjoy! In most of the world, men are killed for believing something different from their neighbor, or for having skin or eyes of a different shade, or for wanting something different in life. You do not know, in your innocence, how rare it is, how precious, this city where all of the peoples of the world mingle, and where anyone can believe what they will without fear. You know her beauty, her wealth, but you do not yet know her true treasures."

"I do," Iras said, and I started. Her voice was clear and strong. "I do. Alexandria's treasures are her ideas."

"Her freedom," I said.

Isis looked at Cleopatra.

She answered, her voice low: "Her people."

Isis nodded. "And that is the core of it. To rule the Black Land, you must love her. From Alexandria Queen of the Seas to the cataracts of the Nile, from the scholars and poets to the farmers in the fields, you must love her. Can you do that, daughter of Ptolemy?"

"Yes," she said, and it seemed to me that Cleopatra stood a little straighter.

"It will not be easy," She said.

"I have my sisters to help me."

Her eyes glanced over us again. "You do," She said. "And they can help you carry this burden, and walk each turn with you, if they are willing."

"Willing to do what?" Iras asked.

"To be My hands," Isis said. "To walk the Progress of Isis. This is no easy time, daughters of Ptolemy. The things that have been built are fragile indeed, and easily lost. Cities fall. Crowns fail. Even the gods themselves may die."

"What can kill a god?" I asked, as I had never imagined such. Even in the stories where gods die, they are always reborn.

She smiled, but Her smile did not touch Her eyes. "You would call it Apophis, the serpent who devours all. Unbeing. Uncreation. Things becoming nothing. You cannot imagine what Nothing is like." She looked at me again, and for a moment I thought She was unnerved. "When men destroy wantonly, they are the servants of Apophis. When men burn books for the pleasure in it, cut down trees to see them fall, kill because they enjoy it, and care for nothing but that the world should make a splendid conflagration, there is Apophis. And against that stands all that We prize, all love, all learning, all joy. All of the people of the earth, under heaven. From the frozen wastes of the north to the shores of seas you cannot yet imagine, every man fights Apophis when he builds and defends and cherishes. But when he tears things down, he opens a door. And he lets Apophis in."

"And that is happening now," Iras said keenly.

Isis nodded. "Again," She said. "It has happened before, when all was very nearly lost, and all about this Middle Sea cities fell and men died, until there were only the remnants of people, living in hardship and pain, most without even the letters to write or more to give them hope than the vague memory of a time past when there was enough food. It could happen again. And We will do anything to avert it."

" 'We'?" I asked.

She smiled. "The gods of the peoples of these lands, We who love you. We do not want to see Our children suffer. Mother of the World you have named Me, and Mother I am. I do not want to see any people suffer."

"The Black Land is a bulwark," I said slowly, and it was as though I remembered something I already knew. "The Black Land is strong. It is here that You must make a stand."

She beamed at me like a teacher when a very young student has found a difficult answer. "It is here. The ancient roots of the Black Land, and the bright beacon that is Alexandria. Together, this is where We must make Our stand."

"I'll do it," Cleopatra said. "I'll try my best. What do I have to do?"

"I will too," said Iras. Her face was grim as a soldier's.

"I will," I said, and my voice was quiet. "What do we need to do?"

"You will know," She said, and She glanced at me sideways, out of Her long painted eyes. "You will know."

Before I could so much as blink, She was gone. We stood in the chapel, my sisters and I, holding hands. The moonlight came through the sungate, and the brazier smoldered sullenly.

Iras drew a quick, sharp breath. "Was that real? Did you see Her?"

"Yes," I said.

Cleopatra nodded, and her face was white.

"She was beautiful," I said.

Iras tilted her head. "I'm not sure I would say that," she said. "She looked like Asetnefer, only older. Like She was from Upper Egypt, dark-skinned and tall, dressed like a widow in mourning, with a veil over Her hair."

Cleopatra laughed. "That's not what I saw at all, Iras! She was fair and plump, with Horus at Her breast and a himation around Her shoulders."

"No, She wasn't," I said. "She was our age, and beautiful."

We all stared at each other.

"I wonder what that means," Iras said thoughtfully.

"We all saw something different," I said, understanding. "Like the pictures on the walls." I looked at Cleopatra. "You saw the Mother of the World with Horus, and Iras saw the Lady of Amenti. I saw Isis Pelagia, the Goddess of Love."

"Each of us saw what we reflect," Cleopatra said, her voice taking on the same tone that it did when wrestling with an interesting problem.

Iras put her hands on her hips. "So I wonder what happens now."

"I don't know," I said.

For a time, it seemed that nothing was different. The Inundation ended and the planting season began. Iras turned fourteen. Our days went on as they always had, until I began to wonder if it had been a dream and we had imagined it together at night in the chapel. We did not speak of it, not to one another and certainly not to Apollodorus. None of us wanted to be taken for fools.

News and rumors came from the north. Auletes had mortgaged Egypt to Pompeius Magnus for an enormous sum of money. He had bought Gabinius, the Roman governor of Syria, and marched overland against Pelousion with an army. No, surely that was not true. Archelaus, the husband of Queen Berenice, was in Pelousion with the Royal Army. He would hold Pelousion against any comer, fortified as it was. And everyone knew Auletes was no general.

In Bubastis, nothing changed. Bastet had a feast day in the planting season, when the statue of Her from the inner sanctuary was carried out in a great litter painted like a barge and carried on the shoulders of the priests to bless the fields. It was also known as a blessing on women who were with child, or who wanted children and were unable to conceive. Cats bear their kittens purring, and there is no animal who is a better mother. Consequently, crowds came from all around to line the streets where the barge would pass to receive Bastet's blessing.

We had no parts in the festival, other than the work Iras and I must do in the kitchens afterward, cleaning up, so the three of us and Apollodorus hurried out to find a good place just outside the gates to watch the spectacle.

The story of Cleopatra's generosity to the melon farmer had spread, and he was not the only one who offered us a place to watch the procession beneath a shop awning. Smiling, she took a place beneath his, bending down to talk to the little girl, whose eyes seemed clear and normal now. Iras and I looked out, trying to see where the music was beginning. There was a flourish of trumpets from the temple gates. The crowds pressed forward in anticipation.

A man shouldered his way under the awning, an ordinary man with a clean-shaven face, wearing the clothes of a tradesman. "Princess Cleopatra?" he asked.

Something seemed wrong to me, a prickling at my back, cold and sharp, as though someone had just laid a cool hand on my shoulder. Apollodorus was in conversation with the melon farmer, and Cleopatra was still bent over behind me, talking with the child. I felt rather than heard Iras half-turn. "I am Cleopatra," I said.

Now, She whispered behind me.

I flinched. I moved. I had half an instant before the knife went in. And then all was chaos.

Someone screamed, loud and high, like a seabird. Perhaps it was the child. I don't know. Apollodorus cursed, and he grabbed at the knife, unschooled in war as he was, as it rose again dripping with my blood. It scored across his forearm, but he blocked the blade.

The melon farmer, half-tripping over me as I fell, lunged for the man's knees, bringing him down in a cascade of rolling green melons, ripe and sickly sweet.

Cleopatra flung herself to the floor beside me, Iras landing on us both, covering us with her body. "Oh sweet Isis," my sister said. "You took a knife for me."

"Shut up and get down," Iras said, her arms covering my face and her back sheltering Cleopatra's bent head.

There was a great deal of screaming and cursing, but I could make little of it. It seemed to go on forever. Time seems to stop somehow in moments like these.

"Of course I did," I said.

I think it was the melon farmer who subdued the man, even before the temple guards arrived. They were not much soldiers, more used to keeping order at festivals and breaking up fights than dealing with royal assassinations.

I was half-fainting from the blood loss before they carried me back to the temple. I remember Cleopatra walking beside me, almost running to keep up with the bearers of the litter, her face set in a frown, my blood all down her white dress as though she had made the feast day sacrifice.

"Iras...," I whispered.

"She went with Apollodorus," Cleopatra said tightly. "To see about the man."

The Greek doctor came then, and laid me on the bed in Cleopatra's room, where they got my chiton off to see how bad it was.

He had meant to stab me in the gut, a horrible way to die, but I had turned at the last second, and so the thrust he meant for my lower belly scored instead along my hip, a long jagged wound that laid my hip open to the bone and trailed off into the flesh of the upper part of my thigh. The doctor probed it wordlessly, and I could not help but scream.

"Not life threatening of itself," he said. "Unless it turns septic. It does not seem to have broken the bone."

"She's lost a lot of blood," Cleopatra said. Her face looked white.

"And will lose more while I clean it and stitch it," he said. "That's what the distilled alcohol and linen thread are for. Hold her arms when I pour it in, so she cannot fight."

I tried to shake my head to show I understood as Cleopatra took my wrists in her hands, but he poured the alcohol straight into the wound, and I fainted.

WHEN I WOKE, I was still in Cleopatra's bed, though it was night now, as the fretted lamps were lit. My leg was a blinding pain.

It must have been her voice that awakened me. She stood in the curtained doorway, her back to me, one pale arm holding the folds of the curtain back. She was talking to someone, Apollodorus and a man I did not know.

"Princess," he said. "I have come with Master Apollodorus from the magistrate. The man has been put to question, and we have been very specific in asking if he was hired by any person, here or in Alexandria, to harm you. He has insisted under greatest duress that he was not, and that his actions were solely his own, intended to restore to the throne what he terms the rightful rulers of Egypt, the dynasty of Nectanebo II."

"Nectanebo lived and died more than three hundred years ago," Cleopatra said, "killed by the Persians."

"Yes, Lady." The man shuffled a little. "But memories are long in the Black Land, as your Ladyship knows."

Apollodorus cleared his throat. "The magistrate says that it is up to you what is done with him, Princess."

I saw her head lift against the light in the next room. "Execute him," she said.

"Your will shall be done, Lady," the guardsman said.

I WAS A long time convalescing. The wound did not take septic, thanks to the ministrations of the Greek doctor, but it took a long time to heal, being both deep and straight into the muscle.

"What possessed you to say you were me?" Cleopatra asked me later, as I sat propped in her bed eating porridge. It did not escape me that she only wore one bangle now.

"I don't know," I said, though of course I did. I had played the incident over and over to myself in my mind, remembering each phrase, each movement. I had known something was wrong. Isis had told me. "I think...," I began uncertainly.

"Think what?" my sister asked.

"Nothing," I said. I didn't want to seem foolish to Cleopatra. After all, since the night in the chapel we had not spoken of it.

"What?" she said. "Charmian, I know you're thinking something."

"That it was Isis," I said reluctantly. "I think She warned me."

"Oh." Cleopatra looked startled.

"I heard Her, just a moment before he stabbed. She said, 'Now,' just one word, but I knew what it meant. I knew what was happening. And that my blood was the price for your life. My life for yours, freely offered."

"It wasn't your life," she said. "And I will bless Her name forever for that! Charmian, you must never do that again."

"I am your handmaiden. It's what I'm supposed to do," I replied.

AT FIRST, during that long winter while the crops grew and Cleopatra turned fourteen, either she or Iras stayed with me all of the time. Later, as I grew stronger, they went about their day, returning to me often to see if I needed anything. I stayed in Cleopatra's room, and she persuaded one of the temple servant girls to look in on me in the morning, when she and Iras were both at the Morning Offices. I dozed, and when I could I read from one of the scrolls Iras found for me in the temple archives. The Adoratrice, it seemed, had warmed to me when she heard I was willing to die for my mistress.

One morning, early on, I woke from terrible dreams in which a great weight rested on my chest, a crushing weight of water pinning me down, water on top of a steel breastplate that cut into me, holding me under. I struggled up from the dream to find there was indeed something on my chest. A cold thing touched my nose, and I opened my eyes.

A small gray cat was sitting on me, her nose against mine. Her green eyes blinked at me.

"Hello, cat," I whispered.

She uncoiled gracefully, her soft little paws against my chest. She must be one of the temple cats, I thought, though I had never seen her before. Leaning down, she butted against my chin.

I raised a hand and petted her. Her fur was clean and warm, and she kneaded me delicately, her claws pricking but not breaking the skin, purring like a lion.

"Hello, sweet," I said. "Bastet and Sekhmet alike, aren't you? An iron fist in a silk glove."

She settled down against me, leaning in and washing my cheek with her rough tongue.

We were thus engaged in the adoration of cats when the servant girl came in. "Oh," she said with some surprise. "You've found Sheba."

"Is that her name?" I asked. "I've never seen her before."

The girl nodded. "She's not usually around. A snake killed her litter of newborn kittens, and since then she hasn't let anyone touch her. I'm surprised she hasn't taken your hand off."

The cat watched her, her ears forward, but she did not hiss.

"She's been perfectly friendly to me," I said. She purred under my hand, though her eyes did not leave the girl, and her claws pricked through my thin chiton.

The girl looked back at her, careful to stay out of range of her claws. "Bastet's favor, I suppose."

"Perhaps so," I said.

Through the rest of my convalescence, Sheba was rarely far from my side. She slept beside me at night, or prowled about the room hunting. She brought me dead rats from the temple granary, which I suppose she thought a delicacy. She would bear the other girls in the room, but she would not let either Iras or Cleopatra touch her.

I tried to accustom her to them, but Iras smiled and shook her head. "She's yours," she said. "You earned her."

I had never had something before that my sisters had not. Now I did. Sheba's love was both unconditional and exclusive. It made me afraid. What should happen to the three of us when some greater love should come between us, a man who could not be shared?

I turned fourteen in the spring, just as I was able to get about again. I would have a terrible scar that would show in the bath, marring my looks forever, but it seemed a small enough price to pay for Cleopatra's life. And she was not likely to forget it, with the scar staring her in the face in the bath each day.

Not that she would anyhow. Lately it seemed that we were all shifting somehow out of true. Iras was cranky and sullen before her blood, Cleopatra was given to fits of temper that were most unlike her, and I dreamed long and intricate dreams in which a beautiful eunuch tempted me with things I could not do, lacking a manhood to do them with, and in which two faceless strangers enfolded me on a couch deep with pillows, stroking me and sucking on my breasts, one to each side, their bodies hard and yearning against me.

Perhaps it was that we were all fourteen.

We might have said things we regretted ever after if the messenger had not come. A swift scout ship came upriver from Pelousion with the news, Pharaoh's banner flying from its stern.

Ptolemy Auletes had indeed hired the Roman Gabinius with Pompeius Magnus' money. Gabinius had fought Archelaus outside the walls of Pelousion, and killed him in battle, utterly crushing the Royal Army in the process.

The messenger stood before us and the Adoratrice in the Inner Court, and his voice rang off the columns painted like trees. "Pharaoh Ptolemy Auletes is restored to his palace in Alexandria, where he has executed his perfidious daughter, Berenice. He sends his gratitude to the Adoratrice of Bastet in Bubastis for her loving care of his daughter

Cleopatra, and bids us to place ourselves at the service of the Princess, that her return to Alexandria may not be long delayed. He also asks me to convey the sad news that her elder brother died of a fever at Ephesos. Proper sacrifice should be made to his memory."

I looked at Iras, and she looked at me. I saw her throat work. We both knew what this meant, what we had asked for, and yet when it came we could hardly believe it.

Cleopatra stood straight and tall in her white dress, like the queens carved on the wall behind, as though she had half-expected it. She did not so much as glance at the Adoratrice. "I will obey my father's wishes as quickly as possible. Philopater he should name me, for in this as in all things I have proven myself the lover of my father."

The messenger almost smiled. "My Princess," he said. "I am sure that would make a fine throne name."

She had left Alexandria an unregarded third daughter. She returned the heir to the throne.

ꜣ Amenti

Isis spread Her hands on the arms of Her chair and leaned forward. "And do you think if you had told the Adoratrice of your dreams that she would have laughed?"

"No," I said slowly. "I think if I had told her I might have been trained as a priestess, as an oracle as was my birthright. I might have learned to use my gifts in ways that would help us — both Cleopatra and the Black Land. But I was too afraid."

"And what were you afraid of?" She asked gently.

I looked up at the high ceiling, disappearing into infinity. "That people should laugh at me. That people would think me a weak and superstitious woman."

"And do you think the Adoratrice of Bastet would think so?"

"No," I said, and regret swelled in me. "I think of all the places in the world, this was one where I would have been understood, and valued for the things that made me different rather than despised. Where I should have been cherished, if my gifts were true. But I was afraid of her, and I had been laughed at for my blond hair and pasty skin, so I didn't say anything. Even when Sheba came to me I said nothing. I did not trust myself."

Beside Serapis' throne, the lean hound stretched, His legs lengthening as He stood up on two legs, a man with a hound's head. Anubis spoke from the shadows beside the throne. "And yet you took a knife for Cleopatra without hesitation."

I shrugged, looking at Him with surprise. "Wouldn't anyone?"

He laughed, and I saw an expression pass between Him and Serapis. "Indeed, anyone would not. There are some lessons you have learned well, Companion."

"Companion?"

"Do you think this is the only time you have served Cleopatra, or the only time you have stood before these thrones?" Anubis smiled, a hound's openmouthed smile. "Three times before you have walked into the dark places at Pharaoh's side as he came forth by day. And not three hundred years have passed since you took Companion's oaths together, not three hundred years since you swore yourself to the service of Egypt and the House of Ptolemy. And in fulfillment of those oaths, you returned as a member of that same House, of the same blood, no less than your sisters."

I bent my head. "She is Ptolemy, the first of our line who came to the Black Land. I have always known that."

"Just so," Isis said, stirring on Her throne. "She has tried to fulfill her oaths, as have you."

"And yet it was not enough," I said, and tears welled again behind my eyes. "All we did was not enough."

"Then let Us see where you have gone wrong," She said. "You are brave enough to bear it."

"I am not brave," I said. "Gracious Lady, do not think me so! I am no hero, no leader of men, nor have I aspired to be." My voice broke. "All I have ever wanted was to be with those I love and to have good work to do. If I have had any strength, it is in those things. It is in the beauty of the Black Land, in a child's smile or the play of light on the water, in the beauty of the night or a word written well, or in my lover's eyes."

"It is in love," Isis said, and Her eyes were like stars. "Tell Us then, how you have loved."

THE FLUTE
PLAYER'S TWİLİGHT

W̄e came home to Alexandria, Cleopatra, Iras, Apollodorus, and I. I stood at the rail in the morning light, Sheba perched on my left shoulder like a child, watching Pharos rise out of the ocean to greet us. If we had thought it would be the same, we were wrong.

Cleopatra's old rooms were not good enough for her, now that she was the heir to the throne. Instead of the comfortable old sitting room where we had had our lessons, and the little bedchamber off it, she had an entire suite facing the Royal Harbor, with a small dining room of her own, a grand bedchamber with windows to the sea, and best of all, an archive room with cubbyholes built in along the walls and a huge worktable, so that she might keep her own correspondence and studies in peace.

There was a bath chamber with a round pool about my height in diameter built of white marble. It was waist deep, or a little more, as I was not tall, and a bench ran around the sides. Above, an oculus opened to the sky. Peering up, I saw that there were two large mirrors suspended in it, with cords that came down from them. A little experimentation showed that they adjusted the angle of the mirrors, so that sunlight might be directed on the pool all day long to heat the water. I was more concerned that someone might climb in through the oculus, and made a note to myself to talk to Apollodorus about it.

There was also a separate room for me and Iras near the bedchamber, with a large comfortable couch and a small window that opened onto the terrace. I looked at it for the first time as we were coming through the rooms, leaving Cleopatra exclaiming over the archive room. A young slave girl stood on a stool, hanging pale blue linen curtains from the clips above our window. They billowed and trembled in the fresh sea breeze.

"Let me help with that," I said, coming and holding the fabric for her.

She looked down at me, half-horrified, and I saw that she was a good two or three years younger than me. "Thank you. But you really shouldn't. We've been told that you and Iras are the Princess' handmaidens, and that you're not to touch any of the domestic work. We're to take instructions from you at any time regarding her things or her pleasure."

"Oh," I said, surprised. "Who told you that?"

"The Master of Pharaoh's Household, when he assigned us this morning. He said that the Princess instructed that you and Iras were to be obeyed in all things, and that the guard should allow you access to the Princess or her rooms at any time of the day or night on any pretext." She frowned. "That is right, isn't it, Lady?"

"Yes, of course," I said. I had never been addressed as "Lady" before. But then I had never before been principal handmaiden to the heir to the throne of Egypt.

I went and found Iras, where she and Cleopatra were investigating the bath chamber.

"Of course we can still use the main palace one," Cleopatra said, looking round the pool with satisfaction. "And we'll probably want to for hot water. But it's nice to have, isn't it?"

"Iras," I said urgently, "did you know that we're the principal handmaidens to the heir to the throne and have charge of all her things and household?"

Iras blinked at me.

Cleopatra laughed, splashing one hand in the water of the pool. She looked incredibly happy to be home. "Who else would be in charge of my household?" she asked. "Apollodorus is my Major Domo and you and Iras have charge of my rooms and my things. Who else should I trust besides you?"

"We're fourteen!" I said.

At exactly the same moment Iras said, "But what about our studies?"

Cleopatra put her damp hand on Iras' shoulder. "I thought you'd want to have lessons with me like you used to. But if you'd rather go to one of the symposia, I don't see why you shouldn't."

"How will we have time for that when we're running your household?" I asked, thinking of all the work involved in two sets of bed linens and the modest clothes we'd had in Bubastis. There were four beds now, fifteen windows, three dining couches, and the gods knew what else.

"Well, there are twelve slaves to help you, aren't there?" Cleopatra said. "I mean, you're in charge, but it's not as though I think you're going to do the wash yourself."

"Go to the symposia?" Iras looked as though someone had just shoved a sticky pastry into her mouth and she was trying to swallow it all at once.

Cleopatra nodded. "I wish I could, but Father says it's too dangerous. I can send for any scholars you recommend, though, for private lectures and lessons. You could pick out anyone you want who lectures two or three times a week and go, or go to discourses at the Library or experiments at the Museum, whatever you want. But if it's really interesting, I want you to let me know so I can learn it too. Father's got two or three people lined up already to teach me geography, literature, and rhetoric. And of course I'll be going on with Aramaic." She looked at me. "You can join me if you like, or not. I know Iras doesn't want Aramaic."

"I do," I said. I grinned. "I don't suppose that means Dion."

"I don't see any reason to change tutors," Cleopatra said loftily, but there was a gleam in her eye.

I looked around the spacious rooms. They had belonged to Tryphaena before, when we were children. I suspected she was murdered here, though I really didn't want to know exactly where. Everything was clean and light and airy, and so very big. Twelve slaves. Food tasters, laundresses, bath attendants, cooks, and carpet cleaners. "How in the world am I going to learn how to run a household like this?" I said.

Cleopatra met my eyes. "The same way I'm going to learn to be a queen. We have to grow up, Charmian."

I nodded.

She looked at Iras. "And when I'm Queen, you will handle my correspondence and keep my purse, all of the diplomatic correspondence, and all of the money the Royal Household spends. Charmian will run the palace, all of the slaves and entertainments and banquets, all of the audiences and festival clothes and progresses, and the Royal Nursery."

"Oh sweet Isis!" I said.

She put one arm around each of us and drew us close. "You are my sisters," she whispered. "You're the ones I trust. If we are the Hands of Isis, I need you. To make everything we said become true. It's what you were born for."

THUS WE BEGAN a new life. My apprenticeship had really begun in Bubastis, but now I had to take it up in earnest. That first night, as Iras and I sat in our beautiful new room, she said the first thing that brought a chill to my heart, and would ever after.

"Charmian, what do we know about these twelve slaves who work in her rooms? Were any of them previously with the Queen's household?"

She didn't mean Berenice's people. Indeed, they had little enough reason to want to harm Cleopatra now. She meant the servants of Pharaoh's wife, the mother of Arsinoe and her young brothers. The thing that now stood between them and the throne was Cleopatra.

If Auletes were to die, the throne would be held jointly by brother and sister monarchs, Cleopatra and the older of the two boys, another

Ptolemy, known as Theodorus. But he was barely seven years old, and it would be a very long time indeed before he could be expected to wield any real power. Cleopatra could wield it in a year or two. She was nearly fifteen. If anyone had reason to hate her, it would be Theo's mother, her stepmother.

I shuddered. "I hadn't thought," I said. "There could be."

"We have to think," Iras said, and I knew she was as irritated with herself as with me. "If we don't think, who will? We'll have to think about every slave, every craftsman, and every dish. Where did they come from? Who sent them? Whose hands have been on them? Every last one."

"Forever," I said. The weight of it hit me like a giant block of granite. "She has put herself in our hands for the rest of her life."

Iras looked at me, and there was something of the soldier in her glance. "We're Ptolemies too. Her job is to rule Egypt. Ours is to guard her and her children while our life and breath lasts."

CLEOPATRA HAD COME BACK from Bubastis with three chitons, and none of them was fit for court. An hour after sunrise I had the best seamstresses in the palace in her sitting room, along with four cloth merchants highly recommended in the city. They spread their wares on couches and tables in a glistening array. There was linen of every sort, fine and light, in every pastel shade. There were bolts of printed cloth with designs of whorls and fish from the Carian coast, with bright geometric patterns from Meroe and Elephantine. There were wools from Tyre and Damascus dyed crimson, and the rich purple color that is worth more than gold. There were cottons from Hyderabad drawn so thin that the light passed through, making it look like a weft of silver, detailed with gold and silver embroidery in intricate borders a handspan deep. One merchant had even brought three bolts of fine silk from Chi'n, two years upon the road through Samarkand and Babylon, in a dark, rich turquoise embroidered with fantastic beasts.

Cleopatra looked about in a kind of dismay.

"You are dressing the heir to the throne of Egypt," I said. "You are dressing a goddess on earth."

On most of their faces I saw nothing but avarice, but one of the seamstresses nodded, a dark, wizened woman nearly seventy. "Then you will want this," she said, picking up a length of plain white linen, light as a cloud and so fine that it seemed to have no texture. "This will hold a pleat the way the robes do in the old carvings: skirt and collar and cape. This will make you look like Nefertari, Great Ramses' queen."

Cleopatra held it up, and one could see her face clearly through it. "Am I not too fair for that?" she asked worriedly.

The seamstress came around the table and put her hand on Cleopatra's waist, feeling the shape of her body beneath the loose chiton, squinting into her face gravely. "You'll need a wig, but the queens of old always wore wigs. That's the way it was done then. Half of it's jewelry and bearing, Princess."

Cleopatra nodded seriously. "Do you think I'm pretty enough?"

The seamstress looked her up and down, while the others hastened to assure Cleopatra that she was a vision of loveliness. "You could be taller," she said critically. "You've got nice eyes, but the Ptolemy nose is unfortunate on anyone. Good skin. Nice hair, though a bit average. A good figure, though not enough breast to really shine. I can do something with you."

"Good," Cleopatra said. "Because you're now the Royal Seamstress. After you've finished fitting me, I want you to do some clothes for my handmaidens. I think they've got nothing but the chitons on their backs." She looked at me and Iras through the crowd of merchants pushing one cloth and another, over the three other seamstresses exchanging distressed glances. "Pick out whatever you want. Anything. Your word is enough for them." Then she looked at the disgruntled seamstresses. "You're going to attire the rest of my household. Come back tomorrow and Charmian will have my Major Domo for his fitting, and others that I require."

They moved toward the door, and Cleopatra smiled at the seamstress with what was for once a genuine smile. "Let's pick out some cloth."

"I like this pink from Hyderabad," I said, lifting a length. It was thin silk shot through with gold thread, a dark saturated pink like real roses. It would make her skin glow.

THAT AFTERNOON Dion turned up. Pharaoh's guards called me over to the door to identify him as he stood behind crossed spears in the outer corridor. I almost didn't recognize him.

"Dion?" I said doubtfully.

The boy I remembered from three years before was gone. He was seventeen now, and seemed to have shot up two handspans, tall and thin. He wore a neatly trimmed dark beard around the edges of his chin, and his short dark hair fell in endearing curls over his forehead. He was, I thought, breathtakingly handsome.

"Charmian!" He pushed past the guardsmen and embraced me like a kinsman. The top of my head barely reached his chin. He smelled like incense and old scrolls. His beard was scratchy against my face as he kissed my cheek. "It's been so long. You've missed a lot of plays."

"I imagine I have," I said. Dion felt wonderful pressed against me. I had never thought he might. Before I had time to decide exactly what I thought, he let go much too quickly and stood back, grinning.

"Do you still want to learn Aramaic?" he asked.

"You know I do," I said. His grin was catching.

"Where's Iras?" he asked.

"Here," Iras said, coming out the door smiling as though her face would crack.

He bent to embrace her, and I felt a stabbing pain of jealousy run through me. Was it my imagination, or did he hold her longer than he held me? Was he pressing her a little closer?

"So what have you been doing, Dion?" I asked, pushing my hair back as we all went into the sitting room together.

"A little of this and a lot of that." Dion threw himself into one of the chairs as though he hadn't a bone in his body. "I'm teaching mathematics now to a bunch of snotty-nosed little boys, and I'm working with Philo in astronomy. He's calculating the vectors of parabolic orbits, and how much speed you would need when accelerating away from a large body."

Cleopatra had come in, and she poured watered wine for him. "And what can you do with that?"

Dion shrugged. "Go to the moon. Do you want to go, my Princess?"

Cleopatra laughed. "Is the moon made of silver, Dion, that I should replenish the treasury of Alexandria?"

"No one knows what the moon is made of," Dion said seriously. "But if I had an engine of sufficient efficiency, I have the mathematics. Perhaps in a century or two it will be possible. Hero has done some very promising things with his aeliopile."

"Aeliopile?" Iras sat down beside Dion on the nearest couch, reclining on the arm as she leaned toward him.

"It's powered by the steam of boiling water," Dion said. "It can make a ball spin faster than the human eye can see it, around fifteen hundred times per minute. It compresses air through a copper tube and expels it in a way that causes tremendous energy to be released. If there were a way to build a tube large enough that a vessel might be attached to it, then it might create sufficient force to lift that vessel clear of the air and into the aether that separates our celestial sphere from that of the moon."

I felt a chill run down my spine, as though someone had whispered to me long ago. *I would build a ship of moonlight and silver, and we should sail beyond the baths of stars and far away, to strange islands in that ocean where men have never walked....*

I had lost the train of the conversation, but no one had noticed.

"And are you married, Dion?" Cleopatra asked.

Dion blushed. "Not yet." He ducked his head, and I noticed that his eyelashes were thick and dark. "But I have a lover."

"Oh!" Cleopatra leaned back in her chair, clearly enjoying being the picture of sophisticated adulthood. "Who is he? Tell us all about him."

Dion looked up at her. "His name is Doriskos. He's twenty-six, and he works in Pneumatics. He's from Corinth, but he's come to Alexandria to study. My parents don't really know about him."

"You look happy, Dion," I said. It had not really occurred to me that while we were in Bubastis, Dion might have found someone. But of course he had. He was three years older than I was, and very handsome.

"I am." Dion blushed even more. "There was never a more ideal erastes in the history of the world, and that's saying rather a lot."

"I'm very happy for you, Dion," Iras said. Her voice was cool, and I was sure I had imagined warmth between them a few minutes before.

"I am too," I said. But the jealousy did not die.

UNFORTUNATELY, we had worse troubles than Dion's new erastes. It was true that Ptolemy Auletes had mortgaged the country to Pompeius Magnus. The Roman Gabinius had indeed defeated Archelaus in order to restore Ptolemy to the throne, but had practically destroyed the Royal Army in the process. It was necessary to keep Gabinius and his mercenaries on for still more pay until somehow the army could be reconstituted. In the meantime, the first of the hefty payments was due to Pompeius, through his banker, Rabirius Postumus. It amounted to a huge sum.

Still, the Ptolemies were not poor. Auletes scraped together the first payment from the treasures of the palace. Gilded lamps and golden plate, fine cedarwood chests full of treasures made their way to the docks for shipment to Rome.

Gabinius guarded them closely. He and his men were billeted within the Palace Quarter, in the barracks that should be reserved for the Palace Guard, if we *had* a Palace Guard. It made me more than a little nervous to think that we had Romans for our guardians.

"We've set the jackals to watch the henhouse," Cleopatra said grimly, and said no more.

"We'll find the next payment when the harvest comes in," Iras said. "There will be export taxes on the grain. That will cover it."

"It will," Cleopatra said. "But it won't cover anything more."

"Like rebuilding the army," I said.

"There are the Royal Jewels," Cleopatra said.

Iras bristled. "The Royal Jewels will not leave Egypt! Some of them are two thousand years old, meant to grace the necks of Pharaohs for all eternity on their funeral beds, plundered by the Persians and returned to us by the grace of Alexander! Auletes will send them to Rome when the seas freeze to ice."

I was less sure of that. Auletes would do whatever he needed to.

Still, as long as we had them, we should use them. When the Alexandreia approached, I sent word to the Treasurer that all of the jewels suitable for a queen should be sent to Cleopatra's quarters that she might choose which ones to wear for the festival. She was fifteen, and would be walking in the great procession with her father, as the heir to the throne should.

The Treasurer was taken aback by the request, so much so that he went straight to Pharaoh. We heard that Auletes laughed, and said that his daughter should have what she liked.

The next day the Treasurer came to Cleopatra's quarters, with fifteen guardsmen and a dozen slaves bearing boxes. Piece by piece, he spread out the contents of the Treasury. I had no idea there was still so much.

Each piece was dazzling by itself. Together, it was almost unbelievable. There were broad necklaces that covered one from throat to waist, with counterweights in the back made of solid gold, pectorals of lapis and carnelian, earrings of glistening peridot, star rubies from India carved as scarabs and set into a bracelet, cabochon sapphires, and a gold ring for a man's thumb bearing the cartouche of Seti the First. There were amulets of turquoise, strings of pearls from the depths of the Aegean, golden bracelets in the form of snakes, and a glass locket containing a lock of Alexander's hair.

And of course there were crowns. She was trying on a very light golden one, a simple circlet with the rearing cobra of the uraeus in front, when there was a knock on the door. With all of the treasure spread out as it was, the guardsman challenged aggressively. "Who is there?"

"Pharaoh Ptolemy Auletes," he said, and sounded amused. "Cannot I visit my own daughter's chamber?" The Treasurer had them draw back the bar immediately.

I had not seen Auletes in person since we had left Alexandria for Bubastis, and I was shocked by the change in him. Auletes had always been a plump man with a ruddy complexion, a bit too hearty and cheerful, like a merchant trying too hard to strike a deal. Now he seemed older and grayer. Thinner, he should have looked better. Instead, he looked as though he had shrunk. Time had not been kind to him.

We all bowed to the ground, except Cleopatra, who bowed from the waist. He came over and raised her, so that we might stand as well, looking at the uraeus on her brow. "It suits you," he said.

"Thank you, Father," she replied.

"It takes a certain amount of cheek to want the entire treasury," he said, but he was smiling.

"I suppose it does," Cleopatra said. "But I would not have us displayed before all the world at the festival looking humble."

"You do not look humble in the least," he assured her.

She didn't. Cleopatra was wearing one of the new chitons, violet cotton that moved like silk, with deep borders of violets and hyacinths, and over it all of the necklaces and bracelets she had been trying on, topped by a queen's crown. Half-Greek and half-Egyptian, she was dazzling.

"They will never think us weak while I live," she said.

Auletes smiled. "Or poor," he said.

"It's the same thing."

I thought that he would laugh. Instead, his eye fell on me, poised as I was with a box of rings. "You seem familiar."

I lifted my eyes to his. "I am Charmian, the daughter of Phoebe the Thracian, my Pharaoh, whom you may remember."

He nodded, and raised one hand to touch my face. "I do. You have her eyes."

"So I have been told, my Pharaoh."

"Just that color," he said, and I wondered for the first time if he had been grieved when she died. I had never thought about it before. "Are you content with your lot, Charmian?"

"Very content," I said. "I could wish for nothing more in life than to serve the Princess Cleopatra as I do."

"Charmian is dear to me," Cleopatra said, coming to stand beside me, her bracelets clanging together. "She took an assassin's knife for me in Bubastis."

"Very like her mother," he said, his eyes still roaming my face.

"She is a Ptolemy," said Cleopatra. "I would expect no less from the descendant of so many noble kings."

Auletes laughed, a bark of actual mirth. "I do not mean to take her from you, Daughter. Winter does not meet spring without looking utterly ridiculous." Cleopatra colored. "Go on then," he said, gesturing to the finery. "Look as magnificent as you will. I am less Serapis these days than before, but with such a splendid Isis beside me the world will tremble. I would that I had the world to lay at your feet, Daughter."

"I do not need the world," she said. "Only Egypt."

"Now you sound like our forefather Ptolemy Soter," he said. "Who stole his fire and kept it."

"There are worse things to do," she said, and she smiled in return.

"Indeed there are, Daughter," he said. Pharaoh turned, as though to leave. "The difficulty is keeping it." He glanced at the Treasurer. "My daughter is to have whatever she wishes from the Royal Treasury, whenever she wants it, either treasures or money. You do not need to ask me. Her word is absolute." He turned and walked out, leaving the Treasurer spluttering behind him.

Iras looked at Cleopatra, her arms adorned with twenty bracelets, wreathed in golden snakes. "I think you have bracelets enough now, my Princess."

FLAWED ALABASTER

E
ight days later we attended the great festival. In the past I
would have enjoyed it, the crowds, the people, and the holiday festivities. Almost all of the shops and businesses closed
for the duration, and on the eve of the festival the city was alive with
lamps, people running from door to door, bringing moon-shaped
pastries of almond cream to neighbors and friends. The children
were wild, of course, and their shrieks and games could be heard
everywhere.

I, on the other hand, was dressing Cleopatra for the feast at the palace. She had a chiton of pale yellow silk worn with a massive collar of
turquoise and peridot. Iras and I had matching gowns of saffron linen,
our shoulders clasped with turquoise scarabs. One or the other of us
would stand behind Cleopatra all of the time, tending to anything she
might need, watching over her plate, and refilling her cup only from
the common vessel. We would take turns, since the banquet could be
expected to last three or four hours, start to finish, not counting the
drinking and games of kottabos at the end.

If this were a Greek party, indeed she should not be present at all,
but things were done differently in Alexandria. The Egyptians have
never closeted their women, and in Alexandria unlike in many parts
of the world, it was usual for respectable women to have their place at
public functions and banquets.

The banquet room was huge, with a good breeze off the sea coming in through the spaces between the columns, and bronze lamps hung from each one, giving off the sweet scent of terebinth resin as well as light. The couches were arranged in multiples of three on the dais, with Pharaoh upon the best one. His queen was beside him on a couch of her own, and Cleopatra on the third. I noticed that the Queen did not look at all pleased, and resolved to watch carefully everything that made its way to the inlaid ebony table that sat at Cleopatra's left elbow.

I watched for an hour or so, through the speeches of welcome and the propomata going around, oysters stewed in red wine with coriander, salt fish from the Bosporus, little bits of cheese rolled around coriander seeds and ornamented with dill fronds, and a great many other things. Then I traded with Iras, that she might stand and wait on Cleopatra while I went behind a carved screen that concealed the trays for dirty dishes, sat down on a stool, and ate a little.

When I came back, we were already into the second round of main dishes and the fish had been taken away. Cleopatra had a succulent slice of pork glazed in a reduced pomegranate glaze, but she was hardly eating it. This was the first time she had had people coming up to pay their respects to her throughout a banquet, and she looked mortally afraid of being caught with her mouth full.

Iras nodded to me, and we traded. Cleopatra had no wine in her cup, just water, and that came from a pitcher that Apollodorus held. I stood beside him, looking out over the hall. His new robes were lavishly embroidered, though there was a gray hair or two on his head now. I imagined the three of us had been enough to give him gray hair.

The Romans were seated together in a clump to the right. Gabinius was hard to mistake, with the crimson cloak of his office about him, even though they did not wear their harness. Most of them were reclining comfortably, talking among themselves and tucking into the pork with great enthusiasm.

One young man, though, only toyed with his meat. He was cleanshaven, with a square jaw and close-cut brown hair, and eyes that roved restlessly over the room and the diners. He took everything in, the lamps and the hangings, the duck being served to the Patriarch of Alexandria and the other Jewish notables instead of pork, the girls bringing watered wine around. But his gaze kept returning to the dais, to Cleopatra.

I sidled closer to Apollodorus. "The young man," I whispered. "The one who is always looking. Who is he?"

Apollodorus had the knack of answering without seeming to move his mouth. "One of Gabinius' tribunes. His name is Marcus Antonius. He leaves for Rome tomorrow."

DESPITE OUR GOOD SHOW at the festivals, the finances of the realm were in no better shape. There was discussion of debasing the coinage by reducing the amount of silver in an Egyptian stater, the first time we should have ever deviated from the standard set in the time of the first Ptolemy. The Mareotic Canal required dredging, an enormously expensive task, but absolutely necessary to the economy of Alexandria and of all Egypt. If the grain harvest could not get to port, we should lose our most taxable export. Ptolemy chose the canal and defaulted on the third payment of the loan.

Pompeius Magnus' reaction was swift and predictable. A month later his banker, Rabirius Postumus, arrived in person in Alexandria to collect the debt. I imagine he expected to be rebuffed, instead of given a royal welcome as though he were the dearest friend Auletes had. It was a matter of days before Auletes appointed him Chief Tax Collector of the realm, a position of tremendous authority with considerable scope for personal profit.

Iras was furious. She paced about Cleopatra's sitting room, looking like nothing so much as Sheba lashing her tail. "I can't believe he's appointed that corrupt man to collect our taxes!" she said. "He'll steal us blind, and our people too. What can Pharaoh be thinking?"

Cleopatra looked up from the scroll she was reading, a smile playing about her lips. "He has a plan, you know. He's not stupid. He knows perfectly well that Rabirius Postumus is corrupt, and that he'll steal everything that's not nailed down. Just wait and see."

"Do you know what the plan is?" Iras challenged.

"No." Cleopatra closed the scroll, her pointer still in place. "But he's not a bad ruler. He may not be a general, but he's a Ptolemy. We're clever, the three of us. Can't you trust that we got it from somewhere?"

I half-thought it was only that she hated to think ill of him, but I was pleased when it turned out she was right. Within four months, Rabirius Postumus had made himself so hated in Alexandria that a mob attacked him and burned his house, and he fled with his life only because of the fortunate intercession of the Palace Guard.

"What can I do?" Ptolemy asked Pompeius Magnus in a letter. "I allowed your man free rein to collect the debt I owe you, but not only did he do no better than I have done, but he now owes his life to me. You must understand that we need time to repay you as you deserve."

Whether or not Pompeius was comforted by this I do not know. Perhaps he was. He knew Ptolemy Auletes less well than I.

MEANWHILE, I had other things on my mind. In addition to learning the running of Cleopatra's household, I continued my studies. I did not have either the time or inclination to give them most of my attention, but I saw at least one tutor each day for an hour or two. And of course I had my lesson with Dion.

Afterward, while Cleopatra went to her father to discuss affairs of state, where she should be well guarded by Pharaoh's own men, Dion and I could go about town. More often than not Iras joined us. Sometimes we walked in the parkland over the tombs of the Palace Quarter, but more usually we went to plays, or wandered about the city seeing the sights, shopping or dining off the street, or in one of the many neighborhood taverns that catered to a respectable crowd. There were lots of these, and as the city had quarters that held as many different kinds of men as there are on the earth, there was always something new to try.

There were Carians and Greeks, Lydians and Jews and Palmyrans, Romans and Numidians, Nubians and Babylonians, even Ethiopians with their spicy bean dishes that one ate wrapped in flatbread, and some Andalusians from far-off Hispania with their goat cheese and green olives. Once every ten days or so we stayed late into the night, laughing and disputing with Dion and his friends in a mock symposium on the nature of love, or the truth inherent in beauty.

I turned sixteen, and found that beauty had its own truth. While Dion might not notice me, leaning as he did on the arm of his newest friend, their brows bound with vine leaves, there were plenty of young men who did. My coloring was considered exotic, and even I could find nothing to dislike in my deep breasts and curving hips. Iras was taller and slenderer, and she did not encourage attention the way I did. I liked to see the way young men drew breath more sharply when I came near, the way a casual hand against their lap when leaning across a table would cause them to moisten their lips nervously. It was a kind of power. Was this, I thought, what my mother had felt when she captivated Pharaoh?

There was one in particular, a young scholar named Lucan who worked with Dion, who I thought beautiful. He had very full, very pink lips, and no matter how often he shaved a dark shadow showed around his mouth. When I watched his lips, he got nervous. Sometimes when we left dinner to begin walking back to the Palace Quarter, he would drop back to walk at my shoulder.

I did most of the talking, as at first he seemed to have little to say. He was working with a noted lecturer in Pneumatics, which seemed to involve the complex process of making automations that moved or made certain sounds when air was forced through various tubes and pipes, a very specialized form of engineering indeed. I gathered that Dion had lately become fascinated with it, but I found it much less interesting. It was, after all, impressive to own a mechanical bird that sang when you pressed a lever, but it seemed of less practical use to me than ships or canals. On the other hand, as Lucan pointed out, there was a lot of money in Pneumatics, as wealthy people wanted all manner of interesting automata.

He had a lot of money to spend for a young man, and took to bringing me little things—flowers or painted papyrus fans, things that I supposed would have been impressive to most young women. But most young women did not live among the riches of the Ptolemaic court, with the entirety of the Royal Treasury at their disposal. I was more interested in his regard than in his money. I did not need a well-off husband.

Unfortunately, what I did have was Iras. She stuck to me as though we were joined like twins, her arm around my waist as we reached the parks about the tombs. Everyone knew it was a popular place for lovers to go apart. I brushed her hand off, but she got between me and Lucan smiling and chatting, and then the moment was gone. Lucan and the others were off with Dion, who walked with his arm around his beloved's waist.

I dragged Iras out of the earshot of the gate guards. "What did you do that for?"

"Do what?" Iras asked loftily.

"Keep me from going apart with Lucan. I'm sure he would have if we had been able to fall back together."

Iras raised an eyebrow. "I thought you were interested in Dion."

"I would be, if he liked girls at all." I shrugged. "Lucan is perfectly nice, and he's interested in me. Why not see what it would be like?"

"I see," Iras said. "One man is as good as another. You must not care about Dion very much, then. I can see how your heart is broken."

I tossed my hair back. "We're not Greek maidens, bound to virginity as our only worth. We belong to Cleopatra. We're slaves. Nobody expects us to stay virgin. And because we belong to Cleopatra, we can pick and choose as we want. We don't need to lure rich husbands with our virginity."

"Is that all it means to you?" Iras snapped. "You can't think of any reason not to fall into bed with the first boy who likes you?"

"I don't why I shouldn't enjoy myself," I said hotly. "Of course I don't want to get pregnant right now, but there are plenty of things you can do without getting pregnant. I've asked around."

Iras' lips compressed in a tight line. "I thought you had good sense. Are you determined to be a whore like your mother?"

I slapped her across the face. Then I turned from her in horror and ran inside.

CLEOPATRA WAS GETTING READY for bed, one of the junior maidservants combing out her hair. She looked up at me as I stormed in, still shaking. "Charmian? Are you all right? What's happened?"

I burst into tears.

Dismissing the girl, she got up and came over to me, sitting down next to me and putting her arms around me. "Is it about that friend of Dion's you've talked about?"

I buried my face in her neck, nodding. I couldn't answer.

"Has he hurt you?" she asked very quietly.

I shook my head. "No," I choked out. "Nothing like that. It's just that…"

Cleopatra took a breath. I felt her chest tighten beneath mine. "If it's that you're in love, and he wants to marry you, you know that I would free you if you wanted me to. I can do that. I would hope you'd stay with me as an attendant or something, because I would miss you. But I can't fault you if you want to marry, to have children and a normal life." She put her cheek against mine. "I expect Pharaoh would give you a dowry if it mattered to his parents."

"I don't want to marry Lucan," I said. "Why should I want to do that?" I sat up, spreading my hands on the cushions.

Cleopatra blinked at me. "Most women do," she said. "Most women want to marry, and he seems like he's kind and stable."

"'Kind and stable.'" I smoothed out the fabric cover of the cushion absently. "He's both of those things. But is that all I can want? Dion doesn't have to settle for 'kind and stable.' Dion has a different friend every three months. Or sometimes he just ends the evening on another couch, when Dionysos is kind. He chooses to love when he likes and not when he doesn't."

"Dion is a man," Cleopatra said.

"Is that what it comes down to then?" I fought back tears. "That this woman's body is a prison? Dion can choose as he likes, because he is a man, but I cannot?"

"Most women marry," she said. "Of course you don't have to. There are women who don't, priestesses and hetairae, scholars and slaves. But most women want a normal life."

"Why would I want a normal life?"

"Charmian, I don't know what to say," Cleopatra said. "I would hate for you to go away from me, but I want you to be happy. What is it you want?"

I looked up at her, my eyes blazing. "I want to fuck him, all right? I want to kiss him and go apart with him into the tombs and get my clothes up and have him! I want him to touch me and tell me he worships me and that I am a goddess on earth to him and that he is never happy except in my arms. I don't particularly care if it's true or not. I want to find out if the things I dream can really happen, if I can stop being twisted into a wad of desire and longing. I don't want to marry him and I don't want to go away from you. Iras is right! I'm a whore, just like my mother." I choked again, and flung myself against the pillows.

For a long moment there was silence. Then I felt her hand against my hair, brushing it softly like a child. "Iras shouldn't have said that."

I felt as though my heart would crack open.

"Asetnefer went to Pharaoh reluctantly, because it was her duty. We know how to serve, in the Black Land, and Pharaoh is the anointed of the gods. But Phoebe went laughing, and she came from Ptolemy's bed naked, wearing jewels and his seed on her. It was said he carried the marks of her teeth on him for days after each time. It's remembered here. Iras heard and told me, and I asked her not to tell you. I didn't think that kind of old gossip and jealousy would do you any good."

"My mother was a whore," I said into the pillow.

I heard her take a breath. "There's no shame in doing well the things put before you in life. Would you want a man to be a soldier who had no love of battle? Or a scholar who took no pride or interest in learning? Like your mother, you belong to Aphrodite Cythera. Do you not remember the rite we did at Bubastis? We all saw Isis differently, remember?"

I nodded. "You saw Isis the Mother of the World, with Horus on Her lap."

"And you saw Isis Pelagia, the Lady of the Sea, who the Greeks call Aphrodite Cythera. No man owns the Sea Lady. No man ever brings Her home to his house. She chooses where She wills." My sister put her hand over mine. "We took on the responsibility to be Her hands and Her faces. The face you wear is the Queen of Love. Of course you want to go apart with Lucan. Of course you want to come into your power. Do you think I do not want to come into mine?"

I put my head to the side, wondering what it was she desired so much.

For a moment Cleopatra looked almost embarrassed. "I want a child. Were I an ordinary woman, I could marry and perhaps there would be a baby in my lap by now. When I see young mothers with their children, my heart leaps into my throat, and I am so envious, Charmian! I am so jealous. But I can't do anything about it. My children will be the heirs to the throne, and my maidenhead is too valuable a playing piece." She swallowed roughly. "I know when it's time, it won't be a man of my choosing. It will be for politics, and because it is useful to Egypt. I hope it won't be bad, and that I can take some pleasure in it. But I can never hope for love as you can."

I closed my eyes. "I want to choose, not be chosen. If I were a man, I could even have Dion!"

"So could I," my sister said quietly.

I looked at her sharply, and she gave me a little smile. "Do you think I don't notice him too? But it is impossible. I understand that. I would share him with his male lovers if he were interested in women at all, but he is not. And in any event, I cannot choose as a prince could, as Pharaoh can. If I could, I should marry for Egypt and love where I willed, one love to last a lifetime."

I nodded. I had always known that about her. She was made for fidelity, as I was not.

"You can choose," she said. "You are my handmaiden, and you always have a place, you and any children of yours. Yes, you can marry if you want. But you don't have to. If you want to choose, you can. And the same is true of Iras."

I thought again of Bubastis, of what Iras had said she'd seen. "Isis before the Veil," I said. "The Queen of Amenti, unengendered and unengendering." And how terribly hard, I thought. How lonely, to forever forsake the mortal loves of husband and children for the love of the mind! I could never do it, I thought. "I slapped her," I said guiltily.

"You shouldn't have done that," she said.

"I know."

I heard something in Cleopatra's voice and looked up. Iras was standing uncertainly in the doorway. Her eyes were red. "I'm sorry," she said.

"I am too," I said.

And then we flew together in a flurry of arms and kisses, tears and apologies, crying into each other's hair while Cleopatra put her arms around both of us.

"I'm sorry, I'm so sorry."

"Can we have peace now, dear sisters?" Cleopatra said.

We did. Though, like flawed alabaster, I knew where the cracks were.

I WENT WITH LUCAN nine days later, among the tombs of my ances-tors in the park, walking alone in the fragrant night, his arm around my shoulders tentative and gentle, as though I were some rare crea-ture of moonlight that might vanish like a dream. We lay down on his cloak beneath a cypress tree that shaded the entrance to a tomb. The white marble gleamed coldly in the moonlight.

His lips were warm, and the body I pressed against was as hard and needy as I desired. We explored with hands and lips, touching, caressing. It was not all I had imagined, but it was pleasant and warm. I could not help but feel there must be more that was missing, some spark that should leap from one to another, rather than this indolent dream of moonlight.

Kindle it, I thought. Shape it from shadow, from the light on stones. Shape desire from the pale breadth of his chest, pushing him down beneath me, licking and sucking at his nipples as though he were a girl, hearing his breath catching as his hardness pressed against me. Shape passion from his moans, rubbing against him, straddling his thigh with my skirts lifted, rubbing that tender pearl back and forth against his flesh, my head thrown back, looking down to see his eyes as wide as if I were Aphrodite Herself. I spent against him as I had so often in my own hands, reached for that hard, aching length. He groaned something that might have been my name, and I closed my hand around him, smiling.

When he came in my hands he called out as though he were dying, and afterward he lay on my shoulder like a lost child. Having a lover was not quite all I had imagined, but it certainly was nice. Perhaps next time we should progress to defloration.

"Good," Lucan said, and nibbled at my ear.

I stretched, cramped by lying on stone. The names over the door of the tomb were just visible in the moonlight, relief marking out the dead. I touched the nearest one. HEPHAISTION SON OF THE HIPPARCH LYDIAS AND HIS WIFE CHLOE, FAITHFUL SOLDIER OF PTOLEMY SOTER, FALLEN IN BATTLE IN THE TWENTY-FIRST YEAR OF HIS LIFE... She must have been a woman of some note, to have her name with her husband's on her son's tombstone.

Young men warm and loving go down to the shades below, to Death and His Queen.

Lucan sat up, pulling his cloak around me. "Charmian? Does it bother you to be among the dead like this?"

I smiled. "Why should it? What do we have to fear from the shades of those who have gone before us, who surely loved us?"

———

Unfortunately, within a few weeks I had other things than love to think about.

I had enjoyed a pleasant night out with Lucan, Dion, and their friends while Iras remained with Cleopatra, doing some entirely routine dinner. We traded off those nights that were not affairs of state, so that we did not both have to be there unless it was a great matter. Lucan and I had progressed farther along, though it was not as pleasant as I had hoped. While it didn't exactly hurt, it wasn't comfortable, and the awkwardness fell like a damp sponge on the pleasure I had felt until then.

Lucan left me at the palace gate, where the guardsmen made their usual flirtatious noises. I came in with a pleasant haze of wine around me, interrupted the moment I entered the palace.

One of the messenger boys came rushing up to me. "Lady? The Princess Cleopatra wants to see you in her rooms right away. She says it's most urgent."

I went at a run. It was not like Cleopatra to say that.

I burst into her chambers, but the dining room and sitting area were empty, and so was the bath. I heard Apollodorus' voice coming from our room, and ran to the door.

Cleopatra was talking with an older man, whom I recognized as Pharaoh's personal physician from the Temple of Asclepius. One of the young slave girls held a basin beside the bed, where Iras lay pale and shaking, her limbs trembling and palsied.

"What has happened?" I asked, feeling my pulse beating suddenly in my head.

Cleopatra turned, her eyes shadowed. "Iras got the poison that was meant for me," she said.

THE WOLF'S HEIRS

I f she lives a day, she will live," the physician said. "I have done all I can with the emetic."

Cleopatra nodded. "I see that you have done your best."

The physician knelt down beside Iras on the couch again, pressing his fingers to her wrist. "She is a strong young woman," he said. "And her heart rate, while elevated, is steady, not weak and thready. She has a good chance, Princess."

"What happened?" I demanded. Guilt gnawed at my heart. I had been having fun with Lucan, laughing with my friends, while...

Cleopatra sank into the chair beside the window. "Nothing unexpected. It could have happened anytime. Iras took the portion prepared for me at dinner, and served me a second portion with her own hands. The one prepared for me was poisoned. She took sick before the dinner ended, and we sent for the physician."

"Who?" I said, and did not mean the doctor.

Cleopatra raised an eyebrow. "Who do you think?" She did not wish to say more in front of the serving girl.

"I should have been here," I said.

"And what would you have done?" she asked. "It could as well have been you."

I knew that, but it mattered anyway. I did not sleep until the poison passed from her, and it was clear Iras would recover.

*   *   *

PHARAOH CONDUCTED his own investigation. Five days later, the Queen was sent into exile in Ephesos.

"You must understand," he said when he spoke to her, "that nothing is more important than my heir." I heard so from Asetnefer, who heard from a servant who was there. Auletes would not risk the kingdom again.

I sat beside Iras in the archive room, the scrolls on the table around us, as I told Cleopatra. She nodded gravely.

"I don't understand why she tried it," Iras said. She was feeling almost entirely well now. Whatever the poison was, it had passed out of her body. "Her son would already inherit with Cleopatra. Ptolemy Theodorus will already be Pharaoh. I don't see what she gains so much by getting rid of Cleopatra and having Arsinoe with him instead."

Cleopatra began rolling the scroll neatly and tightly. "She knows Theo has no spine and he'll do anything she wants. I won't. And Arsinoe will play whatever game she's told."

I shrugged. "You're stuck with Theo no matter what. He's only nine, so at least you won't have to marry him for a while."

"Not for five or six years," Cleopatra said. "A lot can happen in five or six years." She tied the cord around the scroll and put the label on, then looked up as if eager to change the subject. "So where are you going tonight?" she asked me.

I shook my head. "I'm ending with Lucan," I said. "I belong here."

HE TOOK IT WELL, I thought. I explained to him that my sister was very sick, and that I had no idea when I would be able to see him again, that he was wonderful and would make someone very happy, but I could hardly hold him when I knew that my duty led me to be apart from him. I thought it was flattering, and as kind as one can be.

After all, what discontent was there to voice? Lucan was considerate and his company was enjoyable. He was handsome enough and more than smart enough. How could I say that I did not love him as he wished to be loved?

If I were a man, I thought, I should love as men do, able to go from one house to another freely, pursuing youths and maidens alike as the whim took me. If I were Ptolemy Auletes, and could have anyone I wished, I would enjoy beauty in all its forms, fair and dark, curved and hard, spiced or pleasing. I should sample all of the delights of the world.

And there were so many. It almost staggered me sometimes, how many forms of beauty there were. I saw it in the broad shoulders of a guardsman, in the handsome dark face of a young doctor from Elephantine, in the lissome movement of a eunuch dancer, in the knowing gravity of Masters of the Sciences from the Museum old enough to be my grandsires. Each, in their turn, looked aside at me, and I felt their eyes following me.

It was not that I was beautiful. When I looked in the mirror I could not see that it was so. My face was symmetrical, only marred by the Ptolemy nose, and my eyes were blue. But so were the eyes of others. There were plenty of young women as fair, with rounded breasts and sweet curves. It was, I thought, something more.

It is an old maxim that Aphrodite gives beauty to women who love Her. Like most young girls, I had thought that meant that those who give offerings will have their skin clear up. Now I understood better. Those who love Her gifts are always beautiful, no matter what they look like.

There were women too who caught my eye. I saw it in the quiet girls with a way of moving that suggested depths of sensuality they had not yet plumbed, or the way some women tossed their heads, beads on the ends of their braids clicking against the smooth honey skin of their necks.

I understood my father better then. With all of the beauty put before him, how could one not sample a little of each? And he, I thought, would understand me.

But I was neither a man nor Pharaoh, so I threw myself into my work. I had the feeling that the time to learn was running out.

Ptolemy Auletes must have felt the same way. He made his will, and keeping one copy in our archives, sent the other off to Rome, to his great ally. "My kingdom I leave in joint trust to my eldest son and daughter alike, the Twin Gods Cleopatra Philopater and Ptolemy Theodorus. It is my wish that they should marry when both have come of age, and from their union should continue the heirs of my kingdom. I therefore establish the executor of my will to be none other than the Republic of Rome, thus to defend the realm of Egypt for my heirs in their minority."

Rome, of course, meant Pompeius, the First Man of Rome. It would be in his interest to balance the Queen, should Auletes die soon. The Queen would not wish to give over the regency to Pompeius Magnus.

Or perhaps what Auletes planned had less to do with some future hypothetical regency, and more to do with defaulting on the fifth payment of the loan. He had paid the fourth, but when the fifth came due there were other things more pressing, including the repair of the breakwater around Pharos. Instead of the money, he concluded a treaty with Rome, promising that forthwith Egypt and Rome should be the sturdiest allies. Egypt should contribute to Roman expeditions in the east, and Rome should defend Egypt against all enemies.

THE INUNDATION CAME. It was a good year, but the flood was high. Many banks and sluices were overrun, and when the water came down they had to be repaired. Day by day, Auletes looked thinner and grayer. He no longer visited the harem, and he complained constantly of a pain in his side. The physicians examined him and looked grim, prescribing rest and care.

The waters receded, and Iras turned eighteen. Dion's most recent friend went to study in Athens, and he was alone again. He moved out of his parents' house, though, to rooms nearer the Museum, supposedly because his astronomy required he keep late hours, but actually because he was tired of assignations in odd places.

There were bills for naval stores, and to repair the walls of Pelousion where Gabinius had breached them for Ptolemy so long ago. We defaulted on the sixth payment of the loan.

This time Pompeius did not send his banker to collect the money. This time he sent his son.

A T T H I S T I M E Gnaeus Pompeius was twenty-four, and though he was well built, he was not handsome. He was the oldest son of Pompeius Magnus, however, and might in due course of time become, like his father, the First Man of Rome. He did not remind me of a wolf, but of a jackal, decidedly untrustworthy.

The son of a devoted friend could not have greeted Auletes more smoothly, or with greater graciousness. He did not drink excessively in public, and when he was invited to use the palace baths, he displayed a body that was honed to perfection by military life.

"Watch him for me," Cleopatra said. "There are half a dozen attendants in the bath at any time. No one will notice you in particular if you dress like the others, and stand about holding towels. I want to know what you think of him. Candidly."

So I went to the baths and stood about the pool, moving jars of oil from one place to another and watching while Gnaeus Pompeius splashed about in the pool and lay on a cushioned couch for a slave to massage him. When he turned over so that she could work on his front, his phallus was already erect, glossy and surrounded by dark curls. I averted my eyes, so that I should not seem curious, glancing beneath my lids.

She worked on his legs. It was Philene, one of the best girls, and the most professional. She displayed no embarrassment as she worked. He was so swift I hardly saw it as he grabbed her wrist, his other hand slipping between her legs and grabbing her by the pubic hair. Philene squeaked, more with surprise than alarm.

"There's a use for all this oil," he said, sliding her oiled hands onto his manhood; she was caught on one knee, unable to back up, held by the hair.

Her mouth opened as he sat up, drawing her down hard onto him in full view of every bath slave. The two boys who sluiced bathers off gaped. He thrust hard while Philene tried to find the rhythm, to keep her composure, biting down on her lip. With each thrust he withdrew almost completely, driving hard. There was no sound in the baths except the slap of his skin on hers. It only took him a few minutes. He came with a groan, drawing out of her, his hands leaving red marks on her hips. Her distended nether lips seemed to clutch at him, moist and full and purpling.

I felt it deep in my stomach, my answering arousal, and with it the horror. I had never been taken like that, as though I were nothing, before half the household, and I imagined I should like it no better than Philene did.

Gnaeus Pompeius took a towel from the stack and cleaned himself off, while Philene stood mute, clutching the edge of the couch.

Tossing the towel on the couch, he strode off toward the dressing room.

I found my voice. "Myrtle," I said to the steadiest of the attendants, "tend to Philene, please. You are both dismissed from your duties today." I did not trust myself to touch her.

I TOLD CLEOPATRA everything, everything except my arousal. That was nothing she needed to know.

She looked away, out the window that faced the sea. "Oh sweet Isis," she said.

"I know," I said. "He had no business. Philene's not in the harem. And she hadn't done anything to encourage him."

Cleopatra nodded. She seemed abstracted. "He can't send for her. Tell her that, and the Master of the Baths too. That's not her job. And tell her she can slip out if he comes into the baths." She walked over to the window, and I could not see her face. "Sweet Isis."

"It's a message," Iras said. "Everything that's here is his. It's about politics, not Philene."

"I know," Cleopatra said. "But there's no other way to sweeten the deal enough this time."

"What do you mean?" I asked.

"No," Iras said at the same moment. "No. Absolutely no." She stood up, her hands clenched. "Auletes can't mean to do that. That old pimp!"

"We don't have any other choice." Cleopatra turned around, her chin high. "The only thing that will sweeten the deal enough to keep him from his father's mission is me."

"You can't do it," Iras said, grasping at straws. "You're supposed to marry Theo."

"Theo is eleven years old," Cleopatra snapped. "He's no help. He's nothing at all. The only other thing Auletes could do is throw Arsinoe at him, but she's three years younger than I am, and she's not the heir."

"Gnaeus could marry Arsinoe," I said. "And take her away from here where she can't be the focus for her mother's faction anymore."

"Except that he already has a wife," Cleopatra said. "A woman named Appia. I don't like it. But I don't see any other way."

"I won't permit it," Iras said, her face flushed.

Cleopatra walked toward her, and put her hand to Iras' shoulder. "Dear Iras," she said, "you are not my brother."

"I wish I were," she said. "I would never let you do this while you have breath in your body."

"There isn't any other way!" Cleopatra dropped her hand and spun about. "Don't you see that? I just have to make the best of it. If he calls in the whole debt, we have no way to pay. The economy will collapse. It's worse than it was in my great-uncle's day, when he melted down Alexander's golden sarcophagus and replaced it with a glass one. If I don't do this, we're going to have to start robbing the dead. It's either that, or rob the living."

Iras and I looked at each other. I opened my mouth and then shut it.

"I need you to stand behind me," Cleopatra said, her back to us. Her voice sounded odd. "If you can't do that, I need you to leave."

"I'm with you," I said. "You know that I am."

Iras nodded. "I'll do what you need me to do," she said.

I took a step toward her. "You know we would never leave you."

She nodded. One piece of hair had fallen from her pins. "It can't be worse than a bitter draft, can it?"

"And maybe sweet can come after," I said. "After this, you could pick your lovers as you wished."

"I doubt I can ever do that," she said.

FOUR NIGHTS LATER, Pharaoh entertained privately in one of his small dining rooms, three couches, one for Cleopatra, one for him, and one for Gnaeus Pompeius. When the evening was over, she came back to her bedroom.

"Brush out my hair, Iras," she said. "And bring me a silk robe. The pale pink one."

Iras went to find it, and I knelt beside her, pressing her hand to my lips.

"Does it hurt?" she whispered.

"Not so badly," I said. "It's better if you're wet first."

She nodded.

"I liked it," I said. "After a while. But Lucan was gentle."

She nodded again, looking over the cosmetics arrayed on her table. "Take that oil there," she said, "and put it where it needs to be. Quickly, before Iras gets back. It will upset her."

I took the glass bottle and poured some out, still kneeling. She lifted her chiton and spread her legs while I warmed the oil in my hands, attar of roses, the oil we had used to anoint the goddess' image back in Bubastis. "Like a goddess," I whispered.

She gave me a tiny smile.

I worked the oil into her nether lips, sliding one slick finger just inside, making sure it was where it needed to be. She did not resist my fingers at all. I felt the soft skin there flush in my hands.

"It will be better if you can touch yourself some," I said. "When he's with you." I didn't look at her face.

We had never talked of such things directly, Iras, Cleopatra, and I.

But we had shared a room long enough to know the sounds in the night that come when one thinks one's sisters are asleep.

She nodded, straightening her chiton as I sat back on my heels. I slid the stopper into the bottle.

Iras came in, holding the robe. "It's one of your best," she said.

"I know."

There was a knock at the door. I went to it, and called to the guardsman outside. "Who is it?"

"Gnaeus Pompeius seeks entry, Lady."

Cleopatra stood up, the robe falling in graceful folds around her. "Please let him in. Then you may go."

DEBTS

n the morning, I waited until I heard movement in her chamber
before I went in. Cleopatra was awake and standing beside the
window, draping her pink robe about her. She put her finger to
her lips.

Gnaeus Pompeius was sprawled across her bed, sleeping. He was
completely naked, except for one of the bedsheets tangled around his
feet. It had a bloody stain, no more than a few drops.

She tiptoed across the room to me, and did not speak until we were
outside and the door was closed behind us. "Leave him be. Let's go to
the palace baths. There won't likely be anyone there this early."

I wondered why, when she had her own bath right here that she
usually preferred, but then if Gnaeus woke up he might decide to
bathe too.

We went to the palace baths, which were indeed empty except for
one old slave who was putting clean cloths out. She got in the warm
bath, and I settled to washing her hair. Cleopatra leaned her head back
onto the rolled cloths at the edge of the pool. As my fingers worked the
lotions through her hair, I saw her face begin to relax, the tight lines
around her mouth fading away.

I did not ask how it had gone.

After a while she sighed. "It was not as bad as it could have been,"
she said. "I suppose it could have been much worse. Now comes the
hard part."

I raised my eyebrows. "The hard part?"

"I have to keep him interested until he forgets about the money. For as long as it takes, I must play the lover."

"How long?" I asked.

"Until we can pay Pompeius his debt, or until something happens." Cleopatra closed her eyes. "Sooner or later, something will."

AND SO we bought a little time. Gnaeus Pompeius made himself comfortable as the honored guest of Pharaoh Ptolemy Auletes, dicing, hunting lions in the desert rather fruitlessly, attending one banquet after another, and of course dallying with Cleopatra, who kept an eternally bland smile on her face. He had no interest in the running of the realm, in the business and internal politics that continually demanded the attention of the ruler. As far as he was concerned, Egypt governed itself as nothing more than a big moneymaking arrangement. Pompeius Magnus might be the First Man of Rome, and famed for his political prowess, but his eldest son seemed to understand little of governance besides force. He spoke no more than a few words of Koine, seeing it of little importance to understand what people might say around him. It was a good thing that Cleopatra, Iras, and I had studied Latin. He expected everyone to speak it to him.

Meanwhile, by day, Cleopatra immersed herself in the running of the realm. No detail was too small or complicated to study, that she might see how it was done, or how the men who attended to it served her. How should she know if it were done wrong, at some future time, if she did not know how it was supposed to be? So she spent her days learning about canal dredging, talking with scientists and priests, with the Patriarch of the chief synagogue of Alexandria, with the Treasurer, and with the Horologers who measured time and set the calendar, predicting when the Inundation would come.

When the next payment came due, Gnaeus Pompeius wrote to his father.

Though it is clear that Ptolemy Auletes intends to repay his debt in good faith, it has been a difficult year in Egypt. The harvest was poor, and the revenues have been much less than expected. Consequently, it is impossible for him to send the payment at this time without imposing great hardship on his people. As a wise farmer tends his fields so that they may yield more in the long run, we must wisely allow him to husband his people, so that in due course of time our investment may pay greater dividends.

Gnaeus Pompeius sent the letter, but no one doubted that the words were Cleopatra's. Certainly Pompeius Magnus did not doubt it. The next month a letter came from him to his son, stating it plainly.

I know that you greatly enjoy the hospitality of Ptolemy Auletes; however, I hope that you will remember your duty to me. If it is difficult to collect the debt, then you must lend your energy to its collection, and not accept any idle excuses you are given.

Gnaeus Pompeius took the letter straight to Auletes. Auletes put his hand on Gnaeus' arm, his eyes shining with unshed tears. "So might a father speak, to such a son as you! Alas, if I had so worthy a son, my burdens would be lighter! But I am only an old man, whose health is failing, and the prop of my throne is Cleopatra. True, she is nineteen, and her beauty and wit are unsurpassed, but she is only a woman! You must not blame us if all is not done as you would wish. Your mercy on my failing age, and her feminine foibles, dear Gnaeus! Would that I had a man such as you to follow after me, as her consort and husband!"

Iras got Gnaeus Pompeius' reply for his father before it left, and made a clever copy so that we all might see.

Most esteemed father, I hear and reverence your words. I have come upon an opportunity too wonderful to pass by — it seems that Ptolemy Auletes is ailing, and his eldest daughter is much taken with me. Would it be possible, do you think, for you to pro-cure a divorce for me from Appia? If so, I could promise you always the riches of Egypt at your disposal....

Before a reply could come from Rome, the worst happened. Ptolemy Auletes died.

His death was hardly unexpected. We were prepared. He had been ill for months, and his last sickness went on for weeks before he drew his final breath. By that time we could only hope he would go soon, and suffer no more. At least that is what I hoped. I loved him, I suppose, for all that he only regarded me a little. He had done well by me. I had not lacked for anything it was in his power to give. Those things that were not within his power, I did not begrudge him.

I walked in the funeral cortege, far in the rear, with the other women of Cleopatra's household, my hair covered with a white veil. About me, Iras and the others set up ritual wails.

Now I should never know, I thought. I should never know what he had felt, who he had been. Was my mother as little to him as Lucan was to me? Who was he, and what might he have said, if things had been different? Of all his children, Asetnefer said I was the one most like him, the one who might have understood.

If I had been born a boy, I should even now stand as a contender to the throne. Auletes himself had been a son of the harem. He would not have hesitated to raise me to the throne beside Cleopatra, a much more compatible consort to her than Theo, now known as Young Ptolemy. If I were a boy, would it be I who even now walked beside his bier, beside my sister in mourning? Would it be I who stood as Horus, the son of Serapis, the promised Falcon of Egypt?

Something in me whispered that I could do it. If I were a boy, I should be her consort, the prop to her throne, her general. I should exchange fashion for a sword, and the meticulous dance of court events for the swirl of the battlefield. Instead of provisioning funeral feasts, I should provision armies. And I should do it well.

I inclined my head. Through the trumpets and drums of the funeral procession, I heard Isis' voice speaking softly behind me. *That is not the task I have set before you.*

Auletes lay in a crypt in the royal parkland, long prepared for him, in a sarcophagus of Carian marble, his mummy wrapped in fine linen and encased in gold.

"It's only gold leaf," Cleopatra whispered to me after. "Over cartonnage. We can't possibly afford gold."

"I'm sure it's beautiful," I said, thinking how it was like Auletes, to look fine beneath something that was essentially no more than paper, the kind of coffin used by ordinary people. Even in death, he still owed money to Pompeius Magnus. Unfortunately, that debt still hung around our necks.

"How are you going to find the money?" I asked Cleopatra. There would be Theo's counselors to deal with as well as the men who had served Auletes. His tutor was a man called Theocritus, whom I didn't like, and his household was run by a eunuch named Pothinus, who had come to us from Tyre. They would have a great deal to say, I imagined.

"I don't know yet," she said, and shook her head.

In a few days, I saw how at least she meant to delay.

"You must stay with me," Cleopatra said. She reclined beside Gnaeus Pompeius on the dining couch, lifting a morsel of meat to her mouth. "Now that I am bereft of my father, what shall I do?"

Gnaeus Pompeius raised his wine cup. "I'm sure my father will make certain that Rome supports the terms of the will. And supports your claim to the throne. I suppose you must marry your brother, as your father intended."

"But Theo is only twelve," she said, gazing at him adoringly. "And there are factions and factions here at court."

"You don't need to worry," he said. "I will see you crowned. And then perhaps I will see if I can find you a better husband than your little brother."

"That would please me greatly," she said, dipping her head and smiling at him.

"She cannot think to marry him," Iras fumed in native Egyptian. "He is nothing, nothing except the spoiled son of a rich man who does his father's bidding badly. She is the daughter of kings, of the noblest line in the world."

"I do not think she means to marry him," I said. "But she certainly means to be crowned. And I doubt that the Queen's faction would wish it."

Though the Queen was gone, her faction among the nobles was alive and well. And Theo had a full sister, Arsinoe, who could be his queen as well as Cleopatra. I wondered if she should have Arsinoe killed, but dared not say anything about it to her. I was sure she would not do it. Not until something happened to make Arsinoe less innocent. She would not be Berenice. That I knew.

Of the coronation, I cannot say as much as I should. Mostly, I remember the tremendous amount of work. A coronation is a complicated affair, and the priests of the Temple of Serapis and Isis were very firm on what must go into it, that it should conform to the formulae of previous coronations. There were huge crowds lining the streets from the gates of the Palace Quarter to the Serapeum, cheering and shouting, throwing flowers. For although this was their fourth ruler in five years, the people of Alexandria loved a festival.

Meanwhile, Gnaeus Pompeius had some bad news of his own. Not only was his father pressing for a loan payment, but it seemed that Pompeius Magnus himself was in great need of money. His feud with this Caesar, which had at first seemed some sort of falling out between men closely allied by marriage, had gone further. Caesar was in arms against Pompeius, or against Rome itself, depending on whose letters were most reliable. In any event, Pompeius was raising an army, which is never a cheap endeavor. Toward that end, he was sending Gnaeus some very probing letters, pushing for funds immediately.

After as great a delay as possible, Cleopatra sent as little as she could. Still, it was talents and talents of gold, money we might have better spent in Egypt. And not enough to more than put off Pompeius Magnus for a short time.

On top of this, the harvest in the north was poor. Cleopatra directed, in the name of the joint rulers, the Twin Gods Ptolemy and Cleopatra Philopater, that the grain surplus from Upper Egypt should be sent to Alexandria immediately. If the price of grain in the city went too high, we risked the kind of riots that had originally cost Auletes his throne.

———

Iʀᴀs ᴘᴀssᴇᴅ her twentieth birthday, and then Cleopatra did, in the winter when the fields of the Black Land greened. And as the year turned, the days measured by the Horologers getting almost imperceptibly longer, Gnaeus Pompeius received yet another letter from his father.

While Gnaeus was out hunting, Iras and Apollodorus worked on the letter, carefully steaming loose Pompeius Magnus' seal without damaging it. Cleopatra paced around the room.

"Not more money," Cleopatra said, stopping by the windows, her himation hanging over one arm instead of about her shoulders. "Not more money now. It's not possible. We're bleeding money right now on grain."

"We have to," I said from where I sat in a chair by the table. "It will be months yet before the new harvest, and the city has to have grain. If you don't keep the price down, it will be a disaster."

"I'll have to think of something to keep Gnaeus busy," Cleopatra said. She was silhouetted against the light from the windows, and I couldn't see her face. "His father is pressing him hard."

"I have it," Apollodorus said, and carefully he and Iras unrolled the letter.

"Is it money he wants?" I asked.

Iras shook her head, bending over the letter, her brows knitted. "No. Troops. He wants Gnaeus to take all of the men he brought with him and come to Greece immediately. It seems that Caesar has driven him from Italy, and Pompeius intends to make a stand in Greece. He directs Gnaeus to set out without delay, as any delay may be critical." Iras looked up. "That's a mixed bag."

"We get rid of Gnaeus, anyway," I said, glancing toward Cleopatra.

"And his troops," she replied. Cleopatra turned, leaning on the window ledge. "Which leaves us with nothing but the mercenaries Auletes hired, and no actual Royal Army except for them. And their loyalty is for sale to the highest bidder."

"Reconstituting the army would take money," I pointed out. "Especially since the mercenaries have to be paid."

Cleopatra stretched back on her arms. "Sometimes I hate Auletes," she said. "He managed to mortgage the kingdom and destroy the army at the same time!"

Iras laid the scroll carefully on the table. "What else could he have done?"

"Nothing!" Cleopatra began pacing again. "It's as well to be rid of Gnaeus, and that's a pause at least in the relentless demands for money, but his troops..."

"Are what secured your throne," Apollodorus said. "Gracious Queen, if I were you I would be very careful."

"I mean to be," she said.

THREE WEEKS AFTER Gnaeus Pompeius sailed for Greece, we were all placed under arrest by order of Pharaoh Ptolemy Theodorus.

THE MIRROR
OF ISIS

I looked into the mirror, and the Queen of Egypt looked back. Beneath the heavy black wig with its hanging plaits, eyes rimmed in kohl gleamed under shadowed brows, the green malachite paint on my eyelids drawn out to the very corners. My lips were red, my skin pale, more a mask than a face in the formal paint.

"Try this," she said, and I felt the weight as the uraeus settled upon my brow. The gilded cobra seemed almost to move in the dim light.

"You'll do," Iras said. Her sharp dark eyes met mine in the mirror as it tilted, her face beside mine. "You'll do if no one sees your eyes in the light."

Cleopatra bent, tilting the mirror again. "No one should see her that closely," she said. "It will be dark, and she will have her head inclined a good part of the time."

Iras grimaced. We had played The Game for amusement, but now it was deadly earnest. If Cleopatra stayed in the palace, it was only a matter of time before some assassin succeeded. It might be that she was only kept alive until after the holy days, because if she were not able to do the Queen's part in the ceremonies there would be talk. On the other hand, the ceremonies themselves might be the focus of an assassination attempt. An attack by a seeming madman, cut down by Pharaoh's guards in the full view of the city, would deflect suspicion from him.

When I had taken a knife for her in the past I had only a moment to think on it. Now I should deliberately and coolly provoke it.

The rites of Isis, like those of the other Egyptian gods, required the ancient dress of the Black Land. The gown was sheer linen, almost translucent, pleated into dozens of folds that almost concealed the opening at the front from hem to waist. It would not swing open unless I ran or moved carelessly. It belted tight beneath my breasts, and a long semicircular, pleated linen collar fastened around my neck, falling to the waist front and back. On that was placed a great jeweled collar set with malachite and turquoise, faience, and bits of ruby glass. It weighed tremendously. If I did not stand very straight it threatened to pull me over on my face, even with the counterweight attached at the back.

Iras fussed at every pleat, as she did for the Queen. I stood still.

Cleopatra circled me, her brows furrowed. When she saw my expression she smiled suddenly. "You do look very like me," she said. "The stamp of the Ptolemies is fairly unmistakable."

THE CEREMONIAL PROCESSION wound its way out of the Palace Quarter, between parks and guesthouses, beneath wide arches and porticos, beneath the broad gate itself. On ordinary days, the Queen should be borne this way in a litter, but today we were all postulants of Isis. I walked shod in gilded sandals, surrounded by four of the most junior attendants on the Queen, who were in turn surrounded by Pharaoh's guards. Always surrounded by guards. Ostensibly, they were to show his sister honor. Yet no matter how respectful their salutes, how gilded their ornament, I was under no illusion I was not a prisoner.

My steps were proud and slow, dignified as befitted the Queen of Egypt. Let them watch. Let all eyes be on me. Eyes that are upon me are not seeking elsewhere. If everyone knows where the Queen is, in the full view of all Alexandria, no one will wonder at the movements of two servants, slave girls who might go to the markets or about their mistress' business on any day. No one would notice Iras and Cleopatra, leaving even now, their himations over their heads as they went to make their devotions at some smaller temple this feast day.

We passed through the shadow of the great gate. Its shade fell over me, cool and pleasant. Above, the first Ptolemy looked out from the wall, his carved face seeming somehow amused. Do you see what I do? I thought. Do you watch this game among your descendants? Do you dwell in paradise in the deathless western lands of Amenti, or are you born again, walking the streets of this city you built?

The procession turned into the Canopic Way. Wide enough for four carts to pass abreast, lined with fine buildings, the Canopic Way stretched straight as an arrow through the heart of the city, from the eastward gate almost to the city wall at the Inner Harbor. Past the Museum and the great Library, the Street of the Soma gave southward, to the Temples of Serapis and Isis, and the tomb of Alexander.

The glare was almost blinding. Those buildings that were not faced with white marble in the Greek style were built of light-colored stone in the Egyptian, some faced with gypsum to seem grander. The street was clad in pale sandstone, washed clean before dawn of the previous day's filth. Each building along the processional way had been prepared as well, votive statues given a good scrubbing, and I noted with some amusement that the massive statue of Ptolemy Philadelphos that stood halfway along lacked his usual crown of lackadaisical seagulls. Normally, they kept a raucous commentary on the events in the streets below, swooping down to snatch up anything dropped that bore the slightest resemblance to food.

My eyes watered against the light, even shadowed as they were by kohl. The wig weighed a thousand talents. On my brow, the uraeus warmed in the sun.

Past the great sweeping colonnades at the front of the Library, the procession began its turn into the Street of the Soma. Ahead, between the steel-tipped spears of the escort, I could see the high dome that marked where Alexander lay in his sarcophagus of glass.

And then we passed into blessed shade, into the portico of the temple. Girls came forward with basins of clear water, holding them that we might bathe our hands before we stepped into the temple itself. One of the maidens assisted me, unfastening jeweled sandals and washing the dust of the city from my hennaed feet.

The inner courtyard was crowded, and likewise the temple itself, dark after the street outside. Resinous smoke billowed up from two great braziers before the altar, myrrh and frankincense and kephri, dark and fragrant as the night of Her search, touched with lotus and something more sweet beneath the scent of funerals.

One of the guards stumbled, momentarily blinded by the sudden darkness.

The Queen's place was at the front, and the crowds parted as they should, our party passing through, stopping just before the right-hand brazier, the guards coming to rest with their gilded spear butts against the stone floor.

High up on the walls, the shadows shifted with the faint movements of flame in the braziers, old gods seeming to walk along the walls. Thoth inclined His head to the throne, where Isis sat beside Her husband. Ma'at suspended a feather and a heart. The Lord of the Dead stretched forth His hand. Silence filled the temple.

I inclined my head. I could hear my own heart pounding in my chest. The braids swung forward, half-hiding my bent face. Perhaps it looked like piety. Perhaps no one else was really paying attention. I closed my eyes and rested in the perfumed darkness. Even the faint sounds of the people about me faded away.

Mother Isis, I thought, the most impious of thoughts, let me get away with it!

Then in the darkness there was a voice, whether the voice of woman or boy I could not tell, high and pure as heaven's arch. "If I do not bring you solace, then at least I bring you light. Hope is more precious than the brightest gold. If I do not bring you solace, then at least I bring you love. Hope is more precious than the brightest gold."

The story was older than time, old as memory, and I had learned it as a child like everyone does, celebrated it each year. In that long ago night, the Widow wandered, Her husband slain and His body dismembered. Lost and alone, She wandered in the swamps of the Delta. Only the stars shone down on Her with pity.

"If I do not bring you solace, then at least I bring you light. Nothing is more precious than hope." The voice soared, filling the temple with its bright solo, clear and strong as starlight. In the depths of the swamp, in the depths of despair, Isis sought the parts of Her husband's body and quickened it, lay with Him for one night only. "Nothing is more precious than hope."

And now the sistrums began, on the same note as the children's choir, their voices pure and light. "If I do not bring you solace, then at least I bring you light!" I opened my eyes and I saw them singing as they'd been taught, their mouths opening and closing with the exaggeration of children who have been told to enunciate. "Hope is more precious than the brightest gold!"

In the darkness of Her despair, She gave birth to a son, infant Horus who would restore the world, whose bright eyes opened like the rising sun.

Through some marvel of engineering, fire ran down the long channels at the front of the temple, pouring like liquid into the vast bronze cressets, the entire front of the temple blazing forth suddenly with the brilliance of leaping flame.

"If I do not bring you peace, then at least I bring you love." The men's choir came in, their strong voices ringing, and behind them the deep drums like a heartbeat, old and fine.

The sun rose over the steaming swamps of the Delta, a Prince who should return to save His people, Horus, the Son of the Widow. In His bright ascension we are made whole, and life begins anew.

"For nothing is more precious than hope," they sang, and my heart filled. I felt the uraeus warm on my brow, not a burden but a weight, as though it too quickened in the pulse of the flames.

Mother Isis, I thought, please help me do what is best for Egypt. Please help me do what is best for Your people.

I heard Her then, as if She kissed me softly on the brow. *They are all My people.*

I closed my eyes, not against the darkness but against the light, long lashes sweeping my cheek for a moment.

The priest was coming down from the high altar with the oil in his hand, his shaven head slick. The children were singing, their sistrums shaking, each bronze disc glittering in the leaping light. I felt his hand on my forehead for a moment, rose and myrrh of the anointing oil. Of course the Queen should be the first, and the Hierophant himself should tend her.

"Thank you, Father," I said.

"Peace be to you and yours, Cleopatra, Lover of Egypt," he said.

By the time I returned to the palace, it was almost evening. I changed back into my own clothes, being careful to remove every trace of the heavy makeup, and put the wig neatly on its stand. Cleopatra's room was quiet and tidy, nothing out of place. I stood looking out the windows toward the harbor, waiting. I should have to do this before I fled, to set the time that Cleopatra left. I felt vaguely nauseous.

As soon as the sun set, I walked to the main doors and pushed them open, running past the guard outside toward Pharaoh's rooms, calling out for Pothinus.

The guard caught me at the entrance to his chambers, grabbing me about the waist. "Here now," he said, as I struggled feebly.

"I have to see Pothinus," I said. "Please let me in. It's very important."

"You can't just barge in there," the guard said.

"It's very important!" I sobbed. "I have to see Pothinus!"

In a moment he came out to me. I had never liked him, but he looked every inch the courtier, polished and well bred. "Is there a problem?" he asked mildly.

The guard let go of me.

I fell to my knees before his fine leather slippers. "Forgive me, oh gods! Let not your wrath fall on me!"

"What has happened?" There was a note of alarm in his voice now.

"The Queen is gone!" I gasped. "I helped her disrobe after the ceremony, and she sent me to fetch wine and food for her, and when I returned she was gone, she and Iras! Oh gods, they have left me to feel Pharaoh's wrath!" I pressed my face against his toes.

"What?" Pothinus kicked me accidentally as he grabbed my elbows. "What?"

"The Queen is gone!" I sobbed. "Fled with Iras! Oh mercy upon me!"

"When?" I thought irreverently that Pothinus was being a bit slow on the uptake, as I had to keep repeating lines. "Tell me, girl!" He shook me.

"Just now I think," I said. "I wasn't gone long. Just long enough to go to the kitchens. And I put her wig on the stand and shook it out first. She wore the heavy wig for the ceremony, and it has to be blocked right away. It's very expensive, you know."

"Just now." Pothinus looked about as though he expected Cleopatra to materialize from a shadow. "You, fetch the captain of the guard. Search the palace! The Queen must not be allowed to escape!" He dropped me and I collapsed to the floor, sobbing where I fell while over my head the guards ran about, mustering and giving orders. It seemed to go on forever. I hoped I was forgotten, and that no one would think to question me more closely until later.

The stamping feet began to die away, and Pothinus had gone to join the hunt, keen to direct matters himself. I made myself not run toward the portico of the bathhouse. I would not go to my room. If Pothinus wanted more information from me, that was where he should look first.

Among the linens and towels was my bundle, tied up to look like the rest. I got out the dark cloak, put the bundle under my arm, and slipped out of the bathhouse window into the night.

Quietly, I made my way into the park. There were no search parties there yet. Obviously, they thought she was still in the palace. And in any event, one could not leave the park without going through one of the gates and the guards there.

The tombs and mausoleums gleamed in the moonlight. We should have waited for a moonless night, but we did not think we had half a month. I tried to stay in the shadow of the trees, making my way among the older tombs closer to the harbor gate.

Silver droplets played in the air from a fountain, and I came to crouch behind it. The basin was a massive stone sarcophagus once belonging to Nectanebo II. Ptolemy Philadelphos had it drilled as a fountain that caused the water to play in the night air, spreading a sweet mist about. I knelt there, one hand on the stone. My heart beat so loudly I thought it must be audible at a distance, but part of me was exhilarated. The night was cool, and the plan was working.

I heard running feet and froze. There was a sound, and then a body dropped on top of me. "Ooof!"

"Dion?" I tried to sort out his splayed limbs while he righted himself.

"I didn't know you were already here," he whispered.

"I'm here," I replied. "And Cleopatra, Iras, and Apollodorus are away. What about Apollodorus' family?"

"His wife and the four younger children are at my aunt's house," Dion said. "And the oldest two are at my cousin Gorion's. Or Yusef. Or whatever his name is this week." Dion gave me a sideways grin. "He can't ever decide if he's using his Hebrew name or his Greek one. They'll all be safe. My family will hide them."

I nodded. Cleopatra could hardly flee with Apollodorus' family, the youngest not but six, but as soon as Apollodorus was seen to be missing his family would probably be arrested and questioned. Better that they disappear into the Jewish Quarter.

Dion looked up. "Now don't you think we'd better get started? I've got us passage up the Mareotic Canal on a trade ship. I told the captain I was eloping with a Gentile girl, and my parents would be furious."

"Well," I said. "I suppose I can pretend to be madly in love with you."

"Work at it," he said, and helped me to my feet.

We approached the gate on the palace harbor side together, his arm around my waist, with me leaning on him and looking at him adoringly, strolling along in plain view of the torches. There were guardsmen I knew, men who had whistled or called to me before, but it seemed there were many more of them on the gate than I ever remembered seeing.

"Hold there!" one called.

We stopped full in the light.

"What's going on?" Dion asked, as one of the guardsmen came forward.

"Where have you been?" he replied.

Dion and I exchanged loving glances. "Just...around..." He gave the guardsman a wink and a grin. "You know. Paying our respects among the tombs."

I blushed furiously as one of the guards catcalled, one who had always called out to me before.

"This is Charmian," Dion said. "One of the Queen's maidservants. You know her."

I tilted my head up in the glare of the torches, letting the cloak fall back and uncover my light hair.

"That's her," the guard said. "Fancy a real man next time, love?"

"I've got a real man," I said, twining my arm around Dion.

"We're going for a bite to eat," Dion said. "Any problem with that?"

"Bring me some of what you've got," the wit said.

"No problem," the senior one said. "Mind you come back in the open. There are some who are jumpy and will hit first and ask questions later."

"Thanks, my friend," Dion said.

We walked through arm-in-arm, winding our way down the street toward the harbor, our heads together. I'm sure we made a pretty picture.

"Oh my God," Dion whispered, "I nearly had an accident."

I started giggling. And then I couldn't stop. I was sure they could hear it at the gate, and it made our story all the better.

"Will you shut up?" Dion hissed. "It's not that funny. It's not that funny at all."

"My poor little boy," I said, leaning on him and slipping one hand down toward the front of his tunic. "Do you need to go take care of that?"

"Charmian, for the love of…" Dion grabbed my hand, and then he couldn't stop laughing either. He took my hand and we ran all of the way to the boat.

L O R D · O F · T H E
B L A C K   L A N D

W e followed the Mareotic Canal all that night, the barge
making its way slowly upstream under the stars, drawn
by oxen on the shore plodding steadily. A boy walked
with them, sleepily driving them along the bank. The commerce of
the land of Egypt did not stop when the sun set. Perhaps it once was
so, but now the great grain barges went back and forth all night.

I did not think I could sleep, but I did. When I woke just before dawn
all was quiet. I was stretched out on the deck toward the bow, and Dion
sat beside me. He clasped his knees as if he were a boy, with his head
tilted back, looking up at the stars. He glanced down at me, and seeing I
was awake, spoke softly. "Do you suppose the stars have changed?"

I smiled, looking up. The night air was cold. Above, the dawn stars
winked brightly away from the haze of the city. "Why would they
change?"

Dion smiled up at them as though they were old friends. "Every
year the Earth moves a little differently on her axis, like a top not quite
spinning true. It's an infinitesimal part of a degree each year, but over
two or three thousand years, it should change quite a bit. Do you suppose any of the old temples up the Nile have a star painting?"

"They might," I said.

"Still, that wouldn't account for it," he mused.

"Account for what?"

Dion glanced at me. "I remember different stars."

A chill ran down my back that had nothing to do with the night's breeze. "Remember what?" I asked gently.

Dion tilted his head back again. "Sitting under a night sky like this, on a beach where the tide was coming in. Just sitting. Looking up at the night. But the constellations were all different."

"Tell me about it," I said.

"Just that," he said. "That's all." He smiled at me. "I'm not like you."

"Like me?"

Dion settled closer to me, as though he shared my couch at a party. "In another age you'd have been a seer, a prophetess. Touched by the gods."

"I don't know anything," I said. I knew what a real oracle was, what one should be, and I was not that, someone who lived for the gods.

"You believe," he said. "And you know what you believe. You know who you are."

I leaned against him. "I just am, Dion. There's nothing special about it."

"There is," he said. "You're someone who can see the pattern clearly. But we don't really believe in things like that anymore." Dion grinned. "Alexandria, the city where you can believe in any gods you want, as long as you don't take it too seriously!"

"Surely most people believe in the gods," I said.

Dion shrugged. "Educated people don't. Philosophers don't. Courtiers don't. I'd bet any amount of money there's not one of the council who actually believes in the gods, except for Cleopatra."

"Politics is ruled by self-interest," I said. "But surely most people are better than that."

"You think?" Dion raised an eyebrow. "I think most people just look after their own. And that's not malice. It's just that most people don't think about anyone outside their circle. They don't want to think about grain farmers in Upper Egypt, or orphans in Ashkelon, or people burned out by wars in Cyrene. Unless they know them personally, or they're kin. How many people would take in an orphan who wasn't their relative?"

"The temples do," I said. "The Temple of Bastet in Bubastis had a bunch of orphans."

"But that was a temple," Dion said. "Presumably a temple is run by people who make it their business to care about others."

"Isn't it everyone's business?" I asked. I had never considered that it might not be. From my earliest days on, we had always thought of Egypt and her people. But now that I considered it, I wasn't sure why that was so. It wasn't in our lessons, really. The three of us had decided upon it, as surely as we had chosen to be the Hands of Isis.

Dion looked at me very seriously, as though weighing something important. "No. Not everyone makes it their business." He took a deep breath. "I do. Make it my business, I mean. I took oaths. I took a sacred vow to work to build the Temple with all my strength and power in this life."

"An oath to whom? The Hebrew god?"

"Well, to one of His servants, actually," Dion said, shifting his arm about me, his voice low. "To one of His angels, Mikhael. He was the angel of the Lord who defeated Sennacherib the Akkadian seven hundred years ago."

I looked up at him, my head to the side. "I thought the Pharaoh Shebitku defeated him at the Battle of Pelousion."

"With the aid of the angel Mikhael," Dion said smugly. "And then Shebitku restored Jerusalem to its people. He has long been the defender of peace in this part of the world, though he is a warrior at need."

I leaned back against Dion. It seemed to me I had heard this story before, somewhere. "But you are not a warrior, Dion."

"I don't fight with a sword," he said. "But what else would you call it, helping the Queen escape Alexandria and fight for her throne? What else would you call it when I spend my life seeking things that will improve the lives of all mankind? That's the purpose of all my studies. Like Archimedes, I want to create things that feed people and give them healthy water, that save backbreaking work and that add to the store of knowledge. Because through these things, sure as anything else under the sun, we are all elevated."

I swallowed, feeling tears start in my eyes. "Dion, I made an oath too. To Isis. I…we…promised to defend this land, and to love the Black Land and govern it for the good of all its people."

"'We'?" I did not answer, but Dion laughed, bending his head against mine. "You and Iras and Cleopatra. There's only one 'we' for you."

I nodded. "Isis agreed that Cleopatra should be queen, if she would swear her own oath to govern always for the good of Egypt, to keep the bargains of the first Ptolemy."

"'The bargains of the first Ptolemy'?"

There was an odd sound in Dion's voice, and I craned my neck to look up at him. "The first Ptolemy made oaths," I said slowly. "He made a bargain with the gods of Egypt. He would protect Egypt and govern her justly…"

"…and the gods would make him Pharaoh as of old, Horus Come Forth by Day," Dion said.

I nodded again. "Yes. How did you know that?"

Dion shrugged. "I've always known it. Perhaps I was there with you and don't remember it."

"I remember it," I said. "Dion, I've always remembered it. Even when I tried to forget. Sometimes I feel like there's a thin veil between me and all the rest of it, and it would be so easy to just sweep the veil aside and look."

"Why don't you then?" Dion asked. His curiosity was always insatiable. "I would."

"Because I'm afraid," I said. "I don't know what would happen if I did. I don't know who I'd become." I moved closer, taking comfort in the warmth of his body.

"I think you'd only become more yourself," he said gently. "But you shouldn't do it if it frightens you so. Not now. Not when our big question is what we do next."

I took a breath. "We find an army. We find money. We keep Gnaeus Pompeius sweetened enough to back Cleopatra with Rome, we retake Alexandria, execute Pothinus and Theocritus, and exile Arsinoe to Ephesos."

"Well, that ought to be easy," Dion said with a smile. "Nothing to it, really."

"The first problem is finding an army without any money," I said.

Dion took a deep breath, his chest against my back. "No, the first problem is convincing the authorities in Memphis not to pack Cleopatra straight back to Alexandria as a prisoner."

"That would be the Hierophant of Serapis," I said. "His name is Memnon, and he has a reputation for being a fair man, but one who drives a hard bargain. I think we can work with him."

Dion nodded slowly. "And then of course there's my more pressing problem."

"What's that?"

"I forgot to bring a blanket," he said sheepishly.

I stifled a giggle. "Dion, trust you to plan the perfect escape from Alexandria without a blanket. You can share mine."

"You don't mind?"

"Of course not," I said, and went to sleep with Dion pressed against my back, his arms around me.

At Naukratis we left the barge and changed to a fast boat, one of the sailed passenger ships that plied regularly up and down the Nile. It was much more comfortable, and would get us to Memphis faster. Cleopatra should be far ahead of us, since Apollodorus had arrranged a swift sailing vessel for her from the beginning.

We had seen no sign of pursuit. Not a single royal scout ship had passed the barge. It seemed that Pothinus and Theocritus had logically concluded that Cleopatra had either departed by sea to join Gnaeus Pompeius, or intended to make for Pelousion, which had been Auletes' stronghold. Indeed, those were reasonable choices, and the choices Auletes would have made. Their mistake was assuming that Cleopatra was like Auletes.

Dion was a child of the city, and had never before left it, except for a brief trip to Canopus, and the farther we got from Alexandria the more obvious this was. As farms and fields unrolled along the riverbank beside us, he watched all with unabashed enthusiasm, but he had no idea how to barter in the native Egyptian for our supper from the market vendors of any medium-size town where we might stop. To me, it was Bubastis again, and I realized exactly how much I had learned. Strange to say, I had missed Bubastis just a little, when we were back in Alexandria. Though we were on the westernmost branch of the Nile rather than in the east, it seemed much the same. And I was nearly as excited about seeing Memphis as Dion was.

In earlier days, Memphis had been the capital of Egypt, but had lost place to other cities, to Sais and Thebes, to Avaris and Tanis, and most recently to Alexandria. It was ancient beyond imagining. Outside of the city, the great pyramids stretched toward the sky, tombs of kings who had reigned twenty-five hundred years before. I could hardly begin to imagine twenty-five centuries, or what life must have been like for people who lived then. I wondered, like Dion, if even the stars had been strange.

Of course not all of Memphis was ancient. It was a modern city too, with baths and apartments, markets and shopping, and a commodities exchange where grain and other things were bought and sold on speculation. There were temples of course, from the old Temple of Ptah to the massive complex of the Serapeum, where the divine Apis bulls lived and died and were buried. There were separate quarters of the city for Jews, Greeks, and Carians, with their own temples and shops and markets, all enclosed within a massive wall nearly five miles in length. The dikes along the river that protected the city from the floodwaters when the Nile rose were five times the height of a man, fashioned of clear golden stone.

We came up to one of the stone quays along the river and departed the boat in the bright light of morning and made our way to the Serapeum. That was where Cleopatra should be, if she had been received as a guest, not a prisoner.

WE FOUND CLEOPATRA in the receiving rooms of the Hierophant Memnon, a big sunny room with chairs of carved cedar sitting in a semicircle. Cleopatra's was ornamented with gold, and beside it stood a table weighted down with scrolls. Several men and a woman I did not know sat in chairs, and one woman I recognized immediately.

"Adoratrice?" I said incredulously.

The Adoratrice of Bastet from Bubastis looked at me with amusement. "Good morning, Charmian." I immediately felt as if I were twelve years old again.

Cleopatra looked up from the scroll on her lap, and her eyes filled with tears. I only saw them for a moment before she came and embraced me and then Dion. "Welcome to Memphis," she said. Then she turned and faced the room. "Eminences, this is my principal handmaiden, Charmian, who has risked her life to cover my departure from Alexandria, and also Dion of the Museum, a scholar of the general sciences and also my tutor in the language of the Jews."

We inclined our heads politely, I farther than Dion for I could surmise who some of them must be. The old man with the shaven head and the skin of a cheetah about his shoulders must be the chief priest of Thoth, while the woman beside him with the elaborate wig and old-fashioned pleated gown might be the Great Wife of Amon from Thebes, a largely ceremonial role now rather than wielding the secular power it once had, but significant for all that. I knew the Adoratrice of Bastet and Apollodorus. The man of thirty-some years wearing Greek dress, his hair cropped short and his face shaven, was a soldier even though he wore no harness or arms in the presence of the priests. I had seen him before. He was the eldest son of the governor of Pelousion. There were two other men I did not know, soldiers or nobles, one dark and one fair.

In the central chair sat the man who was obviously our host, Memnon, the Hierophant of Serapis, chief priest of the Lord of the Dead. He was a sturdy man in his prime, likewise shaven to expose a strong head with a square jaw. He had broad shoulders, like a laborer, though he was clothed in the finest linen and a pectoral of lapis and glass lay across his chest. He returned our courtesies gravely.

"We are discussing strategies," Cleopatra said as Dion took an empty chair, the one farthest from the center and most junior, and I came to stand beside Iras behind Cleopatra's seat. "Eminences, I have no secrets that are not shared by Charmian and Dion in these matters. You may continue to speak freely."

Memnon and the Great Wife of Amon exchanged a look, and then she spoke, obviously picking up a thread that had already been teased out. "We do not doubt anything that you have said, Lady, nor do we doubt that you regret as deeply as we do the troubles brought upon our land by Pharaoh Ptolemy Auletes' unfortunate loan from the Roman. But this loan is not the crux of our troubles, nor is it the beginning of the difficulties we have faced in Upper Egypt."

Cleopatra sat forward in her seat in a position of flattering attention. I did not miss that while the Great Wife of Amon addressed her respectfully, she did not address her as Queen.

"Since Ptolemy Philopater, the fourth Pharaoh of your dynasty, the attention of the Great House has been ever more increasingly confined to Alexandria and the immediate needs of Lower Egypt. Canals and ports, trade and temples, marketplaces and buildings of all kinds, irrigation projects—all these have primarily benefited Alexandria and Lower Egypt. While it is true that Ptolemy Eugertes conducted some building projects at Edfu, and some other minor things were undertaken since then, Upper Egypt has been neglected. Indeed, it does not escape us that all of the Black Land outside of Alexandria and a few Greek towns are referred to as the Chora, the Hinterlands. There is more to Egypt than Alexandria, Lady."

Cleopatra glanced at the Adoratrice, and held her in the corner of her eye as she replied. "I am well aware of that, Eminence. As you doubtless know, I spent much of my youth in Bubastis. The tongue of the Black Land is as familiar to me as Koine, and I reverence the ancient gods of the Two Lands as I reverence the gods of the Greeks, and respect the gods of all lands." She glanced about the room, and her voice was strong for all the slight girlish body it came from. "I am Queen of Egypt. I am the avatar of Isis, born to champion my people. All of my people. From Alexandria to Pelousion, from Memphis to

Elephantine, from the western deserts to the Middle Sea to the Great Cataract, wherever Isis stretches Her wings under the barque of the sun, I too shall keep guard for my people's well-being. You know that my kindred and my dynasty have done much for the Black Land. We have improved the irrigation technology so that men may keep their crops with greater ease. We have built roadways, and brought the Faiyum Oasis under cultivation, and opened trade with the world, bringing money into Egypt. But we have not done enough, it is true. These last years have been hard, and too much of our time has been spent contending with Rome and other outside powers. I have said already, and will say again, that we must regain our ancient strength. We must rely on no outside lands or rulers."

"Not even Gnaeus Pompeius?" the son of the governor of Pelousion asked, one eyebrow raised.

Cleopatra did not blush, nor did she bat an eye. "Most certainly not Gnaeus Pompeius, nor any of his kin. If I had meant to rely on Rome, I should have gone to Rome, not Memphis." She leaned forward, her hands on the chair arms. "Eminences, we cannot get rid of Rome. But we must use her, rather than be used by her. If we are to regain our true independence, we must leverage what we have, whatever coin it may be."

"Whatever coin?" the chief priest of Thoth asked. "Your sister asked a Seleucid prince to come and marry her, gave him command of the army, and sat him beside her in the Great House. If we wished to be ruled by a Seleucid who has never set foot in Egypt, we could simply surrender to them."

"I am married already, to Ptolemy Theodorus," Cleopatra said.

"And Ptolemy Theodorus may not survive long," one of the soldiers said. "We want no foreign overlord. If we choose to throw our lot in with you, Princess, we are not yours to give away to any blooded princeling or Roman of your choice."

Memnon raised an eyebrow, but it was Cleopatra who answered. "I will set no man beside me on the throne of Egypt who is not of the royal blood of the Ptolemies. Would an oath to that effect satisfy you?"

"It would," he said.

"Then I shall give it gladly," she replied.

Memnon clasped his hands together before him. "The first Ptolemy, like Alexander before him, like his son and grandson after him, was crowned in the old manner. In recent years, however, that rite has been neglected. Pharaohs have ruled in Alexandria, and some have ruled well, but none has walked through the darkness and come forth by day properly tested by the gods. The Lords of the Two Lands have always borne this test, since Osiris Himself went down into the West, into the Halls of Amenti. If you would truly reign in Egypt, Cleopatra, you must be properly crowned."

The Adoratrice snorted. "That's impossible. To do it properly as it was done in ages past would require her father's tomb. Auletes is buried in Alexandria."

Dion spoke up directly. "That is true," he said. "But in the absence of the required object, the symbol may suffice. If we do not have her father's tomb, we may yet use some appropriate place that is in a symbolic sense her father's tomb."

The Great Wife of Amon leaned forward. "And by what authority do you speak?"

Before Dion could answer, Cleopatra forestalled him. "Eminences," she said, "I shall rule all of the people of Egypt, and thus must be crowned by all of the gods of Egypt. Dion represents the god of the Jews, and is a magician of no little note."

My surprise must have showed in my face, as Dion looked sheepish. I thought perhaps Cleopatra was puffing him up just a bit.

Memnon met the Adoratrice's eyes across the room. "Abydos," he said.

Dion nodded. "The tomb of Osiris Himself. Or of Serapis, if you prefer." He forestalled the Great Wife of Amon's comment. "Lady, let me remind you that while she is to be Pharaoh of Egypt, she will also rule over Alexandria. Like Great Alexander and the first Ptolemy, all that is done must work in both systems."

"We are speaking of the strongest magic," the priest of Thoth said.

"And of the strongest political symbols," the Adoratrice said. "If Delta and Upper Egypt alike are to rally for Cleopatra, it must be carefully done. Abydos is acceptable."

Memnon took a deep breath. "I am the Hierophant of Serapis. This is something that would fall within my duties, though of course I will welcome your thoughts." His eyes sought Dion's, including him too. "It must be acceptable to all the gods."

Dion nodded gravely.

THE · GATES
OF AMENTI

W e were three days longer in Memphis before the messenger came by swift ship, sent by the Patriarch of
Alexandria, who it seemed was also in correspondence
with Memnon, and with Cleopatra as well. He was drinking watered
wine, and I arrived in the hall only moments before Cleopatra herself.
She came in almost at a run, her Greek peplos sweeping behind her.

"My Queen," he said, his forehead pressed to his knee. "Pompeius
Magnus is dead."

Her eyebrows rose.

"How?" I blurted out, though of course it was not my place to ask
questions. "Did he lose a battle?" Perhaps if he had we should have
Gnaeus out of the way permanently too, though that presented its own
problems. Gnaeus was our one way of manipulating Rome.

The messenger looked nervously at me, but Cleopatra nodded at
him to answer. "He did lose a battle, Lady, but that was not the cause
of it. It is said that he met Caesar at a place called Pharsalus in Greece,
and that he was utterly defeated. Gnaeus Pompeius was also there, but
he fled his troops almost as soon as the battle was joined, and it is said
that he escaped to Hispania. In any event, Caesar was victorious, and
Pompeius Magnus fled Greece on a commandeered grain ship."

I was hard put to not snort. For all Gnaeus' posturing, he was
proved a coward in the end.

Cleopatra, of course, had focused on the political implications.
"Pompeius was my father's great ally. Where did he go?"

"The Patriarch said to tell you that because of the things his son Gnaeus had related, he assumed he would find a warm welcome in Egypt, and that he would be able to call in the remainder of the loan, using that money to buy himself a new army and continue the fight against Caesar."

"Oh Mother Isis!" Cleopatra said. The last thing we needed was Pompeius in person calling in the loan.

"He landed in Pelousion, where Pharaoh and his advisers were, and asked to speak with Pharaoh. A council meeting was called immediately. Debate went back and forth. General Achillas said that Pompeius should be sent away, as allowing him to land would anger Caesar and bring the man who was now the most powerful of the Romans down upon us. Pothinus said that to send Pompeius away was folly, because he would go elsewhere and raise an army, and then we should have an enemy rather than an ally, and that in any case Pompeius was bound to favor you because of his son."

"And Pharaoh?" asked Cleopatra grimly.

"Pharaoh said nothing, my Queen. At last Theocritus spoke, and he said that we could afford neither to send him away nor welcome him. We could not repay the loan, and we could not afford to make an enemy of him, nor of Caesar."

That sounded like Theocritus, I thought. I could see where this was going.

"So they invited Pompeius Magnus to come ashore and have an audience with Pharaoh. As soon as he landed from his boat on the beach, he was slain by two men. The remainder of his party sailed away when they saw what had happened, and it is not known where they have gone."

This changed the entire political constellation, and I could almost see it spinning, like an armillary sphere out of control. What it would mean for Egypt, for us, was still in motion.

THE NEXT DAY we left for Abydos. This time we did not travel on barges, or on a fast ship, but on a large and comfortable river galley belonging to Memnon. Abydos is in Upper Egypt, a long way upriver from Memphis, not quite so far as Thebes but far enough that it would take us the better part of a week to get there with favorable winds pushing our sails and oarsmen at their work all through the day. We sailed south, into the heart of Egypt.

I could not help but feel that we sailed into the past as well. Each morning, the sun rose in vibrant power out of the east, chasing away the shades of night. Each day, beside the river, we saw people going about their work, many of them as they had since the great pyramids were built, sleepy oxen working the irrigation systems, while the fields were greening with the fruit of the Inundation. Each night we watched the stars of heaven wheeling overhead like some vast dance, calm and impenetrable.

Before we reached Abydos there was a council to explain the preparations for the coronation. Already news had been sent upriver ahead of us, inviting those it was deemed politic to include, but the entire population of Abydos should also bear witness.

We sat on deck beneath white awnings while the oarsmen beat on. I came around with sweet cakes, and served the Adoratrice while Iras poured well-watered wine.

When we had all been served, Memnon began to speak. "The difficulty is this," he said. "Our new sovereign is a woman."

"I believe we know that," Cassander, the son of the governor of Pelousion, said, shifting restlessly in his seat.

Memnon didn't even blink. "This creates a considerable liturgical problem. You see, a reigning Pharaoh is Horus. He is the Son of Isis, the Falcon of the Sun, and in a very real sense is expected to be the avatar of Horus on earth. He takes up this role in a symbolic sense, and whether or not you believe that Pharaoh may become a channel for divinity, the symbolic role is of considerable political importance."

Cassander subsided. He was a courtier, and doubtless thought this mere hand-waving, except for the politics of the matter.

"When Pharaoh dies, the essence of Horus that has been indwelling in him must leave and move to a new, living host. The dead Pharaoh must be transformed into Osiris, so that he may dwell in Amenti.

In large part the funeral preparations and the coronation preparations are entwined. During the seventy days of the dead Pharaoh's embalming, all is made ready. The purpose of the funeral is not just to bury Pharaoh, or to secure his safe passage to Amenti, but to transform his son into the new Horus. His son must walk in the darkness and come forth by day tested and worthy to be the avatar of Horus and the shepherd of his people. In order to do that, the indwelling part of Horus, that which has lived within his father, must leave his father's body and join instead with him."

"What about Isis?" Cassander asked.

Cleopatra said nothing, so I assumed Memnon had told her all of this before.

Memnon steepled his hands and looked at Dion, who straightened. "Isis is the wife of Osiris, the mother of Horus. She is the Widow, bereaved of Her husband. Isis journeys in the marshes, seeking the scattered parts of Osiris' body that Set has dismembered. In Her wanderings and Her grief, She finds each part of Him, and restores Him to life for one night only. Thus is Her son Horus conceived. Isis is very important in this, but She is the Widow, not the Widow's Son. Pharaoh's mother is Isis, and in the old days no one in the Black Land was more honored than Pharaoh's mother. It's she who is the avatar of Isis." He looked at Cleopatra, sitting quietly in her chair. "Our gracious Queen cannot be Horus. And Isis' path is very different."

"Osiris lies in his tomb in Alexandria," Memnon said. "Auletes is dead. While he lived, he reigned with his daughter-wife, but now he is gone. Isis has come to Upper Egypt, alone and bereft, while Her life is sought by many. You asked that she swear she would set no man beside her on the throne of Egypt who was not of the blood of the Ptolemies. That is as it should be. She will raise no man to the throne of Egypt except for Horus, her son."

At this a flurry of exclamations flowed out.

"You do realize that you're disinheriting Ptolemy Theodorus and her other brother, don't you?" the Great Wife of Amon said. "I'm not sure we can get by with that."

"Who's to say she'll have any sons?" the Adoratrice asked. "Or who their fathers will be?"

Cleopatra spread her hands, her himation gracefully around her shoulders. "Eminences, I am twenty years old, and enjoy good health. While I cannot of course guarantee that I will bear sons, there is no reason to think I may not. My mother was a fertile woman who bore five living children, and my best years are ahead of me. I do not think there is reason to fear that I shall not bear a son. As for who my son's father may be"—she glanced sideways at the priest of Thoth—"the rite will be enacted in symbol only," she said. "I am sure Isis will provide a suitable consort to get a son on me soon enough."

The Adoratrice stirred in her chair, and I was reminded for a moment of how my cat Sheba would sit when paying close attention, with only the tip of her tail twitching. "Of course," she said, "it is by no means to be literally taken that Pharaoh should sire a son after death. The heir must already be a young man of a reasonable age in order for the coronation to take place."

"If we had Theodorus...," Cassander began.

"Do you think we can keep Ptolemy Theodorus?" Memnon asked Cassander.

"If he were separated from his advisers."

"And should he forgive us for that, or do anything beyond build another faction against us?" the Adoratrice asked. "We have had Berenice and Tryphaena already. Before that, in Auletes' generation, he was the only male heir left after Ptolemy Alexander murdered his sister Berenice and then was killed in turn." She stood up, and I could almost see the sharp ears rearing above her head, the elegant tail lashing. "Egypt has had enough of this! We cannot afford any more fighting between heirs, mortgaging the country and spending lives this way! We have before us an heir who will rule as well as any other, and better than most. Let us put her on the throne alone, and trust that she will raise her son not to stab her in the back."

"She will," Iras said, from where she stood behind Cleopatra's chair.

The Great Wife of Amon raised her eyebrows. "Can you be sure of that?"

Memnon leaned forward. "I don't think we can debate fruitfully the actions of an heir not yet conceived," he said mildly. He raised a hand to forestall the next question from the Great Wife of Amon. "Nor can we debate who his father should be. Let it suffice to say that whomever he will be, he will not sit on the throne of Egypt."

He will have no need of Egypt's throne, She whispered inside me. *Already he is coming, as the day follows night, already he is coming like fire from heaven.*

THE OSIRION at Abydos is a temple like no other in Egypt. For the most part our temples are open to the sky, with courtyards and columns and many buildings inside the sacred perimeter. The Holy of Holies is covered, it is true, but it is not isolated or secret. Even the most sacred images are brought forth on certain festival days and shown to the world. The Osirion is underground.

From the outside, it looks like a strange garden behind the great temple that the Pharaoh Seti built more than a thousand years ago, a grove of tamarisk trees on a green mound covered with grass and flowers. However, if one goes around and to the side, one comes to a door leading down into the darkness. Above it are the carvings found on tombs. It is a grave, a womb, a Gate to Amenti. Within these hidden chambers Cleopatra would be tested.

Cleopatra should see nothing of it beforehand, nor any of us taking part in the rites. It is tradition that Pharaoh's heir be accompanied by two kinsmen who stand at his side as his champions. Of course it was irregular that Iras and I should stand beside Cleopatra, as the champions should be male. However, as Cleopatra pointed out, there were no male heirs present, and if the heir were female, surely her companions could be as well. It felt strangely right to me that it should be so, as though I had stood beside Pharaoh before, clad in white.

C·OMING FORTH
BY DAY

We assembled outside the door. The old priest of Thoth stood in front, his cheetah skin wrapped about his shoulders. A young priest with a censer stood beside him. The rich scents of kephri and myrrh flowed back over us. Cleopatra stood silent in her simple white linen gown, looking as though she could have walked out of a painting from the pyramids. Iras and I stood behind her.

The priest of Thoth looked at us gravely. "You are resolved to do this, Daughter of Egypt?" he asked.

Cleopatra nodded. "I am."

"And you will accompany your kinswoman, as Bastet and Anubis accompanied Isis in the marshes?"

"I will," we said. Bastet and Anubis, I thought. Cat and dog, the two creatures that stay with humans for love, since the earliest days. Sheep and goats and cattle stay because they must, but only dogs and cats love. I wondered which of us was which, but then I knew. Sheba had come to me, and I wandered farther from Cleopatra's side than Iras ever had, but I always came back. I should be Bastet and she Anubis.

I looked at Iras and saw that she had decided the same.

We went down into darkness. Behind us, the Horologers cried out the first hour of the night. Ahead of us, the censers walked slowly, the smoke rolling back over us, redolent and heavy. The passage sloped gently down. In the flickering dim light, the pictures on the wall seemed almost to move. Ma'at, the Goddess of Justice, reared life-size, Her profile crisp and lifelike.

Then she stepped forward, between the censers and Cleopatra, and I saw it was a priestess gowned as Ma'at. In her hand were her scales, and her dress was red as sunset. "Daughter of Egypt, why do you seek the Halls of Amenti?"

"I seek my lord Serapis, whom You name Osiris," Cleopatra said. "He brought justice and peace to the Black Land, and now He is dead."

"Will you serve Me here and above?" Ma'at asked. "Will you serve out justice to your people, and weigh their hearts when they are brought before you as righteously as you may?"

"I will," she said solemnly.

"Then pass, Daughter of Egypt," Ma'at said, and it seemed She stepped back into the wall, though I knew it was only an alcove that stood in shadow.

The priest of Thoth led a song of thanksgiving then, and in the chamber his voice was curiously magnified, a lovely strong voice. The smoke washed over me again.

We went on, through the darkness. How long could this passage be? I wondered as I walked beside Iras. Surely not so very long. And yet it seemed we went on for hours. The paintings on the wall beside me showed peasants at work in their fields, plowing with their oxen beneath a painted sun, fishing in the river. I almost missed the beginning of the next tableau.

A young man and woman came forth, he wearing nothing but the plain linen skirt of the laborers, wreaths of grain on their heads. "Daughter of Egypt," they said. "We are the peasants of the plains of Wernes, those who dwell below in everlasting sunlight, who suffered in life many cruelties and illnesses, and now live in fields of plenty. In the world above, our misery was unrelieved. But the gods are merciful. Why should we let you pass, Daughter of Egypt?"

Cleopatra licked her lower lip, as she had as a girl, and in a moment I felt a powerful wave of love crash over me. I was not here because I must be, but because I loved her. And I knew what she must say.

"I am Isis, and My heart is heavy too. I am seeking one who has gone from Me, and I shall only find Him through the Halls of Amenti. As the gods are merciful to you, be merciful to Me and let Me pass."

The love was real, not pageantry. She had loved Auletes, flawed as he was. We were cut of the same cloth, and we had all loved Egypt.

"Pass, Daughter of Egypt," the man said, and stepped back.

"Pass," the woman said.

We went on through the darkness. It seemed the passage ahead had no end. There was only the singing and the rushing smoke. Beneath the song, I thought I heard the sound of running water. Surely that was not possible?

The passage took an abrupt turn, and suddenly before us there was space. The sound of running water was loud, and as the priest stepped aside I heard Cleopatra gasp. A dark figure, snake-headed, reared up before her. Unthinking, I stepped ahead of her.

"You have come to the river," he said. "And Death waits for you."

It seemed to me I saw a real snake, grown to monstrous size. I felt Cleopatra's wrist tremble in my hand, and knew she saw it too. I spoke without thinking. "Go back," I said. "You may not touch her, creature of Set."

"By whose authority, Little Cat?" it asked.

"Cats kill snakes," I said flatly. "Try my teeth and claws."

For a moment I almost heard a chuckle, and knew it was Dion beneath a mask. "That I will not do."

"Snakes are not Death in dreams," I said, and felt I had said it before. "You will have to try harder than that."

The snake reared up for a moment, then stepped back, vanishing from our way.

In that moment, shuttered lamps opened, and the light leaped forth, dazzling our eyes. The walls were hung with saffron, and the smoke was resinous, the sky arching blue above. We stood on the edge of the desert, under the endless blazing sun.

I closed my eyes, blinking with tears in the sudden brightness. "The

Fourth Hour of the Night. You have come to the edge of the desert, and there is no escape. Here, you will wander eternally, sorrowing."

I couldn't see a thing. The light was too bright, after so long in darkness. Cleopatra also must be blind.

"Here," Iras said, and I felt her take both our hands. "You know that I am the hound, and I track by scent. The desert holds no terrors for me. There is nothing I have lost behind me. It is all ahead."

I let her lead me, still blinking at the tears running down my face, and in a moment it was blessedly dark again. When I opened my eyes, I could still see spots of light. We were in a cool corridor, and ahead the sound of water was stronger still.

A woman in green waited for us, and her eyes were painted with gold. "I am Nepthys," she said, "Lady of Sorrows." She held out a goblet. Cleopatra took it and drank, then passed it to me and Iras. The goblet was solid gold, and heavy enough to take two hands. It was dark good wine, and I drank thirstily after the smoke that had seared my throat.

"Why do you weep?" she asked.

Cleopatra, remembering what she was supposed to be doing, replied, "I am mourning Osiris, who has passed beyond the world. I seek Him in the Halls of Amenti."

"The dead will not return to us," she said. "And sorrow will follow You all Your life."

"Still I must search," Cleopatra said. "For I have hope, and under that bright star must continue. Sorrow will not stop Me."

"Then search," Nepthys said, and led us on.

It seemed that we went through an endless series of corridors and small rooms, seeking in tiny cells of stone, turnings that went nowhere and walls that blocked us. All the while the sound of water came, moisture in the air, as though we approached some great underground river.

At last we came to the riverbank. We stood on a stone embankment far underground. A vast dark pool lapped at our feet, at massive black stone columns rearing to the ceiling. Away, in the midst of the dark pool, there was an island of stone, steps going up from a tiny platform. A faint light came to me across the water, as though a single torch stood in an iron stand in that distant place beside a dark sarcophagus.

"How do we cross?" I wondered aloud.

"There," Iras said, pointing. At the side of the pool was a tiny reed boat such as peasants use in the marshes. Like the ones in the paintings on the walls of pyramids, it was barely big enough for three people if we were very careful.

I looked down at the dark water and felt a frisson of fear. Who knew what waited in its black depths.

Now a man approached, a priest stepping out from one of the columns, and I saw that it was Memnon. His shaven head shone with oil, and he wore the skin of a cheetah across his shoulder. "The Sixth Hour of the Night. You have come to the edge of the Primeval Water. Once, the world lay in darkness, and waters covered all that was. There was no dawn or sunset, no stone or fire, no green things that grow or animals that creep. There was nothing except the dark sea. There were no beginnings or endings, no light, no time."

I shivered, and it had nothing to do with the coldness that settled around us.

"And Isis moved like a breath over the waters, and where She was, winds troubled them, and the clouds stirred. Through the clouds might be seen at last a single star, and then the breadth of the heavens, where all of the stars sang for all eternity. And where She was, the clouds were troubled, and they brought forth rain. And where She was, storms rolled over the depths, lightning striking the seas and quickening them. Isis is the Mother of the World."

Somewhere behind us, among the pillars, a choir began to sing softly, voices soaring in eerie descant.

"And when the world was green and beautiful, She and Her husband Osiris came and dwelt in it. They came to the first men and showed them how to tame the wild goats, how to plant grain and to grow fruits and good things of all kinds. She taught men writing, and

Osiris gave them law, that they might dwell in justice together and that no man might harm his neighbor. But nothing endures forever, and Osiris' brother Set was jealous, and He wished to be Pharaoh. He murdered His brother and cut His body into many pieces, that He might conceal the deed. Thus He became Pharaoh, and Isis fled from that place. She searched land and sea, and at last found all of the scattered pieces of Her husband Osiris, and brought them together. Will you seek Osiris across the stormy seas?"

"I will," Cleopatra said.

Together, the three of us climbed into the tiny boat, me in the front and Iras in the rear with Cleopatra between us. Cleopatra took up the single paddle, and we set out over the dark water.

It seemed that somehow the pool was much bigger than it could have been, that the island was much farther and the shore more distant. A dreamlike silence descended. All I could hear was the quiet strokes of the paddle, as though we did indeed row into the past, or into a dream.

I could not see my sisters behind me, and it seemed the water went on and on. At last we came to the shore, and I scrambled onto the platform, reaching back for Cleopatra's hand. Everything seemed to take a very long time.

Together, we mounted the steps to the platform. At the center of it lay a huge sarcophagus of black stone. Above us, the vault of heaven stretched uninterrupted, stars prickling in the firmament. I wondered, with some part of my mind that was still awake, how they had managed that effect.

"We have come to the grave of Osiris," Cleopatra whispered.

Iras sank to her knees beside the sarcophagus, her hands reaching upward, and for a moment I thought we stood in the Soma, beside the tomb of Alexander.

"No," I whispered. This was the tomb of Osiris, not Alexander.

Cleopatra bent stiffly over the sarcophagus. I could not tell if she read the marks inscribed there, or if she spoke some words.

I caught at the edge of the stone, leaning on it. Above, the stars wheeled, seasons spinning forward at an incredible rate. And in the wrong direction.

It seemed to me that a king lay in state on the lid of the sarcophagus, his brown beard laced with white, a red dragon banner across him like a shroud, covering his death wound, while a man with a censer wove patterns in smoke above him, speaking Latin to his shade. "Rex quondam, rexque futuris…"

No, it was instead a red-haired queen, her elaborate copper curls belying the deep wrinkles of her face. The stars spun.

A sword spun around and around, as though caught in a whirlpool, now a Roman gladius, now a long straight sword, now a sharply curved sword with a guard ornamented with ivory elephants, now a heavy two-handed sword, now a half-moon of steel in a red and black enamel case, now a fine thin straight sword like lightning, now a sword with a cross hilt engraved with golden bees.

The king lay in his sarcophagus of marble beneath a huge dome, light streaming down from the ceiling, the floor still echoing from my footsteps.

"Back," I whispered, my hands grinding into the stone, trying to halt this wild progress into the future. "Back. Back to Cleopatra." I held to the memory of my sister's face, whirled around and around in the maelstrom.

"Be still," I cried, and all was dark.

I DREAMED, and in that dream I walked insubstantial as shadow through the pickets of a great camp. Horses stood sleeping in their lines, tents spaced just so, sentries moving quietly through the dark.

I did not hesitate. I knew where I was going, drawn by him as though by an invisible light.

A lean, balding man in a red tunic sat at a writing desk, a scroll unwrapped before him. Behind him, the walls of a tent rose, lit by lamplight.

"What wind is it that blows the lamps?" he asked, looking up as the flames stuttered.

"The wind from Egypt," I said. He had dark, lively eyes, and a face that seemed readily given to either laughter or sternness. "I have come for you, my Lord. The Black Land is waiting for you, as for a lover."

"Why have you come?" he said, and he rose up and walked toward me. "Have you come from Pompeius?"

"I have come from Cleopatra," I said. "I have come to bring you home."

"The world is my home," he said. "And thus I can never be away."

"Your home is in Alexandria too," I said, my voice strengthening, "and by your relics I call you. The Black Land needs you. By those who love you, I call you. By those who have died for you, I call you. By your bones resting in honor in Alexandria and Thebes, I call you. Come to Alexandria, Son of Amon!" I raised my arms, and it seemed they were white in the lamplight. "You are the wind of the world, and the wind is blowing!"

"Isis Invicta," he said, and it seemed to me then that everything spun around once again.

I closed my eyes tight. After a few moments the sensation of movement ceased. I moved my hand and felt stone beneath it. I opened my eyes.

CLEOPATRA LAY on the lid of the sarcophagus, her eyes closed, her face turned up toward the stars, while Iras knelt beside it, leaning against it, one hand raised as though stilled in the movement of reaching for her. She lay like a carving on a tomb, her hands closed around crook and flail crossed on her breast.

I moved my hand. I lay on the stone some little distance away. I shook my head, trying to clear it. Across the water, I could see torches, see the movement of people.

I tried to speak, and a faint croak came out. I swallowed and tried again. "Iras?"

I saw Iras stir, and I crawled across to her, taking one of her hands in mine. "Sister? Iras?"

Her eyes flickered open and I saw sense return. "I'm here," she said.

I found my feet would hold me and I got to them, leaning over my sister Cleopatra, my heart seized with a sudden dread. She looked so pale, so lifeless. I could not even see the shallow movement of her chest. "Sister?" I reached out to touch her throat and saw the tremor of pulse there. Her lips opened, and her lashes trembled. She opened her eyes, and for a moment they looked wide and dark, reflecting the painted stars on the ceiling in a way that assuredly they couldn't.

Iras put her arm behind her and helped her to sit up. "Can you speak?"

"Yes," she said, and looked down at the crook and flail in her hands, symbols of divine kingship as old as the Black Land. "Where did these come from?"

I blinked. "I have no idea. You must have picked them up after I fainted. What did you—"

Cleopatra raised a hand and stopped me. "Not now, Charmian. Not yet. It's too new."

Iras nodded. "Then let's get back in the boat."

It was I who rowed on the return journey, while Cleopatra sat in the front with the crook and flail in her hands, still as an effigy carried on a feast day. As I rowed, I felt life returning to my muscles, my head settling without so much as an ache. I could not explain what had happened, and like Cleopatra I thought it was too soon to talk.

When our boat touched the shore, Memnon's deep voice rang out, echoing in the far corners of the chamber. "All hail Isis, Lady of Egypt, Mother of the World, Ruler of the Two Lands! All hail Isis, all hail Cleopatra!"

"All hail Isis," the priestess who had played Nepthys said, beginning the litany. "All hail Isis, She Who Treads the Waves. All hail Isis, who made laws and gave them to men. All hail Isis, who taught us writing. All hail Isis, who quickens the child in the womb. All hail Isis, who rules with justice and mercy."

"All hail Cleopatra," Memnon said as one of the junior priests handed him the double crown of Egypt with the sacred serpent in the front, the crown that Pharaohs had worn for three thousand years. She did not incline her head as he put it on her, heavy though it was. She held her head straight like a painting off the walls of a tomb as it settled upon her hair, Isis born in darkness, coming forth by day.

THE REST OF THE NIGHT was a blur to me. I hardly remembered the rest of the rite, Cleopatra dressed in royal raiment, reborn like the new sun, Dion once again masked as the serpent, leading her back through the desert, or the final rituals in the long exit corridor, in which Iras and I carried the double crowns to the eastern gate, there to await the precise moment of the reappearance of the sun.

At last we emerged from the final passage, from the door of the temple, just as the first rays of the new day broke over the temples and palaces of Abydos, striking fire from her high, gilded crown, from the golden uraeus on her brow. We walked out to the sounds of trumpets.

AFTERWARD, when all of the assembled notables had finished making their respects to Cleopatra, we repaired to the small palace to wash and have the first meal of the day. Clean, and sitting about the remains of our breakfast, we at last had a moment for private conversation. All of us were quieter than usual. I, at least, was very tired.

"You are troubled," she said.

"I had a dream," I said carefully. "When I fainted, or whatever it was that happened. I don't know entirely what it means."

"What was it?"

I thought of the first part, but it was too confusing, too indefinite. I shook my head. "I was drifting through a camp, and then I saw a man. An older man, a Roman I think, from his clothes. I dreamed that I summoned him to Egypt, that I summoned him by his bones where they lie in Alexandria and Thebes." She said nothing, so I went on.

"I summoned him by his bones, to draw his wandering spirit back to Egypt, whatever name or face he might wear now."

"In Thebes," she said. "In the Valley of the Kings. I wonder which Pharaoh?"

"I don't know," I said, though at the same time I could imagine him so easily, a lithe, dark-skinned young man.

Her eyebrows rose. "And in Alexandria."

"In his own city," I said.

"Alexander," Cleopatra said.

"It was just a dream," I said hurriedly.

Cleopatra looked at me sideways. "Charmian, why are you always so quick to dismiss your own gifts?"

"This is a later age, sister," I said, "and we are civilized people. Alexander lies in the Soma, and I have seen him there. Gods do not rise from the grave and walk the earth."

"Why are you so sure of that?" she asked. "You believe I am the Hand of Isis?"

I looked away. "I feel in my heart that you are, but I do not want to be foolish. It was different when we were children."

She shook her head at me. "Charmian, I need you to believe. You may not trust your dreams or gifts, but I do. And I need you to tell me when there is something that matters so much. I will never laugh at you, not if you tell me to get up in the night and sail to Syria."

"I don't want to guide you badly," I said. I hardly knew how to say what was in my heart. "Sister, I am no scholar, no counselor or wise man. I know I have a pretty face and that I can organize a banquet or dress you as a queen should be dressed. But I am not a savant like Dion, or even like Iras. I do not understand the half of what they talk about in the Museum."

"You speak four languages, and compare yourselves to the greatest scholars of the age. It's true that you're no mathematician or engineer. But I have no need of a mathematician or engineer just now! What I need is you. We are all three Her hands, remember? We are royal Ptolemies. If She chooses to speak through you, then She has chosen what is best for the Black Land. Trust it, as I trust you. We will see if your dream is true."

It was nearly ten days later, as we prepared to leave Abydos for Memphis, that the messenger came speeding up the Nile by swift ship.

"My Queen," he said, falling to his knees in Cleopatra's presence, "Caesar has landed in Alexandria."

▽ Amenti

I spread my hands, looking at Isis and Serapis on Their thrones. "And then there was Caesar."

Anubis stirred where He stood beside Serapis' throne, His pointed ears twitching. "And your fates became entwined with one of the Great Stories."

I looked at Him, His eyes bright as amber stars, and I dared to ask a thing I had always wondered. "Gracious Lord," I said. "What is he?"

Anubis smiled like a hound, while Isis and Serapis exchanged a look. "What do you think he is?"

"I do not know," I said slowly. "Perhaps he is some god's avatar or a god himself. He comes, and he leaves a changed world behind him. I do not know what he is, Caesar or Alexander. I do not know."

It was Isis who spoke. "He is a man. An extraordinary man, who has become so often the focus of men's hopes and dreams. And yet, if he wished to remain disincarnate and take his place among the other spirits who have become more than men, he could. But he is bound instead by his desire for the world, by his longing for all there is in it. He is imperfect, bound and binding. He blows through the world like a wind, reflecting the spirit of the age, leader of men and yet their mirror. Ahmose and David, Kyros and Alexander, Caesar, and more whose names you would not recognize, for they have lived and died in lands that are strange to you. And in his wake you are blown about, you and the other Companions who have tied your fate to his at some point."

"And yet ships driven far from home by the storm may discover new lands," Anubis said. "In the wake of the fires that burn the grass, flowers bloom and new worlds are born. You called him to Alexandria. Why?"

I shook my head, trying to find the words for what was in my heart. "We needed him," I said. "We could not go on as we were without being consumed by Rome. The kingdom of the Ptolemies had to change to survive. In Caesar we had a chance. And I knew he should love the Black Land as she loved him. I thought it was best." I lifted my eyes to the thrones. "And we needed a father for Horus, someone who was worthy of Osiris' place, and who should take on that role willingly. Caesar knew what he did, I think." I stopped for a moment, thinking of how best to say it. "We needed Alexander. We needed that sacred fire. Gracious Lady, did I do wrong? Was it I who courted ruin when I called him?"

"The Great Stories are always perilous," She said. "And yet their outcomes are shaped by men. You brought Egypt into his tale once again, for good or ill. Tell us what befell when Caesar came to Alexandria, and perhaps you will find the truth in it."

THE WIND OF
THE WORLD

C aesar had come to Alexandria while Ptolemy and his advisers were still in Pelousion, chasing a rumor that Cleopatra
had decamped to Gaza. They hurried back to the city by
sea just in time for Ptolemy to be welcomed to his own palace by Caesar, something that was no doubt awkward. If they had hoped that
Caesar should be mollified by the death of Pompeius, and, his mission in Egypt accomplished, simply sail away again, they were gravely
disappointed.

Caesar was furious.

"Apparently," Cleopatra said tartly, "it's only Romans who are
allowed to murder Romans."

Instead of sailing away again, he announced that he was in Alexandria on behalf of the Senate and people of Rome to mediate the dispute
between Ptolemy and Cleopatra, and to make certain that Auletes' will
granting the throne of Egypt to them jointly was honored.

As she read that part of the message out, Cleopatra put it down on
the table before her, looking thoughtful.

"He wants the money," Iras said.

I was glancing ahead at the page. "He's brought two legions, but
they're not up to strength. Maybe five thousand men, the Patriarch
says. And he says one of the legions was Pompeius' that Caesar par-
doned and signed on. And that they haven't been paid."

"He wants the money," Cleopatra said. She started pacing again. It seemed like she did that every time money came up, and it was turning into a familiar gesture. "Everyone wants to milk us like an old cow, drawing more than there is."

"They don't have it," Iras said. "Pothinus and Theocritus can't find it any more than we could."

"Mediate the will?" I asked.

Cleopatra shook her head. "It's an excuse to get into the middle of it." She turned to Apollodorus. "Find out everything you can about Caesar. We need to know what he wants, what his ambitions are, what he enjoys, what he eats for breakfast. Anything might be important. Anything might give us an edge."

"He's not going to be like Gnaeus," I said. That at least was already clear. At fifty-two, Caesar was no green young man to be dazzled by sleight of hand. "You can't handle him that way."

"That's something of a relief," Cleopatra said. She paced away again. "We need to go back to Memphis. It's important to be closer to Alexandria."

"And a better place to raise your army," I agreed.

OF COURSE all of the world knew Caesar and his story in later days, but at the time I knew comparatively little. He was fifty-two, of an old noble family that traced its lineage back to ancient gods, an able soldier and an active ruler.

Once, he had been Pompeius Magnus' father in law, Pompeius' third wife having been Caesar's daughter, Julia. Perhaps if she had lived there would have been peace between them. But she had died some years earlier, delivered of a son who did not live more than a few days—Caesar's only grandchild by his only child, a younger brother I am certain Gnaeus would not have welcomed. Indeed, knowing Gnaeus, it was impossible for me not to suspect...

If I thought of it, no doubt Caesar did too.

But such things are unknowable, and certainly it is possible for an infant to die of all manner of natural causes. It is just that we consider such things, in the House of Ptolemy.

In any event, Caesar had spent years conquering various Keltic tribes, away north of Massalia. At some point, things had come to a rift between him and Pompeius. Pompeius, styling himself the legitimate representative of the Senate of Rome, and Caesar, styling himself who knows what, had come to blows. The echoes had reverberated from one end of the Inner Sea to the other as they fought, first in Hispania, then in Italy itself, and most lately in Greece.

Now Pompeius was dead, and it was uncertain what Caesar would do next. Would he return to Rome and be recognized as their king? Would the nobles of Rome raise another army against him, under some younger and more vigorous general? Whatever might happen, he should need money. If he lingered in Egypt now that Pompeius was dead, there could only be one reason for it.

Still, if he had no reason to support Cleopatra, he had no reason to hate her. Whether his anger over Pompeius' murder was real or feigned, she had no part in it. And Ptolemy Theodorus did.

It was little surprise, then, that Caesar sent a messenger to us in Memphis, inviting Cleopatra to return to Alexandria, where he would "fairly and fully" mediate the dispute between Queen Cleopatra and her brother, Pharaoh Ptolemy Theodorus.

The response of her de facto council was swift. "You can't do it," Memnon said. "Not when you're raising an army and your legitimacy in Upper Egypt rests on being Pharaoh, the avatar of Isis and the sole heir. If you recognize Theodorus as Pharaoh, your support will evaporate into thin air."

Dion nodded from where he lounged by the door. "And right now that's the only support you've got."

"There's the Patriarch," I said.

"Who has Caesar camped on him with five thousand men," Iras snapped.

Cassander, the son of the governor of Pelousion, took a deep breath. "Do you have any concept what five thousand Roman legionaries can do? Even if you had two or three times as many troops at your disposal, you would have levies from Upper Egypt. Unarmored archers. Spearmen with no shields who have never drilled together. Volunteers who haven't been properly trained. There's no way those men could stand against even the two understrength legions Caesar has, even if they outnumbered them three to one."

Cleopatra nodded. "We cannot make an enemy of Caesar," she said. "Even if all the gods smiled upon us and we held him off, he would simply return with more troops and an ample reason to annex Egypt as a province, as Rome did lately in Judea." She steepled her hands before her chin. "No, we must make a friend of Caesar. And make Theodorus his enemy."

Thinking of Caesar's displeasure at the murder of Pompeius, I said, "The thing about Theo and his advisers is that if you give them enough rope, they'll hang themselves."

"But to give them the rope," Apollodorus said, meeting Cleopatra's eyes across the room, "you have to be in Alexandria."

WE RETURNED to Alexandria on a merchant ship, embarking by night, Cleopatra, Apollodorus, Dion, and me. Memnon and the rest of the council stayed in Memphis with Iras. They would sail north two days later on Memnon's great barge. Iras would play the Queen. Meanwhile, for the journey north, Cleopatra would play the serving girl, the handmaiden of a young Greek woman traveling with her husband and her father.

Apollodorus found the role difficult, and had to be constantly reminded to ignore his daughter's slave. Dion, however, enjoyed himself immensely, telling Cleopatra to come and go, and to fetch and carry things. She made a grand production of it for Dion, bowing and scraping as though he were a god on earth, as though he were Pharaoh. They made such asses of themselves that on the third day one older woman among the passengers took me aside and told me that I mustn't take it to heart if my husband's eye strayed. Obviously the girl was a hussy, and I should sell her at the first opportunity in Alexandria!

I was as embarrassed as if it were true, but Cleopatra and Dion thought it a grand joke.

And what if it were? What if Cleopatra stretched out her hand to Dion? Would he come to her as he had not come to me? Such jealousy ill became me, I thought. And it made me happy to see my sister laughing and jesting for once, as though she were only a young woman of twenty-one, not a queen.

If she were the handmaiden, would she be happier?

Pharaohs are not made to be happy, Isis whispered. *Pharaohs are made to serve.*

CAESAR WAS NOT STAYING in the palace itself. He was staying in one of the guesthouses in the park, the best one, surrounded by a high wall with a defensible gate of its own. And of course it was Dion who thought of a way to get in.

"Tradesmen come and go all the time," Dion said. "A merchant with something Caesar has ordered should be able to pass the gates and go to him. If Apollodorus stays in the part of a merchant and takes a large package, like a carpet, with him, the Queen could be inside it."

"Caesar won't be alone," I pointed out. "He'll know he hasn't bought a carpet."

"That doesn't matter," Cleopatra said. "Once we're inside the gates it will be all Romans. They'll take me to Caesar, not to Theo or Pothinus."

"Does it have to be you?" I asked.

I didn't expect for her to throw her arms around me. "Dearest Charmian," she said. "I know you would if you could. But think what Caesar will feel when he finds out he's been talking to the wrong Cleopatra! If we make a fool of him, we make an enemy." She put her hand to my cheek. "It has to be me. Do you see?"

"I do," I said.

WE WAITED IN THE PARK, Dion and I. After they passed the gate, we could see and hear nothing. We stood in silence under the trees, while the night wind played around us. After a bit, I put my head on Dion's shoulder and he put his arm around me.

"We can still get clear," he said. "If it all goes wrong. No one will look for us."

"I know," I said.

If it did, I would. There was nothing I could do for them from here. Memnon would still have a bargaining chip. He could claim that Iras was the real queen, and that the Cleopatra Caesar held was a fake.

We waited for what seemed like half the night. I suppose it was a few hours. The Roman watch changed, at any rate.

At last Apollodorus came out with two Romans. They did not touch him, and seemed to accompany him rather than escort him.

Dion stepped out of the shadow. "What's happened?"

"We're to return to the palace and make the Queen's quarters ready for her. Caesar intends to enforce the terms of Auletes' will, and reinstate her as Queen of Egypt. He is meeting with her now."

I saw how the men tried to follow the conversation, but apparently they did not speak Koine. Still, my answer was carefully gauged. I nodded deeply. "It is my honor to prepare my Lady's things."

We fell in with them, crossing the park and the street beyond, walking along beneath the trees in the starlight. The moon was rising, and not yet a quarter grown.

One of them, the one on my side, seemed to be trying to follow the very formal conversation between Dion and Apollodorus, his eyes flicking back and forth from one to the other. They were hazel, almost green, and, unlike any Roman I'd ever seen, he wore his hair long and caught behind him in a chestnut-colored tail. He also wore trousers, faded buff woolen ones beneath a scarlet tunic and leathers. The sword that hung at his side seemed longer than the others I'd seen.

Making my Latin more halting than it was, I asked, "Are you Roman?"

He nodded. "Decurion Aurelianus, of the Seventh Turma of Pollio's Lancers." He gave me a sideways glance. "We're cavalry. That's why we don't wear steel."

"Oh," I said.

"I'm Aremorican," he said, as if that made it all make sense.

"Oh," I said again. "Where's that?"

"We're a tribe in northern Gaul," he said, with a tone that suggested he'd explained it a hundred times. "Along the coast, on a peninsula jutting out into the sea."

"That's very far away," I said, forgetting that my Latin was supposed to be halting. "Why are you here?"

"We hated the Arverni," he said. "So when Caesar raised an auxiliary cavalry legion of eight hundred men to fight Vercingetorix, I joined." Aurelianus shrugged. "It seemed more exciting than raising sheep. I've seen a lot of the world in the last six years."

"Your Latin is very good," I said.

"So is yours." He glanced at me sideways again. His eyes were actually green, not just greenish. "But I'm not following the Greek very well."

"You'll learn Koine if you stay in Alexandria long," I said.

"That will be as Caesar commands," he said.

We were at the doors of the Queen's quarters. Aurelianus stopped. "I'll be here. Caesar has my turma on guard duty. Cavalry's not much use in the city, and we've been with him a long time." There was pride in his voice. "I imagine your Queen will be along in a few minutes, with Constantius' turma. You can rely on us."

I certainly could, I thought, to obey Caesar's orders rather than Theo's, which was something. The others went in ahead of me, but I stopped in the doorway. "Shall I ask for you if we have any difficulty?"

He nodded briskly. "Just ask for Decurion Aurelianus. What's your name?"

"Charmian," I said. "Principal handmaiden to the Hands of Isis, Cleopatra of Egypt. I'm in charge of all her staff and personal arrangements."

"Oh." He looked a little taken aback. Then he smiled. "So you guard her back."

"I took an assassin's knife for her once," I said, and gathered my robe at my side to show him, the scar jagged and ugly across my white skin. "We are not as soft as we look."

"I would not make that mistake, Charmian," he said, and his eyes were warm.

"Nor would I," I said.

His smile grew. "Then I believe we understand one another."

"I think we do," I said. With an answering smile I stepped in and closed the door.

CLEOPATRA RETURNED within the hour, looking tired but not displeased. "Wait," she said, as Aurelianus closed the door behind her. We followed her, Dion, Apollodorus, and I, out onto the small terrace, where the wind from the sea whipped in, forty feet over the breakwater below. No one could overhear us there.

"We can work with him," she said. "He's determined to enforce Auletes' will, and for us to rule jointly."

"The money," I said.

Cleopatra nodded. "He says he put up seventy million sesterces of the money that Pompeius loaned to Auletes. And that he'll forgive thirty million if we can pay the other forty immediately." She put her hand up to forestall Dion's question. "It doesn't matter if it's true or not. The proof is in Rome, even if it is. It's about twenty percent of what we owed Pompeius, and then the debt is completely cleared."

"We can't find forty million sesterces right away," Apollodorus said. "And neither can Pothinus."

Cleopatra paced to the brink and looked down at the waves. "He has to pay his troops. About half his men are from the Sixth Legion, which only came over to Caesar after Pharsalus. They haven't been paid in months. And they used to be Pompeius' men."

"And Gnaeus is still out there," I said.

"And the Senate may or may not accept his victory over Pompeius," Apollodorus said. "Or may raise another army against him."

"What about these Gaulish Lancers?" Dion asked. I was surprised he'd heard that much of my conversation with Aurelianus. I'd thought he was busy with Apollodorus.

"There are only six hundred of them," Cleopatra said. "He's dismounted them on guard duty in the city. I think he's sure of their loyalty, but six hundred on forty-five hundred isn't good odds if some of his troops mutiny. The rest of his are from the Twenty-eighth, and they're very young and were badly mauled at Pharsalus. If I were Caesar, I'd be worried that the Sixth could carry them with them if it came to that."

I thought that was true. If Aurelianus was representative of his men, they'd stick with Caesar, but they didn't even wear steel.

"So what did you promise him?" Apollodorus asked.

Her mouth was hard. "I promised him forty million sesterces if he would make me sole ruler of Egypt. He said he'd consider it."

I shook my head. "And if he takes it, then what?"

"We find forty million sesterces. There are temples in Upper Egypt. If Memnon and the others want the Romans gone, they'll have to sell their treasures." Cleopatra looked out to sea, where Pharos burned golden on the breakwater, symbol of our wealth and our world.

"Perhaps it won't come to that," I said.

THE NEXT DAY in the palace there was a grave ceremony of reconciliation. I stood beside Apollodorus while Caesar, in his carven chair, prepared to read the terms of Auletes' will, that his heirs should together rule Egypt in peace and harmony.

At first my attention was on Theo. He looked sulky, though behind him Theocritus and Pothinus were beaming. Crocodile smiles, I thought.

Then Caesar began to read.

His voice was light and cool, his Koine perfectly accented as he read the will. His balding head was inclined to the scroll, but even from that vantage I could see the firm lines of his face, the elegant hands.

"I know him," I whispered. I had seen him in the dream in Abydos. He had been the last vision, the man in the tent. I had summoned him to Alexandria, summoned him by his bones. I stood on my toes to see a little better.

Yes, that was the man. I was quite certain of it. I had not mistaken the keen dark eyes that occasionally scanned the room. He knew the contents of the scroll quite well. He sat with his right foot forward, and he looked like a bird at rest, pausing for a moment only, like the golden eagles his men held at either side. Their cuirasses gleamed.

"I know him," I said, a chill down my spine as though someone stood at my back.

THAT NIGHT there was a banquet in honor of the reconciliation. Theoretically, Cleopatra and Ptolemy were honoring their guest, Caesar, but we all knew the banquet was on Caesar's orders.

It was not a very splendid banquet. Pothinus had hidden all of the best plate the moment Caesar arrived, and we were using the everyday stuff, silver servers and kraters, with fine antique Corinthian pottery, elegant and plain. It spoke of good taste, and the appreciation of generations of Ptolemies for fine things, not of great wealth.

Half of the men present were Caesar's officers. Most of the Egyptian clergy were absent. Memnon and his party hadn't returned to Alexandria with Iras yet, and I wondered if they would. If they did, they should have to acknowledge Theo, and they had just gone to great lengths not to.

Indeed, a great many people were there who seemed not to want to be. Theo left as soon as it was possible without unforgivable rudeness. After all, some leeway is allowed in leaving banquets when they begin to turn into lingering over the wine when one is only fourteen.

Caesar stayed on and on. People kept coming up and talking with him. Cleopatra, whose couch was too far away from Caesar's for conversation, courtesy of Pothinus, began to stop smiling. She was tired, I thought. Bred as she was and trained for the last seven years to these things, even her smile began to fade well after midnight. Yet for all that, Caesar hardly seemed drunk. In fact, either he held his wine exceedingly well or he had hardly drunk at all.

Without Iras to trade off with, I had not been able to sit down, but sometime after midnight, when there were only the sweets that go with the wine left, Apollodorus took my place behind the Queen so that I could eat something.

Some of the couches had been abandoned, but I could hardly go and sit down at a place covered in other people's dishes or their abandoned flowers. I looked around in irritation for a couch that had not been full.

I saw one toward the end of the hall, a young man who seemed to be eating alone, leaning over the bolster and talking to a friend at another couch. One of the Romans. I should be my most charming and diplomatic, since that seemed to be how Cleopatra had decided to play it.

I came and stood beside him. "Is this place taken?" I asked.

He hurriedly shook his head, and I thought that he was younger than he seemed at first. I had thought him my age, but flushed with drink and the blood rising in his face, he might be several years younger. He was strongly built, with hair halfway between brown and blond, and long blond eyelashes and a cleft chin. He looked at me and blushed scarlet.

"I'm not a hetaira," I said gently.

"I know." He sat up, showing me the entirety of his legs in the process. They were very nice indeed. "I saw you standing behind the Queen."

"I'm her handmaiden," I said. "Charmian is my name. May I sit with you and eat for a few minutes?"

"Of course," he said, leaning back again so that I could sit on the couch beside him, my back not touching his body at all.

"Thank you," I said. One of the servants appeared swiftly with wine and sweets. It would have been nice if some of the meats or savories were left, but no. I filled my cup and made conversation. "So which legion are you with?"

I had caught him in the middle of a drink of his own wine, and he swallowed hurriedly. "Neither one. I'm a tribune seconded to Caesar."

"Isn't that unusual?" I asked.

He nodded, and I thought there was something like embarrassment in his face. "My mother's a good friend of Atia Balba Caesonia," he said. "Caesar's niece. She got me the appointment and I joined Caesar right after Pharsalus."

Green, I thought. And owes his rank to his mother pulling strings. No wonder he's down at the last couch. It's that or insert himself among veterans many years his better. Still, he had sense enough not to try it. "What's your name?" I asked.

"Marcus Vipsanius Agrippa," he said, and glanced up at me from beneath those long lashes. "And I'm not like that."

"Like what?"

"Spoiled. Come out east for a little military experience so I can go home and run for office. My brother Lucius was with Pompeius Magnus." He took a gulp from his cup. "I don't know where he is now. But nobody found his body after Pharsalus."

I refrained from asking if he'd joined Gnaeus Pompeius in flight. That wasn't the sort of thing one could ask.

"All my life I've wanted to be a soldier," he said. "And Caesar's the best. When I first met him I could hardly speak. I knew I had to do this."

"How old were you then?" I asked.

He blushed again, his fair complexion showing every emotion. "Ten. I knew I was born to serve him. Does that make any sense to you?"

"I suppose it does," I said. Perhaps I should have found him amusing, but I didn't. The intensity in his eyes made that impossible. *Here is one*, She whispered, *here is one the gods have touched. Here is one like you.*

"Good," he said seriously. "He's like no one else."

"I know," I said. The wine was unwatered, and it made my head spin. And the hour was incredibly late.

"You do, don't you?" he said, looking at me again. "You really do know."

"Yes," I said. I might have said more, oddly enough, in the presence of this all too intense Roman, but at that moment Apollodorus caught my eye. The Queen was preparing to retire. She would not wait out Caesar.

"I need to go," I said. "Good night."

"Good night," he said, leaning forward as I stood up. "Will I see you again?"

One of the men on the next couch called out to another, "Oh, look! Baby Marcus found a girl! She's too much for you, little boy!"

I swept my skirts around me and turned, giving Marcus Vipsanius Agrippa a dazzling smile. "I'm looking forward to seeing you again, Tribune." And I went to tend to my Queen.

SON OF VENUS

F or several days we had very little to do. Cleopatra kept sending word very politely to Caesar that she would like to see
him, and he kept sending word very politely back that he was
too busy, but that he would wait upon the gracious Queen at some
other time. She paced and I planned intimate little meals that seemed
like they were never going to happen. Dion went to the Library and
brought back a case of assorted scrolls, supposedly for the Queen's
amusement.

Cleopatra took one look at them and burst out laughing. "'A
Treatise upon the Physiology of Geese and Ducks'? 'Some Copies of
Documents from Memphis Requested by Ptolemy Eugertes'? 'A New
Method of Calculating the Angle of Navigational Stars'? Dion, what in
the world?"

Dion hastily grabbed for the stack. "There are some other things
in here. There's a copy of the new poems by Catullus." He shuffled
through the end tags and then produced a slender scroll.

"Just what I need. More Romans," she said, but still laughing she
took it and went off to her bedchamber to read.

"It's the waiting that's killing me," Dion said.

I handed him a scroll. "Why don't you read about the insides of
geese and ducks?"

"I think I'll go talk to the guards," Dion said, and sauntered off.

"Fine," I said, and picked up one of the other ones at random.

"Some Copies of Documents from Memphis Requested by Ptolemy Eugertes." I was still reading when Dion came back in a few minutes.

"Decurion Aurelianus is off duty," he said. "I suppose he sleeps sometimes."

"Dion, listen to this," I said, and began to read.

" 'From the Library of the Temple of Thoth in Memphis, from the eighth year of Ramses Usermaatre, the third of that name. Hry, He Who Walks in the Sunlight of Amon, writes: I had occasion to converse with a traveler, one of those Denden from the lands between the Akhiawa and the Hittites, who had journeyed much in the islands, and from that traveler I heard of the Drowned Land, the island that is no more. Three generations before there was a mighty kingdom on an island, with sweet water springs and rich pastures, with vineyards and fields and all else that men might need. There too stood a great city, ruled by powerful princes with many ships. Somehow they angered the gods. It is not known what crime they might have committed, but in punishment the gods destroyed their land utterly. The land itself heaved up, and the mountain upon which the island was built exploded in a rain of fire and ash. The land heaved and crumbled and fell into the sea. All that was left was tree branches and ash, and bits of bone floating on the waters. The plume of smoke of its burning could be seen from far away, appearing a pillar of smoke by day and a pillar of fire by night.

" 'This traveler had been there, and affirmed that nothing was left of the island except a narrow beach and springs, and that beneath the sea could still be seen the ruins of houses and temples. I have written this down, that it may be compared with an account from the reign of Ramses the Great, second of that name, because like broken shards of pottery do the stories fit together. In that day, there appeared on the northern horizon a vast pillar of smoke, and all of the water rushed out of the Sea of Reeds, leaving the sea floor barren, that men might walk upon it as upon dry land. Pharaoh ordered his chariot men to investigate, and they drove upon the bottom of the sea. Suddenly, with a great rush, the water came flowing back into the sea in a mighty wave, and all who had driven out were drowned. The sea returned to its normal place. However, for many days it could still be seen on the northern horizon, a pillar of smoke by day and a pillar of fire by night.'"

I stopped reading and looked at Dion. "Isn't that amazing?"

He sat down next to me, leaning over the scroll. "Everybody knows that story, Charmian."

"I don't," I said. "You mean you've heard it before?"

"You're not a Jew," Dion said. "We all know that story. It's the story of the Exodus." He put his head back, as though thinking. "I only know it in Hebrew, of course. So it's not exact. But I can tell you the story."

"Please," I said.

"Once, we were slaves in Egypt, and God raised a man called Moses, and told him to go to Pharaoh and tell him that the Lord required that we should go free. Pharaoh refused, and God visited ten plagues on the Egyptians before Pharaoh agreed that we could leave." His voice changed to the slow cadence of translating in his head. "But the Lord hardened the heart of Pharaoh King of Egypt, and he chased after the Hebrews, who were going away defiantly. The Egyptians chased after them, and all of the horses and chariots of Pharaoh overtook them camping beside the sea, beside the place where the reeds grow. When Pharaoh got closer, the Hebrews looked up, and saw the Egyptians chasing after them and were terrified. They cried out to the Lord, and they said to Moses, 'Are there no graves in Egypt that you have taken us out to die in the desert?' And Moses said, 'Fear not! Stand firm, for the Egyptians you see today you will never see again!' The Lord said to Moses, 'Tell the people to move on. As for you, lift up your staff and extend your hand toward the sea and divide it, so that the Hebrews may go through the middle of the sea on dry ground.' The angel of God who was going with the people moved and went behind them, and a pillar of cloud stood behind them. Moses stretched out his hand toward the sea, and the Lord drove the sea apart, and made it dry land, the water forming a wall on their right and on their left. The Egyptians chased after them and followed them into the middle of the sea, their horses and their chariots. The Lord looked down from a pillar of smoke and said to Moses, 'Extend your hand that the waters may flow back together.' So Moses stretched forth his hand, and the sea returned to its normal state. The water returned and covered the chariots and the horsemen. Not one who had driven on the bottom of the sea survived. And they journeyed up by Sukkoth and camped in Ethan, and the Lord went before them, a pillar of smoke by day and a pillar of fire by night, to give them light."

"It's the same story," I said, "only with the part that's embarrassing to Pharaoh taken out of the Egyptian version."

"All of those people," Dion said wonderingly. "An entire island full of people, with cities and houses and ships. And to us, it's all about the Hebrews."

"I don't believe that any god would destroy an entire island to provide a pillar of smoke," I said. I put my hands on the scroll. "No god is so cruel."

"We can understand it all," Dion said. "Given time. Give us world enough, and time. We will understand it all."

"Except for one thing," I said. "How did Moses know?"

THREE NIGHTS LATER Caesar made his move.

I awoke when the doors to Cleopatra's outer chambers opened with a crash. Still half asleep, I ran out into the sitting room in nothing but a tunic. It was full of armed men, in steel and full harness, methodically forcing all of the doors. One whirled about, his sword flashing up toward my belly.

"I've got her," a voice behind me said in Latin, its owner sweeping me back against his chest. "She's one of the handmaidens." It was Aurelianus, his usual leathers augmented by a helmet.

I twisted in his arms, kicking. I would not go down without a fight. I clawed at his face, hitting the chin guard of his helmet hard enough that it must have hurt.

"Charmian!" he shouted, trying to pin my arms.

I heard screams, but could not tell whose they were. I kicked, but connected with nothing but unyielding leather.

"Charmian!" He had my wrist now, my other arm pinned painfully against his side. "Stop! I'm not trying to kill you."

"Need some help?" another voice asked him, a legionary in full breastplate and greaves.

"I've got her, thanks," Aurelianus panted. It was good that I was at least winding him.

"What is the meaning of this?" Cleopatra's voice rang out across the hall.

One of the legionaries, a man ten years my senior, replied. "Lady, you are all under arrest by order of Caesar. You and your servants are to come with us."

"Very well." Her chin was high. "If you will be so kind as to unhand my handmaiden, we will accompany you. We have nothing to fear from Caesar."

Aurelianus let go of me with an apologetic shrug and I shook off his hand. My wrist was numb where he had held it. "I'm sorry," he whispered.

"It is my duty to die for her," I hissed.

"I respect that," he said.

WE LEFT THE PALACE through the main doors, crossing the street and the park toward the guest villa where Caesar had been staying. Arsinoe and Theo were already there, and it seemed as though there was a substantial crowd, what with the Romans and their servants.

Arsinoe rounded on Cleopatra the minute she entered. "You! This is all your fault!" Arsinoe was sixteen, and her long dark hair fell on her shoulders in pleasing disarray. "You with your bedding Romans! You're as bad as Father!"

"I'm not aware that anyone is bedding Romans here," Caesar said mildly. Of course he understood Koine perfectly.

"What do you want with us?" Theo asked. He stood straight and pale, his lips set in a thin line. I thought that he had never looked more like a Pharaoh.

"I believe the issue is General Achillas' army," Caesar said. "The Royal Army." He replied to Theo, which followed, as we had never had control of the Royal Army at all. Achillas was Theo's man. "The Royal Army has marched from Pelousion with twenty thousand infantry and two thousand cavalry, I understand. It has marched on Alexandria. I should like to know by whose orders, and to what purpose."

None of the royal children replied, Arsinoe because she had more sense, and Cleopatra because she didn't know. Theo said nothing.

Caesar nodded shortly. "You will send envoys to Achillas telling him to disarm and return with the Royal Army to Pelousion. If Achillas disobeys, he is in rebellion against Pharaoh."

"And if I do not?" Theo asked.

"Then you will no longer be Pharaoh." Caesar crossed behind his writing table. "I expect you to choose sensibly."

"And what shall I do, Caesar?" Cleopatra asked evenly. "What shall I do while you and Ptolemy Theodorus tear up my country between you?"

"Nothing," Caesar said. "You and the Princess Arsinoe will remain my guests." She might have said more, but he forestalled her. "Agrippa, you will give the Queen your room."

The young man from the banquet, wearing a scarlet tunic and leggings beneath a leather breastplate chased with gold, stood up. "It will be my pleasure, Gracious Queen," he said in accented Koine. "I will escort you."

He fell in beside us as we were escorted out. Various other officers were to give up their rooms for Theo and Arsinoe. I followed Cleopatra, her head held high.

Agrippa's room was small, with a third-story window and balcony that looked out on the park. Over the tops of acacia trees we could see a sliver of the Royal Harbor, and beyond it Pharos gleaming on its island.

"I'm sorry it's a mess. I didn't expect to have a queen in it," Agrippa said, hurriedly throwing what appeared to be his laundry into a trunk before he departed.

Cleopatra looked at me over his bent back. "Where is Dion?" she mouthed.

I shook my head. Dion hadn't been at the palace, which meant he was somewhere in the city. Dion was more than capable of looking after himself. Cleopatra and I might be prisoners, but Dion and Iras were both free. We knew they would not desert us.

Cleopatra sat down heavily on the couch, Agrippa's blankets still thrown across it helter-skelter.

After a moment I sat beside her and put my arm around her. "I could seduce Agrippa," I said.

She put her hands to her mouth and laughed, then hugged me tight. "Charmian, what should I do without you?"

"I don't know," I said. I put my forehead against her shoulder.

She turned my hand over, looking at the purpling bruises in the light. "Aurelianus?"

I nodded. "He does his duty and I do mine. I could go after Agrippa. He's young, and I think he's attracted to me. That might be worth something."

"We need Caesar," she said.

"I don't think I can seduce Caesar," I said.

She laughed again, her cheek against mine. "I think that will have to be me," she said.

"He's no Gnaeus Pompeius," I said. "He won't be easily diverted."

"Diverted from what?" she mused. "That's the real question. What is it that Caesar needs so badly that he's still here?"

"The money," I said.

She nodded. "It must be very bad. His legions must be on the verge of mutiny."

"And the Senate has declared him a rebel," I said. "Caesar stands or falls in Alexandria. If he loses control of his legions…"

"They'll loot the city," Cleopatra said. "Five thousand soldiers out for plunder in a city of half a million innocent people. We must avoid that at all costs. So we must help Caesar keep his legions."

"Pothinus thinks he'll sail away. That's got to be the game that Theo is playing," I said.

"It won't work," she said. "Not if he's that desperate."

"I know," I said. I looked down at my wrist. Aurelianus. Agrippa. Caesar. I put my head upon her shoulder and closed my eyes against her. "What is it you need me to do?"

"Bring me Caesar," she said.

I T WAS NO EASY THING to talk to Caesar, as we had already discovered. Any visit to the Queen would be done with dozens of witnesses, and every word of their conversation would be repeated and parsed by the entire court. Also, he was constantly surrounded by people. While it was doubtful that the huge Germans who formed his personal bodyguard understood Koine, there were soldiers around him at all times, reporting and meeting and dining and conferring. I wondered how he, like any ruler, managed to tend to his bodily functions in private!

For three days I tried to find a way to see him, without success. Theo's emissaries had left the city to see General Achillas, but as yet we had had no reply. We remained Caesar's guests.

Blessed Isis, I prayed, if You have a plan, then help me speak with Caesar!

The third night I could not sleep. I lay tossing and turning on the mat on the floor beside Agrippa's bed, trying not to wake the Queen. At last I got up quietly and went out into the hall. I needed fresh air, if only for a few minutes.

Agrippa was standing with the guard on the side door, but he came to me when I neared. "Is there something that the Queen needs, Charmian?"

I thanked him for his courtesy, and replied that no, there was nothing. "It's only that I can't sleep," I said. "Do you think I could walk in the garden for a few minutes? Or on the balcony?"

He hesitated, no doubt wondering what scheme I was trying.

"It's only the balcony," I said. "Tribune, it's a three-story drop to the ground! And then I should be in a garden with a wall four times my height, with gates guarded by legionaries! How should I escape?"

He hesitated again, and then smiled. "I suppose it would be all right," he said. "Just the balcony." He let me out.

This villa, like so many, was built to catch the sea breezes. In better times, doubtless it was a lovely place to set out couches and little tables, and dine in the sea air, with the soft scents of the garden below. There were no couches or tables now, only a sentry at each end of the building, the cressets unlit, as they would interfere with their night vision over the shaded garden. Still, the waning moon was bright enough that it hardly mattered.

I walked out to the rail and took a deep breath, clear and cool, like drinking moonlight.

I was not alone. His hair was a loose cap of silver, and he stood by the rail as well, some little way away, looking out over the garden. From the other side of the villa we should have been able to see Pharos and the sea, but this side looked the other way, toward the Mareotic Canal with its long lines of barges, bringing the grain of the Black Land endlessly to the sea. It was Caesar.

"Who's there?" he said sharply, one hand dropping to his waist, to a dagger I did not see. Romans have assassins too.

I stepped out into the bright moonlight, my open hands held well away from my sides. "It is only I, Imperator." My white himation shone in the darkness. No assassin would wear such.

His hand stilled. "You are one of her handmaidens," he said. "I've seen you. Charmian, is it?"

"It is," I said, inclining my head. I wished he did not know my name. It was better to be anonymous, a shadow behind Cleopatra. But then, Caesar noticed such things. "I did not mean to disturb you." I looked away. "It's only that it's so close in the villa, and I felt if I did not get some air I should scream."

"That would hardly do," he said with a strange half smile, the left side of his mouth pulling more than the right. "I expect it would alarm people."

"It would," I said.

He lifted my chin with one hand. "You have the look of her." His hand was warm, and he turned my face as though it were some work of art.

"Ptolemy Auletes was eclectic in his tastes," I said. "We were born the same year."

"Her sister as well as her servant? Interesting." The Roman raised one eyebrow. "You are loyal to her, then?"

"Would I tell you, Imperator, if I were not?" I asked. "Surely you cannot expect naïveté from someone who serves Cleopatra Philopater? If we were any of us naïve we should be long since dead." His face was very near mine, and the moonlight made each wrinkle a deep gravure, but his eyes were bright as stars, light reflecting. It seemed that I had dreamed this once, or perhaps that I dreamed still, sleeping beside Cleopatra and wondering how I should speak with Caesar. It was that sense of dream that made me bold. "She is the living Isis, Her Hands on earth. You must put her on the throne of Egypt. It is what she was born to do."

"No doubt it's what she wishes," Caesar said dryly, releasing my chin with the same unminding caress one would use for a cat. "Your mistress has many estimable qualities."

"Does she fascinate you, Imperator?" I asked.

"As she means to?" He turned, one eyebrow rising again. "You can tell her yes, of course she does." He looked out over the garden. Somewhere out there in the night, the river was flowing beneath the stars, the Nile rolling ever seaward, as it always had and always would. I said nothing, just waited for him to drink his fill of the night. "The pyramids are two thousand years old," he said. "So they tell me. How old are your gods?"

"Do you care for gods, Imperator? I didn't think Romans put much stock in such." Certainly Gnaeus had not, and I had not known so many others closely. They seemed a supremely practical people.

"I am a priest of Jupiter," he said lightly. "Or had you forgotten?"

"I did not know," I said. "Perhaps there is some small flaw in our intelligence." I came and stood beside him at the rail, looked sideways at his face. "Do you believe in pothos, like Alexander? Fata, leading you by the hand?"

"It's a foolish man who scorns Fata," he said. "I don't think even my enemies have called me foolish."

"No," I said. "That's not the thing they've named you." Rebel, traitor, tyrant, a man with no regard for law, a man who would be king—all those things had been said and more. But no man had called him foolish, at least not in a very long time. But what did he believe? If anyone knew that, they did not speak of it.

Caesar looked vaguely amused. "And does Cleopatra wish a second Alexander to swoop down upon her enemies like a plunging falcon? To raise new temples in her honor? A royal wedding and a Caesarid dynasty?"

"You have named it, not I," I said, but a shiver ran down my back.

He laughed, a pleasant enough sound. "She wishes to know these things. Why does she send you to ask me?"

I must gamble. The stakes were too high not to. "Because you will tell me," I said, certainty in my voice.

"And why will I do that?"

"Because you have known me for a thousand years. I have died in your service. I have saved your life when your enemies sought you, and I have killed a man across your funeral bier." I held his eyes, and in his face I saw it again, the funeral cortege making its way down a mountain road. "We carried you to Memphis in a coffin of gold and laid you among the sacred kings, beside the bulls of Serapis until your city was ready. You may not remember, waking, this side of the River, but I think that you do know. I think you know much more than you pretend."

Caesar tilted his head to the side, his face unreadable. "Strange," he said quietly. "You look Greek, with your fair hair."

"I am all Egypt," I said. "Egypt as she is now, Black Land and Red Land and Alexandria together. You have come home to your place, Imperator, and she greets you as a lover long absent and much missed. Do not scorn Fata, or the words of the gods."

"Now you are the voice of a goddess, not a slave?"

"We are all more than we seem, Divine Julius, the Son of Venus," I said. "Are you not descended from Venus through that Trojan tossed over sea and land by the enmity of Juno, until at last he came to Italian shores and took up his long destiny?"

He threw his head back and laughed, long thin throat exposed. "I should take this then as a caution against sparring with Cleopatra. If the handmaiden is so practiced in arms, I should beware your mistress!"

I inclined my head. "Perhaps you should. But you have not answered my question."

"Nor will I. Now," he said, and smiling walked away.

I waited until he was gone. He had answered. I knew what I had come to find out.

FIRE

A chillas killed one of the emissaries, and the other returned to Alexandria badly wounded, having been left for dead and saved by the intrepidness of his servants. Achillas, he said, was determined that Ptolemy was not in control in Alexandria, and he marched on the city to liberate Pharaoh and people both from the Romans. Unfortunately for Caesar, the city guards agreed. They let him into the city without a fight, and Caesar was besieged in the Palace Quarter.

In that day, the Palace Quarter, palaces, villas, and park, were surrounded by a wall with gates. There was also the small Royal Harbor, with the docks for our private ships just south of the Lochias Peninsula, where Caesar had brought in his ships. It was not large, and to sail, one had to go through the main harbor and out around the breakwater and the island of Pharos, but it did still give him a way to leave.

Perhaps that is what a sensible man would have done. I do not know. I do know, however, that I did not like the smell in the air in the villa. The legionaries stood together when off duty in quiet knots, and there was little laughter or dicing. Only the Gaulish cavalry in their thin leather harness went about their business with calm gravity. The legionaries on our doors were replaced by Aurelianus and his men again, presumably because the infantry were needed on the walls, and there was little use for dismounted cavalry, but I thought also that it was because they were steadier. They spoke their own languages among themselves, and obeyed their own officers.

Fighting broke out near the docks. Achillas was pressing in, pushing the infantry back street by street and house by house. It was only a small area, mostly warehouses and inns, but my heart bled at the thought of fighting in our city. Meanwhile, we were trapped.

On the second day of the fighting, Caesar came to see the Queen.

He wore harness like his men, but it was gilded steel over leather, Medusa's head embossed on the chest piece, with gilded greaves and the full infantry kit, save the helm. I thought that beneath the fine clothes his legs were rather skinny, and that was where he showed his age. He was, after all, nearly as old as Auletes.

Two German bodyguards accompanied him, huge blond men looking as though their muscles had been carved from stone.

Cleopatra rose from her chair. She did not incline her head, and neither did he. "So you have come to see me at last," she said.

I busied myself pouring watered wine into cups, but of course Caesar did not take his, nor did the Queen.

"As you can guess, I've been busy," he said.

Her gown was a shade between rose and purple, and brought color to her cheeks. "So I understand. Caesar, let me be sure we understand one another. You want money to pay your men. I want my city undamaged."

"I thought you wanted to be sole ruler of Egypt," Caesar said. One eyebrow rose.

"In order for you to get your money, I must be," she said calmly. "You will not find that money in Alexandria, and you will not be able to raise it in taxes and payments from Upper Egypt while the country is in civil war. It is in your interest, now and in the future, to have Egypt as a firm ally at your back, a source of wealth and support. You will not get that from Ptolemy Theodorus, and you can get it from me."

"What makes you think I cannot get it from Ptolemy?" he asked, his cloak over his arm as though he were a rhetoretician.

"From the men who killed Pompeius?" One of the Queen's eyebrows rose in mirror of his. "Will you ever be certain, if you turn your back for one moment, that your will shall be done or promises kept? Do you plan to stay in Egypt and collect taxes yourself?"

"And you will pay promptly and without quibbling?"

Cleopatra nodded. "If the terms are reasonable. I will not beggar my country, not for your aid or anyone else's. If I should, then I should be a poor ruler indeed."

"And the price of this invaluable assistance?" Caesar smiled, as though now it were down to bargaining, and he was sure of getting what he wanted.

Her reply wiped the smile from his lips. "Put me on the throne of Egypt, where I shall rule jointly with the son you will get on me."

"My dear lady, it isn't that I'm not flattered by your proposal, but it is quite impossible," he said. He paced toward the wine table, while the Germans exchanged looks behind his back. They might seem to be carved out of stone, but they understood some Koine, at least. I, for my part, nearly dropped the cup in the krater.

"In all my years of life, I have never sired a son. One child, and one alone, my daughter who is dead...." Caesar turned and spread his hands. "Believe me, I have had many women with varying degrees of pleasure, but they do not quicken."

"Perhaps you have never lain with a goddess," Cleopatra said, seeming unperturbed.

"I have not," he said. I looked for amusement on his face, but there was none. "But I will not have the child of some slave foisted off upon me as my get. If I would not take the son of Publius Clodius, I will take no lesser."

"I have more dignity than that, I assure you. Do you think I would raise the son of a slave to the throne of the Ptolemies?" Cleopatra said icily. "Should you lie with me, we will get a son, a Horus for Egypt. Isis wills it."

"And what does Cleopatra will?"

"That does not matter in the least."

He looked at her and nodded shortly, as one swordsman will to another. "Perhaps you are a ruler after all."

"I am Pharaoh," she said, and there was Egypt in her cool eyes. "I am Isis."

Caesar put his head to the side, and this time his smile was real. "I had thought the Ptolemies were Greek."

"Egypt changes men who have their will with her," she said. "Conquerors come, and go away changed."

"Alexander did not," he said.

"Alexander already knew who he was before he went to Siwah." Cleopatra crossed the room in a whisper of soft silks, and took the wine cup from my hand. "Do you, Caesar?"

He laughed. "I'm Caesar," he said.

"They say you visited the Soma," she said.

"Don't all travelers? It is, after all, Alexandria's most famous sight."

"They say you wept," she said. "Why, Caesar?"

"Do not many men?" He met her eyes. "Are not many moved at the sight of such devotion, that friends should treat a corpse with such reverence, should kill across his bier?"

He did not look at me, but I sucked in a breath.

"Certainly of all the Companions Ptolemy at least was true," she said.

"Loyalty is a rare thing in a ruler," Caesar said. "Or in anyone." He glanced behind at his bodyguards. "I take it where I find it, in whatever guise."

"As do I," she said.

His eyes shifted to me. "Then you are well served."

"I know," she said.

Caesar nodded. "I will consider your proposal, Gracious Queen."

"I will await your response, Imperator," she replied. And the interview was at an end. Caesar swept from the room, his Germans behind him.

A FEW HOURS LATER the doors opened to admit Dion, and I flung my arms around his neck. "Dion! How in the world did you get in?"

Dion grinned. "Aurelianus. They have orders not to let you out. Nobody said anything about not letting me in."

Cleopatra rose up from the chair at the window. "What's the news in the city?"

"Not good." Dion bowed gracefully. "Most of the city is in Achillas' hands, and it's business as usual. But the neighborhoods along the harbor north of the Soma are still full of people. They slapped the cordon down so fast that people couldn't get out. And that's where the fighting is."

The Queen looked grim. "Who's winning?"

"Right now, Achillas. There's still a corridor open from here to the harbor. They could still get to their ships. But there are Egyptian ships in the main harbor that answer to Achillas, and the batteries of ballistae on Pharos' island. Caesar's not going to get any supplies by sea."

Cleopatra looked at me. "What if we've miscalculated?"

"Then we're finished," I said.

Dion looked from one of us to the other. "Miscalculated about what?"

It was Cleopatra's to answer, so she did. "Telling Caesar that I would bear him a son to be Pharaoh of Egypt in return for his backing."

Dion let out a long whistle through his teeth. "That's interesting," he managed.

"Caesar has no sons," I said. "He never has. One daughter years ago, but no other children. Do you suppose he can't do it?"

Dion grinned. "I think that's unlikely. You should hear what his Gauls sing about him. 'Lock up your wives, Romans! Here we come with our balding debaucher! He'll take them fore and aft, and finish up in their mouths for good measure!'"

Cleopatra burst out laughing. "Where in the world did you hear that?"

"Aurelianus," Dion said. "And his friends call him Emrys."

"Do you count yourself one of his friends now?" Cleopatra asked, smiling.

"Unfortunately not yet," Dion said. "I'm pretty sure the Romans aren't supposed to explore Greek vices. Though they say Caesar did.

Some wit years ago called him 'every man's woman and every woman's man.'"

"I remember that," Cleopatra said. "It was Curio, wasn't it? When Caesar was such good friends with King Nicomedes of Bithynia."

"I think so," Dion said. "But that must have been twenty years ago."

"More like thirty," I said.

"Well, that sounds promising," Cleopatra said dryly. "Romans aren't supposed to do anything of the kind. They think that men lying with other men is wrong, and that it turns men into soft cowards."

Dion raised an eyebrow. "What, like Alexander the Great? If you lie with men, you may only conquer most of the known world? If you don't, you might do better?"

I shrugged. "Maybe Caesar slept with Nicomedes or maybe not. I don't see how it matters."

"It matters in what other Romans think of him," Cleopatra said. "They don't accept that normal men enjoy sex with both men and women."

"I have no idea what Gauls think," Dion said. "Anyone?"

Cleopatra laughed. "I think that's your research project, Dion. Please report back to us on your conclusions!"

"Provided we're all here to listen," I said.

Dion put his arm around me. "Caesar will pull it off. You'll see. He's been in tighter spots, so Emrys tells me."

WE WOKE TO FIRE. Smoke crept into the room, choking and acrid. I got to my feet and went to the window. The sky was pink, a strange, nacreous glow lighting all of the usual haze. There was more than usual; something enormous was afire.

I shook Cleopatra. "Wake up! You must get up! The city is burning!"

She wriggled and sat up, choking and coughing. Her eyes were wide.

I flung the door open.

The Roman sentry stood still, his sword at his side. The smoke was less in the corridor, where there were no windows.

"What is going on?" I demanded. "What is happening?"

It was only a moment before Aurelianus came running.

I leaned out into the corridor again, the smoke following me. "What is burning?" I yelled. "You must let us out. We will suffocate in our beds!"

"Caesar is burning the Egyptian fleet," Aurelianus replied, his green eyes bloodshot. "There is a sortie out to do it. The wind is blowing this way, so we are getting the worst of the smoke."

Cleopatra was at my elbow. "If the smoke is blowing this way, then the fire…"

"Some of the buildings along the harbor have caught," Aurelianus said. "The warehouses along the main harbor just past the Gate of the Moon. Achillas is having to use his men to put the fire out."

"Caesar doesn't put out fires? Only start them?" Cleopatra asked tartly, and I knew she was thinking of her city, of the families whose homes and whose livelihoods were in those neighborhoods.

"Caesar can't get to it, Lady," Aurelianus said evenly. "That area is entirely held by Achillas."

"Wonderful," she said, and whatever else she might have said was lost in a fit of coughing.

"We can't stay here," I said. "The smoke is too thick. Aurelianus, ask Caesar if we can be moved somewhere else."

"Caesar isn't here," he said. "He's out with the sortie at the Gate of the Moon." The smoke was so thick that he began coughing as well.

"Surely he does not mean to kill the Royal Family from smoke inhalation," I said.

Aurelianus opened his mouth, then shut it again. He turned to the guard. "Escort the Queen and her handmaiden out into the park. I will inform General Pollio that we are moving, and that the other members of the Royal Family should be moved because of the smoke." He strode off smartly.

The guard stepped aside. "Come," he said.

With my himation held to my nose and mouth, we followed him

down, through the garden and out into the park. Perhaps it was that the trees broke up the smoke, or that we were a little farther, but the air was cleaner. We sat by the fountain made of the sarcophagus of Nectanebo and wet our himations in the clear running water. Breathing through the damp fabric was much easier. After a few minutes, some of the other guards joined us, escorting Ptolemy Theodorus with Pothinas. Since we hardly had anything to say to one another, we said nothing. Above, the sky roiled with clouds, their undersides glowing from the fire. In the city there must be shouting, desperate people running. Somewhere, in the chaos, Agrippa drew the first blood of his life in some courtyard, while at the Gate of the Moon Caesar watched to be sure the gate held.

Here, among the tombs, all was serene. This must be, I thought light-headedly, what it is like to be already dead.

Another decurion came hurrying up to Aurelianus. "Where is the Princess Arsinoe?" he asked.

Aurelianus spread his hands. "I don't know. She's never been in the care of my turma. Is she still in the villa?"

"She's not in her rooms," the other decurion said. "Perhaps she was moved somewhere else because of the smoke." He started back to the villa again.

I looked at Cleopatra and she looked at me. Perhaps Arsinoe had taken advantage of the opening we had not. Whatever her flaws, cowardice was not one of them.

We waited in the gardens until dawn came, a flawed dawn with a pall of smoke hanging over the city. All in all, several hundred buildings had burned, mostly warehouses and shops near the harbor, as well as the massive drydocks that served the fleet. Those would have to be rebuilt at no small expense.

"Caesar will understand if I deduct the cost of my drydocks from the money I have promised him," Cleopatra said grimly. "If he is to burn our docks, he will pay for us to replace them."

One building that had burned was irreplaceable. The Library had not been, since the second Ptolemy's time, housed under one roof.

Four buildings clustered together, and then about them, among the halls and lecture theaters of the Museum, there were three more buildings, including the Ascalepium, the great medical library with its teaching facilities and dissection rooms. It was one of these satellite buildings that had burned, the one containing part of natural sciences and eastern literature and thought. Original manuscripts of Aristotle had been housed in that building. So had books from the Sind and other parts of India, including an incredibly beautiful scroll in Sanskrit about a hero named Arjuna.

I wept when I heard it, as much as I wept for the city and her people. These things were as precious as any human life, as impossible to duplicate.

Cleopatra was furious and white-lipped. When Caesar came to us in the morning to tell us that we might move back into our rooms in the palace rather than the villa, she told him in no uncertain terms that his carelessness was criminal.

"What am I now, a god, that I might command the winds?" he asked. "Sparks blew and the roof caught. I regret that it happened but I could hardly prevent it."

"Surely Caesar can tell which way the wind is blowing," Cleopatra said tartly. "If you burn our treasures, you will get little money. I expect that Caesar will pay for the dockyard, and for the reconstruction of the Library building, at least, since our men, priests, and scholars labored all night to put the fire out. I understand that one elderly master carried water with a bucket until dawn, at which time he sat down upon the stones, laid his hand upon his breast, and died in the ashes of his beloved library."

"My men have died too, all night long," Caesar said. "It is the price. You are old enough to know that."

"I am old enough to know that my duty is to guard my people," she said. "And to guard our precious treasures, our way of life, and our gods."

"Surely your gods can guard themselves," Caesar said.

"Our gods work through us, Imperator. Is that not the way of it in Rome?"

"It is indeed," Caesar said, and laughed. "I will reduce the amount you owe me by the cost of the dockyard. It is certainly true that we will need it in the future."

Cleopatra raised one eyebrow. "Then you have agreed to my proposal?"

"In theory," he said, and took a step closer. They did not touch, merely stood too closely together for casual conversation. "Though I will not fault you if you do not bear a son. I prefer to demand the possible."

"Should we all get out of this alive," she said.

"That's the trick, isn't it?"

"Always," she said. She did not step back nor turn. She would not until he did.

I do not know who would have moved first, had Agrippa not come up behind. "Imperator," he said, "Princess Arsinoe and her tutor, Ganymede, are gone. They escaped in the confusion."

Caesar sighed. "I suppose that is not too much damage."

Never underestimate a Ptolemaic princess, I thought. Arsinoe was as clever as the rest of us, and she would play her own hand.

She did, of course. Before the day had ended, she was with Achillas, who proclaimed that he served at the pleasure of Queen Arsinoe and Pharaoh Ptolemy Theodorus, a legitimate enough cause. It made Caesar's position infinitely worse.

And ours as well. Queen Cleopatra, it seemed, was no longer necessary at all.

CAESAR WAS ON HIS FEET from morning until night, and there was no chance to speak with him in the next day. We were in a state of siege and for now the Palace Quarter held. That would not continue forever, though it seemed to.

"Do you have reinforcements?" Cleopatra asked, as they supped together in the evening cool the next day. I had finally been able to plan an actual meal, with Caesar present and sitting down, something I considered a personal triumph. It was an intimate meal, in the sense there were only the six of us—Caesar and Cleopatra, me, two

German bodyguards, and Caesar's taster. I stood behind the krater at Cleopatra's elbow, the two bodyguards stood behind Caesar's couch, and the taster knelt on the floor beside Caesar's table. It was a very private meal, and quite informal.

"I hope I do," he said.

I was beginning to learn that Caesar often put something humorously when it was deadly serious and not to his advantage, hoping that people should remember the tone of his words rather than their content.

"You will not tell me?" Cleopatra turned her cup round in her hand. It was painted Corinthian ware, a century old.

"I don't know," he said smiling, seeming undistressed by this turn of events. "I devoutly hope so."

"I devoutly hope you do too," she said.

"Regretting our bargain already?" he asked lightly, but there was something serious in his dark eyes as he looked over the cup rim.

"As I recall we have yet to seal our bargain," she replied.

His eyebrows rose. "You intend to stand or fall with me? If you tie your cause too closely with mine, you are closing your options."

"I have already closed the option of reigning with Theo," she said, and I knew she spoke of Abydos, which she had not told him. "A son for whom we could both strive would hold us to a common cause. Today, tomorrow, and the next day are the days I am most likely to conceive. If it is to be done, let us do it."

"And that is all? Something to be done?" Caesar rested his chin on his steepled fingers.

"I am Cleopatra, and you are Caesar," she said, but there was a faint flush creeping up her face. I knew how intensely embarrassing it must be, to play as coolly as she had with Gnaeus. "It is a matter of state."

"You have never had a lover?" They spoke as if they were alone, and why should they not? The taster, the Germans, and I were part of the furnishings, like the silver krater or the fine ebony tables that stood beside their couches.

The color rose higher in her face. "I do not have that luxury," she said.

Caesar leaned back on his couch, and for a moment I could see in his grace the youth he must have been. "Gnaeus Pompeius was a matter of state too, I suppose."

"Could you imagine that I should want that boor for anything else?" she asked.

Caesar laughed, leaning back on his cushions and laughing so hard that tears started in his eyes. "I beg your pardon, dear Queen," he managed at last. "I know Gnaeus Pompeius, and I am deeply sorry for having insulted your taste!" He took a quick drink of the watered wine. "I suppose I am his step-grandfather in some sense, but I am in no way responsible for his upbringing!"

"I hardly thought you were, Imperator," she said. Her voice was calm, but I saw her hand shake.

"Imperator? Perhaps under the circumstances we could move on to Caesar," he said. "Just as a matter of informality, while we are getting a son together. I find 'Imperator' a bit off-putting in the bedroom. I would not dream of suggesting you dispense with decorum altogether and move on to Gaius, or perhaps even to 'my honey,' but sticking at Imperator feels as though you intend to report very seriously how things are going on your end."

"If you wish it, Caesar," she said sweetly. "I cannot pretend to have your vast age or tremendous and varied experience, so I do not know how these things are done."

Once again he roared, and kissed his fingers to her in his laughter. "You scored that time," he said. "Vast age is something of an understatement. Still, I will try not to disappoint." He rose to his feet and held out his hand to her. "Shall we be about it, then?"

She took his hand and let him help her to her feet, turning toward the bedchamber beyond. "Charmian, you will not be needed," she said quietly.

I bowed silently.

"And that goes for you too," Caesar said to the Germans and the taster. "I do manage some things on my own."

They closed the door behind them, leaving the tables, couches, wine, and us. The taster shrugged, got up with a belch, and wandered off into the hall. With a sigh, one of the Germans picked an olive off Caesar's abandoned plate and, chewing, walked over to stand on guard at the bedroom door.

The other caught my eye. "It is better to laugh together, yes?" he asked in his broken Latin.

PROMISES AND
DREAMS

Outside the city, the harvest began to come in, the first
fruits. The coolest days of the year were upon us, pleasant and cloudless. In Rome, ice storms might blow down
from the mountains, but in Alexandria we needed no more than a
cloak at night.

Caesar held. So, unfortunately, did Achillas.

I had rather expected that, their bargain kept, we would see little
of Caesar, and that there should be small love lost between them. To
my surprise, they took to dining together almost every night, sometimes with his officers and sometimes not. Often, after the meal,
Caesar would return to his work, conferring with his maps and his
men far into the night. Sometimes, perhaps one night in three or four,
they would retire together into the Queen's rooms. It surprised me, as
either his seed had taken or it hadn't, and I should altogether be the
first (or second) to know when the Queen's blood came.

Perhaps Caesar wanted his money's worth, though unlike Gnaeus
he was never crude. They dined on separate couches, with no unseemly
pinching or squeezing. Often, several of Caesar's officers joined them,
talking of science or literature, with no jests that should not belong in
decent company.

I particularly liked the young general, Ansinius Pollio, who,
though not but twenty-eight, commanded Caesar's Gaulish cavalry.
He wore his hair a little longer than the fashion, though he did not

entirely adopt the long ponytails of his men, and was always high spir-
ited, with a toast or some matter of friendly conversation. His men
were dismounted, because light cavalry was of no use while besieged,
and their fodder was obtained only by slipping out into the marshes
by night and cutting reeds that could be dried on the rooftops in a
poor substitute for hay. They were far from home, and their prospects
were not bright, but Pollio never seemed to flag at all.

Tiberius Nero, Caesar's Chief-of-Staff, brooded. Often his conversation lagged, and he stared moodily into his wine cup. I could hardly
blame him. If I had charge of the logistics for this great crowd, I should
brood too.

Sometimes Agrippa was there, but he hardly said anything.
Everyone ranked him; he knew better than to put himself forward.
He would try to catch my eye from time to time, and I confess that I
found it flattering to be seen by someone as something other than an
appendage of Cleopatra.

We were still guarded by Pollio's men, as they were the troops Caesar could spare, and I saw a good deal more of Aurelianus than I had
expected. He was learning Koine quickly, and he often sat his watch
with Dion, trading words back and forth in Koine and Keltic.

A FEW DAYS LATER, Aurelianus came on the watch and greeted us.
"This lady says she is to see the Queen," he said.

"Iras!" I had barely seen her before I threw myself into my sister's
arms. "Thank all the gods that you're safe!"

She bent her head against my neck, and I felt her smile.

Dion came up, and wrapped his arms around us both. "Welcome
back," he said.

"I slipped in through the marsh," she said.

"One of my men nearly shot her," Aurelianus said. "But she said that
she was here with a message for the Queen. I take it you know her."

"She's my sister," I said, my voice choking with tears. I had not let
myself realize how halved I had felt without Iras.

"Oh," Aurelianus said. "She could have said that."

"I need to see the Queen," Iras said, stepping back. "I need to tell her what's happening."

"Of course," I said.

It seemed that Arsinoe and Achillas' friendship was short-lived. Already, there were rifts between them, and it seemed that it might come to an open breach. If so, the mercenaries who had formed the bulk of the army would stay with Achillas, the professional soldier whose reputation they respected. However, the Egyptian peasants who had rallied would remain firmly with Arsinoe, championing the House of Ptolemy.

"And what do they say of me?" Cleopatra asked her as we stood in her rooms. "What do they say, Memnon and the Adoratrice and the rest?"

Iras shook her head. "They believe you are the Roman's hostage. That you are powerless to do anything, as is Pharaoh. That they must go on with what they have, since you are unable to act, and probably will be killed when you become inconvenient to Caesar."

Cleopatra nodded slowly. "That will not happen."

Iras met her eyes. They widened with understanding. "Oh no. Not again."

"He is no Gnaeus," I said swiftly. "Caesar is nothing like that."

"He is a Roman," she said. "And he holds our city hostage. That is all I need to know."

"It's more complicated." Cleopatra shook her head. "Much more complicated. Iras…"

"Must you do this? Must you?" Iras' hands were clenched. "Surely there must be some other way to deal with Rome than you prostituting yourself to every general who walks into Alexandria!"

"We have a bargain," Cleopatra said, though spots of color were showing in her cheeks. "I shall keep my end of it, and he will keep his."

"Do you really believe that any Roman will keep his word to you, a woman and an Egyptian?" Iras' eyes were snapping. "Do you not know you will be the butt of every bawdy joke from one end of the Inner Sea to the other? That men will laugh at how Caesar conquered Egypt with a big prick?"

For a moment I thought Cleopatra would slap her, as I had so long ago. But she did not. Instead her voice was ice. "You may go. I will send for you when I require you."

Iras paled. I thought in many ways a slap would have been easier. "Yes, Gracious Queen," she said, and, bowing, left us.

Cleopatra sat down in one of the chairs, her back to me. I wavered, unsure what to say.

"Do you think that as well?" she asked. Her voice was even, and I could not see her face.

"No," I said. "But then, I have seen Caesar and Iras has not. It is easy to think he is like other men, until you see him."

"Do you still believe then, that he is Alexander returned?"

I wet my lips. "Yes," I said. "And perhaps I am a fool for thinking so. But I feel it in my bones."

"I pray that may be true," she whispered, and I knew in that moment she had her own reasons for wishing so.

SHE TOLD CAESAR before she told me. She didn't need to tell me anything. I had charge of her clothes and her linens. Each day that passed without blood told me everything I needed to know. Three days late, a week. Two weeks. Three weeks.

A Horus for Egypt, a child who would be my nephew, my king, my charge, my god. Or else something that would slow us, would doom us if it all went wrong and we needed to flee.

Four weeks passed before Iras said anything to me. She dealt less with the Queen's clothes than with her papers, and she had been away so long that she didn't know to the day when it should have been. "Is she pregnant?"

I nodded. The court did not know. I had said nothing to anyone, not even Dion, and apparently Caesar had told no one either. It was early days yet, and perhaps he was superstitious that too many wishes of good fortune would be harmful. Or perhaps he was wary of the more practical harm that might come from increasing the Queen's value as a target. Either way, I approved of his silence.

"Well then." Iras took a deep breath. "Whatever you need me to do." She met my eyes. "You know I'm with you."

"I know," I said, and embraced her.

"Not that I think it's a good idea," she said. "Women are judged differently than men. The Romans will smile and joke about it, another exploit of Caesar's. They will call her harlot and whore, and hate her."

"It should not be that way," I said.

Iras took my wrists in her hands. "Charmian, it is. Whether we like it or not, whether or not it's fair, that's how it is. This isn't an exercise in rhetoric, or something you can dismiss by saying 'Who cares about Plato!'"

I laughed, as she had meant me to. After all, that was how I had dismissed Plato's certainty that Iras was not the intellectual equal of a man or a Greek, woman and Egyptian as she was. But it was not all that funny.

"Whether or not that's how it is," I said, "we must live according to what we believe, not the beliefs of others."

"The beliefs of others are not irrelevant, not when they shape the world we live in!"

"I didn't say they were irrelevant. But they will never dictate my judgment or my decisions," I snapped back. "Because others believe something does not make it true. You are not stupid because Plato says you must be, nor is Cleopatra a whore because some Roman wit will say it. I will never trust any learned opinion more than what I see in front of my face."

"Not even to the nature of the gods?" Iras asked. There was comfort in the familiarity of philosophical debate. It was less personal.

"Not even to the nature of the gods," I said. "No priest can stand between my soul and the divine."

"That's what priests do," she said.

"No," I said. "That's what some priests say they can do. But whether we stand in the Halls of Amenti before Ma'at and Serapis, or in Hades before the throne of Persephone, we stand there alone and are judged by our own hearts."

"Then you will never be part of anything," she said a little sadly. "You will never truly belong anywhere, standing apart from society as you do."

"Yes," I said. "I am a cat, and I belong to no one, even those I stay with for love."

Iras put her arm around my waist. "And does that bring you peace?"

"Yes," I said slowly, "I rather think it does."

THE SIEGE CONTINUED. Arsinoe had Achillas killed, but that broke nothing, save perhaps that the Royal Army was less well commanded than it had been. We thought that Caesar would move against them, but he did not.

"He does not have the troops," Dion said to me quietly at night, as we walked in the park among the tombs, a place it was unlikely we'd be overheard. "He's still outnumbered at least three to one, and in the city there's no way his cavalry will be any use at all, so Emrys says."

"You and Emrys seem to be doing a lot of talking," I observed.

"A lot of talking and nothing else. He's a friend, Charmian," Dion said.

"I see that," I said. I had never before seen Dion as the pursuer rather than the pursued, and he seemed to be finding it harder than he thought. Perhaps the role of erastes did not come as easily to Dion as the role of eromenos.

"He's traveled half the world in Caesar's service," Dion said. "And I've never been further than Abydos. Oh, I know the theory of things! I've seen the maps and I've studied the books, but I've never even been on the ocean, not even so far as Pelousion, as you have. I've never seen snow, or mountains, or anywhere different from Egypt. Emrys' been in Hispania and Greece. He's been in Athens, Charmian! He's crossed the Alps, and voyaged the seas four times. He took a shoulder wound after Caesar crossed the Rubicon, and was laid up two months with a fever in Massalia. He's never been to Parthia or India or among the Scythians or Britons, but says that if he did he's sure he would find men like him."

"It sounds like you're in love," I said.

"I am," he said, and his dark eyes were very serious. "Even if nothing ever comes of it. They're not supposed to, in the Roman army. The penalty can be death. Under the circumstances, Caesar would probably give him a slap on the wrist instead, but he'd never rise higher than decurion."

I was a bit bemused. "He can't read, Dion."

"Not more than his own name, no. They don't have a written language where he comes from, except for the priests. They name their months by the trees, and they follow Druids who make no temples besides groves beneath the stars. Where he comes from, there are huge boulders along the seashore that were raised by giants before men came into the world. They stand looking out to sea, half-covered with flowers in the summertime, and the sheep graze among them."

"Why in the world did he follow Caesar then?" I asked.

"Because it seemed more interesting than raising sheep." Dion laughed. "I suppose it is."

THE SIEGE DRAGGED ON.

One night, while Dion was called upon to translate for the Queen and Caesar as they spoke with some Jewish dignitaries, I walked back and forth on the terrace, looking out at Pharos. It was so near and so far, the great lighthouse that guarded our shores, a wonder of the world with its towers stacked on towers, and its magnificent lamp that was visible for miles out to sea.

I heard a step behind me and turned, but it was no more than Aurelianus. I supposed I should begin to think of him as Emrys. It is more polite to address people by name in their own language, even if you know no more of it than that.

He relaxed when he saw me, the wariness leaving his face. "It's you," he said.

I nodded. The siege was wearing on all of us. "Are you on duty?"

"Just came off the watch," he said. "Why?"

"There's something I want to show you," I said, as a thought occurred to me. "Come and see."

"See what?"

"I'll tell you when we get there." I wondered if he would follow, but he did. I did not expect him to trust me enough to follow me through the dark and winding passages of the palace, to follow me under the trees of the great park, skirting the walls and the very edge of the siege. But he did.

There, in a courtyard between a burned-out building and one of pristine white marble, we halted. In front of one of the lecture halls of the Museum, we stood silent, side-by-side.

Taller than a man, gleaming in the moonlight, the orrery turned, spheres inside spheres, tracing the paths of the wandering planets in the night sky, bronze glittering like electrum under the moon. The sun turned slowly on its unseen clockwork, and like dancers they turned and dipped in their slow and endless dance.

Emrys reached up, one hand brushing Mars as it swept past. "It's beautiful," he said. "What is it?"

"It's an orrery," I said. "It shows the paths of the stars."

"As the gods must see them," he said, and the moonlight turned his eyes to peridot, clear and light-filled.

"Yes," I said. "I knew you would understand."

"The love that moves Dion," he said. "Science. Understanding what the gods have made." He reached up, but his fingers did not quite touch the ribbon of bronze that held Jupiter suspended, turning through the night. He looked up at the stars dimmed over the great city. "Is it another sea, I wonder?"

"So they tell us," I said, standing beside him and looking up as well.

"A sea of aether, where the air gets thinner and thinner until it cannot be breathed, as it is on great mountains. But some scholars think the aether pools around the stars, and that after one reached a certain point of ascent, one would turn and then descend into another pool, through thickening air until one reached the ground."

"On another world," he said. Mars swung by again, and he stepped back.

"Yes," I said, and for a moment it was as though I looked down incalculable years to a different young man, his limbs long and wasted from pushing only against thin air, his ship an envelope of steel and silver that answered to his mind, wings of gossamer filament extending at his thought, like the wings of a bird, turning in bright reflected sunlight in the void of the high aether.

Woman of Earth, he said. *Oceans in her eyes.*

For a moment I thought Emrys had spoken, but of course he had not. He was still looking at the orrery, walking around it and tracking the pattern of Mercury.

"I thought you would like it," I said.

"How do we know they move in circles?" he asked, his fingers brushing Jupiter's path.

"Ellipses, actually," I said. "Astronomers in Egypt have observed the stars every night and kept records for thousands of years. They can calculate the paths of the planets fairly accurately now. The bodies that move around the sun, that is. The other stars are much more difficult."

Emrys nodded, his eyes still lifted to the spheres. "Druids do that too. There are places where a certain star appears on a certain night of the year, or where the sun rises on certain days."

"We have that too," I said. "Sungates in temples where the sun shines on the altar on a certain day of the year, things like that. Though of course the sun never stands directly overhead in Alexandria." Emrys looked confused, so I continued: "The angle of the sun is seven degrees, twelve minutes off the vertical at midsummer," I said. "That's how Eratosthenes measured the circumference of the Earth.

He knew that it was five thousand stadia to Syene, a town in Upper Egypt where the sun is directly overhead at midsummer, so therefore five thousand stadia must be about one-fiftieth of the circumference of the Earth, which is two hundred fifty thousand stadia."

Emrys blinked again. "And why do we need to know that?"

I grinned. "Because all of the known world is much smaller than that. From farthest Nubia to the Isles of Britain is less than a quarter of that. From the Gates of Hercules to India is about a quarter. So everything we know, all of the lands we have ever discovered, are less than a quarter of the whole world."

His eyes lit, and I saw that he had it. "So what's in the rest?"

"We don't know," I said. "But we know it's there. Out there beyond the Gates of Hercules across the wide ocean, or over the Hindu Kush mountains, there are other worlds to find."

Emrys lifted his face to the stars. "And there are men there like us."

"Probably," I said. "Eratosthenes writes that a ship was lost outside the Gates of Hercules, on the coast of Far Hispania, and driven across the ocean to come back with strange tales of another world. And merchants in Marakanda and Alexandria Eschate tell that there are trading routes north of the Hindu Kush to kingdoms twice as far away as India."

Emrys looked at me keenly. "And why do you want to know these things? You are no ship's captain or explorer. What use is it to you?"

I shrugged. "I like to know things. Like Dion."

Emrys glanced away, studiously watching the orrery. "You and Dion are very close, aren't you?"

"Dion is a brother to me, a kinsman," I said, so that there could be no mistake. I knew Dion was in pursuit, and the last thing I wanted to do was to imply to Dion's quarry that I was his wife or betrothed or some such.

"Then you know him well," Emrys said. "I wonder..." His voice trailed off, as though he searched for the words he wanted in unfamiliar speech.

"I do know him well," I said. "What is it that you wonder?"

"I wonder...," he began, then started over with a deep breath. "General Pollio, he is very good. He is young and he has been in Gaul with Caesar since he was seventeen. He is a good general and we all like him."

Emrys looked at me and I waited expectantly for him to go on, not sure what Ansinius Pollio had to do with anything.

"He said when we left Gaul many things that are helpful. And he said that when Romans say one particular thing, it is not the thing we think it is. That what we do among ourselves, he does not care, but we should know that when a Roman asks us if we like to do it, it is grave insult. That Romans would not do such to another man unless he were a dog or a slave, someone without honor. And that we should not go with Romans, even if they ask, because they offer insult. I am wondering what Dion...sometimes I think he is asking something, but then I think I do not know, that I am misunderstanding. And I do not know which he would mean."

I took a deep breath, trying to keep my face absolutely serious. If I had not misunderstood, Dion was spending a lot of time courting when a simple question would have done as well!

"Dion is not Roman," I said carefully. "Dion is Alexandrian. We are not Roman, and we do not think of such things between men the way the Romans do. I am certain he offers you no insult, but rather that he is interested in you and is not certain if you would be insulted by that fact. He knows as little of Gaul, you see, as you do of Alexandria."

Emrys' face cleared, and I thought he was indeed very handsome, pretty enough for Dion's somewhat exacting tastes. "It is not insulting here? Men with men? I'm sorry, I do not know a polite word."

"Not insulting in the least," I assured him. "Most men try it when they are young, though not so many are like Dion, and do not like women at all. Once a boy has become a youth, and is entered in the gymnasium, around sixteen or seventeen, he can be courted by one older than he, what we call an erastes."

"That is what?"

"A man a few years older, twenty-five or so, who becomes his lover and instructs him in how to live as a man, in arms and in civilized arts. How to have a conversation, how to behave at a symposium, all the things a young man needs. He introduces him into society. It's not just if he's rich. It's anybody—students, skilled craftsmen, soldiers. In fact, it's looked down on to have an erastes far above your own social class. It looks crass."

Emrys blinked, and I realized I'd used a word he didn't know. "It looks like you can be bought for money," I clarified. "The eromenos, that's the younger man, is supposed to be choosing a lover out of love, not for the boost to his career. Of course some do, but people talk." I looked at him curiously. "What do they do in Gaul?"

Emrys shrugged and looked away, at Mercury circling nearby. "Usually it is friends of the same age. Lots of boys try it. It doesn't mean anything, good or bad. It's just one of those things. Sometimes they promise blood brotherhood, and stand together in war forever, but blood brotherhood has a lot of obligations. It can't be taken back, and it makes you kin, as though you were born brothers. Sometimes boys promise when they are fifteen and then regret it." He smiled at me, expecting me to understand. "It looks bad to have someone too much older or younger. Like you say, people talk. It's usually friends of the same age. Is that what Dion is asking?"

"I think so," I said. "You and Dion are about the same age, which is unusual here, as Dion is old enough to find an eromenos of his own. He's getting a bit old to play the youth. And I know he thinks you are very handsome and very interesting."

A slow blush rose in Emrys' cheeks. I thought he was handsome and interesting too, but clearly Dion had beaten me to the finish. "That is good to know," he said very seriously. "I should not want to offend Dion."

"I'm glad," I said.

THE ROMANS CELEBRATED their Lupercalia and began their new year. In Upper Egypt, the grain harvest was coming in, but we should see none of it. And Caesar should see no profit in it. Here was the money to pay his men, in the wealth of Egypt passing down the Nile to Alexandria and hence into the rest of the world, our grain, gold of the Pharaohs.

And still we waited.

To our surprise, envoys came from the Egyptian army for Caesar. I stood behind the screen while he spoke with them, a gesture of good faith from Caesar to Cleopatra, who of course could not be present. I did not recognize their voices or their faces, which in itself told me something. They were not of Memnon or the Adoratrice's party.

Egypt, they said, needed Pharaoh. If Caesar would release Ptolemy Theodorus to them, Pharaoh would call to order his sister Queen Arsinoe and her tutor Ganymede, and would restore peace to the land. Surely Pharaoh would honor agreements with Caesar made in good faith, the siege could end, and most important, the grain harvest could get to market. This would be in the best interests of Egypt, and of course in the best interests of Caesar as well.

I told Cleopatra what I had heard while she paced her chambers. She was four months gone now, and when she was nude one could see it, though the drapery of her clothes would conceal her pregnancy a little longer. Her doctor had been brought in on the secret, and pronounced her in the best of health, saying that in a few weeks he should be able to hear the baby's heartbeat through a tube placed against her belly, and that any day now she would begin to feel the baby move.

"He will tell them no," Cleopatra said. "It's a ploy and a fairly transparent one."

Pharaoh Ptolemy and Queen Arsinoe. It was a situation that would satisfy everyone. Except Cleopatra, who had played a card that made her invaluable. Caesar had no living child or grandchild.

"He will tell them no," she said. "I know he will."

INSTEAD, he told Theo that he would be delighted to release him to his own people, and that he would send him off with many gifts, that

Pharaoh might return to his city shortly as a friend and ally of Caesar and Rome.

I thought that General Pollio should have to be treated for apoplexy, and that Emrys would break a blood vessel. Even the Germans looked at each other with frowns, as if wondering if Caesar had at last lost his mind.

The Queen said nothing, at least not in my presence. If Caesar had betrayed her, she said nothing to anyone but him. Tight-lipped and pale, she kept up her daily routines of meetings and work as though everything were as it had been. For a few days the palace was very quiet.

Then the word came that Pharaoh had taken charge of the Royal Army, and called upon all Egyptians to drive Caesar into the sea. Oddly enough, they seemed to be doing this by lightening the guard on the Palace Quarter. While the siege wasn't lifted, their sorties were fewer and lighter, and in each place where they were tested their defenses were thinner.

Dion shook his head, and said he could make nothing of it.

"I can," Emrys said, dropping his voice as he sat with us, eating bread and fish beside one of the columns of the portico. "They're pulling troops out. That means they have to face something else somewhere else."

One of the legionaries hurried up. "Master Dion? Caesar and the Queen require you immediately."

"I'm coming," he said, dusting the bread crumbs off his robe. He cast Emrys a glance. Emrys did not follow him into Caesar and the Queen's presence without being asked, but I did.

They were in one of the little dining rooms, and the man who stood before them was dripping wet, having swum ashore under cover of night from a fishing boat that had passed out to sea, daring the defenses on Pharos Island as too small and insignificant.

"Imperator, Gracious Majesty," he said to both in Hebrew, inclining his head. "I am Benjamin bar Micah, of the city of Ashkelon. I am sent to you by His Reverence Hyrcanius bar Alexander, Ethnarch of Jerusalem. At his request, and yours, we have assembled three thousand Jewish cavalry at Ashkelon, there to meet with the nearly six thousand infantry of the Twenty-seventh Legion that you sent marching from Greece. Mithridates has joined us with nearly a thousand Nabatean horsemen, and two thousand infantrymen." He paused for a breath, while the Queen waited, impassive, until he continued.

"Together, under Mithridates and our commander Prince Antipater, we have crossed Gaza and taken the fortresses that guarded it. We have laid siege to Pelousion, where Antipater personally led the assault. I am pleased to report that the garrison of Pelousion has fallen, and our armies have advanced into the Delta as far as Memphis. At Memphis, the gates were thrown open in the name of Queen Cleopatra, and Antipater and Mithridates are the guests of Memnon, the Hierophant of Serapis."

I bit my lip until I thought it would bleed, not to cry out in tears of thanksgiving.

"Prince Antipater and his son, Prince Herod, send you their most cordial greetings, and ask if you will sally forth immediately, that we may catch King Ptolemy's army between us on the Saite branch of the Nile."

Caesar smiled, and I thought it was the most terrifying thing I had ever seen. "Good work," he said. "And a brave man to carry the news! Bring wine for this soldier now!" He stood and poured a cup for the man himself, and laid his own cloak about the man's dripping shoulders.

Then he turned. "Pollio," he said, "get every man you've got still horsed mounted up. I need archers to the top of the Gate of the Moon now. Tell Arcavius to light the Greek fire for the ballistae. Send a tortoise from the Sixth straight through the gate, and if the resistance is light enough, I want you to charge through the resistance and get the city gates. Alexandria will be ours tomorrow."

He bent over Cleopatra's couch as men clattered about, running for orders and subordinates. I heard because I stood behind her.

"I told you to trust me," he said.

"I didn't," she said. "But I will in the future."

"The dice are thrown," he said. "Now we will see if it is the Venus throw."

THE VENUS THROW

I had not realized before just how quickly they could move. They were gone before the hour was half done, in a clatter of steel and stamp of feet. Two hours before sunrise the palace was quiet. The fighting would be at the Gate of the Moon, not here.

The Queen paced back and forth, her arms crossed over her chest. At last she turned with a cry I had not heard from her before. "I can't stand it! Charmian, go to the gate and see what has happened."

I ran.

The tortoise had done its work, veterans of the Sixth Legion, their shields locked together, around them and over their heads like a great turtle bristling with spears, advancing through the besiegers, the entire scene lit by the sudden eerie bursts of light from the Greek fire, as at long last the pair of ballistae cut loose.

And then with horrible high shrieking calls, the gates burst open behind the tortoise and out swept the Gaulish cavalry, five hundred of them on their little horses, with Pollio in the front, long hair and cloaks flying behind them. With the thunder of two thousand hooves they resolved themselves into a flying wedge, a lance tip with a single point. I had read my long-ago ancestor Ptolemy describe it, but I had never thought to see it. I stood on the gate with my heart in my throat and it was beautiful.

Straight past the tortoise they went, splitting in two to pass around and reforming on the other side, the wedge unbroken, and overhead the ballistae gave one last volley to clear their way. Eldritch fire flashed over them. Emrys was in that charge, and I yearned with all my winged soul to join them.

For one moment it looked as if the defenders would hold, but then they broke, running for the safety of side streets and the courtyards of buildings. The cavalry went straight through, all the way to the Canopic Way, peeling off by turmae, some left and some right, to secure the main city gates of Alexandria.

Out of my sight. I could see no more because of intervening buildings. So I went back to the Queen, tears on my face.

The sun rose on a city that was ours.

AND THEN WE WAITED. Caesar was gone. All of them were gone, save some men of the Twenty-eighth Legion that Caesar had left to hold Alexandria. We waited.

Which suggests we had nothing to do. Rather, it was the opposite. Alexandria had been without its Queen these many months, and now at last Cleopatra could return to the job of ruling. There were the dry-docks to be rebuilt, the streets around the Palace Quarter mended from the damage of the siege, the streets near the harbor cleared of rubble and rebuilt. The people who had lost their homes must be tended, and while many now lived with kin, the Queen offered compensation for those who had lost their homes in the fire, the money to come from that which the Queen owed Caesar.

At last the barges moved again, and by day and night they made their way down the canal from Lake Mareotis to the sea, grain by the measure and the barge load. The harvest in Upper Egypt had been good this year.

We ate new cucumbers pickled in rough vinegar from the south, because Cleopatra craved it, and those cucumbers were like the breath of life, tart and fresh, the gift of the Nile from Philae and Elephantine and Thebes. Mornings dawned cool and clear, and Pharos glimmered against the dawn before the great lamp was doused for the day.

We went among the people. We went to the great Temple of Serapis and Isis. The markets opened, and a Tyrian ship loaded with cloth came into the kind of exotic profits that a merchant might dream of once in a lifetime. Whether or not they had loved us before, they did so now. The beautiful young Queen walked in procession beneath an ivory shade, her saffron gown pleated like Isis on a temple wall, her swollen belly an ornament of her beauty, the land giving forth fruit. The braids of her wig swung back, and could not hide her smile.

What is there not to love, among people such as us, when youth and beauty and charm combine to make her all at once everyone's daughter, everyone's granddaughter and wife, everyone's honeyed dream of remotest childhood? Crowds screamed her name as though they had never loved anyone else.

"Isis! Isis!" And at last it was not her name they called at all, but Isis. She was a goddess on earth.

I would have thought there was no art in it, were I not the one responsible for the saffron gown, for the wig with its malachite and gold beads, for the cloak she wore of cloth of gold, pleated and with sticks in the seams so that it moved like the wings of Isis when she knelt, not crumpling, but folding like a bird. I would have thought there was no art in it, except that I had seen Auletes school her. I would have thought there was no art in it, except that the flutists who suddenly burst into joyful music had been hired by Iras.

And yet it actually was magic. When I saw her turn, pushing past the careful cordon of guards, to lay her hand in blessing and healing on the brow of a pretty girl child who lay in her mother's arms, her eyes smiling into the mother's with sudden understanding — then, oh then it was really magic.

İT WAS A MONTH before the news came, and by then we had expected it. Caesar had met Theo and the Royal Army on the banks of the Nile. Caesar and his men had routed the king completely, and in their retreat the galley carrying Ptolemy Theodorus had capsized. Pharaoh had drowned.

Caesar and his column approached the city by the main Canopic

Gate, which was thrown wide before him, flowers raining down upon the bemused heads of the German bodyguards. Cleopatra met him on the steps of the Soma, six months filled and smiling. He went down before her on one knee, his head bent before Queen and goddess.

For a moment I thought the Romans would protest, but the Germans followed Caesar, dropping to their knees behind him, and in the next breath Pollio knelt, his scarlet cloak swirling around him, one hand tugging at Tiberius Nero. The Gauls went down like a wave of grain, and for a moment I could at last pick out Emrys, standing beside his horse with his hand on the bridle, and then he knelt, one of the first, with the quick glitter of tears on his face.

And then the Romans knelt, though they cried "Ave Caesar!" not "Ave Isis!"

Toward the back some one of them shouted loudly enough to be heard over the general din: "Ave Caesarion! Hail, Little Caesar!"

Caesar turned sharply, as though to see who said it, but then the whole crowd of Romans took it up. "Hail, Little Caesar!"

"Sweet Isis," I whispered, "please do not let the baby be a girl." But I knew it was not even as I prayed it.

Cleopatra bent over Caesar and said something too low for me to hear, taking him by the hand and raising him so that he stood beside her, one step lower on the steps of the Soma. She raised their joined hands in the air. I doubt anyone other than he could have heard what she shouted above the noise of the crowd, but the gesture was enough. Straight off a temple wall, Isis crowned the victor with Her love.

Two hours later, flushed and hot, trying to make sure there was cool watered wine for everyone in the largest hall of the palace, I found myself beside Dion.

He put his head to the side. "The art of magic," he said.

"Yes," I said.

"It was so in Abydos," he said. "It was art, rehearsed and planned. And yet…"

I looked to see why he trailed off. Emrys was coming through the crowd toward him, excusing himself to people who stood in the way.

"I'm back," he said, and his eyes lingered on Dion's face.

"I see that," Dion said. He had forgotten all else with his forgotten thought.

"I hope you've been well," Emrys said.

"Yes. Fine. And you?"

But that was not what their eyes said.

I went to check on the platters of olives and almonds that were going around, with neither actually noticing me. How good it would be, I thought, for someone to come home to me. For someone to have missed me. To be greeted by someone who had yearned for me, who would murmur my name with his hot breath, say that he had dreamed of me on some awful field somewhere. I was meant for such.

Instead, the party went late, though Cleopatra and Caesar did not wait it out, but went to her rooms with the Germans at the door and Iras to sleep in the antechamber. The dawn star was rising when the last guests were chivvied out the doors, drunk and sleepy. I went back and forth, entrusting a valuable krater to a trustworthy man to wash, getting the slaves about sweeping up the crumbs and scrubbing the tiles, taking the linens to wash later in the day, scouring the corners for stray cups.

The rooms were baking hot from the press of bodies, and I threw open the terrace doors to let the night breeze in. I walked outside, breathing in the cool air.

The stars were beginning to pale on the far horizon.

"What is that star?" he asked, and I turned to see Agrippa standing beside one of the tall painted pillars.

"We call it the Daystar," I said. "But it's not really a star. It's a planet."

"Venus," he said. The dawn breeze stirred his fair hair. "I suppose Aphrodite to you."

"Yes," I said, and stepped closer. His face had the kind of pure, austere beauty that the Greeks loved to carve in ancient days, not pretty but strong. He was young still, and not quite entirely grown into his bones. In a few years he would be a handsome man, with the rugged looks that would last until he was older than Caesar.

"I dreamed about you," he blurted out, and the color rose in his face. "I dreamed that you told me you had loved me since the beginning of the world."

It wasn't polished, but I did not smile. "Perhaps I did," I said. "Who can remember the beginning of the world?"

"A poet," he said. "There's a poet I met in Neapolis when I was there with my mother who said that he could remember the first men in the world, in Arcadia. He said that he had met me beside the River of Memory, and knew that I had been a wanderer and an exile and a king. He wasn't any older than you, and he said that he remembered me."

"I think perhaps he was coming on to you," I said gently.

"Not Publius Vergilius Marc," Agrippa said. "It wasn't like that. He was very serious."

"I see," I said, and smiled.

"Are you laughing at me?" He put his head to the side, and I thought he might blush.

"Never," I said. "There is nothing in you to laugh at. Even Achilles was young once."

"More Patroclus than Achilles," he said. "I've never wanted to be Achilles."

"Or Alexander," I said.

"I don't want to be a king," he said. "I mean, it's not easy, is it?"

"No," I said. "It's not easy at all."

Agrippa took a breath. "Better to be a loyal man, and to be true as best one can. As you do."

"I try to," I said. No one had ever said as much to me, named me for what I was, that way.

"I mean, you're a Companion, aren't you?"

"Yes," I said, and knew exactly what he meant, as though he had seen my heart and put a name to what was there, surely as though he had known me most of my life.

Agrippa leaned back against the column, the wind lifting the hair from his forehead like a mother's touch. "So am I," he said. "I live to serve."

I believed him. And whatever dreams he might conjure, right now he was no dream of starlight, but a flesh-and-blood young man.

"Do you think there can be happiness in that?" he asked. "Do you think if one is true, one will be happy?"

"I don't know," I said. "Maybe." I took a step closer, my himation almost brushing his arm. He was taller than I, and he still had a lot of growing to do. "If you steal your fire where you find it."

"Oh," he said, and bent his head to me, too shy to quite kiss me.

I leaned up into his mouth, warm and soft with the faint stale taste of wine on his tongue, a slow, sensual kiss, showing him all it could be.

Our lips parted, and his brow furrowed as he gazed into my face. "What did that mean?" he asked.

"Come with me," I said.

I DREW HIM DOWN beside me in my room, and he kissed me with raw passion I had not expected. There was no art in this, only desire and need, fire leaping to kindle fire. His touch was rough and reverent all at once.

"I've never done this before," he whispered.

"I know," I said, straddling him, my skirts lifted. "Don't think so much," I said, my belly pressed against him, feeling his hard body against mine. "Just remember." I took the pins out of my hair, watching his face while I did so, watching his lips part as the cascade of my hair fell around my shoulders. I unpinned the clasps at my shoulders, baring breasts pale as shells in the moonlight, my nipples dark with my arousal.

"Oh," he breathed, and I slid my wetness against him.

"Remember," I said, and drew my nails across his chest lightly.

His body knew if he did not, knew what he needed, and he cried out when he spent, his arms tight around me and the need was almost unbearable. I showed him what I wanted, working myself against him to find release in the waves of sensation that washed over me.

Afterward, he lay against my shoulder, his face against my arm, and I felt the tears on his face.

"What's the matter?" I asked, stroking his hair with one hand. That was better than it had been with Lucan, so much better.

"I am broken," he said, "and I'll never be whole again."

"Aren't maidens the ones who are supposed to say that?" I teased.

"Do you think women are the only ones who feel?"

"Not hardly," I said, and gathered him close. "Come here, dear." I stroked his back gently. "Was it so bad, then?"

"It wasn't bad at all," he said. "But now I will want it always, and never be whole without it."

"You are a very handsome young man," I said. "I can't see that you'll ever lack lovers if you want them."

The first rays of the sun picked out each golden hair on his chest with a distinct shadow, and he closed his eyes. "I love you forever," he said, and fell asleep against my breast.

WE SAILED for Memphis in glorious weather on the largest of the royal ships. Egypt, Cleopatra said, was more than Alexandria and they must know that she knew it.

Caesar came with us. The skies were blue overhead as we sailed south. At each town along the banks groups of dignitaries came out to meet us, strewing flowers on the riverbanks and making speeches, choirs of children singing as though this were one of the annual processions of a god.

At each stop Cleopatra had a great deal to do, talking with all of the village elders in their own tongues to their vast surprise, since they had never met a ruler before who spoke Egyptian as well as Koine. Bubastis, I thought, and remembered our long apprenticeship there, at the feet of the Lady of Cats who had taught us what the Black Land was. At each stop there were offerings and meals, and then we were off again, the Nile winding behind us in a ribbon of light, shrunken with the dry season.

I stood behind Cleopatra on the high deck, arranging the awning over her so that it would not get too hot, rose pink and white stripes making patterns on the deck. She lounged on a couch, gravid and sleepy now, while Caesar sat next to her, for once quiet and unmoving.

She gave him half a smile out of the side of her mouth. "You see? Is this not better than going to Siwah?"

"I don't need to go to Siwah," he said, and closed his eyes against the sun. The reflection off the water played over his face, casting him for a moment in strange light, as though he rested underwater, already remote and beneath glass.

I took a sudden sharp breath.

Cleopatra twisted about to look at me. "Something wrong, Charmian?"

"My foot has gone to sleep," I lied.

Osiris must pass into the west. It is the story.

Cleopatra smiled at me. "Then go and sit down for a while," she said. "You don't have to fuss over me. I'm fine."

I went and sat with Agrippa in the bow, where he dangled his legs over the side. He put his arm around me, and I leaned into him. "Hello, darling," I said.

Marcus Agrippa looked back toward the stern, his expression as unreadable as Caesar's. "Have you been to the Soma?" he asked.

"Of course," I said. "Many times. Did you go, when we were in Alexandria?"

"No." Marcus looked out over the water. The reflection of our ship wavered, the waves of our passage disturbing the water too much for it to reflect like a mirror, even in the bright sunlight of midday. "Is it very bad?"

"It's beautiful," I said. "The most beautiful tomb Ptolemy could build, marble and gold, with painted walls so real you would swear they were windows into other lands."

He shook his head. "I can't imagine it. But I'm glad I didn't go."

"Why?" I asked.

"I don't want to think of Alexander as dead." Marcus leaned his head back. "If I saw him lying there, he would be dead to me."

"It's not like that," I said. "There's nothing gruesome about it. You can't really see anything."

"You are Egyptian," he said.

"Yes."

"That's easy to forget," he said. "You don't look Egyptian. But there's something macabre about it, isn't there? Worshipping the dead and preserving their bodies forever, looking at their embalmed faces. All of those tombs in the Palace Quarter where you can just go in as though it were a dead man's bedroom."

"We don't worship the dead," I said irritably. "And it's not as though we unwrap their bodies and look at them all of the time. The dead stay buried in a seemly manner. But they are the people who brought us where we are. There's nothing frightening or cursed about them. When I walk among the tombs of my ancestors, and among the people who built the city, why should I be afraid of them? Why would their spirits do me any harm, loving the thing they built?"

"When you put it that way I suppose I can see it," he said. "Like the Lares and Manes."

"The Lares and Manes?"

Marcus nodded. "Household gods, I suppose you would say. The gods of a family. Our ancestors, kind of. We don't embalm our ancestors; they're cremated. But we keep a wax mask of their faces, and there's a shrine where they go. I mean, the masks are for the Manes. The Lares are sort of more general household gods." He looked vaguely confused, and it seemed strange to me that one could be confused about one's own religion.

"Don't you worship the Olympians?" I asked.

"Well, yes." Marcus drew me closer with one arm. "But it's not as though They take a particular interest in me. I'm not like some who don't even think They exist. But it's not as though Capitoline Jupiter is going to notice what I'm doing or care."

"Why not?"

"They're the gods of the Roman state. They may pay attention to Caesar, but They don't bother with everybody, with people who are nothing special. If you take an offering to Venus or Mars or something you may be able to get Their attention about something specific, but other than making sure all of the rites are done correctly, They just aren't that interested in people. Unless people are either Their sons or have offended Them in some way, the stories of the gods don't usually have people in them at all. Except sometimes Jupiter notices beautiful women." He blushed, and I wondered what all of those stories might be, though I could lay a fairly good guess, if it resulted in sons.

"You mean your gods don't love you?" It was hard to imagine. Of course some gods took a greater interest in some people than in others, but...

"Why would the Olympians love me?" Marcus looked blank.

"They don't even know who you are?"

He shrugged. "Well, maybe. I do all of the rites as I'm supposed to and I made the offering when I came of age. But why would They love me?"

"Isis loves you," I said.

"Why would Isis love me?" he asked, perplexed. "I'm not even Egyptian."

"She's the Mother of the World. She loves you and She loves me and She loves the humblest bricklayer in Elephantine and the richest man in Rome. She loves everybody."

"But they aren't Her people," Marcus said.

"That doesn't make any difference," I said. "We're all Her people. A mother may have a lot of children, and they're all different from each other, but she loves them all alike and they're all hers. Her compassion is for everybody."

"Why would you want a god to be compassionate?"

He looked so honestly bewildered that I leaned against his shoulder and ruffled his hair. "Because we aren't all best and greatest. Because there are a lot of people who are sad or who've had terrible things happen. Who do you think slaves worship and what do you think they pray for?"

"I've never thought about it," he said. "Their own gods, I suppose. But their Gods can't be very powerful or they wouldn't have become slaves."

"And if you were sick?" I asked. "Or if your mother were sick?"

"I'd make an offering to Asclepius and ask for His favor," Marcus said. "But I don't expect it would work."

For a long moment he turned away from me, looking out over the river, at our spreading wake. When he spoke again his voice was different, as though he was thinking of something for the first time. "I don't think I've ever needed compassion."

"Then you have been very lucky," I said.

"Perhaps I have," he said, and his eyes were troubled.

IN THREE WEEKS we were back in Alexandria. Cleopatra wanted to sail as far south as Philae, or at least Thebes, but Caesar reminded her that he still had a civil war to conduct. Egypt might be won for him and stand at his side as an ally, but in Rome the Senate still named him rebel and organized armies. Not that he would leave Cleopatra undefended. He would leave three of his four legions with her, the Twenty-eighth that we had come to know and two others, their size cut in half by casualties, that had come with Mithridates. Caesar, his Germans, his Gauls, the veterans of the Sixth Legion, and the Fighting Jews would march eastward through Gaza and back through Jerusalem for Syria.

The Queen was eight months gone with child. It would have made more sense for him to stay, I thought. But the weather was against it. Soon the heat of summer would make the march more difficult. That was the official reason, of course. I remembered that his first wife had died in childbed, and also his beloved daughter. If something happened, Caesar would hear it far away, in a tent somewhere on campaign, when all this was as though it had happened to another man.

Marcus Agrippa, of course, would go with him. So would Emrys.

And so I stood with Dion atop the Gate of the Moon and watched them go, my gray cat Sheba perched on my shoulder. The Queen did not come. There would be no public good-byes. Whatever they had to say to one another, they had said in private, and if the Germans had heard they were conveniently deaf to Koine.

"Good-bye," I whispered, and the sun glinted off Agrippa's shining helmet, his white plume.

Dion put his arm about my waist. At least, I thought, I could publicly carry on. Dion could not without getting Emrys into a lot of trouble.

"Stupid Romans," I said.

Dion laughed, and Sheba's long tail whacked him in the face as she turned about. "We'll manage, won't we, my friend?"

"We will," I said. And of course we did.

İt was the Queen who noticed first, naturally. Being attuned to it herself, she stopped me in the bath as I held the towel for her, her body huge now with the child due any day. "Charmian." She put her hand on my arm. "You too?"

I nodded. It was only a few weeks. It might be a mistake. It might just be the weather or something I had eaten. Though I knew it was not.

She put her hand to the side of my face, smiling. "They will be the same age, then. Perhaps your son will stand beside mine as you have always stood beside me. Anyway, who? Agrippa?"

"Yes," I said.

"Do you want me to write to Caesar and ask him to send Agrippa back here? There are plenty of positions with the legions here for a tribune."

I lifted my chin. I did at least have enough pride not to have my sister send for him. "He will not thank me for taking him from Caesar or from his chances of promotion to sit in a garrison in Alexandria. And it would hardly be fair for me to have what you and Dion cannot."

"Oh, Dion," she said, laughing again. "I had never thought to see him really in love. And who would have imagined a wild Kelt?"

"Who indeed?" I said. "Yet they seem to do well enough." And turned the conversation neatly from her feelings and from mine, I thought. I stood as close to her as anyone, and yet I would never know what she felt for Caesar, or didn't. My heart was always plain to the world.

"It is a good thing," I said, "that you are the Queen."

She put her arms around me, the hard mound of the baby tight between us. "You always have a place here with me," she said. "You and any child of yours. You are mine."

"Yes," I said.

HER CHILD WAS BORN on the second day after midsummer, a week before the helical rising of Sothis should signal the beginning of the season of the Inundation. The child was born at high noon, after a night of labor, when the sun stood straight in the sky overhead. I stood at her head, a damp towel in my hands, and when the doctor drew it forth I saw as soon as anyone else.

"Oh Gracious Isis!" I said, as the first sputtering wail shattered the air, and saw my sister turn her face to me, sweat rolling down her cheeks, even before the doctor spoke.

"Gracious Queen," he said, "you have a perfect son."

He lifted the child into the light from the window to see to tie and cut the cord, an ordinary enough baby with thin dark hair and the beginnings of the Ptolemy nose, kicking feet, and eyes shut to scream.

"Ptolemy Philometor Caesar," she said. Cleopatra pushed up on her elbows, trying to see him better. "Horus, for Egypt."

"Caesarion," I said.

ISIS ENTHRONED

I had not expected to fall in love. Perhaps it was because I was pregnant myself, or perhaps it was simply that I had never been around a young child before, since I was one, but I fell madly in love. I had thought of him before as an important playing piece, a necessity to the succession, or even a hindrance that would prove our downfall if Caesar failed.

Now he was a person. He was a warm and squirming baby that snuggled against my ear, twisting his tiny fingers in my hair and burrowing against my neck. His eyes, when he opened them, were a sea blue that would darken in time, and his thin hair was soft and fragrant, exactly the color of his mother's. There was something in the set of his eyes that reminded me of Auletes, but the high handsome cheekbones beneath the baby flesh were pure Caesar. When he clung to his wet nurse's breast I felt something stir within me, some primal craving soon to be satisfied.

My child would be born in the winter, Caesarion's cousin. Holding him in my arms, I could imagine that other child there, and when it first moved within me it was in response to Caesarion's mewing and trying to nurse from breasts that were not yet ready.

I cupped my hand around his soft head. "Not yet, little one," I said. "I haven't anything for you yet. But you can share when your cousin comes, if you want." Since he was hungry, I handed him back to his wet nurse, and wondered if I had really felt it, a stirring beneath my breasts as though the child bumped against the wall above.

"When they are old enough," Cleopatra said, "your son will join mine in the schoolroom the way you joined me. Apollodorus will find a tutor for them, and they will learn to write together, just as we did."

My eyes pricked with tears. That was how it was supposed to be. They would sit at the table together in a white city by the sea, reading Ptolemy on the original scroll, two little boys who were his long-removed descendants, learning to love the city he had built. Caesarion would learn to rule fairly and well, and there would be an end to the fighting among heirs the House of Ptolemy had known. He would be loved, and hence moral. And when his mother at last passed the Gates of Amenti, he would rule as Horus, Ptolemy Caesarion, Pharaoh of Egypt. We would have peace, and the Black Land would endure. We would have peace, and the city would spread her wings wide to the world. These would be the days to come.

Of course, for Cleopatra, there was much more than the nursery. I might spend a great deal of time watching over this small life, but she had all of the lives of Egypt to attend to. She bound her breasts against her milk, and suffered through it while Caesarion took to his wet nurse. She could not nurse every few hours for months at a time, not when Egypt was finally hers to rule.

And there was so much to do. The Inundation was scarcely over before she must make the trip upriver to Thebes and attend to the business of the kingdom there. Caesarion, hardly three months old, stayed in Alexandria with me while Iras accompanied the Queen. There was no question of taking him, not in the season after the Inundation when fevers multiplied and took the young and old. He must stay in Alexandria, in the fresh sea air, far from the swamps and quagmires of the Delta.

By the time the Queen returned to Alexandria, I was a month from my delivery and the stars of winter were rising.

Of course she had written to Caesar, and he had replied. Whatever he had said was for her eyes only, and the scroll had not been turned over to the Royal Archive. Subsequent letters were more public. Caesar congratulated the Queen. If he stopped short of calling Caesarion his son, he stopped little short, and he inquired constantly about the boy's health, eating habits, and temperament. "Yes," we replied, "Prince Caesarion enjoys perfect health, except for being fussy about teething as all babies are. He eats with great enjoyment, and has begun to take small meals of porridge mixed with milk, as well as the flesh of peaches well mashed to a pulp. He is in all ways a sunny child, sleeping well and laughing when tickled, responding to hiding behind the corner of a himation and popping out with hysterical giggles. He chews cloth, and burrows into the breasts of any woman who holds him, the bigger their breasts the better."

I thought the latter would make Caesar smile.

Truly, there was little enough to. After he had left Egypt he had marched straight to Syria where he defeated King Pharnaces of Pontus, who had crossed into lands the Romans claimed now that he need not fear Pompeius. Now he might fear Caesar instead. However, while all this occurred, Gnaeus Pompeius and his brother Sextus had raised an army backed by many prominent men in Rome. Caesar had crossed again to Africa, near what had once been Carthage, and tried to come to grips.

It was from there that the first letter came for Dion, which he shared with me as with a sister.

Hail my friend,

I am learning to write. We are in Africa. Many thanks to your Queen whose generosity has sent ships with grain for us. We like the grain, but better still the fruits and other good things. I have your letter. You say it is the fourth, but the first I have. The horses like it better here.

The battle at Zela was not easy. I have hurt in my leg, but it is healing and I do not think I will limp when it is done. Now we have these sons of Pompeius to defeat, though I do not think much of them, having seen how Gnaeus ran at Pharsala when we charged him.

You ask me how I am, and what I am thinking. I am thinking that now it is cold at home, and that the sun grows small in *the southern sky, the nights long and endless long. Yet I am here, where there is no difference and the sun is as hot as ever. The trees are green where there is water, and the dates are fat. Are the waters that wash these shores the same as the ones that come to the cliffs where I grew? Are the winds the same that blow over you, where you are in Alexandria? The world is very big. And also very small when it can be reached across by the heart.*

We will beat the sons of Pompeius. Then I do not know where we will go. Back to Rome, I expect. Caesar must. And some men are tired and their discharges overdue. I wish we might come back to Alexandria. But one thing I have learned is that the Black Land is not going anywhere.

Farewell,
Emrys Aurelianus, Decurio

I had no letters from Marcus. At first I worried that he did not write, but after he was mentioned four or five times in the official dispatches, I knew that he was well. I would not allow myself to be angry. After all, I had not really expected that he should remember me. What is a slave woman, the lover of a little less than three months, that one should remember? An episode in the life of a young Roman gentleman, a pretty face to figure in some future story when he was old and gray. "Once I knew this girl in Alexandria…"

Still, I needed nothing from him. I lacked for nothing. I had my sisters, the Queen's own doctor, and I had my small nephew. I should not want for money or food or care because Marcus forgot me. It was best that I should forget him too.

I stopped writing to him after five letters. There was no point, if he would not reply. It only made me pathetic, a woman who continued to pursue a man who has long since moved on. There was no need to tell him about the baby or how it grew. Why should I share any of that with him, pour my heart out in letters that he would toss aside? Better instead to give my time and attention to those who loved me, to Caesarion and Dion, to my sisters and my friends. Marcus Agrippa should be no more to me than I to him, a story of a handsome young soldier I had once desired.

MY DAUGHTER WAS BORN at dawn, seven days after the winter solstice, at the end of two days of difficult labor. Iras held my hand as she had held the Queen's, and I looked into her eyes in those last long moments, seeing her will holding me up, inflexible and sure as the pillars of the universe.

"A perfect daughter," the doctor said with satisfaction, and turning her about laid her in my arms. The slither of the cord pulsed a few times more, and then he cut it and she lay against me crying, her small fists pounding.

Pounding fists were good, I thought. She will never stop fighting. And I closed my eyes and slept exhausted against her hair.

THE NEXT WEEKS PASSED in a haze of nursing and sleeping a few hours at a time, but as she grew and slept more I could find myself again. Demetria looked less like me than Caesarion, I thought. Her hair was darker than mine, more like Agrippa's, and instead of the Ptolemy nose she had the look of him in the square forehead, the wide-set eyes. Only they were not brown like his but sea blue, like mine and my mother's. She would not, I thought, be a great beauty, but her features were regular and pleasing. Perhaps she would not need to be a great beauty.

In the spring Caesar crushed the sons of Pompeius, and by summer he returned to Rome. Cleopatra had a letter every week, witty and clear, Caesar's personality stamped on each line. Dion had a letter too, sent from Ostia to a merchant who did business for me at the palace.

Hail my friend,

I am in Rome now to ride in Caesar's Triumph. Nobody before has had four in a row. It is truly something to see. But I do not think you would have liked the Egyptian Triumph much, with a statue of your Nile god enslaved, though the model of Pharos with flames shooting out the top was good. Your Princess Arsinoe walked in chains and I would not have known her if it weren't for the placard saying who she was, so changed she was. I did not like it. I did not like it when it was Vercingetorix, who my tribe hated, when he walked with his head up through the excrement they threw at him, and at the end walked into the cellar where they killed him. They did not kill your Princess. I think she is in prison. It would not look good to behead a young woman. No one minded when they beheaded the rest of the prisoners.

You say that I am Roman, but I am not. We kill or do not kill, but we do not make a spectacle of it. We do not watch suffering and call it entertainment.

You will no doubt say something full of sophistry about how we can know what is right. I don't understand, and won't.

I can kill, Dion. I'm good at it. Unlike you, it's not a matter of rhetoric. There is no library like the sword. But I have never hurt a human being for the pleasure of it, or enjoyed watching anyone raped or killed or cut to pieces. I cannot cheer. Let my enemies die if they must die, but let it be properly and swiftly, by the garrote of a priest in some private place.

I do not know when I will return to Alexandria. It all depends on Caesar. I have eleven more years of my enlistment, so I am almost half done. When I am done, I think I am done with killing. I will be thirty-seven then, and have, if the gods wish it, many good years ahead of me yet. I would like to do something else.

Sigismund, my friend the bodyguard who you may remember, says that he could make a lot of money in a short time as a gladiator, and then retire to live rich. I think that is not a good plan. But then he is bigger than me.

I am glad to hear that Charmian has a daughter. Should I congratulate you?

> *Farewell,*
> *Emrys Aurelianus, Decurio*

Dion showed me the last, laughing.

I put my head on his shoulder. "I don't know, Dion. Should he?"

"Don't you dare!" Dion grinned. "I've never done anything of the kind!"

"Not for want of admirers," I said. Dion was both handsome and educated. Lately, his parents had been trying to arrange a marriage with every pretty young Jewish girl in town. I could have told them that it was hopeless. "You could tell your mother Demetria is yours," I suggested. "That you had a torrid affair with a Gentile slave, and that you couldn't dream of being unfaithful to your true love."

"That might work," Dion said thoughtfully, scratching his beard. "Better than to say I'm true to a Keltic cavalryman I haven't seen in a year."

"You can't really be faithful." I snorted.

Dion gave me an injured look. "I'm faithful in my heart!"

I laughed and hugged him. "I'm sure you are."

He bent his head against mine. "And what about Agrippa?"

"What about him?" I said, trying to keep my voice even. "I don't expect anything, Dion, not really. It was one of those things that blooms and dies swiftly. I don't imagine he will forget his first woman, but it will be enough if he thinks of me fondly. I don't need anything from him."

Yes, there had been that lightning sense of connection, that spark. But I did not really know him, not enough to miss him. And if sometimes at night I wished he were there, or wondered who he would be if I actually knew him, I did not cry for him. I had my friends and my sisters, Caesarion and Demetria. I had charge of the Royal Nursery and the Queen's wardrobe and personal plans, while Iras had the Royal Household and Apollodorus the Ministry of State. There were not enough hours in the day for all that needed to be done. I had no time for a love affair, and no particular inclination to look for one. A few hours now and again with a handsome man would be pleasant, but not worth the risk to my heart.

"Perhaps," said Dion, "you would do it if there were someone worth it to you."

"Yes," I said. "Let me know when you see someone worth it." Besides him, I thought. But that was categorically not going to happen.

THE HARVEST CAME, and then the spring. Caesarion was changing from baby to child, walking on his small feet and chasing my cat Sheba, who ran away and retaliated by hissing at him from the tops of cabinets or other high places. Demetria was learning to talk a little, though she was far behind him. Six months is a vast gulf at that age, though it would close as they grew older.

Caesar went to Hispania. It seemed that Sextus Pompeius had escaped from the ruin of their plans in Africa, and waited, one last foe.

Emrys wrote to Dion from Corduba, a letter weeks on the way and half-illegible from seawater.

> Hail my friend,
>
> I cannot think of anything you would like better than making an astrological ceiling for an entire temple, and I liked hearing you tell about it though I do not know the constellations you name. I suppose every people sees the stars differently and tells different stories about them. In Gaul they are not the same as the Roman ones. We have the Wain and the Hammer, the Swan and the Wolf. The Germans tell me they have the Dragon, which is some kind of great flying lizard that a hero killed once and their gods put into the sky. Sigismund swears to me that he has seen the skull of a dragon that one of the great chiefs has, pulled from the earth, and that the teeth of the monster are longer than a man's hand, but I am not sure if such a thing can be true.
>
> We will be leaving Hispania soon. I think we would be already gone, except that Caesar is ill. He had some kind of fever, but it is not just that. Lately he has been sick more often, and sometimes his headaches are so violent that he must stay in the dark all day. I think he is feeling his age.

We will be back to Rome soon, I suppose. I do not know whether to hope that we go by sea or land. By sea is quicker, but there is no misery like a horse transport in a storm in the Middle Sea. By land we will go along the coast, and will come at last to Massalia, which though it is far from my actual home, is beginning to seem like it. It was the first big city I saw when I joined up. I thought it was the grandest thing in the world. I had never seen a sewer before or a gutter for the rain, or a hundred ships at once.

You ask me if I intend to marry. It's forbidden during our enlistment. We can't until after we get our discharges. Even if I could, how could I leave someone else waiting for me and wondering where I am? Perhaps with a child to take care of? That is what I think of when I am wanting home comfort and a warm bed, a woman to love me and need me. It would not be fair....

"Oh, Dion," I said, when he showed it to me. "How did you find the good one?"

"I don't know," he said, and smiled ruefully. "I'd share him with a woman if he wanted. I know he likes women too. But..."

"I know," I said. "Who knows when you will see him again?"

"Not even the gods," Dion said. "It's one of the things you learn as a magician. The gods may know more than we, and understand things that are beyond our learning, but They do not know the future."

"Beyond our learning? Not beyond our understanding?"

Dion nodded. "That's one of the first laws of Hermetics, of the teachings of Hermes Trismegistus. The created universe operates according to natural laws, and all things obey them, even the gods. We, the younger children of time as we are, may not understand how they work, though the gods do."

I shook my head, fascinated. "Like what?"

Dion grinned as he always did when he had something he enjoyed to explain. "For example, I can take this scroll and drop it on my foot. I can do it a hundred times, and do you know what I'll have learned?"

"That it's heavy?" I grinned back. "What will you have learned, Dion?"

"That it falls down. Every time. You could take scrolls, rocks, feathers, bones, anything you wanted, and drop it and it would fall down. Why?"

I blinked. "I don't know."

"Neither do I," Dion said. "Nor does any man. But anyone, from the village fool to the most learned man who ever lived, can tell you that if you drop something it will fall. It's a law of nature."

"Unless something else acts upon it," I said.

Dion nodded. "Exactly! If I throw a rock, it will go some distance before it falls. If I sling it from a catapult it will go farther still. And if I put a piece of metal on the ground and hold a lodestone above it, it will fall up. There are other laws in play. The Law of Attraction, for example. Some things are attracted to other things, like the metal to the lodestone."

Dion was, I thought, a rather good teacher with a knack for making complicated things simple. No wonder he was well liked at the Museum.

"It's observation," he said. "If a thousand men have all seen the same thing, there's something to see."

"Suppose five hundred see something and five hundred don't?" I asked.

Dion looked pleased. "Then you have to figure out what the difference between the men was, rather than conclude there was no phenomenon to observe. Why did some see it and some not? Like the gods. Every people in the world has gods, and every people has those who talk with Them. If thousands of people all over the world in every age have observed something, it's more logical to assume there is something to observe that requires certain abilities to perceive." He nodded at my quizzical look and went on. "For example, when you sound the highest string on a kithara many men can't hear it. However, it's rare that children can't, and more women can hear the very high notes than men. Is it that there is nothing to hear, or only that for some reason we don't understand, children and women can hear high notes better than men?"

"The latter is more logical," I agreed.

"So Hermes Trismegistus teaches us that the understanding of natural law helps us understand the entirety of the created world, including the gods. There is no separation between the material and the numinous."

I put my head to the side. "Dion, do you think you could teach me?"

"I don't see why not."

SUMMER CAME. Caesarion was two. The floodwaters rose and began to fall. The Inundation was high that year, and many marginal fields were deep in life-giving mud. The harvest would be good and the grain would pour in, refilling granaries emptied of their surplus in lean years. Isis was enthroned, and the Black Land was at peace.

It was only a few weeks before another letter came from Emrys, this time from Rome.

. . . we are back in Rome and camped outside the city. We are with the bodyguard, at Caesar's country house, where he is ill again. He's getting better, and I've seen him outside and up and about with my own eyes, though he looks thin. They say he's rewriting his will, that this illness has scared him. I don't think dying scares Caesar, except perhaps for leaving things undone.

You ask me why I love him, and I have thought about it. He's Caesar. He sees people and things for what they are, not for what circumstances surround them. He sees the worth in a man regardless of his family or friends, of the language he was born speaking or his name. He sees things around him the way they are, not the way they should be or the way we want them to be. And when you stand next to him, you see it too.

You ask me, is he good? I do not understand what you mean. He is honorable, surely. He has kept faith with those he has given his word. That is the measure I know. Remember, I do not know how to debate ethics, or play those kinds of games about which god gives better commands. You say that your god forbids you to kill, yet we would have been dead in Alexandria if not for Antipater and the Fighting Jews. It must not be as forbidden as all that.

I am glad you have never killed, and I hope you never have to. If, as you say, you cannot value your own life high enough to say that you would kill rather than be killed, then that is what will happen. But I would be sorry if it did.

Or perhaps one day you will find something worth killing for.

> *Farewell,*
> *Emrys Aurelianus, Praefectus*
> *(As you can see, I am a praefectus now, with command of an ala of four hundred men.)*

Caesar's letter was equally to the point. "Come to Rome," he said. "Come to Rome, and bring the child. I should like to see Ptolemy Philometor Caesar."

R⊙ᴍE

We came to Ostia, Rome's seaport, on a beautiful early fall day. The passage had been smooth and uneventful, our great ship carried along by moderate winds, the two warships in our escort more for show than for protection. It had been many years since Pompeius had defeated the pirates and secured the shores of Sicilia and Campania. It was hard enough to outfit two ships properly. We had still not recovered our navy well enough from Caesar's fire.

Our galley was the first of the new ships, with five banks of oars and eight decks, and cabins large enough for the Queen and all her household. This was necessary, as Caesarion should come, and therefore I should too, as well as his nurse and all of the other servants. Iras came to take charge of the Queen's personal arrangements, while Apollodorus stayed in Alexandria to oversee things there. Dion also stayed, as now he was teaching at the Museum, and could not leave except to the detriment of his career.

Demetria also came. She was not quite two and I was loath to be separated from her, but I also hated to risk the dangers of a sea voyage, not to mention the uncertain airs of an unfamiliar place when she was so young. Still, Caesarion must come. Caesar had never seen him. And at least Demetria could bear him company and be a familiar playmate from home. He was two and a bit, and the age difference between them was beginning to close now that they could both walk.

For my part, I understood Asetnefer better now. The daughter I had carried and the nephew I had not seemed equally mine. I looked at Caesarion and Demetria together on the floor with some toy, seeing the children as refractions of us, different facets of what it meant to be a Ptolemy. In truth, Caesarion was more like Iras than his mother or me, while in Demetria I saw the clever persistence of Auletes.

As we came into port in Ostia, I saw Cleopatra tweaking aside the curtains at the window, searching for Caesar. Of course he was not there. If the Dictator of Rome were to come to Ostia, it should be an act of international significance, as though Rome bowed to Egypt.

"He would come if he could," I said, seeing her face as she let the curtain fall. "I think he would. But he is more than your lover, the father of your child."

"He is Caesar," she said, and lifted her chin. "And I will have no less."

I nodded, and helped her with the clasp on her necklace.

If Caesar could not come himself, he had at least sent his representative in great state. Some of the arrangements had been made before we departed Alexandria, through Iras' lengthy correspondence with Apollonius, Caesar's slave and secretary who handled his affairs as Iras handled the Queen's, so we were not surprised to see the great crowd at the wharf.

There were a dozen covered litters, white curtains moving in the breeze, a full escort of soldiers in steel and harness, and behind all a parade of wagons for the Queen's things. I was pleased to see that the soldiers looked like the familiar bodyguards we had known in Alexandria; they were Caesar's own men, and he trusted them. And of course a crowd had gathered on the wharf and behind, idle spectators of Ostia who were curious about the Queen of Egypt.

Waiting at the front of the crowd, just before the bodyguard, were two young officers and a senior officer. He did not wear a helmet in the sun, and his brown hair curled over his forehead. He was nearly as tall as the bodyguards, and the military harness he wore in the heat bared his legs, which were very muscled indeed. There was something vaguely familiar about him, but I could not place his face.

One of the junior officers came forth to talk with Iras, arranging the precedence of the welcome in a few words. Iras nodded, and walked back to join us behind the curtains. "Caesar has sent one of his closest associates, his former Master of Horse, a man named Marcus Antonius. He is to escort us to Caesar's villa just outside the city, where Caesar will join us this evening for an official reception. The villa is to be ours for the duration of our stay."

I glanced over her shoulder at Marcus Antonius, who was waiting in the heat. Now I recognized him. He had been a young officer with Gabinius, when they returned Auletes to power. Ten years ago. The years had certainly been kind to Marcus Antonius. Even Iras gave him a glance beneath her heavy eyelashes.

Cleopatra nodded. "Is it agreed whether Antonius will bow?"

"He will bend but not kneel," Iras said. "It's not their way. They are so proud of having no kings."

Cleopatra nodded. "That will suffice. After all, I do not come to Rome as a suppliant, as Auletes did. I am Caesar's guest."

"I hope they understand that," I said, looking about to make sure Caesarion had not gotten his white chiton dirty already.

"If they don't now, then they will soon," she said serenely.

Antonius greeted her properly, bowing deeply enough and holding it long enough that it was clear he had been well rehearsed. "Gracious Queen," he said, as he straightened, "I bring you the personal greetings of Gaius Julius Caesar. He regrets that he is unable to meet you at the harbor himself, but sends his own vessel to bring you upriver. He hopes that these humble conveyances may be enough for your comfort, and that his house will be pleasing to you. He will join you in the second hour of the night, that you might dine together and that he might bring you greetings from the first men of Rome."

All very unofficial, I thought. From the first men of Rome, not from the Senate. From Gaius Julius Caesar, not from the Dictator. He has enemies, I thought. And things of which he is not certain.

Cleopatra nodded once, gravely. "Please convey to Caesar my pleasure in accepting his kind hospitality. As I am traveling merely as a friend, not as the sovereign of Egypt, I am happy to dispense with tiresome ceremonies, and will look forward to receiving him this evening, and with being introduced to his intimates. Do you count yourself among the evening's guests, Marcus Antonius?"

He inclined his head again, and I could see how his eyes lingered on her face. "I am so fortunate, Gracious Queen."

"Then I shall look forward to speaking with you," she said. "I understand you have been my guest before, in Alexandria."

Antonius flushed, and I wondered what it was about these Romans, blushing like girls. "It is kind of you to remember, Gracious Queen. We did not speak on that occasion."

"As I recall you were practically outdoors on that occasion," Cleopatra said, and I saw her lips twist in a real smile. His couch had indeed been at the very back of the hall.

"I was," he said. "But that was many years ago. And we've both had a promotion or two since then."

"So I see," she said with a glance at his gleaming harness. It was Greek, from the look of it, and faced with gilded lions. Beneath it, his tunic was aqua blue with worked borders, rather than anything he ought to be wearing. But I suppose if Caesar didn't tell him to put on proper uniform, no one else could.

Caesarion twisted, grabbing at the front of my gown. From where he stood it was nothing but a sea of legs, and he wanted to get up where he could see something. I thought it was better to go ahead and pick him up, rather than have him start pulling and yelling, so I hoisted him up as quickly as possible. Of course Antonius saw the movement.

"Is this Prince Caesarion?" he asked, his face lighting with a smile that seemed genuine.

Caesarion, for his part, stared at the gilded breastplate and aqua tassels as though it were the most lovely thing in the world.

"This is Ptolemy Caesar," Cleopatra said carefully.

Marcus Antonius inclined his head gracefully to the boy in my arms. "Hail, Ptolemy Caesar," he said seriously. "I have a little boy of my own just your age."

Caesarion looked at him curiously, his head to the side, and his feet unfortunately digging into my breast. He said nothing.

"A man of few words," Antonius said to the Queen, smiling. "He handles the crowd quite well."

"He has been brought up to it," Cleopatra said.

"My son Antyllus would be screaming," Antonius said. "But then he's not a prince."

"Or a Caesar," Cleopatra said pointedly.

"I don't think Fulvia and Caesar have ever been that close," Antonius replied, laughing. He stopped when he saw the look of icy horror on Iras' face behind the Queen. "Your pardon," he said, stepping back. "I am a plain soldier, and unused to diplomacy."

I wondered if it were indeed the fashion in Rome for husbands to joke about their own disgrace, or if there were a message there—that Cleopatra was not the only woman who had claimed Caesar's favors, Queen or not. Or perhaps Antonius was just putting his foot in his mouth.

WE CAME UP the Tiber in morning, and the bustling business of the river was no surprise to me. It was much like the harbor traffic in Alexandria. Caesar's barge, too, was not surprising, save in its luxury and workmanship. The cushions were of scarlet leather, and the fixtures were gilded. There was chilled wine to drink while we made our passage upriver, though I got none of it. Iras attended the Queen and Antonius, while I tried to keep Caesarion from falling in the Tiber. Demetria knew better, but Caesarion scaled the rail and leaned out alarmingly, yelling at the seagulls that swarmed around the ship hoping for a handout. By the time I had found bread for him to throw to them, and gotten Demetria bread of her own because she was hungry, then found Caesarion bread because Demetria had some, we were passing under the Sublician Bridge and into the city proper.

We did not, however, stay in Rome. While the city spanned the right bank of the river, instead we came about and docked along the left side. There trees and parkland came down right to the water, and above, among the cypresses, I could see the occasional gleam of marble.

"A Palace Quarter?" Iras asked.

I nodded, steadying Demetria as the ship bumped against the dock. "It seems so."

Many of the rich men of Rome kept more than one house, and while an old family home on the Esquiline or Palatine was expected, many had built newer houses outside of the city proper, in the parks and wooded vistas on the other side of the Tiber. One of these was Caesar's.

I had never before been in a house that was entirely new. In Egypt, an old house may be a thousand years old, one floor built on top of another, one wall patched and remade of blocks that were once a city wall or a temple so long ago that the carvings are faded. Even in Alexandria, which is new by the standards of the Black Land, our houses were a hundred years old, or two. Of course new rooms might be added, old decoration torn down and brought up to date, a modern bath affixed to an older building, but a house built entirely from the beginning was a novelty to me.

And yet that is what Caesar had done. Ten years ago this had been a wooded plot on a hillside. Caesar had approved the plans in Gaul, without walking the land himself, and in his absence the trees had been cut to supply a glorious vista of river and city on the other side, gardens and groves cunningly arranged, and amid it all the marble splendor of his new house. There was a hypocaust beneath the floors to provide radiant heat in the winter. The long colonnade facing the river had pots of Indian jasmine, whose perfume would fill the area during the summer. The walls were plastered and painted with scenes in bright colors, precious as a jewel box, as though even the smallest room were the setting for a brilliant play. The furniture was all new, elegant, and graceful, without a single scuff or mark of wear. There were twenty rooms, and each was perfect.

"And this is to be the Queen's bedchamber," Caesar's secretary, Apollonius, said as he showed me about.

The walls were painted green, and on each panel was a pastoral scene—farmers working in fields, hunters with bows shooting at waterfowl, and so on. Through it all a great blue river ran. Boats plowed it, sailing serenely past cities half-imagined.

"It's the Nile," Apollonius said. He shrugged. "Or at least what the artist thinks the Nile looks like."

To my mind it looked more like the Tiber out the window than the Nile, but it was still very pretty, and I said so.

Apollonius nodded. He was a small man with graying hair and the purest Greek possible. Sold into slavery as a boy in Athens, he had been freed by Caesar some years ago. Since then he'd been at Caesar's side from Gaul to Hispania, managing his affairs and writing his letters. He was, I thought, a man of whom to make a friend.

"The Prince's room is across the hall," he said. "The windows are right above the guard post." He looked at me significantly. "But I suppose you are used to guarding the boy."

"We have brought our own guards," I said, "but we are also grateful for the loan of Caesar's men."

"Yes, well," Apollonius said. "It's the Germans. Legionaries can be bribed. The Germans have blood oaths. They believe if they break them that their god will send ravens to eat out their entrails while they are still living. A safe enough guard for Caesar's son."

That pleased me in more than one way. "He means to acknowledge him, then?"

Apollonius sighed. "Caesar has a wife. I take it you know that?"

I nodded.

"And it is also Roman law that no marriage with a noncitizen can be valid, even should Caesar be divorced. So you see he could not marry your Queen, Egyptian as she is. Roman may only marry Roman. He may acknowledge Caesarion, but he cannot legitimize him."

I felt myself coloring. "My mistress is a Queen, and laws can be changed."

"Not in Rome." Apollonius looked at me seriously. "Caesar may convince the Senate to make some special exception, but the people will never accept it, and Caesar knows that. No one who is not born Roman will ever be the equal of someone who is. An affair of the heart or an affair of state in some distant place is one thing. A son who might be Caesar's heir is another."

He must have seen my back stiffen, for he went on: "Not that I don't wish it otherwise! Not that Caesar doesn't. I've been with him nearly twenty years now. I was with him when Julia died, and that poor child who didn't live long enough to be named."

"I am well acquainted with Gnaeus Pompeius myself," I said grimly.

Apollonius nodded shortly. "Then you know everything to be settled to that account. The child was a boy, and there was no mark on him. But a pillow doesn't leave a mark."

I shivered. "I could believe it of him," I said.

"These things happen in Rome," Apollonius said. "But then the House of Ptolemy is not always a loving family."

"Indeed not," I said. "Understand that we are always watchful. Caesarion is the heir to the throne of Egypt. We could not be more careful of his life." I turned, lifting my chiton to show the scar on my thigh. "This I took for the Queen myself, when we were little more than girls. I have belonged to her since we were six years old."

Apollonius nodded gravely. "Then you know how it is. The great ones live as long as they are well served."

CAESAR CAME THAT EVENING, just as night was falling. We had five hours to get the house in order and to get a suitable meal on the table. Fortunately, Apollonius had gotten a head start on things, and the cook was Caesar's own, sent over from his house in the city. What Caesar's wife had to say about that remained a mystery.

I did not see their meeting, in the atrium of the house with all of Caesar's entourage of great men about him and all of our people. I was changing Caesarion's chiton again, which he had somehow gotten soaking wet in the ten minutes before his father arrived.

I jerked it down over his head a little impatiently, rose-colored silk worked with golden borders. He was supposed to be in yellow, to match his mother's gown, but his chiton was now sopping wet. "Now stay clean," I admonished. "Caesarion, you're a prince, not a ragamuffin. Try to look the part for an hour!" This was his fourth clean chiton today. I shoved his dark curls back from his forehead and picked him up. If he could just avoid pissing until it was over. I didn't want to clout him like a baby lest Caesar think he was behind hand, but he hadn't entirely mastered asking to use the pot every time.

"I try," he said firmly, and smiled at me with his big dark eyes.

I kissed him soundly. "Come now, sweet," I said. "Let's meet your father."

CAESAR LOOKED OLDER. Perhaps it was that he stood next to Marcus Antonius, who might have posed for a sculptor as the model of some hero, or perhaps these two years had taken their toll. The lines were more deeply graven around his mouth, and in the skin of his throat one could see the veins beginning to bulge, there and in the backs of his hands.

"Here is Caesarion now," Cleopatra said, and looked at me as the men parted for us.

Caesarion, for a wonder, did nothing at all untoward, just looked at them all curiously, lovely as a rosebud in his pink silk, his dark hair curling across his brow and his eyes alive with mischief.

Caesar took in a single breath. Every man waited to see what he should do.

Caesar came toward him, and he knew enough about children not to reach for him. Babies will tolerate that, but a child who is two and a bit is likely to turn away and clamber. Caesar clasped his hands behind his back and bent toward him like a tutor. "So you are Ptolemy Caesar."

"No," said Caesarion firmly, his favorite word. "No, no, no."

Caesar laughed, and then everyone did.

"We call him Caesarion," Cleopatra said, coming to my side. "He doesn't answer to Ptolemy."

"You should rather be Caesar than Ptolemy then?" Caesar asked. His eyes explored the boy's face hungrily, every line of it. He looked like his mother, yes. Or like any child, round-faced, but beneath the curves of childhood he should have Caesar's fine bones. The resemblance would come. I had seen it in his infant face.

Caesarion looked back, and having seen all day things that were Caesar's decided to gamble. "I want a dog," he said.

"Will not your mother give you a dog?" Caesar asked, looking sideways at Cleopatra.

"You are too young for a dog, as I keep saying," she said, reaching for him and taking him from me, his arm going about her neck. "You may have one when you are older. And it is no use asking Caesar for one."

"So your mother says," Caesar said, and turned to the Queen. One dark eye flickered in a wink at Caesarion, who giggled.

Together, they might have posed for a tableau, Isis in gold, beautiful and smiling, Horus on her shoulder in pink, Serapis by their side, his face graven with care, his white toga about him like a shroud. No, I thought, forcing the idea away from me. Of course he is not young. He was not three years ago.

Caesar turned to Antonius, his voice pitched loudly enough to be heard around the atrium. "What do you say, Antonius? Is my son a well-grown boy?"

"Your son is a fine boy," Marcus Antonius said gravely, no doubt just as he had been rehearsed. An exhalation that was almost palpable ran through the room. "Any man would say so. I think he favors your father somewhat."

As surely Caesar's father had been dead long before Antonius' childhood, I doubted that he could say so with any veracity, but perhaps he had examined a bust or statue.

"I see the Julians there," Caesar said, smiling at Caesarion again. "Descended of Iulos, that son of mighty Aeneas who fled Troy for our Italian shores. It is in his eyes."

Everything said, they went in to dinner. I took the child back, and he looked out from my arms as the crowd passed. A thought arose unbidden: *Wilos' eyes were blue, though the shape of his face was the same.*

EUROPA

The party ended an hour short of midnight, Caesar and the other notables leaving in a long procession of litters, guards about and torchmen before and following. I did not see them go. I was in the kitchen, making certain of the washing up. It was a point of pride that Apollonius should see everything that was Caesar's in good order the next morning. And much was Caesar's, as our dishes and furnishings had not yet been brought from the ship. They would arrive at midday, and then I would have a great deal more to do.

When every fragile cup was stowed and the hearth fire banked, I sent the slaves to get some sleep, and walked out through the front of the house, checking everything for the last time. The white marble floor of the dining room glinted wetly. It had just been mopped.

I was standing in the atrium looking around the dining room doors when I heard the sound of swift hooves, the challenge of the guards outside, the exchange of voices.

It was Caesar. Only four men accompanied him, and I heard them dismounting just outside. The bodyguards did not enter.

I stood a moment longer, hesitating, and saw him cross the atrium with a tread as light as a young man's, saw her meet him halfway, standing together, their foreheads touching, silhouetted against the light that poured in above from the compluvium. It was too far to hear their voices, low as they were, meant only for each other's ears. I saw her smile, and he bent his head to her shoulder, his face against the warm flesh of her neck. Her eyes closed as her arms went around him.

I stepped back into the dining room, heedless of the floor. This was not something I was meant to see, me or anyone else.

I slipped through the dining room and out another door, back toward the kitchen, something like an ache stirring inside me. No one would ever greet me that way, and Agrippa...

If Agrippa wanted to send a message to me, it would be easy. He must guess I would be here with the Queen. And I had had no letter in Alexandria in more than two years. He had of course grown out of his infatuation, the idealistic desire of a very young man, certain he is in love with the first woman who has looked at him and seen a warrior, not a little boy. He had meant the things he said when he said them, but of course he did not now.

I opened the kitchen door, momentarily surprised to see the oldest of the slaves now serving up ham and bread and the remains of the watercress from dinner to three or four men. Of course. The escort.

"Charmian?"

Emrys stood by the hearth, a slab of bread in his hand, his scarlet cavalry cloak tossed carelessly over one shoulder. He grinned at me, and the next instant I hurried to embrace him. He was taller even than I remembered, taller than Dion. My head barely came to his chin, and his eyes were sea green. "Emrys! What are you doing here?"

"I came with Caesar," he said, putting me back to look at me. "My ala has escort duty this week, and I'm the ranking officer. You look well."

"So do you," I said. In truth he did. He looked tanned and fit, his face properly shaved, but with his long hair pulled back in a tail. "Dion will be horribly jealous that I've seen you. He wanted to come, but couldn't without disrupting everything at the Museum."

"I know," Emrys said. "I'm sorry he couldn't. But I expect his experiments are important."

"Yes," I said, wondering if he would think that an odd theory about each material having a specific weight unique to it was worth pursuing. As near as I could tell, it seemed to involve dropping bits of things in a vessel of water and weighing them over and over. I thought Archimedes had already done that.

"Come and sit and eat," I said. "Would you like some wine? Are you hungry?" I drew him to one of the long trestle tables. "I can find a meal for you if you'd like."

"I'm well supplied, thank you," he said and sat beside me, the bread in his hand. "We all had dinner earlier at the barracks. We're just off the Campus Martius. It's not supposed to be allowed to bring troops into the city, so Caesar just has the bodyguards at his house. After all, lots of men have German bodyguards. I think we look a little too much like troops. It's the horses." He grinned at me.

"And the leather," I said. "And possibly the plumes."

In the end, I did not sleep at all. I sat up all night in the kitchen talking with Emrys. Also, I timed the Queen to a nicety. I got up stiffly from the bench just before I heard the footsteps, the slave who slept outside her door moving as the Queen called for something.

Emrys gave me a smile over the long-since-cold remains of eggs we had shared some hours before. "Time to go," he said.

"Aren't you exhausted?" I asked.

Emrys shrugged. "We'll see Caesar back to the Campus Martius, and the Germans will take him from there. They've had a full night's sleep. Then we'll turn in and get some rest. Nobody expects us to run the day around. But you probably have to, don't you?"

I mentally cursed myself for staying up, thinking of the furniture and dishes that were coming from the ship in a few hours. And soon Caesarion would be up. Of course his nurse would chase him, and there were plenty of people to make sure he and Demetria had their breakfasts, but the first morning in a new place they would want me. "I do," I said. "But it was worth it to talk to you, Emrys."

"A friend is good to have," he said, and brushed an errant strand of hair out of his eyes.

A friend. Other than Dion, I had very few friends. I had slaves and masters, sycophants who sought me out for favor with the Queen, relatives and children and all the rest. But I had very few friends.

He stood while one of his men went out and called for the grooms to saddle their horses. The horses, at least, must not stand ready all night. "I know you're busy today, but tomorrow if you can get away for a few hours, I'd enjoy showing you the city."

"Show me Rome?"

Emrys shrugged. "Why not? You showed me the orrery in Alexandria. Let me show you a thing or two."

"I would like that very much," I said.

⊙F COURSE the next day was impossible. Caesar wanted to introduce the Queen to any number of distinguished men, and naturally it was necessary to do so at a private dinner at her house. The Queen could not take any part in the public business of Rome.

Putting on a production of that sort in only a couple of days was a major undertaking. Unlike the men who had accompanied Caesar to the first small dinner, these guests were not friends. They were important, and hence dangerous. Some were actual enemies, but most were leaders of some faction or another whose favor must be courted. Only a few, like Marcus Antonius, could already be counted upon.

The afternoon before I was seeing to the wreaths, with an ear on Demetria and Caesarion plaguing their nurse in the atrium, when one of the door guards called to me. "Domina, there is a gentleman here who says that he needs to see you, and that he is known to you."

I went out into the atrium, wondering if it was the florist with the roses for the feast, and if so why the guard should style him a gentleman.

It was Marcus Agrippa. My heart nearly stopped when I saw him. I had forgotten he was so beautiful.

He was wearing a toga, which I had never seen him in before, and it suited his height and the breadth of his shoulders. He had grown in two years. He was as tall as Emrys now, but more strongly built, with the narrow hips and wide shoulders that sculptors love to give to heroes. His brown hair was cut short, except where it curled across his brow, and his eyes lit at the sight of me.

"Charmian? I hardly knew you."

I came toward him, but did not give him the kiss of greeting, not knowing whether it would come amiss under the circumstances. Instead I greeted him in Latin. "Hail, Marcus Vipsanius Agrippa. You are welcome under the Queen's roof."

He stared at me, a little confused by the greeting, then gestured with his draped left arm. "Oh, this. I thought I should dress properly in case I saw people other than you. I wouldn't want people to think I was being disrespectful of Queen Cleopatra."

"You mean you're here to crash Caesar's party?" I asked, but there was no sting in my voice.

"Is he having one? I didn't know." He took a step closer. With his new height he positively loomed over me. "My father and Caesar aren't really...My father was always Pompeius' man. It's my mother who's friends with Caesar's niece."

"And now you are your family's best chance of clearing up...misunderstandings?" I smiled at him, unable to avoid it. I had forgotten how overwhelming he could be in person, young as he was, how intoxicating the sense of the familiar about him. I had intended to be angry.

"Well, yes." He shrugged. "But that doesn't have anything to do with being here. I came to see you."

"Really?" It is possible that my tone was frosty. "After more than two years with not so much as a note? Suddenly you absolutely must see me?"

"I wrote to you," he said. "I wrote to you from Zela, and twice after that."

"I had no letters from you." Though, to be fair, I thought, only about one in four of the letters Emrys had sent Dion had arrived. It was just that there had been so very many letters.

"I only had one from you," he said.

"I wrote you five," I said. And hardly knew what to say, I thought. I knew then that I was pregnant with Demetria, but should I put that in a letter? I was suddenly very aware of her, splashing and yelling with Caesarion in the compluvium in the atrium, while their nurse stood by. Demetria seemed to think that the atrium pool was put there for the express benefit of the household children so that they could pretend to be ducks.

But this was not the time or place for that conversation. Marcus had not noticed her. Why should he? Children are not the responsibility of young men, and if he noticed anyone it should be Caesarion, who no doubt was the subject of speculation by more than one noble Roman.

"I should have written," he said. "But I didn't know what to say." He glanced away, toward the four cypress trees in pots that screened the compluvium from the door and also sheltered a small statue of Aphrodite. "I'm not good at writing things. The things I mean look silly when I put them on paper."

"I understand," I said coolly. He had said many things he could not have meant later, when he had a chance to think, when the magic of the Black Land had worn off. No doubt it seemed like some enchantment, when it was nothing except the intensity of first attraction, first experience. Or perhaps it was enchantment after all. One did not play lightly with Isis Pelagia, nor with any who might embody Her.

But I did not intend, then or now, to hold him to his declarations of love. I had made it clear I expected nothing from him. Why should I be angry at him for taking me at my word? It was not as though I were some innocent girl of good family, led astray into disgrace. I had lost nothing because of him.

Marcus looked at me, chewing on the inside of his lip. "I'd like to talk to you, Charmian."

"You are talking to me," I said.

"Privately. I mean...I don't mean..." He stopped.

"You mean to talk," I said. "Not to have me."

"No. I mean, of course I'd like...but that wasn't what I meant."

"Do Romans never court women?" I asked bemusedly. "Do you have anything between 'let's take our clothes off' and a visit to her father?"

"No," he said, sounding almost miserable. "And anyway it wouldn't be me meeting with her father. It would be my father." He squared his shoulders as though he were about to explain something difficult. "You see, my family's from Campania, an old family, but nobody ever had anything much until my great-grandfather got in with Marius. He was gifted, or bought for almost nothing, a lot of property—vineyards and orchards and good farmland. He got killed by Sulla, but then my father became a client of Pompeius Magnus, when he was just rising and was getting rid of the pirates. Which is how my mother met Caesar's niece, back when Caesar and Pompeius were family. They stayed good friends through all the ups and downs, and it was my mother who got me a place as a tribune. But my father's still not welcome in a lot of houses. Fortunately, he wasn't a very prominent supporter of Pompeius, but we might have lost the property anyway because of my older brother Lucius—he fought for Pompeius—if I hadn't fought for Caesar. Since Lucius was killed in battle and I wasn't, confiscating my father's land would be like taking it away from me, so we've kept it."

"And so now your father owes you," I said.

"Which isn't how it's supposed to be," Marcus said. "He's supposed to be head of the family. You can't know how it hurts his pride to know that everything his grandfather won would be lost if it weren't for me, and I'm not but eighteen." He turned, looking back toward the doorway. "And my mother goes on day and night with the I-told-you-so and now-your-foolishness-has-cost-us-Lucius. I know it's because she's grieving Lucius and she has nobody else to blame. We don't even have his ashes. We hope he was burned on one of the mass pyres and not just left for the vultures, but we'll never know. I don't know why I'm alive and Lucius isn't."

"Perhaps he simply wasn't as lucky," I said.

"No one ever is," he said. "Nothing touches me. Five battles now and not a single scratch. You'd think I'd be wounded."

"Be glad you aren't," I said, smiling. "Many men would be glad to be proof against swords. It's like Achilles or something."

"It's not." He did turn then, his eyes bright. "It's nothing like Achilles."

I stroked the folds of his toga over his arm gently. "Marcus, it doesn't require a charm or the favor of some god for a strong young man to win through battles. You're bigger than many men you face, and you've practiced hard and learned well. Yes, some is luck, but some of it is your common sense and hard work." And, I thought privately to myself, to have the order of battle set by Caesar instead of Gnaeus Pompeius. In his youth Pompeius may have been a great general, but when he left things to his son there was only one way it could go.

"I do not want to succumb to hubris," he said.

At that moment a very wet something plowed into my knees shrieking. I looked down to see Caesarion, his soaking wet chiton pulled up above his belly, his hair plastered to his head with water. When I looked down at him he collapsed into a giggling heap.

"Caesarion!" I exclaimed, reaching down to catch him. He evaded me and scooted away, rolling across the tiles of the atrium, still laughing wildly. From the other side of the potted cypress trees I heard Demetria splashing, then a rising wail with the tone that meant actual pain, not mere frustration.

I grabbed Caesarion about the waist and handed him to Marcus, then darted between bushes and picked up Demetria. She had fallen and bitten her lip, which bled in a tiny place while she shrieked.

"There now, sweetheart," I said. "It's just a tiny cut. You're all right." She put her wet arms around my neck, nuzzling in, spluttering.

Caesarion. I ducked back around the bushes, Demetria in my arms.

Marcus stood just where I'd left him, looking at Caesarion bemusedly. Caesarion, for his part, regarded Marcus with curiosity, crumpling the border on his toga in one damp little hand.

"Here now, darling," I said, swinging Caesarion back on my right hip. Together they made quite a handful, one on each side. It wouldn't be long before I couldn't pick them up together.

Demetria stopped crying and pushed back to look at Marcus, and I felt my face grow warm.

"Is that Caesarion?" Marcus asked.

"Yes," I said. Truly, I should never have handed Caesarion to someone outside of the household, not even for a moment. It only took a minute to break a child's neck. But in that instant it had seemed as natural as breathing, that of course any child of mine should be entirely safe with Marcus Agrippa.

"I should take them to their nurse," I said. "And I have words for her on leaving them alone near water, even for an instant."

He looked at me, a child in each arm, and I waited for him to ask who the other child was. But he didn't. "I suppose I should leave you to your work then," he said.

I nodded.

"We can talk soon?"

"If you want," I said.

As I carried the children to their nurse I buried my face in Demetria's soft curls, a shade lighter than Marcus'. He did not want to know, I thought. But surely the loss was his.

It was nine days before Emrys and I managed to go into the city. Between Emrys' duty, and the enormous business of setting up the Queen's household and arranging three dinners, not to mention having Caesar in and out nearly every day, it was more than a week before I could take an entire day off.

It was a beautiful day in early fall, with bright sun and the leaves not yet quite changing color on the trees in the park.

"They'll be changing in the mountains now," Emrys said, turning unerringly toward the northwest. "The snowline will already be creeping down the passes, and at home the gales of autumn are beginning."

"Will it snow here?" I asked him. I had always wanted to see snow.

He grinned. "You sound like the children. No, probably not. Or not much. There's some ice in the winter, but Rome never really gets heavy snow. A little bit, maybe."

I draped my himation about my shoulders. It was a little chilly under the trees and out of the sun, though I expected it would warm up later in the day. "Who do you worship, Emrys?"

"Epona," he said, "though I respect all gods. But Epona is who I'm dedicated to." We walked downhill through the last of the parkland, toward the Sublician Bridge, past the shops just outside the gates of the Grove of Furrina, where women were selling seed cakes to give to the sacred doves. "She's a horse goddess, born when the Great Mare was mounted by the sea god, Mann. The Great Mare gave birth to Epona, and it was She who brought horses to men and taught them to ride. To Her we owe our herds, the horses that pull our plows and mount our warriors, our life. Like a mare, She can be gentle to those She loves. And She guards Her children as fiercely as the herd mare will the foals in the herd."

"That's fascinating," I said. "I know almost nothing of horses."

Emrys shrugged. "Horses have been my life. Since the first horses came up out of the sea, there's been a tie between us, my people and horses."

"Tell me that story," I said comfortably as we strolled.

"It's not long," he said. Emrys dropped his voice to a storyteller's tones. "Time was when there were no men. All of the world was dark and held in the grasp of a winter that never ended. The first men awoke in a distant place, and they wandered in the snow, always looking for food or something to hunt. The mountains were dangerous because the dwarves lived there in great caves."

I must have looked blank, because he smiled and elaborated. "Smaller than men, and somewhat like men, but thinking differently and living in the deep places of the earth. They were dangerous, and men had to be wary of them. And so the first men wandered far from the mountains, following the game northward across the plains. Sometimes a false spring would come, and on those plains there would be for a little while tender new grass, so men hunted the animals that lived there. Only it was very dangerous, because the animals were very big, and the men had nothing but spears. They could not keep up when the animals ran, and when they charged, the men had to flee.

"One day, after years of wandering and following the herds, with the high mountains left far behind them, they followed the animals right to the edge of the world. And there, at the end of the plain, was the sea. Now no man had ever seen the sea before, and they didn't know what it was, so they stopped and stared in wonder at the waves crashing on the shore. And they fell to their knees at the beauty of it."

I could imagine that so clearly, a bright day at the edge of the world, a keen breeze off the sea.

"And Epona saw them and She was filled with love for them, and so as each wave began to break, as the white foam sped down its green side, it turned into a great white horse. The horses galloped out of the sea and frolicked on the sand, running and dancing for the sheer joy of it. One of the men who was braver than most stood up, and he walked toward the horses. A white mare stood her ground and waited for him, and when he came beside her she was not afraid. And she let him touch her and feed her, and at last ride her. Thus, horses came to men and with them the end of starvation and need. With horses, the herds could be ridden down, and hunters with spears could take even the largest bison, speeding beside them in their wild stampedes and throwing a javelin to their hearts. With horses, food could be salted and carried, and men no longer depended only on that day's hunt. With horses, the old people did not need to be left behind to die, but could ride with their families, and children and pregnant women could ride at need. All men prospered and revered Epona."

"You tell the story well," I said. "You should have been a storyteller, Emrys."

"I have no gift for music such as bards need," he said, but he did not look displeased. "They tell this story at home. I've heard a version of it from the Batavians, who claim that it happened in Batavia, where the Rhenus River flows into the sea, and that the men had followed the river north from the mountains where the dwarves lived." Emrys shrugged. "It could be that it happened in Batavia. Who is to say that it cannot be true?"

"An endless winter that never turned into summer?" I said. "Dwarves that live in the mountains?"

"In the very high mountains it's never summer," Emrys said. "In the Alpes Mountains the snow never melts on the peaks, and there are rivers of ice that are frozen all year. Summer may come in the valleys, but the mountains are always in winter. I've been there several times. Perhaps these men lived somewhere like that, or perhaps that's where this story began. The Rhenus flows from the Alpes, after all."

"Oh," I said. I tried to imagine. It was hard enough to imagine snow, much less a river of ice.

"As for the dwarves, why not? There are many strange creatures in the world, and there are a lot of stories about the dwarves in the Alpes. I myself have seen caves decorated with paintings far below the ground, bizarre animals and elephants."

"Elephants?" I frowned. Surely elephants lived in India.

Emrys nodded. "You have my word on it. Strange as that is."

I took his arm as we stepped off the bridge and into Rome proper. We waded into the crowds going north toward the Forum, and I was surprised how many women there were afoot. While there were some being borne in litters, most of the women were walking, mingling with the shopkeepers and laborers on their way to worksites, with the business traffic of the city. They were veiled no more than I, with only perhaps a light himation over the backs of their heads, or just about their shoulders, like Egyptian women instead of Greek.

Alexandria was the crossroads of the world. I had seen people of different lands many times before, but as Emrys and I walked through the streets near the Forum, Rome seemed different somehow. We stopped to see the Forum, of course, and the ancient round Temple of Vesta and the House of the Virgins beside it, where within lived the patrician priestesses of Vesta. We could not go in. Instead, we walked along one of the streets nearby, pitched steeply up the side of a hill.

"Are you hungry?" Emrys asked. He stood by the front of one of the shops, where a woman with several baskets was selling pastries on the street.

"Oh yes," I said. The smell of apples wrapped in warm dough was wonderful.

The vendor, a heavy woman of fifty or so with faded blond hair streaked gray, handed me the pastries while Emrys counted out coin. She smiled at me, saying something I didn't understand.

I shook my head.

Emrys replied in that same language, giving over the coins with a nod.

We walked down the street together. The pastries did indeed taste as good as they smelled. "What did you say?" I asked.

"I said you didn't speak German."

"Why would she think I did?"

"Well, you look German, don't you?" Emrys gave me a sideways glance. "Look around you."

I did, and I saw what he meant, what had seemed strange to me since we crossed the bridge. The litters that crossed the Forum were carried by tall blond men, and everywhere in the crowds of shoppers in the markets blond and red hair stood out like banners. Women carrying marketing baskets, skinny children at their sides. Slaves toting parcels. Maidservants and bodyguards following the rich. The unmistakable occasional pleasure slave, her pretty face dressed with cosmetics. I had never seen so much blond hair in my life.

In Alexandria, I was a rarity. Yes, there were blond slaves, but they were few and far between, and Greeks as blond as Alexander, though that was unusual. Here, everywhere I looked I saw faces like mine. The faces of the lower classes. Freedmen and gladiators, bodyguards and cooks and women who cleaned houses, children who swept shops and boys who ran errands, old women who baked pastries and the wary campaign wives of soldiers with too many children—they all had my face, my looks, my blond hair. And there were others as fair as Emrys, with that pale, freckled skin and light eyes, long hair instead of short, chestnut or red.

Faces that were not Roman.

I breathed out a long sigh. "Do they not notice?" I asked.

Emrys shook his head. "No. Roman virtue and Roman custom, Roman ways and Roman honor. Rome belongs to her citizens. But look around you."

"Not more than half," I said. "Not more than half the men I see could be Roman citizens." A litter with parted white curtains passed, two elderly men in togas conversing, the bearers' long blond hair pulled into loose tails, their tunics stretched tight across their shoulders.

"Much less than half," Emrys said. "And in the legions it's maybe one in five. Boys who are citizens don't serve in the legions for twenty years, not except for a few families. They go in as tribunes and get a little experience to help their political careers, most of it somewhere nice and safe."

"Except Agrippa," I said, remembering.

"Except Agrippa," Emrys said agreeably. "He's all right. He's a good enough tribune, and he did his work, unlike a lot of them. He has some talent and he shuts up and listens. But most of them aren't like that. They're like that spoiled brat great-nephew of Caesar's that we got stuck with in Hispania, complaining all the time."

"Does that happen a lot?" I asked, my mind still on what he'd said about Agrippa.

Emrys shrugged. "Often enough. But mostly it just begins to grate. No matter how good I am, I'll never rise very high because I'm not a citizen. I can't become a citizen, and Rome is for Romans. But do they even notice who's fighting their wars and cooking their meals and washing their clothes? Gauls and Germans."

"I suppose it's like that everywhere," I said, thinking of Iras, and how the scholars had frowned at a woman and native Egyptian approaching Greek learning.

"Well, yes," Emrys said. "But that doesn't keep it from grating." He reached up and brushed a piece of soot off my himation. "Where did you get those looks, anyway?"

"My mother was a slave from Thrace," I said. "She was bought in Histria, in Dobruja. I think this was in all that mess in the Third Mithridatic War. But she wasn't born in Histria. She came from somewhere up the Danuvius River. I don't know how she became a slave."

She had never told Asetnefer, I thought. And I had never thought about her that much, Egyptian as I was. Now I wondered. How far up the Danuvius? How far from home had she already been when she was bought by Pharaoh's agent in Histria? What home had she remembered when she went into Pharaoh, her head held high and laughter on her lips? Almost certainly she had seen snow. Had she missed it in a white city by the sea?

"It's a long river," Emrys said. "It rises in the Alpes too, just on the eastern side. You could be Scordisci or Pannonian or Vindobonian. There are a lot of tribes that trade down the Danuvius, some of them German and some of them Keltic."

"I suppose I'll never know," I said.

I must have sounded wistful, for Emrys touched my face gently. "It doesn't matter," he said quietly. "She lives in you, she and all her people."

I blinked, and was surprised to find sudden tears there. I had never told Demetria the story, young as she was. I should. I should tell her from the cradle what I knew of her beginnings, of my proud mother and Auletes, of Agrippa with his mystical streak and stubbornness. I should make sure she remembered.

"Show me Rome," I said. "Your Rome. Not just the Forum and the monuments. Show me the living city as you live it. Show me what you love."

Emrys reached as though he would put his arm about my waist and thought better of it. "I will if you will show me the Alexandria you love, when we are next there."

"That's a promise," I said, and smiled.

WE WENT all over the city together, walking arm-in-arm. No one paid us the slightest attention. If I looked like some freedwoman, Emrys looked like exactly what he was, one of Caesar's Keltic Auxiliaries. It was, after the pomp and ceremony that attended the Queen, a considerable relief.

We visited the markets and looked at the baths, bought food that Emrys swore I should try. I was a bit dubious of seafood stew with apple wine in it, but it turned out to be delicious. We ate at trestle tables under the tree outside a popular little shop. Most of the patrons didn't stay to eat, but took their food along with them, ripe cheese with a thick rind, blood sausages, round loaves of barley bread. Most of them were Gaulish and German, chatting in unfamiliar languages as they came and went. In addition to the food, the shop seemed to have a little of everything, plates and dishes, beads, knives, and various cosmetic things. I lingered briefly over a bolt of wool woven in a checked pattern, dark blue and white.

"Thread dyed with woad," Emrys said. "The design isn't stamped on, like the Greek cloth. The raw wool is dyed before it's spun. So it doesn't fade like the other does."

I thought about buying it, but I didn't have many places to wear heavy wool. In Alexandria it would be exotic, but probably too warm.

"It's like the shops at home in the Jewish Quarter," I said. "Places that sell a little bit of everything to people from their homelands."

"I can find you a kosher butcher if you want," Emrys said. "There are Jews here too. Not nearly as many as in Alexandria, and they're regulated a lot more. But they're here. And there's a Temple of Isis here too."

"Is there?"

Emrys nodded. "I suppose it was Egyptians living here who built it originally, but there are a lot of Romans who go there now too, at least to celebrate the Pelagia in the spring. Some consul or other ordered it torn down about ten years ago, but he couldn't find anybody willing to take on the goddess' displeasure by doing it."

"I should go there while I'm here," I said. A prayer, I thought, O Queen of Heaven, for Your hands on earth.

We walked the last little bit uphill, and the narrow street turned suddenly into a wide plaza. Bounded on three sides by white temples, the fourth side gave onto a steep cliff and a magnificent view of the city. The river curved like a snake through it, and all stood suddenly visible, as though we were at once become gods. A grassy lawn ran right up to the edge, dotted here and there with statues, and the sky arched above. The city lay at our feet.

I turned, clutching at Emrys' arm. "It's glorious," I said.

He grinned and put his arm about me. "This is the old citadel," he said. "Capitoline Hill. Behind us there is the Arx where the augurs take the omens, and the Temple of Juno. And a lot of other temples besides. It's not allowed to build anymore up here because it's already too crowded."

Endless foot traffic moved over the bridges, and the forums were easy to pick out amid the tangle of buildings. I lifted my eyes from the city. Already Rome grew outside her walls. The walls were dark streaks where some streets ended, but the buildings huddled on both sides all the same. Beyond her, I could just see where countryside began, though the city continued some distance along the highways, great radial roads fanning out from the walls.

"It's beautiful," I said, and knew that what I said was inadequate.

In the distance, above the haze from the city, a bird of prey turned on the wind, sliding slowly away on the invisible roads of the air. The augurs would call it an omen, I thought. Or perhaps they saw that same bird here every day.

"I've stood here before with you," I said, and in that moment had the strongest sense that it was true. The river below curling through tree-covered banks, brown and swollen with spring rain, morning light over green trees and the high, endless sky.

I reached for his hand. It was where I thought it would be, and I stood transfixed. The city. The forested valley. It was one.

ET IN ARCADIA EGO ☉

I hardly expected it when a few days later a messenger arrived for me bearing a very formal scroll. "Thank you," I said as I took it.

He folded his hands behind his back. "Domina, my master has asked me to wait for your reply."

"Your master is?"

"Marcus Vipsanius Agrippa," he said.

"I see." I carried the scroll away, to open it in the light that came in through the impluvium. Now, I thought. Now he writes me letters. But my fingers were shaking as I untied the cord.

Hail Charmian,

This comes to you to invite you to visit at the country home of my father, Lucius Vipsanius Agrippa, from his heir, Marcus Vipsanius Agrippa, Tribune. I hope that you will come. It would give me pleasure if you did, and I could show you the house and our farms and other lands. We have many fine cattle and also our goats are well known for the sweetness of their milk, which is because of their pasture, which makes them cheerful and well grown. If this is agreeable to you please reply and say that it is. If it's not, please reply anyhow.

M. Agrippa

I stood holding the scroll, hesitating. I should say no, I thought. I have my duties. And yet.

What would it be like, I wondered, to do something entirely different? To live as a lover, not a sister. To be prized for pleasure, not for my mind. If I wanted, Cleopatra would manumit me. She had promised me so, long since. What would it be like to be instead a hetaira, a companion, prized for beauty and wit? I should leave behind worry about affairs of state, about politics and diplomacy. I should plan private parties for lovers, not state banquets. I should arrange all for the pleasure of one man, not for the good of a kingdom. What would it be like?

Marcus was young, only eighteen. He might not marry for years, and even if he did a hetaira was no challenge to a Roman wife. I had already borne a child. And he was not the kind of man to cut all ties, even if passion waned. I could have a house of my own, manage slaves that were mine, not my sister's. And if Marcus grew tired of me or me of him there would be other men, powerful, interesting men whose acquaintance I would make. I could make my symposia famous, as hetairae had in the past, all of the best poets and statesmen gathering in my garden.

And I should be here, in Rome. I should be here, with Caesar.

The world turned on the fulcrum of Caesar, as it had turned on Alexander. In that day it had been the Athenian hetaira, Thais the Firebrand, who had burned Persepolis in revenge for the Persians burning Athens, who had sat at dinner with Alexander and urged him to it, who had won the love of Ptolemy and had kept it all her life. What would it be like, to be such? To stand among Companions for love alone?

"Wait," I said to the slave, and went to see the Queen.

WHEN I SHOWED HER THE LETTER, Cleopatra raised one eyebrow. "You can do as you wish, Charmian," she said. She took the scroll from me and read it again. "He is not the most eloquent suitor," she said, and I wondered what Caesar had written to her. Whatever it was, he was certainly better at expressing himself. "He almost sounds as though he intends to sell you livestock."

"I don't think that's what he has in mind," I said.

"He is Demetria's father," Cleopatra said. "But do you understand what that would mean in Roman law?"

"Not entirely," I said. Iras was the one who had studied law before we came to Rome, while I had studied custom.

"A Roman father has the power of life and death over his children," she said. "Not simply in the matter of exposing infants, but forever. And while he might acknowledge her, Demetria was born the daughter of a slave. She cannot be his heir. Even if you bear him a son, he cannot be his heir, though he could inherit property in his will, should he choose to acknowledge him."

"I know," I said. "But many companions have done well enough anyway."

My sister looked at me, and her eyes were troubled. "Do you love him?"

"I don't know," I said. "He swore that he loved me in Egypt, but I don't know how he feels now. I don't know how I feel now."

Cleopatra handed the scroll back to me. "Maybe you should go and find out. If you don't, you will regret it. I know you well enough to tell you that!"

I laughed. "You're right. I have to see, don't I?"

"Go and see," she said. "And don't buy any livestock!"

They say that Campania in autumn is one of the most beautiful places in the world, and I cannot fault the beauty of it. We journeyed south from Rome along the Via Appia in a carriage, a slow way to travel but a certain way to see the beauties of the countryside.

At first it was hard to tell we had even left the city. Even after the walls were behind us, the city continued, miles upon miles of houses, shops, and markets. Marcus, seated beside me, pointed out that these were all small villages, with their own names—Pollitorium, Tellene, Bovillae—but I should not have known it. They seemed like one endless city, Rome stretching out long fingers into the countryside, toward the Alban Hills.

We spent all day on the road, following the Via Appia through the hills and valleys and across the Pontine Marshes. It was evening before we came to Formia, and to a taverna there that Marcus said was good. By that time I could have cared less. I was not used to extended travel except by sea, and the continual jolting of the coach had left me somewhat nauseous.

After some miles, Marcus confined himself to saying how wonderful the road was and explaining to me how it was made, an explanation that might have seemed more interesting were we at sea. I had asked why we hadn't simply sailed down the coast in perfect comfort from Ostia to Neapolis, but Marcus looked at me as if I were mad and launched into an explanation of road building that seemed quite at odds with his usual style of talking, as though it were some presentation he had once been called upon to give, concluding with the smug assessment that "no Roman need ever travel by sea unless in some forlorn place where there are no roads."

I nearly asked him why in the world he was blathering like that, but didn't. I should learn to make myself agreeable. After all, a hetaira must. I should have to school my tongue and smile politely when men rattled on about layers of gravel and sand and other aspects of roadbed construction. For his part, I suppose he thought I didn't feel well, for as soon as we arrived at the taverna I put a cold cloth across my eyes and I went straight to sleep.

I woke to the bright light of morning and the sound of endless carts and coaches on the road outside, all of the traffic of the Republic passing by. I went to the window and looked out. The courtyard wall only extended as high as the second floor, so I had a view of the Via Appia, already crawling with traffic. Beyond, the outline of the Alban Hills was still visible, blurred by distance and autumn. I had time to wash my face and breakfast before we went on.

At midmorning we reached the city of Capua, where the Via Appia turned inland to cross the mountains. Instead of staying on it, we turned toward the coast on the Via Popilia, which should take us the rest of the way. I had thought the traffic would be less, but the Via

Popilia was also a major road, and there was it seemed a tremendous amount of trade between Capua and Neapolis.

"It's not much farther," Marcus said. "We turn off the Via Popilia after only six miles. And then it's just a small road to the farm."

I nodded, watching the countryside go by. There seemed to be so few people for the amount of land. In Egypt, one came upon small villages constantly, not even out of sight of one another. Here, fields golden with grain stretched uninterrupted, and I saw why Campania had been considered the breadbasket of Rome before they bought so much from Egypt. Now and then we passed a side road, hardly more than a muddy track, going off between fields, or glimpsed far across the fields a house surrounded by olive trees, the road marked with a line of cedars.

"Where are all of the people?" I asked. "Where are the farmers who work this land?"

Marcus shrugged. "Most of these are estates. There aren't many small farmers left in this part of the country. We have about six hundred slaves who work the land. A lot of it is in pasture for the cattle, but they take work too. There's haying and we grow our own grain for fodder. We also own about a dozen women to do the work in the house."

"Six hundred slaves?" The Great House of Pharaoh owned less than two hundred, all told, and I doubted there was a lord in Egypt who owned more.

"Six hundred." He nodded. "Not so many, really, because a lot of it's pasture. Some estates have a couple of thousand."

"Slaves from where?" I asked, remembering all Emrys had said. I could hardly imagine what one would do with a thousand slaves. Even the pyramids had not been built that way, long ago. The artisans and workmen who built our tombs were free peasants.

"Gauls, Germans, Greeks, whatever," he said. "They can be manumitted eventually, or buy themselves out. Though generally it's the craftsmen who can do that, the Greeks usually. The Germans don't know anything but farming, away over the Rhenus."

"And hunting, I suppose," I said. It was true that it was inefficient, the way the Egyptian peasants divided and subdivided each piece of land, until some parcels were hardly big enough to reach across if they lay in rich bottomland beside the river, litigating and arguing over hereditary leases from Amon. In dry seasons when the Nile did not rise enough, some bits didn't get enough to produce at all, and hunger haunted the villages. Still, I liked it better. They had their families and their gods, their own people and their own names.

Marcus scratched his head. "Actually, we can't let them hunt. It's not done, arming slaves in this part of the country. It hasn't been very long since Spartacus led his slave revolt here. You could still see some of the crosses where Crassus crucified about six thousand of them along the Via Appia when I was a boy. He gave orders for their remains never to be taken down, you see. An example."

"I see," I said, and was proud to say that my voice was calm. That had happened the year before I was born, no doubt to kinsmen of my mother's who had been sold less fortunately than she. She had had the best of it, a pleasure slave to Pharaoh in Ptolemy's white city by the sea. I could not even imagine crucifying six thousand slaves. In Egypt such a thing had never happened.

Marcus looked at me, and his brow furrowed. "I don't know why we're talking about this, Charmian. Every time I talk to you I say the wrong thing. And I don't even know what I said."

"You didn't say anything wrong," I said, fixing a smile on my face. After all, Marcus Agrippa had not yet been born when it happened. He was only eighteen.

"It's not that I like it," he said abruptly. "It's not what I would have done."

I raised an eyebrow.

Marcus looked out the window, toward the hills that rose to the south of us. The sun glinted golden off brazen flecks in his hair. "There are a lot of things that have to change. And only the right person can change them. We've had seventy years of civil wars, one strong man after another fighting each other, like wolves in a pack that have lost their leader. No plan that lasts more than a few years, no one thinking about the welfare of the Roman people rather than their political career. That has to end. I saw that in Egypt." He looked at me. "We need a king."

"Caesar?"

He nodded gravely. "It's treason, and I will speak it. If Caesar wants to overthrow the Republic, I'll stand by him. The Republic doesn't work. There has to be a way to govern besides chaos and blood. We don't have democracy. We have the rule of the richest, where every man spends all of his time competing for power. If the power were once and forever vested in the hands of a worthy house, there would be no need for all that. A king could concentrate on ruling, as consuls may never do."

"A king spends a good amount of time guarding his back, even in an ancient house," I said, thinking of the treasons hatched against Auletes.

"If he is fortunate, a king has loyal men to guard his back." He looked at me pointedly. "Or to take a knife for him."

"I can't dispute that," I said. "But remember, there are good kings and bad kings."

"And good dictators and bad," he replied. "But the former is more sure and less prone to the whims of the mob." He looked out the window at the fields, at a grove of young olive trees along a winding stream. "How can we even think about changing how things are done when all we can do is everlasting politics? There are things that must be mended. Surely this sprawling, ungainly thing is not what Rome is." For a moment his voice seemed much older than a young man of eighteen. "We should have our own free men working their own lands, considering it an honor to serve in the legions and live and die for their people, married to one woman who stands beside them rather than all this divorcing again and again, raising children who grow up in the free country air and have due reverence for the gods."

My eyes pricked unexpectedly. "My dear Marcus," I said gently, "you are dreaming of a time that is past."

"Why should it be past?" he asked. "Why should we abandon the things that we once were?"

"Rome is not a collection of houses by a river with fields and fishing boats and young olive trees. It is a city of half a million people. It's an empire stretching from the northernmost reaches of Gaul to Judea! Rome cannot be a settlement of pious farmers, not when its people speak twenty languages and it covers half the world!" I put my hand on his forearm, filled suddenly with tenderness for him. "You may not like this new Rome, but this is what is."

Marcus looked away. "I wish I lived in a simpler time, when one knew what was right and just did it."

"I don't think it has ever been thus," I said. "I don't think it's ever been so simple."

He nodded toward the window. "Look on that," he said, "and tell me so."

I leaned across him to see what he pointed to, and a chill ran down my back like a cold hand. The green and golden fields sloped slowly upward toward a great mountain, reposing like some vast slumbering beast, quiescent, its peak wreathed in a tiny puff of white cloud.

"Vesuvius," Marcus said. "The forge of the gods."

"A gate," I whispered. "A forge, a tomb, a womb." The mountain terrified and beckoned at once, and I wanted to shout, to turn the coach around; at the same moment I knew that whatever menace it held, it was not for me. Not today.

"You see," he said, and I realized that I was holding his hand so tightly his fingers were white.

I let go. "It's amazing."

"It's beautiful," he said. "And it gives life to this coast. But I cannot ever find myself entirely easy with it."

"No," I said, still looking out the window. "I couldn't either." With a jolt the coach turned off the main road onto a dirt track. "What? Are we going right up on the mountain?"

"Not so far," he said. "Our pastures sit at Vesuvius' feet, while some of our vineyards are terraced above, and that's also where we keep our goats. This is the north side of the mountain. If we stayed on the main road we'd go past the mountain and on into Neapolis, and then to the beach towns on the other side, Pompeii, Herculaneum, and Stabiae. Farther on along the north side, past our estate, you can come around to a view of Capri, and the town of Cumae."

"Cumae," I said, tasting the word and wondering where I'd heard it before.

"Where the Sybil used to live," he said.

"And the Gates of the Underworld," I said.

He put his arm around me. I was shivering. "We don't have to go there," he said.

I nodded. "You're right. We don't."

And yet I could see a future in which I should come there with Caesarion and Agrippa, with the prince and the soldier who served his father, come to the Gates of the Underworld that served Rome as Abydos served Egypt, so that he, too, might come forth by day.

That autumn day it was still possible.

We came to the villa a few minutes later. Set back from the road, with a high wall screened by cedars, it crowned a rise just below the mountain's skirts. I noted, as we passed through, that there was a place where the wall seemed to have been breached and patched, though now it was all covered over by climbing rosebushes. In Egypt, private homes might have walls to keep out vagrants or to keep in livestock, but one did not expect country houses to be besieged. On the other hand, we had no slave revolts either.

Marcus' parents seemed to be away, and the servants greeted him as though he were already the master of the house. I recalled what he had said about his father's disgrace, and that these lands had not been confiscated only due to Marcus. I imagined that if they had been, then the old woman who came to greet him would have been sold on the block. Yes, I thought, watching Marcus greet his old nurse with affection, he was already the master here, if he chose to be. This was clearly his home, and it suited him more than Rome had. And a man who could show affection to his old nurse was a man worth having.

"Demophile," he said, "this is Charmian. It would please me greatly if you could attend to her and make her comfortable. We'll take dinner on the terrace rather than in the dining room, if you do not mind."

The old nurse raised her eyebrows at me, an assessing look.

"I am certain I shall be well taken care of," I said in Koine, giving her a half smile. I knew I should be the same, the first time Caesarion brings home a hetaira for my approval.

I spent the afternoon in the bath, being pampered and polished as well as one might expect in a fine establishment anywhere. Their baths were not entirely new, nor as large as Caesar's, but they were more charming in many ways, with a cool pool that looked out through an arcade decorated with a fine old statue of Diana into a small walled garden. A woman's garden, I thought, from the scale and the love that had been lavished on a huge old rosebush that climbed the wall, nearly hanging from the branches of a dwarf apricot tree.

A woman bath attendant massaged me, and I lay listening to the birds outside in the garden and the soft lapping of the pool. I rarely had time for this, even if I had the inclination. Every day was so busy. A hetaira would have leisure. If I had nothing except the ordering of my own house and the care of Demetria, how many hours there would be in the day! I could get used to spending an afternoon in the bath, to having my nails hennaed and pumice stone applied to my feet by a slave who knew what to do.

The sun was casting long shadows, and most of the garden stood in shade before I went to dress for dinner. After some consideration, I settled on an aqua silk that was very simple in style, the luxury of the fabric and its beautiful drape carrying the effect. I caught it up at the shoulders with a pair of gold pins cunningly worked like dragonflies, their iridescent wings of thin gold. It was, I thought, the perfect dress for seduction, for the end of the chase. It had been so long.

I put my hair up and endured the curling irons, so it fell in soft ringlets from combs and pins, the largest of them a dragonfly that matched the ones on my shoulder. With a himation of sheer white embroidered with aqua butterflies, I thought I at least looked good enough for a hetaira.

Marcus seemed to think so too, for when I came out onto the terrace he caught his breath and all but jumped to his feet.

There were three couches there, little tables before them, but only one was laid, so I came and sat by him, though it took a bit of doing to get him to sit before me. He lay back on his left arm, and I sat at his knees. If I had leaned back it would have been into the circle of his body, but of course he did not touch me, simply waited for the slave to pour the wine, as is proper. There were some sort of grilled sausages, and a relish of olives and parsley in olive oil and vinegar, good crisp bread and finely chopped cabbages dressed with vinegar and celery, all very good and fresh.

I complimented the situation of the terrace, the view, and the way the terraces sloped down the hill in front, as from where we sat we could see over the wall, so far down the hill was it on this side. Before us, Vesuvius reared up, dominating the landscape. One lone shred of cloud clung about its peak in an otherwise cloudless sky.

The terrace lay in shadow. "Charmian," Marcus said, and I heard the hesitation in his voice. "There's something I want to ask you."

"What is it?" I said.

At that moment the slave came along with the main course, pork cooked in a fresh fig glaze, and we could not continue until he had served us and withdrawn behind one of the potted trees beside the door. Automatically, I approved of the well-trained staff.

"Will you marry me?"

"What?" I looked around at him, an uncomplimentary disbelief in my voice.

"I asked if you would marry me." He sat up straight on the couch and caught my hands.

"That's impossible."

"No, it isn't. Listen, I've worked it out." He held my hands in his large ones, his eyes bright. "I've been thinking of nothing else for two years than how to make it work. When I couldn't forget you, I knew there had to be a way. There must always be a way for lovers."

"You can't marry someone who isn't Roman," I said. "You have to marry a Roman citizen. And your parents? What would they say? Marcus…"

"My father can't gainsay me," he said. "He owes me too much. And my mother would never interfere with something that would make me happy. I've worked it out. There's an old man with land near here, a client of my father's. He only had one son, and he was killed at Pharsalus. He's got no heirs now, no family at all. So it would be perfectly natural for him to adopt his niece if she were raised abroad and orphaned. His sister might have been married to a man who did business in Greece, and when they died their daughter decided to come home to Italy and live with her old uncle. It all makes sense. He'll swear up and down that you're his niece. Once he's adopted you, there's no bar at all to our marriage!"

"Except that it's a lie," I said.

"It's a lie that harms no one," he said. "I would never suggest it if he had any relatives living, but the poor old man is all alone. He gains a daughter, a son-in-law, grandchildren. He'd spend the rest of his life treated as a beloved family member. He's not well-to-do, and it wouldn't be an excellent match for me, but it's a respectable one. And given that I grew up here and I love it here, it's easy to come up with a story about how we met one day in the countryside and fell in love."

"You really mean that."

He must have taken my expression for concern that the story would hold, because he rushed on. "It will work! I'm sure it will! We'll say you grew up in Athens, and that you were living very quietly with your old uncle, mourning your parents, when we met by accident. I came to buy some goats from your uncle, or something like that."

"What a lovely story," I said. I felt as though my hands had turned to ice. I heard my voice going on. "And where does the Queen of Egypt come into this?"

"Why would the Queen of Egypt come into it at all?" For a moment Marcus looked confused. "You've never met her." He stopped. For the first time he felt the storm coming, saw the leaves flying before the wind. "You'd be free, Charmian! Not a slave all your life, but free. You'd be the mistress of this house someday. You'd be respectable, a Roman matron, with a station in life and plenty of money."

My voice only shook a little. "I am a Royal Ptolemy." I stood up, stepping around the little table to face him. "I am the descendant of kings, of eight generations of kings since Ptolemy son of Lagos won Alexander's crown. I am the daughter of a slave so proud that men talk about her twenty years after her death, of her pride and her laughter and her beauty. And I am the daughter of Ptolemy Auletes, Pharaoh of Egypt, who gave me to Cleopatra to serve her all her days. I will not pretend to be less, not for you or any man!"

"But I thought that you..." He looked entirely confused.

"Do you not understand that I have charge of the heir to the throne of Egypt? That I am responsible for Caesar's son, who you might have as your king?" And how had I even thought of it, how had I even considered for one moment leaving him? How had I even considered leaving Cleopatra? "I speak five languages. I manage a budget of thousands of talents a year. If I say to the Queen this should be done, it is done because she trusts me. Do you not understand that cities and provinces are taxed on my word? That levees are built and ships made and soldiers hired? Do you not understand that you are asking me to leave off the government of the wealthiest and oldest nation in the world, the governance of which is my birthright, to come and be your wife?"

Standing there panting in the shadows, I could have cursed myself. Lady Isis, I thought, surely it was love or desire that clouded my mind! How could I have ever even considered such a thing?

"Being my wife is not such a small thing," he said, getting to his feet.

"Compared to what?" I snapped, and regretted it almost as the words left my mouth.

Marcus colored. "I have offered you everything."

"If I will pretend to be something I am not," I said. "If I will pretend for the rest of my life to be Roman, to disavow my father and all of the Ptolemies who came before me, leave my sisters and pretend not to know them, and most assuredly of all to disavow my slave mother who was no more than these men who work your lands."

"But you..." He did not need to finish the sentence. His face showed his thought.

"I would be Roman," I said. "I would be the best thing on this earth."

"I didn't say that," he said.

"But you think it," I said. "All of the things that I am are nothing to you, compared to the status of a Roman matron. What in the world could be better than to be the wife of Marcus Vipsanius Agrippa?"

"Then what did you come here for, dressed like that?" he snapped.

"To be your lover," I said. "You see, you have overbid. You did not need to offer me marriage. Kindness would have sufficed to get me into your bed."

"I don't want you in my bed! I want you to be my wife! I've dreamed of nothing but you for two years, been true to you every day."

I shook my head, trying not to let anger turn into sorrow. "You've dreamed of a lovely time we had together, an interlude, a beautiful memory. If you had let it stay that, you should have been happy. Why did you have to ruin everything by trying to turn it into something impossible?" I turned away, toward the mountain, so that he would not see the tears in my eyes. "I thought you knew me."

"So did I," he said. "I'll take you back to Rome in the morning." I heard the sound of his feet on the stones, moving swiftly away.

I bent my head against the pillar and closed my eyes.

TIES OF FLESH

I ras was the first person I saw when I got back. I stopped wearily in the atrium and sat down on a bench.

She came and sat beside me. "It didn't go well?"

"No," I said. I shook my sandals off and cooled my feet against the stone. "Please don't tell me you knew it wouldn't."

"I wasn't going to say that," she said. "I wished you well. I like Agrippa."

"You do?"

Iras nodded. "A lot of the same reasons I like you. He's stubborn and he follows his own code. But the two of you—Ares and Aphrodite, war and love together. He's too much Ares for me. What should Ares have to do with Artemis?"

I smiled at my sister. "And what god should you have?"

Iras leaned back on the bench. "You know who goes with Isis Sophia. Serapis, Dionysos, or none at all. Without that touch of darkness or madness, what is there?"

"I've never seen you interested in someone like that," I said.

Iras shrugged, one strand of hair escaping from her combs. "I have no desire to live in the Underworld, sister. There is too much here, and I have too many responsibilities. Besides"—she looked at me sideways—"if I joined the procession of maenads, where should it end? Those drunk women with haggard eyes, going from tavern to tavern in the middle of the night, begging men to come home with them who have long since sought other pastures? Clinging to artists who have no talent, explaining to their friends that genius will burn sometime, they're sure of it?"

"But does it have to be that way?" I asked. "What about the poets who really are that talented, the scientists who actually are as smart as they think they are?"

"How do you tell the difference if you're blinded by Eros?" she asked. "Doesn't every man look a genius or a hero to the eyes of love?"

"Not to me," I said. "I never mistook Lucan for any kind of genius or hero. And Agrippa…" How should I say that I was certain he was every bit as good as he thought he was, that he was better even than he knew?

"You weren't in love with Lucan," Iras said. "Nor with Agrippa."

"No," I said, "not enough. Not enough to go mad for them or to destroy everything." I looked sideways at her. "Perhaps I never will be. Perhaps the passion just isn't in me, to be willing to live and die for someone."

"And why wouldn't that be a good thing?" Iras asked in her best rhetorical tone. "If you are not sent mad by Eros to the detriment of your child and your own best interests, is that not something to thank Aphrodite for?"

"Agrippa wanted to marry me," I said. "He had some convoluted scheme about getting an old man to pretend I was his Roman niece. It would all hold together nicely, as long as I never made any attempt to see you or Cleopatra or Caesarion ever again."

"Did you tell him about Demetria?"

I shook my head. "I hadn't gotten so far yet. And now I won't. He could claim her completely under Roman law. He could take her away from me."

"The Queen wouldn't allow that," Iras said.

"We are in Rome," I said. "And I won't take the gamble. Not with Demetria."

EMRYS CAME THAT AFTERNOON, grim faced, without Caesar. "Charmian," he said, "I would like to speak to the Queen."

"Is it about Caesar?" I asked, my hand to my throat. He was not young. Illness could come on unexpectedly...

"No," he said. "It's nothing like that. It's about Princess Arsinoe."

It took me a moment to remember. Arsinoe had been brought to Rome for Caesar's Triumph, nearly two years ago. I supposed she must be in prison somewhere, but actually I had not thought of her.

Emrys' face was white and grim.

"What has happened?" I asked.

"Nothing," he said. "Except that I am risking my career in doing this. Now will you take me to see the Queen or not?"

"I will," I said. In the end, I trusted him.

I HARDLY KNEW HER. She might have been a stranger hunched in the corner of the reeking cell, an overturned slop bucket beside her. Her dark hair tangled around her face and her hands were covered with filth.

The Queen stopped in the doorway, her himation drawn about her.

Behind us and Iras, Emrys and the jailer stood in the hall. "She's been here since the Triumph," Emrys said. "When she was paraded in chains through Rome and her lover Ganymede was killed before her eyes."

"Arsinoe?" Cleopatra said, waiting for some flash of recognition.

The woman said nothing, only huddled farther back in the corner, her ragged dress drawn up so far that her privates were visible, caked with dried menstrual blood.

"She had a baby last spring that the jailers took and exposed," Emrys said in his grim, cold tone. "Anyone could pay them for the privilege. Anyone who wanted to say they'd had a Ptolemaic princess. Of course now nobody really wants to. Not with her like that."

"Arsinoe?" The Queen knelt.

Through the matted veil of her hair I saw one eye I recognized, the proud profile of the Ptolemies. She did not spit or cry, just gave one animal keen.

I stepped back into the corridor, my stomach lurching. The jailer shuffled his feet, but Emrys stood between us.

"I thought you should know, Gracious Queen," he said in Koine.

I closed my eyes. I was not here. This was not real. I stood in some other place. My stomach heaved again. Control. Pride. Iras did not do this. The Queen did not. Not in front of that jailer.

Cleopatra's voice cut like a blade. "Iras, Praefectus, attend on me. I am going to speak with Caesar." I heard the door scraping shut, and then her voice at my elbow. "Charmian, you may go home."

"Thank you, Gracious Queen," I gasped, escaping into the bright morning.

I WENT HOME and threw up my breakfast, and then took a long bath to wash the prison stench out of my hair, leaning back in the water and staring up at the ceiling, utterly ashamed of myself.

Mother Isis, I thought, I did not like her. She was not my friend, and in Egypt she would have killed us all if she could. But I would not wish this upon my worst enemy. Mother Isis, she is my sister too. Mother Isis, preserve us. Sweet Mother, save us.

I got up from the bath and dressed. Iras and the Queen were still not back. I joined Caesarion and Demetria in some childish game, fetching the balls they had thrown away and clutching them too tightly when they ran to me, their little limbs clean and strong and their arms confidently around my neck. Nothing would ever hurt them. Nothing, while I had breath in my body.

Mother Isis, I prayed, let me die before I come to that. Let me die.

Caesarion put his face against mine. "Why you sad?"

"I'm not, precious," I said, pulling Demetria in against my other side. "I just had some difficult business this morning. That's all. Let's go into the garden, and I'll tell you a story."

"Dog!" shouted Demetria, who was six months younger and had fewer words.

"Dog," agreed Caesarion. "And prince."

"All right," I said, and we went out and I settled both on my lap, a trick that wouldn't last much longer. "Once there was a prince named Horus, and His uncle Set wanted to kill Him. So Set sent Death to Him in the form of a snake, a cobra that would sneak into the little prince's bedroom and bite Him. But the prince had a loyal dog who slept every night in His room…"

We stayed there until Iras came. I heard her steps on the path and looked up at her in shame.

"Princess Arsinoe will go to sanctuary at the Temple of Artemis at Ephesos," Iras said, and her voice was almost even.

"I see," I said quietly, so as not to upset the children. "Did Caesar know?"

"Caesar professed surprise, and said he had not thought of the Princess Arsinoe since the Triumph. He said that the Queen might do as she liked in the matter."

"I see," I said. An answer that might mean anything. Or might mean just as he said, that once she was no longer important he had forgotten about her entirely. "And Emrys?"

"Decurion Aurelianus will not be punished, if that's what you mean. At least not directly."

"His career," I said. Caesarion was wiggling, and I let him go. Demetria toddled after him like his shadow. I leaned back into the shade of a palm. "Why did he do it, Iras?"

"Because he is a good man," Iras said, and went back in the house.

It was a month before Emrys came to the villa again. Autumn had turned into winter, and the Roman Saturnalia was fast approaching. Even with the hypocaust working, we still found it cold at night, and the endless rain that came down day in and day out was depressing. Iras wandered around bundled in shawls, and the rest of the servants we'd brought from Egypt complained constantly. I did not take it as badly as most, and for once blessed my thick northern blood, although I suppose it was really not so very cold.

Emrys laughed at me when I complained of the cold, though he brought me a heavy cloak of the thread-dyed wool I had liked earlier in the fall, and I wore it everywhere. It was blue-and-cream-checked, with squares of cream alternating with lighter and darker blue, exotic and very pretty. Also warm.

I was coming to appreciate his company more and more, his ironic sense of humor and his good heart. After the disaster that had been Marcus Agrippa, Emrys' company was balm to me. More than once I wished that something might come of it, but I knew too well from Dion that there was no point in wishing for that.

At least the impending holiday seemed to put the Roman Senate in an expansive mood. Treaties were signed with Egypt, guaranteeing a good price on grain and renewing "the bonds of friendship with a faithful ally of Rome." Egypt agreed to supply auxiliary troops for Caesar's next campaign in the east, which should probably begin in the spring when the sailing season opened, and the troops that Caesar had left behind in Egypt would form the core of a new army that should protect Rome and Egypt alike against the Parthians.

"Do they think the Parthians are such a threat?" I asked, when the Queen told me all of this.

Cleopatra put down her pen and smiled. "I'm less concerned about the Parthians than Parthian territory. As long as we have Judea as a buffer between us, it's moot. But Egypt has ancient claims as far north as Damascus, and I mean to see them carried out. Antipater and I can work out Judea between us. The Jews have more interest in the Egyptian sphere than the Roman, and more than anything they want a prince of their own rather than being swallowed up as a Roman province. Antipater's even sent that son of his, Herod, to Rome so that he can make friends. I think they'd rather deal with the House of Ptolemy so that they know where they stand than with the Roman Senate. They haven't forgotten Pompeius."

"Are we going home now that we've got the treaty?" I asked.

The Queen sighed. "Not yet. We'll leave in the spring, when the sailing season opens. When Caesar leaves for his next campaign. There are some things that must be done first."

"Such as?"

"Caesar will be appointed Dictator for life," she said. "That should not take much longer. And he must make a new will."

"I thought Caesarion could not inherit under Roman law," I said.

"Cannot inherit his citizenship or his titles," Cleopatra said. The color stood high in her face. "He may inherit personal property, just as any man may leave remembrances upon his death to freedmen, or to business contacts who are not Roman. That which Caesar wins in the east will be his personal property, and he will take the lands for himself, rather than ceding them to the Senate."

I nodded slowly. "Which gives him a power base the Senate can't control, and Egypt's ancient properties left to Caesarion. That's clever."

"Thank you," Cleopatra said.

I laughed. "Your idea, not Caesar's?"

"Let's say it was a joint idea."

THE DAYS GREW LONGER, the Lupercalia approached. All through the winter we had entertained regularly, usually Caesar and a party of his friends, notably Senators with votes on the important trade treaties who wanted to meet the Queen of Egypt in person, or businessmen who did enormous volumes of trade with Egypt. Sometimes there were women at the parties as well. Unlike Greek women, Roman women did not live sequestered, and while they took no role in public life, there were many who wielded a great deal of power through men.

One woman who was invited from time to time was the wife of Caesar's right hand, Marcus Antonius. Fulvia was a handsome woman in her mid-thirties, with a proud chin and long black hair that she wore in the absolute latest fashions and the air of someone who knows she is a great beauty. Perhaps she had been, fifteen years before, but she had the kind of looks that did not last once youthful prettiness was done. Fulvia, more than any other, set out to make herself charming to the Queen. And it was she who suggested a garden party.

Cleopatra protested that surely it was too cold, but Fulvia laughed. "Just a small party! After all, the weather has turned and we shall have flowers soon. The almonds are budding already. If you bring some braziers out for the fainthearted to gather around, it will be quite warm."

And who's to have the charge of that, I thought. And who will be fretting and worrying over the temperature and trying to make sure the guests don't freeze. Me, of course. It's worrying enough to have a party outside somewhere it rains frequently.

"We always have garden parties in the winter," Fulvia said. "It's too warm in the summer. Besides, your garden is charming."

Caesar leaned back on his couch, smiling. "It sounds as though you must have a party, my dear. If only because Fulvia will not remove her teeth otherwise."

Marcus Antonius, who shared his couch with Fulvia, colored. "She doesn't mean to be pushy, do you, Fulvia?"

Caesar laughed and blew a kiss in Fulvia's direction. "Of course she does. But there's no harm in it, and possibly some good. Your wife has a head for politics, Marcus."

Fulvia reached up as though catching the kiss and pointedly clasped it to her bosom, leaning back against Antonius. "I think it would do the Queen good to be seen by more people, that's all." She looked at Cleopatra. "You could come and watch the Lupercalia procession from our house."

"I'm afraid I don't know what that is," Cleopatra said gracefully, looking for a cue from Caesar. Of course she did know perfectly well. It was in her briefing scrolls.

"It's a fertility festival," Antonius said, shifting on his couch. "There's a sacrifice and a rite. It's special this year because Caesar has created a third college of priests for it."

"Of which you are the first magister," Caesar said, holding out his cup. I refilled it without him even looking around. "Thus guaranteeing a good turnout for the procession. Who among the ladies of Rome will not want to watch Marcus Antonius run nude through the city striking people with thongs?"

Antonius held his empty cup out too. "It's for fertility," he said again to the Queen. "It's a blessing on women to be touched by the whips, so women who are pregnant or who want to be crowd the ropes so that they can be blessed."

"I see," Cleopatra said. "And are you suggesting I need such a blessing?"

Caesar laughed. "I think she does well enough with her own old goat not to need the goats of the Lupercal!"

Antonius roared, his cup shaking back and forth while I tried to refill it.

The Queen arched an eyebrow. "I had not taken you for a priest, Antonius."

"Antonius has been an Initiate of Dionysos for many years," Fulvia said.

Marcus Antonius stilled the cup and shot her a glance. "Not so many years, I hope," he said. "After all, Caesar only legalized the worship of Dionysos in Rome four years ago."

"Of course she means in the last four years," Caesar said, his eyes dancing. "I am certain you had nothing to do with Dionysos before, law-abiding and temperate as you are."

The Queen lifted her cup for me to refill. There was still half the wine left, but then she never liked to drink the dregs. "The worship of Dionysos was illegal?" I imagine she was as shocked as I, though it did not sound in her voice. Of course we had heard of such things, in the past or in barbarous lands, but the idea of rendering any religion illegal in a place so close as Rome, so recently as four years ago, was frightening.

"Oh yes," Caesar said, lounging back on his cushions. "Most of the Eastern religions have been illegal at one time or another. Isis and Serapis were, for a while. The worship of Dionysos was thought to lead women to infidelity, and therefore be incompatible with Roman values. It's foolish, of course, to think that ideas can be banned and kept out, like a man with a leaking boat bailing furiously while the water flows in between the planks." He took a sip. "Better to bring things into the light than to hide them. Darkness is where the rumors of human sacrifice and rape breed."

Antonius nodded gravely. "The worship of Dionysos isn't like that. People don't understand."

"But perhaps you will teach them, Marcus," Caesar said.

"And you are not an initiate yourself?" Cleopatra asked.

Caesar shook his head. "My heart is given to Venus. She is a jealous mistress."

"And surely Mars," Fulvia proclaimed, "powerful in war as you are."

"I hope that I have enjoyed His favor," Caesar said carefully, "if only as His gift for His beloved's son."

Cleopatra said what I would have, as though we shared one thought. "It is dangerous to be the son of the Lady of the Sea," she said.

He reached across from his couch, clasping her hand. "You worry too much, my dear," he said.

HE LIVES
AND REIGNS

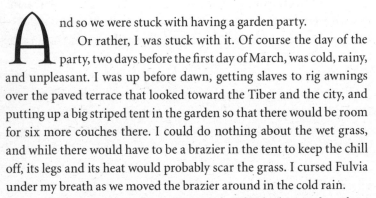

And so we were stuck with having a garden party.

Or rather, I was stuck with it. Of course the day of the party, two days before the first day of March, was cold, rainy, and unpleasant. I was up before dawn, getting slaves to rig awnings over the paved terrace that looked toward the Tiber and the city, and putting up a big striped tent in the garden so that there would be room for six more couches there. I could do nothing about the wet grass, and while there would have to be a brazier in the tent to keep the chill off, its legs and its heat would probably scar the grass. I cursed Fulvia under my breath as we moved the brazier around in the cold rain.

By midmorning the rain had stopped and it had started to clear, though the brisk wind off the river was chilly. The slaves took the couch cushions out and arranged them, six under the tent and six on the terrace, four groups of three. I thought that the damp would damage the good wood, but they were Caesar's, not ours.

By now the scent of roasting meat was excruciatingly lovely. Caesar's cook knew his business, I thought. Since this was an intimate little "family party" Caesarion would have to make an appearance, so I went inside to make sure his nurse had bathed him, and to pick out a tunic for him that would send precisely the right message. I chose one in sky blue, with embroidered borders, but not too fancy or Greek. As I laid it out, I glanced out the window. Yes, it was definitely clearing, and by noon it might be beautiful. I wondered if Emrys would be in the escort today. If he were, I'd have no more time than to smile at him. But in two days I would have a full day off, and Emrys was not on the duty schedule. We could go about the city if the weather wasn't too bad.

There was some little problem in the kitchen just short of noon, so I wasn't there when the first guests began to arrive. By the time I came out again there were eight or so people, standing around the way people always do when they're first to a party and wish they weren't. Caesar wasn't there yet, so there was no point in trying to corner him.

The only one of the party who seemed relaxed was a toddling baby a year younger than Caesarion, who was trying his best to get muddy before the rest of the guests arrived. His mother was chasing him around the garden, her saffron-colored gown already streaked at the hem, but she didn't seem upset about it. I helped her corner him beside the barren rose hedge.

"I'm so sorry," she said, as he trampled on my gown leaving muddy footprints. She scooped him up kicking.

"I'm quite used to it," I said, smiling. "I have charge of Caesarion, so it happens all the time."

"Ah." She put her head to the side, reminding me of nothing so much as a clever, dark-eyed little bird. "Then you'll be one of Cleopatra's handmaidens, the ones who run things."

"I'm Charmian," I said. "And I am grateful for the Queen's trust, yes."

"Roman women are a little more subtle about running things," she said. "I'm Octavia Minor. Marcellus' wife." She cocked her head back toward a florid man in a very formal toga who was bending the ear of a fair youth.

"And how are you…"

"Caesar's great-niece," she said. "Not to be confused with my older sister, the famous wit. She's the one with the symposia full of poets. I'm the one with the kicking child." She attempted to right the boy, who was now hanging upside down over her arm.

I laughed. "And what is his name?"

"Another Marcellus," she said. "I suppose it will be Marcellus First, Second, and Third by the time I'm finished. Admittedly we Romans are not particularly creative in our names. And it does cause a certain degree of confusion, though you can generally tell who someone's family is even if you've no clue who they are."

The florid Marcellus seemed to be expounding on something at length to the youth, who looked bored.

Octavia shrugged. "He wanted to be early, so now he's got nobody to talk to except my brother—Octavian, just to be confusing."

"I've heard of him, of course," I said, putting the pieces together. The young tribune that Emrys had disliked, the one who Caesar compared unfavorably to Agrippa. But surely Agrippa wouldn't be here! He wasn't related to Caesar, and his family was on the wrong side of politics. I looked around quickly to see if he had come with his friend, but I didn't see him.

"Have you?" Octavia smiled. "I suppose you must keep track of it all. And my husband has been here before."

"Yes," I said, "I remember." He had been part of a number of parties of distinguished men, though I did not have the impression he was any particular ally of Caesar's. I wondered how he had come to be married to Caesar's great-niece, but perhaps that predated the current political constellation. Octavia looked to be about my age, and could have been married for some years.

We were interrupted by the arrival of Marcus Antonius, who did have a way of filling a room. Fulvia was with him of course, wearing a gown of so saturated a crimson that it might as well have been purple. The cabochon amethysts she wore were also lovely, if a bit much for a small family garden party.

Antonius was expansive, advancing on everyone and greeting them like old friends, a pretty little boy Caesarion's age on his shoulder.

"Oh yes," Fulvia was saying to someone, "the baby's home with his nurse. But I thought that Antyllus could come since it was just an informal little party, and that he could play with Caesarion."

"Or Marcellus," Octavia said, going to greet her.

"Of course," Fulvia said warmly, but I saw her eyes sweeping the garden over Octavia's shoulder, looking for more important people to talk to. One never wants to be standing alone at these things, but neither does one want to get trapped with someone below one on the ladder.

At that moment the Queen came out, and of course Fulvia dashed off to kiss her and greet her like her oldest friend, while Cleopatra returned her compliments with pretty effusion.

Everyone arrived in a rush then, and there was only one slave taking wraps and cloaks, so I hurried to help her, and then there was a hitch in getting the watered wine poured, so that the gentlemen at least could fortify themselves after coming all of the way across the river. Then Caesar arrived, and there was the usual disarray of a party when everyone is trying to get to the most powerful person in the room without seeming to be doing it. Caesarion won by doing what the others would not and pushing his way among the knees to grab Caesar by the ankles.

Caesar laughed and picked him up. I thought, even from a distance, that the laugh looked genuine. "The boy knows what he wants," he said. "And he's not afraid to be rude about getting it."

"Just like Caesar," Marcus Antonius said, but I don't think anyone else found it nearly as funny.

"So," Marcellus said, lifting his cup in his hand, "when are you planning to retire like Sulla? Isn't it time you enjoyed life a bit?"

For a moment there was a dreadful pause, and then everyone went right on talking just a little bit too loudly.

Caesar laughed again, but his eyes were hard. "I don't think I'm ready to be pastured, Marcellus. I'm afraid you won't put me out to stud just yet!"

The Queen turned to Fulvia, asking her something about an upcoming festival, as though she hadn't heard. Of course the one person missing at this event was Caesar's wife. I imagined there was an equivalent function across town at her house on a different day. It seemed to me much less convenient than Pharaoh keeping more than one wife in the same palace. Of course, it was harder for them to poison one another this way.

Marcellus either didn't know when to back down, or didn't care. "It's this Dictator for life business," he said. "It's upsetting. Even Sulla knew how to preserve the forms."

"Yes, he did," Caesar said. "And in the end he left nothing different than when he began. The moment he was dead the chaos began again. I should be content indeed to retire and to think no further than the span of my years, if I did not have the future to think of." He cupped Caesarion's head in his hand, dark hair so like his, the same dark eyes. "But if I am to think of all our children, then it is not enough to walk away today or tomorrow with our work half-finished, with our borders insecure and our economy struggling. No, dear friends." He shook his head. "Half measures will not do. I am determined to leave Rome on solid footing, so that we can all sleep well in our old age and our spirits rest when we are finished."

"Well spoken," Antonius said, and I saw the great-nephew's eyebrow twitch. Who should be Caesar's heir if not Caesarion? Octavian? Baby Marcellus, struggling in Octavia's arms? Antonius himself? "And it is our friendship with Egypt that secures our trade to the east."

"It has always been the pride of Egypt to be a staunch ally," Cleopatra said, coming and standing beside Caesar. She did not touch him, but with Caesarion between them the message was unmistakable. "I will be saddened indeed to return to Alexandria in a few weeks, when the sailing season begins."

"Oh, do you travel?" Octavia put in.

"Before the Kalends of April, I think," the Queen said. "If the winds are favorable. I have been away from my kingdom for months, and Caesar goes to war."

At that point some other guests arrived, and the conversation became more general. It was an hour or more before I had a chance to take two breaths in a row in one place.

I found myself under the awning over the terrace. Standing just outside the door, his eyes surveying the crowd, was the tall German bodyguard I remembered from Alexandria. "Sigismund is it?" I asked.

He grinned. "It is."

I gestured to a passing slave. "Have you had anything to eat? Do you want anything?"

He shrugged. "Maybe just a bite while I'm standing here. I can't sit down or get too distracted. Not with Caesar in a crowd like this."

I waved the slave over and Sigismund took some bread with pickled fish off his tray.

"It's not much of a crowd, is it? Not more than thirty people, and half of them family."

Sigismund shook his head. "It's not the big crowds we worry about. In the Forum or something like that we've got a cordon around Caesar. There are at least four bodyguards and sometimes the Auxiliaries, and the lictors. And Antonius, who's as good as a bodyguard or two. Besides, it's hard to carry out an assassination in a big crowd. Too uncertain. No, it's at home or in private when we really have to sweat."

"That seems counterintuitive," I said.

"It's not easy guarding a man like Caesar," he said. "What if a man got in over the roof of his own house and jumped down through the impluvium? Or got in through a window when the household is asleep? Or came through these trees here and got up on the terrace?"

I looked toward the edge of the terrace. "It's twice a man's height to the bottom of the wall," I said. "Do you really think someone could climb it?"

"Easily enough," Sigismund said, "if they knew what they were doing. That's why we have irregular patrols in the woods between here and the river, down the slope. Aurelianus takes care of that. It's his ala that's assigned to it. And even when Caesar's in his bedroom, there's always one of us within call." He gave me another grin. "Professional curiosity? Aurelianus said you've taken a knife for the Queen."

"I did," I said. "It was a gut thrust, but fortunately I turned and it went in my thigh."

Sigismund took a bite of the fish paste. "That's lucky, all right."

"Are you with him everywhere?" I asked.

"Everywhere," Sigismund affirmed. "Everywhere except the privy and the Senate house. We're not allowed in there."

I felt a chill run up my spine, as though something had echoed that shouldn't have. "Why not?" I asked.

"Caesar likes his privacy in the privy," Sigismund said. "Thanks for the bite." He stepped out into the sun again, his eyes on Caesar.

It was nothing, I thought, a passing uneasiness. And why not? If these were Caesar's friends, then what did his enemies look like? And where were they at this very moment?

STILL, the uneasiness stayed with me all of the rest of the day, long past the time that Caesarion was returned to his nurse and the guests began to leave. The crowd was definitely thinning when I ducked into the atrium for something and heard voices there.

"I tell you, they do you no good," Marcus Antonius said heatedly.

I ducked behind a potted cedar.

"I have no desire to be king," Caesar said mildly. "And if I did, I should have more sense than to say the word. It's like waving a red flag before a bull to say 'king' before Romans."

"Your men say the word," Antonius said. "They say it in the tavernas and watering holes of the Subura. Every tavern keeper in town has heard it. The Gauls and Germans say it all the time."

"Oh, the Gauls and Germans," Caesar said. "That's just a mistranslation. They take 'Imperator' as king in their own languages, and they don't have any idea why they shouldn't say 'king' in Latin. They take 'Dictator' as something like 'High King,' first among a council of tribal leaders. That's how they see the Senate. They don't really understand our form of government, you see."

"They say 'king,'" Antonius said, "for whatever reason. And people believe they know something we don't. If you say something often enough it might as well be true."

"And what are they saying that you're warning me of?"

"That you intend to be king. That you intend to make Prince Caesarion your heir and put an Egyptian to rule over them." Antonius' voice was hard. "The son of an incestuous foreign whore."

Contrastingly, Caesar's voice was almost lazy. "Cleopatra's marriage with her brother was a marriage in name only."

"That is not the point!" It sounded as though Antonius were pacing. "It's strange. The Roman people don't like anything strange. They don't like anything that seems decadent and effete and Hellenic. Ever since the Gracchi we've had this passion for the common man, for a just plain fellow off the street who hasn't got any airs. Good, plain soldiers who can't tell their ass from a bucket. Why, the gods alone can tell us! But there it is."

"And you do the common soldier better than anyone," Caesar said. He sounded amused. "You, with philhellene written all over you and an education as good as any man's."

"I do," he said. "And so I know what they say and what I hear. It's jealousy, plain and simple."

"And fear," Caesar said. His voice was thoughtful and tempered. "They think we're still some collection of mud huts about to be overrun by anyone who wants to. They have no conception of the real political situation. They act as though this were the First Punic War."

"And Carthage must be destroyed," Antonius quoted darkly.

"Carthage was destroyed generations ago," Caesar said. "And there is no real power in the world that can possibly challenge Rome. Yes, there are tribes on the Rhine that must be kept in check, and it's possible that some new Pontine leader might emerge, or even that the Parthians might make common cause with Liaka Kusulaka, or one of the other Indian princes. But those things are no threat to Rome. They're shadow puppets, Marcus."

"Egypt is no shadow puppet."

"Egypt is thoroughly neutralized, isn't it?" Caesar said. "And will be for the foreseeable future, with my son on the throne of Egypt."

I must have made some sound, for Marcus Antonius struck like a cat, knocking aside the plants I stood behind and grabbing my arm. "Ha!" he said. "Look what I've caught! Who do you serve?"

"She serves Cleopatra," Caesar said. "And we've said nothing the Queen does not know. Hail, Charmian."

"Hail, Caesar," I said, inclining my head.

Antonius let go of my arm. "I suppose it's your job to listen in on private conversations."

"Of course it is," Caesar said approvingly. "What sort of servant should she be if she didn't?" He clapped Antonius on the shoulder. "I appreciate your vigilance, Marcus. But you worry too much. Come and make your farewells to the Queen before Fulvia wears her ears off." He raised an eyebrow at me, and led Antonius away.

In the morning it seemed to me that Iras looked pale and tired, as though she had not slept much. I caught her eye as we were leaving the first meal of the day. "Are you well?" I asked.

Iras shrugged. "Foul dreams," she said.

"Me too," I said.

With one accord we turned and looked after where Cleopatra had gone.

"What did you dream?" I asked.

Iras picked up a scroll from the table, playing idly with the cord that labeled it. She did not look at me. "I dreamed that Caesar was dead."

A chill ran down my back.

"I saw him lying on his pyre, with a cloak across his body covering everything but his face. His face was composed, like the carving on the lid of a sarcophagus and just that pale. Bled white. Antonius stood behind him, and I could see his face tight with strain. He was giving the funeral oration. And then he pulled back the cloak so that everyone could see all of the stab wounds, dozens of them, awful wounds and then people started screaming, tearing their hair and yelling for blood...." Her voice was intense, but her face was as quiet as that of a dreaming child.

I shivered.

Her face changed, the strangeness in her eyes fading. "Iras?"

She blinked. "What?"

"You were telling me about Caesar," I said gently.

She shook her head. "Was I?"

"Yes." I took her arm carefully. "About your dream."

She bent her head then. "I hope it means nothing," she said. "After all, there are always plots, aren't there? We can hardly rush to Caesar and tell him his life is in danger. It always is."

"No," I said slowly. "We can't, can we?"

We will sail on the twenty-first day of March," the Queen explained in Latin for the entire household to understand. "Iras, will you make sure our vessel is at Ostia and prepared on that day? Caesar sails for Antioch in Syria two days earlier. We do not want to create confusion by sailing at the same time. And the wind should be fair for Alexandria then."

"So it should, Gracious Queen," Iras said. "I will see that we are prepared and our ship provisioned."

"That will be all," the Queen said, and the other members of the household began to withdraw, our meeting completed and our instructions given.

I went to the Queen's side. For a moment her face looked oddly blank. "Are you well?" I whispered.

She nodded. "Just a touch of nausea." She looked at me sideways, and her mouth twitched in a tiny smile. I would know what she meant, having charge of her linens and counting as I did. Her blood was more than two weeks late.

"Are you sure you will want to sail in three weeks?" I whispered.

She nodded. "The sooner the better, isn't it? We will be in Alexandria before I am far gone."

"Around the Kalends of November," I said, counting the due date in Latin, half-thinking. "Does Caesar know?"

"Not yet. I'll tell him before he sails."

"He will be pleased," I whispered.

"Yes," she said, sharing a smile with me. "All will be well. Don't worry so, Charmian."

"I'm not worried," I said. "Not at all." I lifted my chin and embraced my sister.

I DREAMED, and in my dream I walked through an empty palace, down echoing halls lit by guttering torches, by lamps half-spilled on the floor. My footsteps echoed in the corridors. The flames burned straight up, never flickering, never changing.

I turned another corner. There was a bath chamber in blue and white tile, a wide pool full of lapping clean water, with fretted screens about a changing area. One white towel lay abandoned beside the pool. A couch drawn close by still bore the indentation where someone had lain.

Panic rose in me. I looked behind the screens, my scarred, calloused hands shaking. There was nothing there.

The bath was empty. Cool clean water lapped against the pretty painted tiles.

I tried a door, ran down a corridor. Somewhere was the smell of burning flowers.

"Babylon," I whispered.

Doors opened onto empty rooms, onto other doors.

There was blood on the floor, blood spilled like wine or wine spilled like blood, red Bactrian wine poured out, the amphora broken.

"Babylon," I whispered again, and charged around a corner. There must be some way out, some escape from the maze.

A light glimmered ahead through some untried doorway.

I ran through it.

"Lydias," someone said, and I spun about.

She stood in the empty throne room, the Lady of Sorrows, Isis with a black veil over Her hair, Her gown all the shifting grays of a land lit by starlight. Her eyes held infinite compassion. "This is Lydias' dream," She said. "His memory."

"Who?" I asked confusedly.

"A person you once were," She said. "When you came to the Black Land with Ptolemy. You are dreaming the death of kings."

"I must save him!" I said. "Gracious Lady, tell me how to save Caesar!"

Her eyes were sad, and when She moved the sound of Her robes was like the wind over the desert. "Osiris must go down into the West. By His death the land is renewed."

"Caesar is not of our land or of our people," I argued. "He is not part of this story and he does not serve You."

"Does he not?" She smiled faintly. "Son of Venus he calls himself, son of the Lady of the Sea. Do you not know that whether Her name is Venus or Aphrodite Cythera or Isis Pelagia or Ashteret, the fate of Her son is the same? He is the Falcon of the Sun, and he must die."

I bent my head, tears smarting in my eyes.

Her voice was more gentle. "Gaius Julius Caesar has known for a long time how his story will end."

"In Babylon?" I said bitterly.

"You speak as though that were defeat," She said. "Do you think Alexander's death a tragedy then?"

"The cruelest imaginable," I said, blinking back tears.

Isis shook Her head ruefully. "And yet through his death, look at all that came to pass! Had Alexander not died in Babylon, there should have been no Successor kingdoms, no white city by the sea. It was the striving of the Successors that opened trade from India to Italy, that gave millions of people writing and plays, chickens and rice to lift them from poverty, clean water drawn from wells instead of stagnant pools, and the concord of the gods. Alexander had made the Choice of Achilles, and in his death the world was remade. Mourn, if you like, for his is a great soul, but do not regret, Companion."

I raised my head. "And Caesar? Has he, too, made the Choice of Achilles?"

"Caesar is fifty-five," She said. "I hardly think his life has been short. It took him longer, to bring the west into this world of the Inner Sea, as Alexander brought the east."

"And yet so many will be carried down into ruin in his wake," I said, and my heart ached for Caesarion, who should scarcely remember his father.

And whom everyone would want to kill. For a moment my heart stopped beating. "And my Queen? Caesarion?"

"That I cannot say. It depends upon the acts of men." Isis took a step away, looking around the empty throne room, frozen in some moment three hundred years ago in Babylon. "The gods cannot control the actions of men like so many pieces on a game board. Take this as a warning: There are many in Rome who should like to see your Queen dead, and many who should profit from Caesarion's death."

"That is not unknown to me, Lady," I said. It hardly took the gods to tell me that. "I will guard my sister with my life, as always."

She turned, and as Her eyes met mine they were sad. "There is always a price, Companion. It may be that you will save her, but there will be a price in blood."

I nodded. I had made that choice long ago. "I understand that, Gracious Lady. If my life would buy hers or Caesarion's, I should consider it well spent."

Isis shook Her head. "It's not always that simple. And the gods cannot see all ends." She looked around the empty throne room again, one little inlaid table lying on its side, as though kicked over in the rush and forgotten. "It's never that simple," She said quietly.

I must try," I said. "I must try."

Iras shook my shoulder. "You must try what?"

I opened my eyes to see my sister looking down at me, her face a mask of worry.

"You were shouting and calling out in your sleep. What's wrong?"

I struggled to sit up. The room was quiet and dark, only a little predawn light coming in through the closed shutters. Iras sat on the edge of my bed. There was no one else there. Of course.

"I don't know," I said. I had dreamed. Something about Caesar. Something bad.

"We had a serious thunderstorm just now," Iras said. "The wind woke me up. Cleopatra's up too, and going to take a bath. She couldn't get back to sleep."

"A bath?"

Iras nodded. "The storm. It's disturbing. But the children seem to have slept through it. I just checked on them."

"Oh good," I said. I still felt disoriented and strange. "Yes, of course it was the storm." I reached for my clothes and put on the first thing that came to hand. "I'll go attend the Queen in the bath."

I was putting on my shoes when I looked up at Iras, something occurring to me. "Is Caesar here?" I asked.

She shook her head. "He left early last night. He had a morning meeting at the Senate today."

Memory flooded back. I leaped up and ran out of the room, ran straight into Cleopatra in the hall. "Caesar mustn't go to the Senate today," I said.

"What?" The Queen blinked at me. "Charmian…"

"She had a bad dream," Iras said, coming up behind me. "The storm."

I took my sister's hands in mine. "Sister," I said, "you told me that you would always believe me. Caesar must not go to the Senate today. You must believe me."

For a moment we looked into each other's eyes, our hands together.

Her eyes wavered a moment. "I believe you," she said, then again more strongly. "I believe you."

My fingers tightened on hers.

"Iras, send a message to Caesar now. Get one of the cavalrymen to carry it. Tell him that he must not go to the Senate today. He must come here. I have never asked anything unreasonable of him, ever. But today he must do this. He must do as I tell him now!"

"It will be done," Iras said, and she ran for a messenger.

THE İDES
OF MARCH

The messenger galloped away toward the Sublician Bridge. We waited. Full morning came, a blustery morning with scudding gray clouds and sudden gusts of wind that sent the dead leaves of fall flying through the streets once more.

The children played and laughed, but my hands shook and I could not still them. The Queen paced.

"We are probably making something of nothing," she said, going to the window that looked on the terrace for the fortieth time. Beyond the Tiber, shadows moved across the city, the flashing shapes of cloud.

"I hope so," I said. I did hope so, though I did not believe it. I could feel whatever it was like lightning in the air, and my hands cramped.

In the third hour a messenger came, cantering up the steep road and stopped by the guardsmen at the gate. Completely careless of propriety, Cleopatra ran out and practically tore the paper from his hand. I was a step behind her.

> *Caesar regrets that he cannot come immediately as per her Gracious Majesty's invitation, as he has business in the Senate that will not wait. He will be pleased, however, to attend upon Her Majesty in the dinner hour, later today.*

It was his own hand, hastily scribbled, and I could see how he had looked as he had done it, bemused, a little surprised that she had sent for him with such urgency. But there were only four more days to accomplish all of his business in Rome before he sailed, and he could not waste a day on idle fears.

"Perhaps it will be all right," I said. "Perhaps it's only stupidity or the weather or something."

"Mother Isis, let it be so!" the Queen breathed. And she went back into the house, leaving the letter in my hand.

I smoothed it out and rerolled it neatly. She will want this, I thought, when he is gone. She will want this, the last words he wrote to her.

I stopped under the portico and leaned my throbbing head against the column. Take this gift from me, I thought. Oh Lady of Stars, take it from me! I do not want to know.

You do not choose what you see, She whispered. *It is what you are, and you can be nothing else. And how could you not know this, when the wave is near to breaking and it tears away the stones beneath your feet?*

What good is it, I thought, to know that such crashing sorrow will come and be able to do nothing to prevent it? To know that now, even now...

Now.

I raised my head, my hand against the cool stone. A stray sunbeam lit the walk, glancing off a white place in the stone. In the shelter of the portico, the dark green spikes of some plant pushed upward through the soil. From the house I heard Demetria laugh, her clear voice pealing out, heard the voice of some maidservant on the way to the kitchen calling to another in the atrium. Far above, among the scudding clouds, a bird hovered on the wing.

Now.

And for a moment the wind stopped, as though time itself ground to a halt.

Now he was falling, now his mouth opened as though he would say one more thing in that rich voice. He would say nothing more, blood on his lips, those wonderful eyes suddenly empty, one hand reaching still.

Above, the bird turned on the wind. Caesarion shouted back to Demetria, and I heard the clatter of the servant's feet in the atrium. The sunlight shifted, golden light splashing across the bulbs that sprouted toward the sun. A breeze lifted my hair. The tree branches waved in the wind of a world without Caesar in it.

I closed my eyes and took one long, deep breath. The pain lifted from my brows. Now I knew what I must do.

I opened my eyes. Nothing had changed. I had stood here only a minute.

I went into the house and stopped the maidservant before she reached the stairs. "Eurydice," I said softly. "Go and pack Prince Caesarion and Demetria's clothes. When you are done with that, begin packing the Queen's things, starting with her state robes. I am going to pack her correspondence. And do it quietly, please. The Queen has a headache and has gone to lie down."

The girl blinked at me. "But I was to clean the baths just now."

"Don't worry about the baths," I said, and was surprised to hear my own voice brisk and businesslike. "That's not important. Do the packing right now. And pack the children's toys first."

"But we don't leave for Ostia for five days."

"It never hurts to start early," I said. "So do it as quickly as you can. I will be in the library."

I turned and hurried across the atrium, into the ground-floor room that served as office and library. How had we gotten so many books? Cleopatra could never resist books, I thought, and we must have acquired a hundred while in Rome, some for her pleasure but more for the Library. After all, it must hold everything of importance to man. And there was all of her correspondence, all of the letters from Apollodorus and others in Alexandria about the business of Egypt. That which was not important must be burned, and the rest taken away.

I went back in the hall and sent a slave to bring me a brazier. He looked at me strangely, as the library was heated very well by the hypocaust. Then I went back inside and started sorting documents.

I WAS DEEP in the task, the afternoon wearing away, a pile of unnecessary papers burning merrily on the brazier, when I heard the scream. I put the papers in my lap aside and hurried out into the atrium. Iras had her arm about Cleopatra, who shook it off, her face white. Before her stood a man in a plain tunic and sandals, who I thought I recognized vaguely. His blond hair gave him away. He was one of Caesar's litter bearers.

"Are you certain?" she demanded.

"I'm certain," he said, his Latin a little halting. "I saw his body myself when they brought it out. He must have been stabbed fifteen times or more. He was bled white. His hands...he'd tried to defend himself, but it was no use. One man against twenty?" He bent his head, his mouth working, and then went on: "They had us put his body in his litter, and they told us to take it to his house, as is seemly. But then people started fighting in the forum, wanting to get to him, wanting to see. So the bodyguards pushed them back, and then one of the Senators, I think it was Brutus, came out and made a speech about a modern-day Aristogeiton, whatever that means."

"I know what that means," Cleopatra said, her voice choked. "Go on."

"And then the crowd rushed him, and the lictors got in front and we had to put the litter down or it was going to be knocked over and his poor body dumped in the street, so we put it down and one of the bodyguards was killed just like that, by a thrown rock. It hit him in the head, one of those big pavers."

I clenched my hands together.

"I didn't see what we could do for him, Caesar, I mean, dead as he was, but I thought we were all going to get killed right there, because the crowd went mad when the awning got torn and they could see him covered in blood. But they went for the Senators instead, all of the ones who had blood down the front of their togas, and two of the lictors were just about torn to pieces. I'd be dead right now if Antonius hadn't gotten in with a bunch of gladiators. I don't know where he got them, but there they were, and he jumped up on top of the steps next to us and yelled 'To Caesar!' and they made a shield wall around us. And Antonius said to take his body back in the Senate house and to send for his wife and his slaves, because there was no way we were getting through the streets to his house. And Brutus and the rest of the Senators got out of there somehow. So we carried him back inside, and then Gallus ran back to Caesar's house like Antonius told us to, and I thought you'd want to know, Domina."

"Thank you," the Queen said. "Iras, will you reward this man?"

"Of course," Iras said, but when she unfastened her money pouch her fingers fumbled on the strings and she dropped it, silver and gold and copper spilling and rolling across the floor.

I picked up a gold drachma and handed it to him. "Here. And thank you."

The man nodded swiftly. "I thought you'd want to know, Domina."

"Yes," the Queen said. "Yes."

"You may go around to the kitchen and get some food and drink if you like," I said, and my voice was perfectly calm. The tears that had rolled onto the burning papers were gone now, leaving ice behind them.

"There's chaos in the city, Domina," he said to me, as Cleopatra turned away. "Chaos. I don't know who'll kill who before the day is out. I heard that Cassius wants to kill Antonius, and that Octavian is hiding because somebody said they'd only killed the head of the snake. And you know Antonius, Domina. He's not going to sit still and be killed."

"I know he's not," I said. "I'm glad we're away over the Tiber."

"Yes, Domina," he said. "There's a mob roving through the city. If you look that way you can see the smoke rising."

"Oh no!" I ran to the back terrace, looking across the Tiber to the city. It was true. Here and there columns of smoke rose, dark against the slanting sun that bathed the city. The sun had come out of the clouds as it moved toward its setting.

Some of the slaves had come to see, and I grabbed the nearest one. "Go get the trunks that are upstairs and bring them down now. And get the two in the library."

There were horsemen on the road. I could see them below in the bright western light, riding unhindered and hell-for-leather up the road.

The guards were gone.

"Oh fuck," I whispered. A king, and a foreign prince to put over us, son of an incestuous whore. That was what they had said. They had only killed the head of the snake.

I flew back in the house, snatching up a long knife in the library, the kind used to cut paper. It was very sharp. Caesarion wasn't allowed to play with it.

Iras and the Queen were still in the atrium.

"What are you doing?" Iras snapped, the Queen's head on her shoulder.

"Horsemen," I said. "Coming hard. And the guards are gone. Their charge died with Caesar."

They sprang apart. "I don't have a knife," Iras said.

"I do." I pulled one of the heavy doors shut, and reached for the other. "Help me bar the doors."

It was Cleopatra at my elbow, not Iras. "Tend to the children, Iras," she said. We hauled the door closed and dropped the bar into place as the hooves clattered across the drive outside. Less than ten horses, I thought. More like six or so. I heard footsteps, and the door shook.

"Charmian? Iras?" The door shuddered under his knock. It was Emrys' voice. "Open the door!"

Cleopatra and I looked at each other, then drew the bar back.

He opened one side. "You've heard then?" His eyes fell on Cleopatra's face, and he bent his head, switching to Koine. "Gracious Queen, please accept my most sincere condolences."

"I appreciate your words, Praefectus," she replied.

His eyes roved from her face to mine. "You have to get out of here," he said. "There's no one in charge in the city. The assassins hold some parts of town, but nobody's sure exactly who was in on it and what happened. Cassius and Brutus, certainly. And probably not Antonius or Octavian."

Cleopatra drew a deep ragged breath, but didn't speak.

Emrys' face was solemn. "Gracious Queen, it isn't safe for you here. I have sent four men to the dock by the Grove of Furrina to commandeer a riverboat. You need to get to your own ship at Ostia." He saw her hesitate, and pressed on. "For the sake of your son. A mob is cover for many things."

The other half of the door opened, and Sigismund stood beside Emrys, a long spatha in one hand and an ax in the other. "We can hold until you go," he said in his halting Latin.

The Queen nodded and I saw her decide. "Yes. Charmian?" She turned to me to order something, but was interrupted by two slaves clattering into the atrium, the chest containing the children's things carried between them. They put it down next to the one with the books and the library papers.

"Already done, my Queen," I said.

She spun away and ran upstairs, following Iras to the children. I well understood her need to clutch Caesarion to her.

"You're packed?" Emrys said to me. Behind him, four other men were walking their horses in the drive, men of the Auxiliaries, all of whom I recognized.

"Yes," I said.

He gave me a smile that was half tears. "How did you?"

"I'm good," I said. "Why are you here?"

Sigismund cleared his throat. "Because honor demands it," he said. "All we can do for Caesar is guard his son. And that we do right."

Emrys nodded. "We'll see you off. The men are supposed to find a wagon and bring it up here as soon as they've got a suitable boat. We'll cover you all the way. And there's also a path down the hill from the terrace that comes out in the Grove of Furrina, if it comes to that."

Iras came hurrying up. "The diplomatic correspondence! That shouldn't stay here."

"Packed or burned," I said. "It's in a trunk in the atrium, ready for the cart when it comes."

"Cart?"

"Emrys has a cart on its way," I said.

Iras looked from one of us to the other, blinking. "Do you do this often?" she asked. We were all reaching that point in the middle of horror where there is nothing to do but jest.

"Only every three hundred years or so," I said.

There was a clatter on the drive, and Sigismund shoved me behind him, but it turned out to be a produce cart, driven by a Gaul with cavalry leathers. "I told the farmer I'd bring it back when we were done," he said, leaping down. "He didn't mind at all when I said it was for Caesar's son. So I've got to take the cart back, on my word."

"Start loading it up then," Emrys said. "This lady will show you where the trunks are in the hall."

I watched them load it, the trunks that were ready and the ones I sent slaves for. Emrys put his hand on my arm and I turned to him, standing for a moment together, our arms about each other. There was so much to say, and suddenly so little time left to say it.

"Tell Dion . . ."

"I'll tell him you love him," I said, blinking.

The cart rumbled out in less than an hour, laden with everything packed — the correspondence, the books, the children's toys and clothes, and Cleopatra's jewels and state wardrobe that would be hard to replace. Demetria went with the nurse in the cart as well. She was crazy with energy, and Caesarion had gone to sleep, so it was easier to send her first, as the nurse could only carry one. Besides, Demetria and her nurse would not be in danger at the dock. An old Greek woman and a little girl were not on any of the conspirators' lists.

Night was falling, the sun setting into a pall of cloud.

I got a bundle of my things together and went onto the terrace. Cleopatra stood there alone. Across the river fires were burning, flames leaping here and there among the buildings. I thought some came from the Forum, but at this distance it was hard to be sure.

"They are burning him," she said quietly. "They are burning him like Achilles."

I nodded.

"Not for him," she said, "the long sleep in Alexandria, the quiet tomb. You will have nothing to summon him by, Charmian."

"I do not think the world will ever need to summon Caesar," I said, and my throat closed with tears. "He will never be far from us."

"I did love him," she said. "I couldn't help it."

"No one could, when he turned his mind to it," I said.

"I know."

Emrys hurried onto the terrace. "There are torches on the main road. I can't tell if it's a mob or troops. But you must go now, down the path to the Grove."

"Praefectus, do you know . . . ," Cleopatra began.

Emrys interrupted her. "Now, Lady! We are out of time!"

I heard them then, and I raced across the atrium calling to Iras upstairs. "Iras! Come on! Bring the child!"

Emrys passed me, running to the doors. Sigismund already had the bar in place. "Go!" he shouted. "The Queen is already on the path!" He drew his spatha.

"Iras!" I looked up the stairs. My sister was starting down carefully, sleeping Caesarion clutched in her arms. "Come on! Aurelianus can't hold them forever!"

I looked over my shoulder at him, side-by-side with Sigismund, waiting for the first blow to the doors.

"Here," Iras said, brushing past me, the child held to her shoulder, his face still in sleep.

"Go!" Emrys shouted, and for a moment I wanted to take my place on his other side, long knife in my hand. But I should do nothing more than distract him from the business of the moment.

I turned and ran after Iras. At the top of the path I heard the bang, the first heavy blow on the door. I ran through the darkness. The path was not lit. Of course not. No one wanted to advertise its presence. Behind me there was shouting and the clash of steel.

I careened into a tree, bounced off, and dodged down the path, hoping I was still on the path. I didn't see Iras ahead of me, but she could run when she needed to.

Don't die for me, I thought. Don't die for me.

Not for me. For Caesar. For my queen. For never being less than we are, I thought. We are Companions, he and I.

The path twisted around some cedars, and suddenly I was in the Grove. Iras was ahead of me, just coming out on the other side, one of Emrys' men helping her, sword in hand.

Caesarion, belatedly, set up a long fretful wail.

I ran after.

And there was the water, the boat waiting, Demetria on her nurse's lap looking out over the river toward the city, her hair pulled back in a tail at the nape of her neck, like one of the Gaulish cavalrymen.

Iras handed Caesarion to the Queen and climbed in. I was right behind her, winded from the run. Above, a flame surged. Torches on the path? Or something catching fire?

"Shove off," the Queen ordered, Caesarion in her arms, and we parted from the shore like a child from its mother. Slowly, reluctantly, the oars bit and the boat drifted out to midstream, turning a little in the current.

With fire behind us on both banks we made our way downriver.

WE CAME TO OSTIA well before dawn and went aboard our warship that waited in the harbor. The captain was surprised, of course. He had not expected us for several days, and nothing was prepared. Besides, there were all these uncertain rumors....

"The rumors are true," Iras snapped. "Caesar is dead. We sail for Alexandria, and we stop for no man."

I thought he might hesitate or ask for the Queen, but he did not. "It shall be as you say," he said, and went to give the orders.

I went below, looking for Cleopatra. Her cabin was not ready, and the mattress lay bare on the floor. She was sound asleep lying on it, one arm thrown over Caesarion, who slept against her stomach. Gently, I took a cloak and laid it over them. I would not disturb them by going through chests looking for blankets. Sleep was the best balm, I thought. Sleep, and the company of her son. And of course that other Horus, the one who still rode beneath her heart. I supposed she had not told Caesar yet, and now he should never know.

I went on deck and watched the anchor raised, the five banks of massive oars deployed. The captain was not even waiting for the tide. We sailed immediately, passing through rows of merchant ships, past the dockyard where Rome's quinqueremes were tied up. They had nearly thirty here, ready to take on troops for Caesar's voyage to Syria, and the captain was taking no chances.

Apparently they had no orders to stop us. I doubted they knew who was in charge in Rome either. Caesar's son was a bargaining piece for any of them, as was Egypt's Queen. But perhaps none of them dared.

The shore faded behind us, a few lights still showing against the dark sea. The breeze freshened, clear and cold. I let it take my hair and stood watching as the winter stars sank into the sea.

By now Emrys was probably as dead as Caesar, with none to mourn him. I blinked into the wind. Dion, I thought. I will have to tell Dion. I will mourn with Dion. The sacrifice was not my blood and yet Emrys, too, would consider the price fair. The tears escaped my eyes and dried in the sea wind.

I stood there until the sun rose, until every muscle in my body was stiff, until in all directions there was nothing to see but the Middle Sea. The captain had decided to steer clear of the Campanian coast.

I should unpack, I thought. I went below.

"Charmian?" Cleopatra's voice quivered, and I hurried into the cabin. Caesarion was still sleeping peacefully, but on the mattress where she had lain and on her rumpled skirts I could see the spots of bright blood, too much blood.

"Oh sweet Isis," I breathed, and fell to my knees beside her. It was a price I had not expected.

♈ Amenti

I bent my head, and could speak no further.

On Their thrones Isis and Serapis waited.

At last I lifted my eyes again. "Gracious Ones, Caesar passed through these gates long ago, into the land of the dead, and the world was changed. You know the reasons for that better than I. I do not understand why it mattered to me so."

"Or why you even considered leaving your queen and your family to go with Agrippa?" Isis asked, leaning forward, Her chin on Her hands. "Did you love him so?"

I shook my head. "No," I said. "I think not. Perhaps I thought I did at the time, but I had not yet learned what love truly is, love that is based upon respect, one Companion for another."

"And yet you might have found it enough," a new voice said. I looked around to see Him standing behind me, a young man with a shaven head glistening with oil, an immaculate pleated shenti around His waist. Behind Him, white wings spread, each feather giving forth its own light.

Serapis inclined His head. "Mikhael, You are welcome to Our court. Though I must ask why You are here, as Charmian stands before Us and she is not one of Your worshippers, nor a follower of Your god."

He stepped forward until He stood close behind me, and His presence was like a heat. "Is not the defendant allowed counsel?" He asked pleasantly. "Charmian has long been a person of interest to Me, since You,

Lady, entrusted her to My care many centuries ago. I have come to speak on her behalf, if You will hear Me."

Isis smiled, the corners of Her eyes crinkling. "I do remember that, and I know the services she rendered You in the matter of this Great Story in ages past. It is possible Your shepherd boy should have died an outlaw rather than a king if not for her. But what have You to do with Charmian, with the mask she has worn in this life?"

"I am Dion's patron, and I have cared as always for Emrys, one of the sons of My heart. Where her story has intersected theirs, there I have been. And thus I will speak on her behalf if I may."

I looked at Him with surprise, and I thought incredibly enough that He winked at me.

"You may," Serapis said. "And what do You put before Us?"

"I put before You that Charmian wielded no inconsiderable power in Egypt, as minister and confidante to the Queen. In that capacity, she used her position to benefit all of the Queen's subjects, Greeks, Egyptians, Jews, and others all alike. She did indeed render mercy to the needy, help to the weak, and safeguard the well-being of all. That is no inconsiderable feat in anyone who rules—to never take advantage of her position to harm those who offended her, or to prefer those who would make her rich."

I looked at Mikhael quizzically. "What use had I for wealth, with the Royal Treasury at my disposal? If I needed for something to be done, I could simply sign for it, or if it were too much money, I should speak to the Queen about it. What use had I for bribes? It is true I did not take them, but it was not a virtue, as I had no use for them or desire for wealth."

Mikhael spread His hands and grinned, looking for a moment like Dion. "You see? One may search far and wide on this earth to find an incorruptible servant, but You need look no further. Any monarch that ever lived should be glad of one like her."

I turned and faced Him. "It's not that I don't appreciate You speaking on my behalf, but You are giving me credit that I do not deserve! There was nothing anyone could give me that I wanted. How could I be tempted?"

"And what was it you wanted, then?" Serapis asked.

"The only thing I have always wanted," I said. "To be with those I love and to have good work to do. And as for the rest, justice and mercy and those in need, I didn't do anything special. I just tried to be fair. I just did my best."

"That is all that the gods can ever ask of anyone," Isis said.

THE MOON VEİLED

A lexandria.
  Home.
  I watched Pharos rising out of the sea at sunrise, glimmering like the evening star, and wept to see it.

The Queen had miscarried on the ship and she was still weak, so we came ashore without ceremony at the palace harbor. The news from Rome had not traveled faster than we, so no one yet knew that Caesar was dead. No doubt a fast ship would come tomorrow or the next day and the entire city would know.

Iras hurried off to talk with Apollodorus, muttering something about the effect on grain prices and the grain markets crashing. The crown must be prepared for the market's reaction when the news came.

I settled the Queen in her own rooms, clean and pristine after so long an absence, and sat beside her while she bathed, talking of inconsequential things. Worn and exhausted, what was there to say? "I'm sorry" seemed pathetically inadequate.

"There is Caesarion," I said.

She turned on me, her eyes flashing. "And that is supposed to make it better? As though one child were as good as another?"

"No, of course not," I said. "I didn't mean it that way."

"It's wrong," she said. "Don't you see it's wrong? I was supposed to bear this child, like Isis. After he was gone." She turned away from me and leaned against the side of the bath. "I failed. And She has deserted me."

"No," I said. "No, my dearest sister. It will all be well."

"Can you restore this child to me or bring Caesar back to life? If not, then leave me."

"Of course," I said, and went as far as the door.

THE NEWS FROM ROME came in bits and drabbles. Antonius had spoken Caesar's funeral oration, and the mob had risen against the conspirators. No, it was not true. Antonius and the conspirators had made common cause. No, that was error. Antonius and Octavian had made common cause, and Caesar's will had been read, naming Octavian his heir.

In Egypt, it seemed very distant. Of course he had named Octavian, and the provinces he would have left to Caesarion had never been conquered, the prizes never won. We expected Cleopatra to be angry in her cool way, to plot furiously. But instead she hardly seemed to care. She slept and ate, bathed and dressed, but her passion was gone.

"Give her time," the doctor said to me as he left her. "Her body will mend from the miscarriage soon enough, but the shock to her soul will take a little longer. She is a healthy young woman, only twenty-five years old. Once she has healed, there is no reason she cannot bear many healthy children. Give her a few months."

"The business of the kingdom will not wait a few months," I said.

"That is what she has you for then," he said sharply. "She needs the company of her son and a few months' rest. I should recommend a progress to Philae. On the river her business will be limited, and the change of scene will stimulate her mind. It will do her good to follow the Progress of Isis, and to do such other things as will remember him."

The doctor had long experience of grief, and his advice was good. If she could not build a tomb, she would build a temple.

And so it was that we sat down with the plans before the week was out, the Caesaraeum on paper, a temple to the god he had become.

It was beautiful, I thought, a square building like the Soma, with a round dome above, pierced to let in the light. Outside there would be a short avenue leading to the Canopic Way, bordered by sphinxes with Cleopatra's face. Most fantastic of all, there should be four great obelisks of red granite, antiques nearly fifteen hundred years old, brought from Heliopolis. That in itself would be the work of a year, and would guarantee the pay of many skilled workmen.

"Let it be so," the Queen said to all the architects might propose. Nothing should be too good or too fair for Caesar, and for her white city by the sea. "And now for my tomb," she said, gesturing to another set of plans on the table as the architects crowded around.

I raised an eyebrow. She had never taken an interest in her tomb before, though many Pharaohs began building their tombs as soon as they were crowned. But then, money had been tight when she was crowned.

"I should like to lie in the Royal Enclosure," she said, "as near as possible to the tomb of Ptolemy Soter. Can you show me what land there is that is not occupied by other tombs, and where there is room enough underground? I know that Ptolemy Physcon lies near."

The architects, sensing a huge commission and ten years of work, all started talking at once.

"If you will each prepare plans for submission," the Queen said, "I will review your work when I return from Philae."

Iras raised an eyebrow at me from across the room. It seemed the physician knew his business.

THIS TIME, I would go and Iras would stay. Financial matters in the capital required her touch, and I should be needed with the Queen. There was no doubt that Prince Caesarion would go as well. His mother would not be parted from him now, and he was turning three years old. It was time that he became acquainted with his kingdom, and his people with him.

The night before we were to go, Iras came rushing into my bedchamber as I was undressing, waving a scroll in her hand. "This is for you," she said, smiling. "And I think you will be glad to see it. There was another for Dion, and I sent a boy to find him at his apartment."

"Oh!" I said, and it came out half a sob, for I could only think of one thing that would come to both me and Dion. I tore the wrappings open, almost tearing the paper in the process.

Hail Charmian,

If you are reading this then you will have guessed that I am not dead. I am in Massalia, with Marcus Antonius. Rome is at war, and if we all must choose a side, I am choosing the side of the man who says he will avenge Caesar. I know from you that it is Horus who is to avenge his father, but I do not think this business can wait until Caesarion is grown.

I did not think that men could murder in cold blood a man they would be afraid to face in battle, even aged as he was, and still call themselves men of honor. Still less can I believe that other men could name them so, or debate over whether they did right or wrong. It is a mystery to me how they can claim any excuse for it, or how people can continue to argue whether or not what they did was lawful. How can killing an unarmed man, twenty against one, be lawful? How can anyone even consider this well done? They talk in pretty words of tyrannicide, and of ancient kings killed for freedom, but this is not that. This is murder for political advantage, and if any king in Gaul tried it, his warriors would be ashamed of him.

There are no pretty words for murder. If I am to march for one or another, let it be for the hand of justice, with Marcus Antonius who is at least doing what is proper. So I have taken my ala over to Antonius. Octavian is no soldier, and he is very young, and Caesarion still a child. So that is why I am in Massalia, where we have withdrawn for reinforcements. We face a Consular army, but Antonius will have no trouble recruiting troops here. Indeed he has already called the men of the Sixth out of retirement at Arelate, whom you may remember from Alexandria.

The battles so far have not been pretty, and there are more to come. I do not know, now, if I will ever come to Alexandria. Even the autumn seems a lifetime away. There are so many things we did not say, and now perhaps never will.

Sigismund sees me writing, and asks to be remembered to you.

Emrys Aurelianus, Praefectus

I read it twice.

"I take it he's well," Iras said, smiling.

I nodded, not trusting myself to speak at this reprieve unlooked for. I had counted Emrys and Sigismund dead.

Iras put her arms around me. "You don't have to pretend to coolness," she said. "I'm glad too."

IN THE END, it was Egypt that healed her. We made the Progress of Isis, the widowed Queen and her young son, traveling by ship through the length of the Black Land. In Memphis, Cleopatra went ashore robed in a blue so dark it was almost black, her hair veiled in a net of silver, and the people cried out to her, wailing and beating their breasts as though they, too, mourned Caesar. At that she lifted her head, and the silver beads rang against each other as she smiled and waved to the crowd. When she picked up Caesarion, and he raised his arms to them like a runner crossing the finish line, I thought they would go mad with screaming.

"Isis! Isis!" The cordon of guards was hard put to keep them back, lest they trample us in their eagerness. But then, Memphis had always loved the Queen.

Isis incarnate, they said, bearing the world upon her slender shoulders, and the beautiful young prince who would come after.

"He is his father's son," she said afterward, ruffling his hair, and there was less pain in her voice than I expected.

"I like them to yell for me," Caesarion said. "They think I'm the prince in the story."

"You are Horus," I said. "The Son of the Widow. They cheer for you because someday you will be their king and protect them from every bad thing."

"That sounds hard," he said.

"It is," his mother said, bending him to her. "It's very hard, baby." There were tears in her eyes, but it was a clean grief, like a wound that bled enough to get the fever out.

He looked up at her, and there was something in his eyes very like Caesar. "I'll help you, Mama," he said.

"You will," she said. "You can help me now. It's time to learn to be a prince."

At three and a bit, Caesarion took up his labors. We had been five, but there had been older children then, and our father lived.

At Memphis the messengers reached us, officers sent by Caesar's friend Dolabella. It seemed that Dolabella had taken charge of the legions Caesar had massed in Syria, and now he squared off against the conspirators, Brutus and Cassius. He asked that the legions that Caesar had left in Alexandria be sent to him without delay.

"Go," Cleopatra said, "with my blessing. Go and avenge Caesar." For a moment her face changed, and I thought her more Sekhmet than Isis.

"That will leave us without troops," I observed privately, when we were aboard ship once again. "We have nothing else to defend us."

Cleopatra's brows twitched. "And nothing to defend against. All the Romans are quite occupied killing one another again." She sighed, looking out over the river. "The flood is rising well. The harvest will be good this year. For once there is nothing to be afraid of."

"For once," I said, and leaned on my elbows beside her.

We traveled up the Nile as far as Philae, to Elephantine where the river breaks over the great cataracts in its wild dash from Nubia and comes boiling out of the gorges to water our land. There is a Temple of Isis there, on an island. When we were children, Asetnefer told us that this was where Isis Herself had come, heavy with Her son, to bear Him in secret and in safety. They tell a different story in the Delta, but it is true that the temple there has power, more than any I have felt anywhere, except perhaps the Serapeum in Alexandria.

Of course, business followed us even there. Dolabella met Cassius in the field and was utterly defeated by him. This left Cassius in control in the east, and we had no troops to face him. Fortunately for us, he had other things to consider, as Octavian had met Brutus, and Brutus had come off the worse. It was said that Octavian was no general, but he had with him a young commander who had managed to pull off a fighting retreat against clear odds. Marcus Vipsanius Agrippa was barely twenty, but he was already worthy of note. Cassius had to leave off whatever he planned in the east and hasten to Brutus' aid.

W E RETURNED TO ALEXANDRIA with the autumn, with green fields beside us and the grain growing long in the rich soil. Demetria would be three soon, and she was filled with curiosity. In Philae she had been much taken with the temple musicians, and now she carried a battered old sistrum everywhere, shaking it at everything that moved. The day Caesarion threw it overboard was a sad day indeed, until one of the rowers leaped over and brought it back, to the Queen's applause and reward.

Caesarion went to bed without supper. "You may not just do as you please even though you are a prince," Cleopatra said. "And you may not take things that are your subjects' only to please yourself."

He cried himself to sleep. Coming in later that night to pronounce him forgiven, I found Demetria curled up sleeping beside him, their arms and legs entwined like so many kittens. She had forgiven him long before the unjust adults.

There was a letter waiting for me in Alexandria.

Hail Charmian,

I am in Rome again. Octavian and Antonius have made common cause, and for now they hold the city together. We hear that

Brutus has fled east to Cassius, and that whatever they plan will be there. For now we are getting into winter, and I do not think much will happen before the spring....

For us, it was the season of the harvest, and the grain came pouring in, as though the land itself were pleased.

I had more work than ever.

When a kingdom is ill served, everyone notices. When there are wars and diseases, when there is little food and it grows more expensive each day, everyone notices. But when a kingdom has peace, when there are doctors and food enough, when an honest workman's wages buy food and good things, no one notices. No one wakes up in the morning and says, "Today I have clean water! Thanks be to the gods who have worked through Pharaoh, through the men of the Royal Engineers, through the scientists who have designed our sluices and gates, through the men who have built our wells! All praise to the woman who oversees the Queen's domestic projects!" Of course they do not. This work is invisible when it is done well, just like the work of a servant. For that is what we are. We are the servants of the people.

MEANWHILE, from Dion I learned other things. He had agreed to teach me the esoteric disciplines he practiced, and now our lessons began in earnest. I had thought that perhaps some of the work of the Magus that he practiced should be forbidden to women, but Dion dismissed that. "Nature contains both male and female, and the gods are male and female alike. Why should women be barred from the study of magic? That's not logical, though it is true that there are some disciplines that seem to come easier to men than women, and the inverse." He shrugged. "I do not know why this is true, but observation indicates that it is."

I learned the four elements and their properties, the names of their guardians and their proper invocations. It was complicated, for Dion insisted that I should learn them in several languages and several systems.

"The concepts are universal," he said, "but just as the Greeks and the Egyptians may use different names for the same gods, people use many different names for the elemental guardians, depending on their need and the nature of the place where they live. In the Hebrew, we use the winged angels, the Messengers of God. The Romans call them differently, dryads and nereids, salamanders and creatures of air. In Egypt, the Sons of Horus stand at the corners, as they do about the bier."

I nodded. "But which is the right one?"

"They all are," Dion said. "Some tools are better suited to one task than another, but they are not better tools! If you need a hatchet and pick up a hammer, is the fault in the hammer or in you? The better you understand all systems, the more tools you have in your workbox. I prefer the Hebrew system for manipulation, the Egyptian for divination. Neither is better. I have a hammer and a hatchet!"

"And some tools," I said, as I understood, "are better suited to one workman than another. I am more useful with the stylus than the plow."

Dion bent and kissed the top of my head. "Ah, but that is because of the kind of tool you are! The gods did not make us all the same, nor give us the same gifts. What good would it do them to have a bucket of hammers and nothing else?"

I laughed. "And what is it that they do with their hammers?"

His face was sober. "Build the world. The world is not a garden, Charmian, but a wild place ill suited to kindness. It has been so since the earliest days, when men and women ate of the fruit of the Tree of Knowledge, and in ceasing to be animals lost their paradise." He put his robe over his arm, cleaning up after teaching. "Look at the lions in the desert, or the cattle in the field. They have no knowledge of good and evil, no understanding of what mercy should be, no sense of justice. They are happy and they live in the moment alone. They do not wonder what next year's harvest should be, nor build granaries against scarcity. They dwell still in paradise."

"And we?" I asked, bending to blow out the lamp on the table before us. "Why are we different?"

Dion lifted it gently for me, careful of the heat of the flame. "We are taught that once men and women lived in Eden, in paradise as I have said. In that garden there was a tree, and its branches held the fruit of the knowledge of good and evil. God had said that they might eat any fruit in the garden save that, but the first woman was curious. Lilit, her name was. And so she ate of the fruit, and when she did all was different. She knew that night would follow day, starvation follow plenty, and pain would follow joy. And in that moment were all the demons born, all the dark thoughts and worries that trouble mankind. For before we knew that sorrow waited, who worried? Before we knew that someday we should die, who regretted? Before we knew that ill could come to us even in the midst of joy, what had we to trouble us? Lilit knew, and she was no longer an animal like the other animals."

Dion blew out the lamp. Its flicker illuminated his face for a moment before it was plunged into darkness. "So she left her band and went apart, dwelling alone as no human did, and her man took another mate. Her name was Eve. One day, she walked alone gathering food, and she stopped beneath the tree. Lilit came to her and she spoke to her, and offered her the fruit. And Eve tasted it. When she did, her innocence was gone, and she cried bitterly for all of the knowledge that had come upon her. What of the child she expected? What if it were sick, or if it were taken by a lion? What if it were lost and she could not find it? What if death came for her son? She cursed Lilit, but she could not forget. She could not be as she was before, an animal."

"So what did she do?" I asked.

"She brought her man to the tree, and begged him taste of the fruit even though it was forbidden. And when the first man put it in his mouth, he gained the knowledge of good and evil as well. But he was made of stronger stuff than Eve."

"Like Lilit," I said.

Dion smiled. "He said, let us build a shelter against the storms that will come. Let us plant grain here by the river against the day when there is no food and the hunting is poor. Let us drive the lions away from here with fire, so that they may not hunt our children. Let us make of this world a better thing than we found. We cannot know less, but we can know more."

Dion put the lamp down. "And so mankind was driven from the garden, and since that day we have all toiled according to our natures, some to build and some to worry, some to put up walls and some to teach."

"And some to go apart," I said, thinking of Lilit. "To go apart and guard the sacred mysteries."

"Just so," Dion said. "And now you are here with me, building the Temple."

I smiled into his eyes and led him out onto the terrace where the clean night air washed over us. The harbor spread beneath us in a bowl, the waves white touched in the starlight. Across the water, Pharos gleamed, each beam of light cutting far out to sea as the vast mirrors turned. "And is this part of it not beautiful?"

Dion put his arm around me. "More beautiful than anything I have ever seen," he said.

WITH THE DRY SEASON and the new year an envoy came from Cassius. The other clients in the east had made their bows to Cassius. Would we? Our tribute to Rome was due, ten million sesterces, payable immediately to Cassius.

I should not have liked to have been the envoy when Cleopatra rose in her chair and handed him a lump of soil. "This is all your master will ever have of Egypt," she said. "I do not pay tribute to dogs and murderers!"

He went away empty-handed, and we armed for war. Some of the money coming in would pay for more ships, and to hire a guard of our own. Wisely, the Queen hired mostly veterans of Caesar's legions, either legitimately discharged, or men who would not serve the conspirators. We should not hold against an onslaught for a week, but we had to begin somewhere.

It was as well we did, for in the summer his envoys came again, demanding tribute and grain.

"You shall have no grain," the Queen said. "The Inundation is inadequate this year, and we shall need all of the surplus we have stored. There is none to give your master." So they went away empty-handed again.

It was true the harvest would be inadequate. Caesarion's first act as Pharaoh beside his mother was forgiving all farmers this year's taxes, that they might not lose their fields if they were in debt, nor mortgage all they had to buy seed for next year. He put his name to the papyrus very seriously, and I watched him biting his lip as he did it, the careful letters that said that they would owe nothing in this hard time, by order of Pharaoh Ptolemy Philometor Caesarion. The ministers and nobles could not help but smile, and say that it was well done.

Hail Charmian,

You will be surprised to hear that I am at Apollonia in Epirus, and wonder why. We have come across to Greece to see if we cannot bring them to bay at last. Antonius is a good general, very workmanlike, and we are in good supply. I also cannot fault Agrippa, who is better than I imagined. He has the talent, and that is saying something.

It is hard to believe that Caesar has been dead almost two years. It seems like a hundred, or a thousand, that he died in some ancient past like Alexander. I am glad to hear your description of the temple for him. They have declared him a god in Rome too, and Octavian has coins minted saying that he is "the son of the God Julius." He is calling himself Caesar's son now instead of his great-nephew, through some Roman custom of adoption, which I think is all very confusing. He is already the closest kinsman of age, and he is doing what he should to avenge his great-uncle. Why does he need to say more?

I wish that I might see you and Dion again, but I fear you would find me greatly changed. War does that.

I expect you will hear from Octavian and Antonius soon, now that you have got a fleet. We need to keep Brutus and Cassius from escaping by sea, when we have finally trapped them....

That request came soon enough.

"The Triumvirs Octavian, Antonius, and Lepidus request that Queen Cleopatra send her fleet through the blockade at Cape Taenarum and into the Aegean, so that the murderers of Caesar may not escape vengeance by sea."

They had sent Rufio, one of Caesar's men who had been in Alexandria before, and he was greeted in the most formal manner in the great throne room, before the Queen and Pharaoh, who sat at her side in white linen, an ancient pectoral across his chest. Caesarion was five years old, and he sat as still as a statue on his throne.

"We will consider your request," the Queen said, the uraeus on her brow, "and give you an answer tomorrow. We know how urgent your business is."

Afterward, the Queen paced up and down in her rooms, Apollodorus and her captains at hand. Iras stood quiet by the window, but her fingers twitched.

"The fleet is ready, Gracious Queen," the admiral said. "I will not say that it is perfected, but it cannot be perfected without battle. Training only imparts so much to green men. I have trained all I can. Now it is time to use what we have learned."

"To run the blockade because these Romans request it?" Cleopatra's tone was mild, as mild as Caesar's had been, and I was reminded abruptly of him. Caesarion was not the only one who resembled him sometimes.

"To put an end to the conspirators," Apollodorus said.

"And is that safer?" Cleopatra asked. "While the Romans are killing each other, we are secure."

"Only as long as no one wins," I said. "Then the winner will turn himself to face Egypt, and ask if we were ally or foe."

"And better that be Antonius or Octavian rather than Cassius and

Brutus," Apollodorus said. "We don't want them to lose. If they do, Rome will be our implacable enemy."

The Queen nodded. "That must be prevented at all costs. Very well, then. We go to war."

With those simple words it was done.

THE PROGRESS
OF DIONYSOS

T he Queen and Iras sailed with the fleet soon after. This time it was I who stayed with Dion and Apollodorus in Alexandria. Caesarion was too young and too valuable to risk, and so I stayed as well.

They were not gone long. An unusual summer gale caught the fleet only a few days out, and the ships were tossed and separated. Indeed, we learned afterward that several had made the Greek coast and there been wrecked on the shore, but most were just driven off course and far apart, though some also sustained damage, principally to their oars. The Queen and Iras were back in Alexandria in two weeks, with nothing to show for the expedition besides damaged ships that limped back into port for a month after, and a case of seasickness that had laid the Queen and Iras prostrate.

I thought to myself that surely I would not have been so sick, but that was easy to say when I had not left Alexandria.

Needless to say, orders were given to reorganize and repair the fleet as soon as possible. While we repaired in Alexandria, the conspirators might be escaping.

They did not. Before our fleet could set out again, news came that Antonius had faced the conspirators at Philippi in Macedonia, and it had been a bloody stalemate, neither side gaining any real advantage. Antonius and Octavian had lost more than sixteen thousand men, but Cassius had been slain.

There were no letters for me or Dion.

"Emrys must not have had time," Dion said. But the messenger had left two days after the battle.

If he were dead, I thought, would I know? His was not the crashing and resounding death of a Caesar. Would I know, only because it mattered to me? Probably not.

I wrote to him and said nothing of it, instead giving only light talk and gossip, news of the children and Demetria's latest doings. Before our messages could even have arrived, there was a second battle at Philippi, three weeks after the first. This time it was decisive. The conspirators were defeated, and Brutus committed suicide rather than be captured.

When we heard, Antonius was already on the move, across the Hellespont into Asia. He and Octavian had divided the world between them, and the East was Antonius'.

The year had already turned when I got a letter from Ephesos.

Hail Charmian,

I write to you from Ephesos, where I am recovering from a wound at the first battle at Philippi. I got a bad slash on my left leg, as that was what they could reach with me mounted. It wasn't bad itself. But then I had blood poisoning, and Sigismund tells me I was mad, but I don't remember a thing about it. He says I called for my wife to see her once more before I died, and hurled invective at my brother-in-law, but as I have neither that seems unlikely. However, I am not dead yet.

Brutus and Cassius are, and it seems we will finally be finished with this war. I hear that we are going into garrison somewhere in Syria to be on our guard against the Parthians. Garrison duty would be nice after so much war. Perhaps it will be so. I only have five and a half years left before my discharge. Maybe I will even get there, though they say that when you start saying that your number will come up.

Farewell,
Emrys Aurelianus, Praefectus

I am now the Beneficiarius, or second-in-command, of the Alia Milliaria. Which is twice as many men, about seven hundred. In other words, the whole unit that is left of us whom Caesar raised in Gaul together. Which means I have staff duties now, but I do not mind that while I am still on light duty.

"Well, that's that," I said to Dion as we shared our letters. "I doubt he'll be in Alexandria any time soon."

"I wouldn't bet on it," Dion said. "The letters came with Antonius' envoy, Quintus Dellius. He's got a letter for the Queen from Antonius. He wants to meet with her."

"He knows where she is," I said. "I expect it has something to do with Judea. You know a lot of people are saying Herod poisoned Antipater himself. The young lion couldn't wait for the old one to die. And Herod has attached himself to Antonius fairly firmly."

Dion raised an eyebrow. "And the Queen?"

"She'll deal with Herod if she needs to," I said. "And Antonius. If we are to meet with him, it will be on her terms. You can be certain of that."

WE WENT BY SEA to Tarsus, on the coast of Asia Minor, where Antonius was wintering. I went with the Queen, and the others stayed in Alexandria, because this time it was my skills that were needed to transform our flagship into a floating palace. No, *more* than a floating palace. A dream.

Our sails were dyed purple, and the rails gilded. The oars were painted pink and gold, and the bow decorated with Triton blowing on a conch shell, done in lightweight wood and painted to look like gold. Her sides were painted as well. All of the female servants arrayed themselves in the rigging and on the rails as we came into the harbor, dressed in pink and saffron gauze, while on her deck musicians played, the sound of drums and flutes echoing over the waters.

Amidships the Queen waited, reclining like Isis Pelagia beneath a pavilion of sea-green mesh held back with golden ropes. Her gown was cloth of gold, pleated in a million folds lest anyone forget that Isis Pelagia ruled Egypt, Queen of the Waters, the Lady of the Sea incarnate.

As we made our way up the river mouth, crowds came to stare, pointing and shouting. In the rigging, our ladies waved back, and I had two pretty youths dressed as Eros go around and light two huge censers that stood well forward, full of second-quality myrrh and copper powder. They burned with a blue-green flame, and the scent of Asia followed us, billowing out in clouds to starboard. Which was a good thing, because otherwise the Queen would have been choking.

People were running along the banks, and I had the trumpeters blow a fanfare. The oars dipped in perfect time, gold tips biting. The sails came down precisely.

"Aphrodite! Aphrodite!" The crowd was yelling as we came alongside the dock. "Cythera!" There were even some shouts of "Cleopatra!"

I could make out the Romans now, ordinary soldiers running and shouting the same as the people of Tarsus. I stood behind the Queen, in a sea-green gown the same shade as the curtains, ropes of seashells in my hair.

"Isis!" someone shouted ashore, but the shouts of "Aphrodite!" were louder. I could see their faces now, townsmen and children, shepherds and soldiers. Even the Romans were impressed.

I nodded to the first of the women slaves on the rail holding to the rigging, and she brought out a handful of silver and copper, coins of Egypt showing Cleopatra as Isis the Queen of the Waters, the lighthouse on the reverse. With a wild wave and smile, she threw them high in the air, some landing on the edge of the dock, but most plunging into the harbor. The other girls followed suit, smiling and laughing like nereids, the coins rising in a glittering shower.

Boys started jumping into the shallow water after them, cheering and splashing. All through the town people were running down to the port to see what was happening, clouds of incense rolling over our bow.

"I expect Antonius knows we're here," the Queen said out of the corner of her mouth.

"Yes," I said, one eye on the girls in the rigging to make sure that all was well.

I saw him then, standing with a group of men in the street above the dock, his head bare and his eyes on us, Emrys well and whole. When he saw me looking he bowed, the acknowledgment of work well done, one Companion to another. My heart jumped.

The trumpeters blew a long fanfare. One of the Queen's officers came forward, flanked by royal guardsmen, as the sailors ran to put the gangplank down and let him go ashore. Two Romans were shouldering their way through the crowd. One of them was Dellius, who Antonius had sent to Alexandria.

The officer thumped his staff. "All hail Cleopatra, Pharaoh of Egypt, Lover of Her Father, Isis Incarnate, Lady of Justice and Mercy, Queen of the Seas. She has come seeking Marcus Antonius, the First Man of Rome."

Dellius was grinning as he pushed his way to the fore and bowed deeply. "On behalf of Imperator Marcus Antonius, I wish to extend every welcome and courtesy to Her Majesty. It would give the Imperator the greatest pleasure if the Gracious Queen would consent to dine with him this evening."

"Our Gracious Lady thanks the Imperator, but would rather be his host this evening."

Dellius bowed deeply again. "I will inform the Imperator of the Queen's kind invitation immediately. I am sure he will be honored."

In other words, I thought, you will make sure he is honored and that he is there. If the Queen can come here from Egypt, Antonius can come down to the dock.

"Now," I whispered, and the boys loosed the golden ropes, letting the heavy curtains swing shut over the Queen's pavilion, and the light mesh over them. Inside, the light was cut to the blue-green consistency of underwater. All of this time Cleopatra had not moved a muscle.

When the curtains were closed she sat up. "It went well. Thank you, Charmian. That was excellent theater."

"You are very welcome, Gracious Queen," I said, smiling at the public praise.

"Will he come, do you think?" She took off the heavy headdress and ran a hand through her damp hair.

"He will come," I said. "And we will be ready."

As royal banquets went, it was fairly small, constrained by the size of the ship, large as she was. Breaking down all of the bulkheads on the main deck except for the very aft cabin, which was Cleopatra's, we could create a sizable audience chamber for a banquet—twelve couches with room between for tables—able to dine thirty-two in perfect comfort, as neither the Queen nor Antonius should share a couch. Since Apollodorus, the captain, and Admiral Alexas should all be present as a matter of course, that meant Antonius could bring with him as many as twenty-nine officers, so for form's sake when I spoke to Dellius in the afternoon I gave him word we could seat twenty-four, so as to leave some room for the Queen's ladies who would be delighted to share the couches of the guests. Dellius took that quite properly as twenty, and sent word around to the eighteen most senior officers who would not be on duty that night.

As soon as the bulkheads were down I spent the afternoon overseeing the final rehearsals of the entertainment, the cleaning and placement of the banquet furniture that had been stored in the hold, the gifts for Antonius, and of course the details of the floral arrangements. We had been limited in the number of food animals we could bring on the ship, but the duck that would be served was our own, so that was one less worry. The cooking was already well begun, the scent of coriander wafting from the grills, and the fruits being sliced on tables in the sun on the foredeck. One of the boys was standing over the tables with a fan, keeping the flies off.

"Nicely done," I said to him as I went by.

By evening the curtains were rigged out on the deck, hiding the wooden sides of the ship with embroidered hangings in green, blue, and aqua, appliquéd together in wave patterns, so that with all of them hung it seemed that one stood in an undersea grotto. There were twelve couches, in four groups of three along the length of the ship, alternating right and left, and separated with curtains of sea-green gauze studded with the aforementioned painted seashells and looped back with golden rope so that there were almost nooks for the couches. Gilded lanterns hung above, their flames encased in cut glass that had a slight green tint.

The couches for the Queen, Antonius, and the one that would be shared by Apollodorus and Antonius' most senior officer were the farthest aft, with the hangings screening them from the stern cabin. The musicians were all the way forward with the big table drum and the seats for the trumpeters. They would move about during the evening, but the wind players, except for the flutists, couldn't be expected to stand the entire time.

My gown was cobalt-blue silk, with wide gold borders at the neck and across the shoulders and on the cascading fabric over my upper arms. The cloth had come from Hyderabad, and it had been intended for a wedding sari, the work of weeks on the loom. The Queen's gown was more fantastic still, sea green and embroidered with pearls. There were more than a hundred large pearls sewn about the neckline and across the shoulders, with more seed pearls worked in. Drops of peridots hung from her ears, and the collar of peridot, turquoise, and gold that she wore above the plunging neckline was so heavy that it had a counterweight attached at the back, like the ancient pectorals that she wore for state occasions.

"You look lovely," I said, examining the work of the hairdresser, who had curled her hair with a hot iron and lifted it with golden combs, so that tendrils framed her face.

Cleopatra took a breath. "Enough?"

"Enough," I said. This was not the feast of a queen, but of a goddess. It must not merely impress. It must stun. And the entire thing was no more than a setting for her. "He will be amazed," I said.

At that moment the trumpeters blew, and I ran to the window and peeked out through the curtain.

Marcus Antonius was carried in a litter with purple hangings, and from what I could see his tunic was purple as well. He wore a gilded breastplate worked with lions, and instead of a cloak, a lionskin hung from his shoulders, like Hercules or the coins of Alexander. Or Dionysos. That was what it was meant to invoke, with his gilded sandals and the procession of other litters behind him.

"He is Dionysos," I said to the Queen, who of course could not be seen sticking her head out the window. "He comes like the new Dionysos, or like a bridegroom."

"Good," she said, and there was something in her voice that made me shiver, as though for a moment some deeper resonance spoke through her. "A sacred marriage, and the marriage of peoples."

I looked about sharply, but she stood there in the reflected light of her pearls, almost too small for the grandeur.

"It will be well, my sister," I said, and was not certain it was to my sister I spoke.

I HARDLY SAT DOWN during the banquet, except for a moment on the end of Quintus Dellius' couch while the tumblers were doing a procession of nereids down the center of the deck.

Dressed in shades of blue, with their faces painted cobalt and bone, they looked strange and beautiful indeed, doing their work to the slow, haunting strains of flute alone. There were no quick movements in this performance. As though they were underwater, they turned and posed, four girls and three youths. Two backbends against each other, and then legs rising slowly in the air, like some strange anemone drifting in the current, then a walkover as languorous as a dream.

Slowly, from the tangle of limbs, the strongest of the youths lifted a girl on his shoulders, her long blond hair falling like a river of platinum, her head thrown back as though in ecstasy. They turned slowly, her arms twining around his neck, and he lifted her to a handstand on his shoulders. She folded like some exotic coral, one leg across his shoulders while the other girls reached up. It was incredibly beautiful, and all the more difficult for its slowness. Everyone always thinks that the quick tumbling runs are difficult, but they are easier than this control.

After they finished, the musicians began a different tune while the servers began bringing around the sweets and the unwatered wine. I slipped out the back curtains where the dancers were toweling off to tell them they did well. They had several routines prepared, for different occasions, but this was the first time they had done this one for a royal banquet.

Emrys was standing by the gangplank, talking with two of our guards. I heard him laughing at some joke in Koine, a smile on his face.

"Lady?" One of the girls was at my back. "Do you want the cheesecakes with the honey topping on them, or on the side?"

"On them," I said, turning away from Emrys. He must be in charge of Antonius' escort. But I would have to speak with him later, when the banquet was over. It was after midnight already. They had been on the couches for nearly five hours. "And garnish them with the mint leaves."

They lingered over the wine for two more hours. The Queen, who did not like to be drunk, nursed three cups in that time, while Antonius must have consumed at least twelve. In any case, I thought, more than was good for him. His voice was getting too loud in the confined space, the curls across his brow had unwound in the heat and lay damply across his forehead, and his gestures were getting bigger and bigger. He had eyes for nothing but the Queen.

I crossed behind his couch on the pretext of getting something. "You are Aphrodite," he was telling the Queen. "You are a goddess in the flesh."

"I know," she said, with a long secret smile.

Antonius looked at her over the rim of his cup. "You do know, don't you? You really think that."

"Don't you?"

He put the cup down abruptly. "Caesar was no god."

"And why do you say not?" Cleopatra rolled her cup between her hands, priceless cameos set into silver on the surface, looking as though this were all part of the symposium — debate Caesar's godhead.

"He died," Antonius said.

"And you think he has ceased to exist? Are you an atheist then?"

Antonius shrugged. "It doesn't matter, does it? Whether or not he has a soul, he is no longer Caesar. He can no longer win battles or share your bed."

She looked as though she were enjoying herself. "And this matters to you?"

"Do you not need a living man?"

Cleopatra's eyes sparkled as she gestured around the hall. "Are there not plenty of men?"

"Not men who are Antonius," he said, leaning forward. "I'm well recommended."

The Queen laughed. "I know. Fulvia said."

That took him aback for a moment, then he leaned forward on his elbow again, speaking like a conspirator. "Fulvia isn't here."

"I can see that," Cleopatra said. "But I have come on diplomatic business, not looking for a stud bull. You will have to do more than brag of your prowess to win Aphrodite." She reached up with one jeweled hand and caressed his cheek, her third finger brushing lightly against his lips.

"What must I do then?" he asked.

The Queen rose to her feet, giving him her wreath as though she were a girl at a harvest feast. "Pray," she said, and with a smile swept out through the curtains.

Antonius followed her with his eyes, holding the wreath.

Yes, I thought, he is fascinated.

"More wine, Imperator?" I asked, holding a golden pitcher in my hands.

"Yes," he said, and looked around the remains of the feast.

It was a strong vintage. I poured it out, but he did not drink, merely held the cup in his hands as he rolled onto his back, looking up at the lamps above. I wondered what he saw there.

THE SUCCESSORS

I t was nearly dawn before the party ended. Or almost ended. Many of the guests did not look like they were leaving. Antonius and several of his officers had not so much left as just gone to sleep where they were, on couches in the banquet hall. This meant that we could not break down the banquet hall at all, but would just have to wait until day, when presumably they would go back to their quarters in the town.

As my cabin had been taken apart to make the banquet hall, and my couch was one of the ones occupied by guests, I got my cloak and prepared to curl up on deck somewhere well forward. Going out into the night air, I saw a familiar figure against the rail, his profile clear against the lights of the town beyond.

"Emrys," I said.

He turned and put his arms around me, holding me tight against his chest, saying nothing.

I leaned my head against his shoulder, my arms under his beneath his cloak. "I've missed you," I said. It wasn't what I meant to say.

"I've missed you too," he said, his face against my hair, and for a long moment we simply stood there. "Charmian..."

"Yes?" I closed my eyes against him, holding him tight. Beneath us, the ship moved faintly on the waves.

"I did miss you. More than I expected to." He sounded almost embarrassed.

"Well, I suppose I missed you more than I expected too," I said. "I didn't imagine I should miss you. But I did. I did."

Emrys squeezed me tighter. "I'm glad of it. Though it was harder, somehow."

"Harder?"

He half-shrugged, his arms still around me. "Harder to go into battle, knowing that you would miss me if I died, that you would wonder what had happened to me, and that you might never know. I didn't want that. I never wanted it. I swore I should never leave a woman waiting and wondering."

"It's not like that," I said, raising my face to his, and seeing there the shadows of some tribal war in Gaul, the mourning women left with ragged children at their skirts, prey for anyone. "I belong to the Queen. I will always have a place there, me and any children of mine. I will never want or lack because of you." I put one hand to the side of his face and said the thing we had been talking around, and avoided all of the time we were in Rome. "I do not need you, Emrys. Even if I were to be your lover. I would not need you."

He nodded, his brows drawn. "Good."

"I simply want you," I said. "There's wanting and there's needing, Emrys. You're like…" I flailed about for a metaphor. "Dessert," I finished.

Emrys laughed. "And you love dessert!"

"A little too much," I said ruefully. It was true that I was plumper than when he had seen me last.

Laughing, he kissed me, sweet and tender, but with a passion beneath it that made me catch my breath. Marcus Agrippa had not known what he was doing, I thought, and for that matter neither had Lucan. I supposed I should thank Dion. At that thought I could hardly keep from giggling.

We came up for air, and Emrys rested his forehead against mine.

"I should thank Dion," I said.

Emrys smiled, and then his face grew serious. "We talked about it, Dion and I. In letters when you were in Rome, and since then. It was his suggestion, actually."

I shook my head. "He never stops surprising me."

"Dion said that he knew I liked women too, and of course he expected me to marry, as most of his friends do. And I told him I couldn't marry, as he perfectly well knew. But he said it would be easier if it were someone he loved."

I put my forehead against his shoulder. "Dion is as dear to me as a brother. I would never want to come between you."

"That's what he said," Emrys said, his arms around me. "That you were a cat who comes and goes, but you should never want to own me."

"Nor be owned," I said. Dion understood me very, very well. "But I do care for you." It came as a surprise to me as I said it. Perhaps I had not realized it myself until I saw him again in Tarsus, how I had come to care for him in those months in Rome, and how I had mourned when I thought him dead.

He bent his head gravely, as though in surrender. "And I you. And I love Dion."

"So do I," I said. "And surely love can make all possible."

There was a smile in his eyes. "I am almost daring enough to think so."

"I'm daring enough," I said, and kissed him again. It was heady and sweet, and I felt the passion begin to uncoil in my belly, growing and filling me, my hand sliding up his thigh beneath his tunic, stroking him there.

Emrys moaned.

"If I had a room," I began breathlessly.

"Don't you?" He felt warm against me, pressed in all of the right places.

"No. I mean, I usually do. But we took out the bulkheads to make room for the banquet, and they haven't been put back yet."

"Ah." Emrys sounded amused. "So where were you planning to sleep?"

"On deck," I said. "It's not that cold. I was just going to find a corner somewhere until morning."

"Find a corner with me, then," he said. "It's warmer for two."

We lay down together in the shadow of the rail, our overlapping cloaks covering us. It was very uncomfortable. At least until I put my head on his shoulder and propped myself around him, hooking my knee over his.

Emrys grunted. "That's warmer." He settled around a bit, trying to get comfortable, my body pressed against his side.

I smiled against him. "I'm going to abduct you," I said. "I'm going to tie you up below, and when we sail for Alexandria you won't have any choice but to come with us."

"Somehow I don't think Antonius will approve of that," he said, but I could hear the note of excitement in his voice.

"We can tie him up and take him too."

"I know he won't approve of that," Emrys said. He licked his lip. "I'm afraid it would be my duty to escape."

I caressed his wrist with one finger, leaning closer. "Even if I tied you up very nicely?"

He took a deep breath. "Now that begins to get more difficult."

"If I had a room…"

"If you did, you could certainly try it." He touched my face gently, turning it up to him. "You have beautiful eyes. I suppose you get tired of men saying that."

"Actually, no one has said it but you," I said. "I think men are a little afraid of me. The ones who understand me at all."

"Just because you're beautiful, brilliant, and have incredible amounts of power?" Emrys laughed. "Nothing there to be afraid of." He put his arms around me again. "I'm used to the idea of ruling queens. Gwendolyn of Corneu, for example. She lived in my grandfather's day." Emrys shrugged. "Of course you serve your Queen, your ruler, and your kinswoman, as best you can with all honor. To do anything less would be wrong. I would never try to persuade you from your duty, any more than you would try to persuade me."

I put my head against his shoulder, half dreaming from the late hour and from the warmth. We lay in silence until I thought he was almost sleeping, beneath the stars above. Sothis burned brightly on his way up the sky.

WE WOKE IN THE HOUR before dawn, more than a little cramped and stiff. Together, we watched the sky pale. The great galley swung gently on the tide. Somewhere in the town a cock crowed.

I shifted against Emrys' shoulder.

"What does your Queen want?" Emrys asked quietly.

"An alliance," I said. "A market for our grain, an ally against any other power in the East, and the guarantee that Rome will not simply take what we have."

For a long moment he was silent. "Rome is good at taking what she wants," he said. "Why pay for something, or bargain for it, if you can simply have it? Rome cannot feed herself." He glanced down at me on his shoulder, the stubble on his chin rubbing against my forehead. "Her fields are plowed by slaves from Gaul or over the Rhenus. In order for there to be a constant supply of new slaves there must be constant expansion of the borders. And the more she grows, the more she must grow in order to keep feeding herself. Here sits Egypt, with more food than anywhere else in the world, with no army to keep off Rome. What is to stop Rome simply taking?"

"Cleopatra," I said.

"Other people have thought that," he said. "Vercingetorix was not the only one."

"Rome cannot be resisted by arms," I said. "We know that. There is not enough money in the world to build the army that could face Rome in the field. The only thing we can do is make an alliance, as we did with Caesar. And as long as Roman fights Roman, someone will need Egypt."

His eyebrows rose. "Antonius and Octavian are in accord."

"At the moment," I said. "But why should not this situation fall out as it did with the Successors of Alexander? Caesar held together this cobbled and piecemeal thing that is Rome, a collection of territories with nothing in common and little desire to work together. Now Caesar is gone. As happened then, lesser men scramble for the remains. Why should not Octavian and Antonius come to the same pass as Antigonus, Seleucus, and Ptolemy? The entirety is too great to be held together by any man except an Alexander or a Caesar. Were it divided, there would be states of reasonable size, and while there might be war between them, it would reach stability when none would have a marked advantage. In the shadow of each brokered peace there could be centuries of civilization."

"And what is your Queen here to offer Antonius?"

"The chance to be Ptolemy," I said.

He was silent for a long moment. "Antonius is not Ptolemy," he said carefully. "And Octavian will not throw his chances away on a desperate gamble, or settle for less than all."

"I know Antonius is not Ptolemy," I said. "But he is the man there is."

THE SECOND NIGHT'S BANQUET was even more fantastic than the first. We used the hangings of saffron silk, looped back with ropes of seashells. The couches were strewn with rose petals, while the best roses whole and intact were woven into garlands and used on the tables. The scent of roses was exquisite. In the warmth of the afternoon, before the guests arrived, the scent diffused throughout the room and it smelled less like a banquet than a temple. Petals floated in the golden bowls of water presented to the guests as they came aboard that they might wash their hands. The dancers wore feathers and nothing else, moving and swaying like dancing birds, or some strange sea creature living among the pearls at the sea bottom in shallow water.

The Queen was in blue, tending toward purple, which would stand out best amid the gold. She wore the uraeus, and a collar of gold and lapis. The cartouche on the weight at the back said that it had once belonged to the mother of Pharaoh Seti. We both hated to take such treasures from Egypt and trust them to the vagaries of the sea, but there was nothing else like them, nothing else that would do for Isis Pelagia.

Antonius was speechless.

WE SAILED FOR ALEXANDRIA on the third day, with Antonius aboard. I do not know how Emrys managed to wrangle a place as one of the few officers sent. The majority of Antonius' men would stay in Tarsus, while some few, including the cavalry, would begin the long march of many months to Egypt. Only twenty or so went by ship. But one of them was Emrys.

We sailed at noon, and watched the sun set over the sea while the Queen and Antonius dined in the open air on the aft deck. He looked at nothing but her, a man entranced.

Emrys stood beside me at the rail. "Do you have your room back yet?" he asked. He glanced sideways at me, and I saw the corner of his mouth twitch.

I laughed. "Yes, and should I tie you up and keep you there?"

"You might," he said, and I glanced sideways to see the real desire in his face.

I leaned against him. "Emrys, I promise you will be a luckier man by far than Antonius this evening!"

"What is she waiting for?"

"Egypt," I said. "It must be on Egyptian soil, this marriage of Isis and Dionysos."

Emrys leaned on his elbows, thinking. "The marriage of Isis and Dionysos. Does Dion say this?"

I nodded. "Yes. Dion says a lot of things." I paused, thinking how much I could tell him, and how much he would think strange or dangerous. "Did you ever wonder how when Caesar died I was ready?"

He looked out to sea, his face still. "I assumed you saw it. Dion said a long time ago that you could have been a seer, an oracle. And that perhaps you were once, in some other time." He glanced at me over his shoulder. "We have the Sight among the Keltoi too, you know. I'm not afraid of it. But I don't want you to see for me."

"I can't do it on purpose," I said, relaxing and leaning against the rail beside him, our shoulders almost touching. "Maybe I could have if I'd been given to one of the temples with an oracular tradition. But I went to Bastet at Bubastis, which isn't one of those. I learned how to run the Queen's household instead. And how to manage the needs of the kingdom."

"Which is important," he said. The sun was setting into the waves, orange and gold, the clouds feathered pink against the sky. "But sometimes you see things anyway?"

"Sometimes," I said. "It's not like seeing. It's just knowing, usually. Just knowing that something is. I can cast lots and know how the dice will fall. I can ask something simple, like show me an odd number if the answer is no, and an even number if the answer is yes. Something easy like that. It works fairly often."

He nodded. "I've seen men do that. It doesn't work for me, though." Emrys smiled sheepishly. "Because the dice usually roll what I want them to. So all I get is the answer I wanted."

"You can roll what you want?"

He nodded. "I'll show you when we're not on a moving deck. I can call a throw and get it about half the time, more when it's late and I'm tired."

"That sounds very useful," I said.

"Not as useful as knowing that Caesar's been killed before anyone tells you," he said.

"Maybe so," I said. I had never thought of it that way before. I did not serve the Lady of Amenti, not in this life. I had pledged my service to Cleopatra when we were children together, sealed it with the sacrifice of my own blood. I belonged to Egypt, to Alexandria, to the things Ptolemy and his men had wrought, to their white city by the sea.

"Emrys," I said slowly, "I think I was there. When Alexander died."

I waited, not daring to look at him. He didn't laugh.

"When Caesar was killed and we were doing things, I knew...,
Emrys, I don't have words for this, but that we'd done this before. You
and I. In Babylon. You were Persian, one of the lords who came with
Oxathres. I can see you so clearly in my mind's eye. Him. You."

"I don't know," he said gravely. "It could be. There are stranger
things in the world. But the gift of memory has never been mine.
Sometimes I go somewhere and the place feels familiar, or I meet
someone and I feel like I already know them, but I don't remember
anything specific." He gave me a sideways glance. "Perhaps I was
bathed in the River of Lethe, and it all washed away. Or maybe it's
somewhere in the back of my mind, and comes only in dreams. I don't
remember anything."

I nodded. At least he wasn't laughing or telling me to be rational.

"You remember things?" he asked.

I nodded again. "A little. Not enough."

"If I were you," he said, "I'd look it up."

"Look it up?"

Emrys smiled. "You've the greatest library in the world at your
fingertips. If you think you were there, if you remember things, you
could look it up. Find him. Find you."

I voiced the thing I had not, not ever. "It's just that people will
laugh at me."

"So don't tell everyone," Emrys said. "You don't have to tell everybody everything you really believe."

I started laughing. "No," I said, "I suppose I don't. But I can't lie
about it."

"There's a difference between lying and not mentioning it. If people will laugh at you or make you feel badly, just don't say anything to
them."

"It's hard enough to be taken seriously already," I said. "There have
been female ministers before, but not many. There have been ruling
Queens of Egypt before. But it's hard. If I stumble, there are always
people ready to say, you see? That is what comes of entrusting a woman
with high office."

"Cleopatra trusts you," he said.

I nodded. "And often that's enough. I don't mean to say it's always bad, Emrys. Most of the men at court respect me. This is Alexandria. They didn't grow up with their mothers cloistered in women's quarters, and there are eunuchs with high office too, like the Minister of the Interior. Even the admirals have worked with people who aren't men before. But it's never entirely the same as if I were a man."

Emrys leaned back, swaying with the movement of the ship. "If I were a woman, I should want to live in Alexandria. I might like that better, I think. Next time."

I looked at him sideways. "Why?"

"I should not have to go to war," he said.

I SLEPT IN THE ANTECHAMBER to the Queen's cabin, which was astern on the uppermost deck, running the width of the ship. The antechamber was also the full width of the ship, but only half that distance across, filled to the brim with things too valuable to risk getting wet in the hold, the Queen's spare linens and curtains, her clothes and other things of that nature. One of the dining couches was wedged in between the bulkheads where it wouldn't shift too much, the distance between the Queen's cabin and the outer door just long enough to fit it in. I slept there, where I could hear Cleopatra in a moment if she needed me, and where anyone trying to enter her cabin unauthorized would have to climb over me in the process. Not that I thought Antonius would try. It would be incredibly undignified to have that sort of bedroom farce.

Emrys was indeed more fortunate than Antonius, though it was a near thing. People kept popping in and out to talk to the Queen until it was very late, and then I fell asleep while Emrys was still on deck with Antonius. I woke when he came in and sat down on the edge of the couch, ducking so that the unlit lamp hanging from the bulkhead above wouldn't hit him in the head.

"Oh," he said quietly, "I didn't think you were sleeping."

"I'm not," I said, still mostly asleep.

Emrys ran his hand over my hair, unbound over my arms in sleep. "It's never the right time, is it?"

"It is," I whispered, and reached up and drew him down to me.

It had been a long time since I had been Marcus' lover, but that had never felt like this, as though we moved underwater, slow and smooth and quiet, our voices hushed so that we would not be heard through the thin partition. I had never been with someone more experienced than I was, not with Lucan or with Marcus, and I did not know how it could feel, the dance of tongues, the gentleness of his swordsman's hands on my skin, the dreamlike warmth of it, of feeling passion rolling like long waves, answering to his touch while he stopped my cries with a kiss.

Afterward, I lay beside him, my head on his shoulder with him crammed against the side of the ship. Above, the lamp swayed with each wave, swinging slowly back and forth.

He closed his eyes, his eyelashes darker than his hair, a long sweep of lash against his cheek. "It feels right," he whispered.

"Yes," I said, fitting against him as though I belonged there.

"Like I've dreamed we've done this before," Emrys said. "The movement of the ship and the sound of the water on the hull, the way you feel beneath me."

"In some dream we've forgotten," I whispered. And I fell asleep against him, listening to the sound of the waves.

WE CAME INTO ALEXANDRIA in evening, with the city alight and Pharos throwing great beams out to sea like Prometheus unbound. A procession came down to the docks, and laughing and waving, the Queen and Antonius stepped into litters twined with vines and were carried to the palace.

I stood at the rail, my arm around Emrys, and I felt the exact moment when he stiffened.

Dion was making his way toward the ship. He looked up.

"Charmian," Emrys said, and I saw the indecision on his face.

I gave him one last squeeze. "Go on, my darling," I said. "He's been waiting for you so long."

I saw their eyes meet, speaking eyes above the crowd. I watched Emrys go down the plank, watched him walk through the public bearers jostling and shouting and proclaiming they gave the best fares to anywhere in the city, guaranteed. I saw them meet, but not touch. Emrys was still in uniform, and still before the eyes of Romans.

And if I cried, it was bittersweet as I watched them walk away together.

İⁿ THE CİTY
⊙F İSİS

A ntonius got what he wanted when they were on Egyptian
soil.

Unlike Caesar, who had had a great deal to do when he
was in Alexandria, Antonius had very little to demand his attention.
The bulk of his army had stayed in Tarsus, and the contingent he had
set upon the road would be months yet before it arrived in Alexandria,
having to march overland throughout the length of the Middle Sea.
He had brought with him no more than a couple of bodyguards and a
handful of officers, men who spoke Koine well and could be of assistance to him.

What did Antonius want? I thought I knew. He wanted a power
base that owed nothing to Octavian and that would be loyal to him.
And he wanted the Queen. That much was desire, not politics. Perhaps
it had been simmering beneath the surface since we were in Rome,
when he could say nothing with Caesar beside her, a living man. But
now Caesar had been dead three years. Even a queen cannot mourn
forever.

Of course she intended it to be an act. It was theater, what we did
in Tarsus. But it is a trap I have noticed often with the actors who can
make you weep at the beauty of their words. They make themselves
weep too. The tears are real. They cannot pretend to mourn Hector
as Priam without drawing deep from some well of human experience,
without imagining that their own beloved child lay thus. They must

believe it. It must become real. So, I think, the trap closed on Cleopatra. In pretending to love, how could she not feel it? Or perhaps Isis, who opens the hearts of all women, played her own game.

In any event, the fourth day back in Alexandria I went into the Queen's quarters in the morning to find them both in the bath, Cleopatra and Antonius. No slave stood by, and when I came to the door I understood.

Antonius sat on the seat of the pool under the wide oculus, with her straddling him, her hands against the flat plain of his chest, his arms on her waist as he guided her up and down upon him. His face was a study in abstracted ecstasy, knowing nothing but her, and her slow, sensual smile was entirely unguarded. The light poured down from above, from the silvered mirrors.

I backed out quickly, hoping they had not heard me. They hadn't, of course. They were lost to everything but each other.

This was not like Gnaeus Pompeius, where I knew too much, or Caesar, where I knew too little. This was not meant for me to know at all.

I left word with the bath slaves that if the Queen wanted me I should be at the Library.

I HAD NOT SPENT AS MUCH TIME in the Library as Iras had, but it was hardly unusual for me to be there. Generally I needed geography or current affairs, the recent histories of nearby peoples so that I might brief the Queen on the lineage of some person she would meet, or upon the history of a tribe or house, or the economy of some particular place. For our trip to Rome, the briefing scrolls had been thirty scrolls long, and covered such topics as the speeches of Cato and Cicero, and the reputed love affairs of Publius Clodius.

This time I wanted older topics. "Excuse me, Master," I said to the head of references. "I am in need of help with a search."

The scholar inclined his head as he recognized me. "I'll do what I can. What city and what people are you in search of?"

"This city," I said. "I am looking for one of the men who came to Alexandria with Ptolemy. A cavalryman. Not a Macedonian, I think, nor a Persian. Someone in the Companions at the time of Alexander's death, but who lived after to see the building of the city. His name might be Lydias."

The scholar must have been perplexed, but good manners kept him from asking why in the world I wanted to read about a man dead two hundred years or so of whom I already knew so little, whose name I might have heard in a dream. "You said he came with Ptolemy. Was he known to him?"

"Yes," I said, nodding. I felt certain of that. Ptolemy son of Lagos had always seemed terribly real to me.

"Then begin with Ptolemy," he said.

So I found myself in one of the study rooms, my hands washed twice to make sure there was no trace of grease on them, alabaster weights holding the scroll unwrapped so that I would not have to touch it, the same scroll that Apollodorus had shown us so long ago on the first day of our lessons, that we might come to love learning.

These are the words of Ptolemy Soter, I thought, Ptolemy son of Lagos, who wrote them when he was eighty years old, that men might remember what he had done.

So many things have been written of Alexander, and many of them are not true. Therefore I must set down what I remember before Death takes me as she has taken so many others down into the Kingdom of Shades. Of those of us who began with Alexander at Mieza, I am the only one left. And so I write this in Alexander's City, Alexandria by the sea...

Five hours later Dion found me thus, the scroll still spread by weights, with ten others about me and a wax tablet on which I scribbled, ink being forbidden in the Library.

I had entirely forgotten that I had last seen him with Emrys, and if he had expected reproach or tears he was taken aback when I looked up, the light of conquest in my eyes. "Dion, have you ever heard of the Hipparch Lydias?"

"What are you doing?" Dion sat down on a stool opposite me.

"I'm looking for the Hipparch Lydias," I said. "He's mentioned over and over, but there's not much about him."

"Who was he?" Dion twisted around, trying to see the scrolls.

"One of Ptolemy's men, the first Ptolemy," I said abstractedly. "He's mentioned here as a Friend of Pharaoh in the last year of Ptolemy's reign. He must have a tomb or grave stela or something. Surely a Friend of Pharaoh had enough money for a nice one."

"I know where it is," Dion said.

I looked up.

"In the park," Dion said. "There's a tomb. I've seen it several times."

I knocked my tablet onto the floor. "Of course there is!" Now I remembered where I'd seen his name. "I saw it when there was the fire. We were waiting by the tomb." I struggled to remember. "I think it was a family tomb."

"Let's go look," said Dion, always keen in the search for something interesting.

IT WAS THERE just as I remembered.

"'Hephaistion son of the Hipparch Lydias and his wife Chloe, faithful soldier of Ptolemy Soter, fallen in battle in the twenty-first year of his life,'" Dion read. The letters cut into the marble were hardly worn at all.

A son who was the pride of his father, I thought, not the oldest child, but the one most like his father in temperament.

Dion was looking farther down the passage into the tomb, another sealed door. "There's a sister here. 'Demetria, daughter of the Hipparch Lydias, wife of Demarios of Cyprus, beloved by all who knew her, laid here in the twenty-seventh year of her life, the year of the plague. Isis receive her. Her children and her parents mourn her.'" Dion ran his hands over the stone carving. "And here's her husband with her. Demarios of Cyprus, died at the same time. He's standing under an acacia tree with his wife, bidding farewell to two boys and a girl."

I came down the passage, trailing my hand on the cool marble. "Two boys and a girl who lived with their grandparents." I closed my eyes. For a moment I could feel again the weight of the child against my chest, a little girl about three years old, clinging to me while her parents were put in this ground here, their wooden sarcophagi painted with the Book of Coming Forth by Day. I could feel her arm around my neck, her face against my chin.

"Demetria," Dion said. "The same name."

I nodded, trying not to let the tears that welled in my eyes spill over. "Demetria," I said. The same name. My baby, named for a daughter I had loved, a daughter I had lost too young.

I sat down on the steps and leaned against the cool stone. I had been here before, with Lucan. I had been here before, with Cleopatra. And much longer ago, I had been here before. What had I indeed to fear from the shades? These were no evil spirits, no dark creatures of nightmare. The only spirits here were those of my family, of people who had loved me.

"I expect the Hipparch and his wife are down here," Dion said, "behind these sealed doors. I don't want to damage anything."

"There's no need to look," I said. I was not there. The mummy that lay beyond, in layers of linen and wood, was less real than these other things. After all, I had never looked on my own mummy or seen my own body wrapped for burial. It was less real than that half-captured day, two months after the plague had run its course, when we laid Demetria, her husband, and their youngest child to rest, while my granddaughter clung to my neck. What do we do now? I had wondered. But the answer was obvious. Start over again, our house full of children in our old age. Begin again, with the tutors and the bedtime stories, the dowry for a little girl with gray eyes.

Dion read it anyway. " 'The Hipparch Lydias, Archisomatophylax of Pharaoh Ptolemy Soter, laid to rest in the fifth year of Pharaoh Ptolemy Philadelphos, the seventy-first year of his age. Chloe, beloved wife of the Hipparch Lydias, laid to rest in the sixteenth year of Pharaoh Ptolemy Philadelphos, the sixty-second year of her age, mourned by her children and grandchildren.'" Dion looked up at me. "It's a lovely carving of Hermes coming and taking them by the hands." I didn't move from my step, and he squinted at the carving again. "Peculiar," he said, bending closer. "It almost looks like Hermes has wings folded behind him."

"He probably does," I said, and the tears flowed down my face. They were not tears of grief, but of gladness. I remembered, and it was real.

We had built this city and defended it and loved it, poured into it all our sweetness and our joy, and dying I had wished nothing more than to return to this place I loved. And I had returned to walk again beneath this sky, to work for her and strive for her in the service of another Pharaoh. When it came time for me to go down into the earth again, I should fear nothing. For what was there to fear? In time, like bulbs sleeping underground, I would again come forth by day, drawn by love as by sunlight.

Dion came and put his arm around me. "Charmian? Are you all right?"

"I'm fine," I said, and embraced him, feeling the warmth, the realness of his skin, cool from the shadows, against my face. Here and now, Dion was my friend. Here and now, this was real.

I will remember, I thought. I will remember this, because I want to.

"Is this about Emrys?" Dion said perplexedly.

I laughed through my tears. "No," I said. "Not in any way that makes sense."

"Who's the Hipparch Lydias?" he asked.

"Me," I said.

WE WENT TO DION'S APARTMENT and sat under the striped awning, drinking wine mixed with fruit juices and spices, slices of lime floating in it. Emrys wasn't there. I assumed he had some duty or other.

Dion and I sat together on the couch eating our dinner, with him reclining behind me. He waited until we had little plates with cheese and olives, and until the cool wine had begun to relax us. The breeze off the ocean stirred the treetops in the courtyard below. We looked out into them, and onto the porches of ten of his neighbors. On the second floor, a man was cooking meat on a brazier. The scent of the spices rose to us, and the clamor of the children playing under the trees in the twilight.

"About Emrys," Dion said.

I leaned back against the couch cushions and closed my eyes. "What about him?"

He reached over me for the cup.

"Do you mind that I lay with him?" I asked, twisting my neck around to see his face.

Dion shrugged. "Yes and no. More no than yes. It's been almost five years. I hardly expected for nothing to have changed, or for him to be true to me." Dion's arm lay around my waist. "I might never have seen him again. Or if I had, it might have proven to have been no more than one of those romances that does not stand the test of time. Either way, there's no point in wasting time on recriminations." He looked down at me and grinned. "I've never seen the appeal of women, but everyone has their own taste."

I laughed and leaned back against him. "I see the appeal of women. How can one not? The beautiful skin, and bared breasts just so, the way nipples pucker and darken in cold water....How can one not notice in the bath?"

"I don't usually take baths with naked women," Dion said.

"So I understand," I said. "If I were Pharaoh, I'd have a harem. And everyone could be in it but you."

"But me?" Dion propped up on his shoulder and refilled the cup. We were drinking rather a lot in our relief. "Why not me? I'm perfectly good-looking."

"You are very handsome," I agreed, "but you have no taste for women, you just said."

"If you were Pharaoh, you'd be a man," he said.

"Well, if I were a man," I said, taking the cup from him, "then you could be in my harem."

"We could be Emrys' harem," Dion said. "That's a thought. He'd laugh so much at the idea."

"He would," I said. "But, my dear, I don't want to take him from you. I should never want to hurt you."

"He loves you," Dion said.

"He loves you," I said.

"He loves us both, and that's the problem."

"Is it?" I opened my eyes and looked at him. "We love each other. Perhaps more like brother and sister than anything else, but it's love. Why can't we share him?"

"We can," Dion said. "I said I was fine with that a long time ago. But it doesn't seem fair. You and Emrys could have some kind of life."

"I don't want to get married," I said. "And Emrys still has years before his discharge. He can't live with either one of us, and he's going to have to leave the minute he gets orders. Why don't we all just make the most of this? We all know it can't last."

"It doesn't seem fair to you," Dion said. "What if you get pregnant?"

"What if I do? I don't mean to, but accidents happen. If I do, the Queen will sigh and smile and I'll be right where I was with Demetria. Dion, I'm not worried about providing for a child. Cleopatra would never let my children want for anything."

"I could marry you," Dion said.

I laughed. "Your mother must be desperate! She's given up on a nice Jewish girl and she'll settle for any girl!"

"She is. But if you needed it, I would. I mean, we both understand I sleep with men...."

I put my arm around him. "Dion, darling. I love you dearly. But I am not going to marry you. Or Emrys. Or anyone else. I like my life just like it is."

Dion looked relieved. "So now all we need to work out is Emrys' schedule."

"As though he were the Apis bull," I said.

By the time Emrys returned, Dion and I had spread papyrus on the table and had drawn out the next two months, all of the banquets and other events that I knew I had to take care of, Emrys' rotating duty schedule, and Dion's classes, lectures, and private students.

"That night's a tough one," Dion was saying. "I've got a session at the Observatory, and it's six miles out of town. And you've got a dinner until the fifth hour of the night. I need to leave before dark, ideally."

"We could let him have a night to himself," I suggested as Emrys came in.

Perhaps he had been expecting to find us quarreling, or perhaps he hadn't expected me to be there at all, but the last thing he'd been expecting was to find us, wine cups in hand, with more than half the jar gone, gesturing wildly over ink and paper. "What are you doing?"

"Scheduling you," I said.

"It's very complicated," Dion said, enunciating carefully. "We all have such complicated work schedules. And we're trying to make sure that we have approximately the same number of evenings per week. Which is a bitch in a week with an astronomical conjunction or a state dinner."

Emrys burst out laughing. "You're what?"

"Scheduling you," I said, waving the wine cup at him. "See? This day and this day you're Dion's, but you're mine the day after."

Emrys looked at the paper, his mouth twitching. "Heaven forbid we have any spontaneity."

"It wouldn't be fair," Dion said, and kissed him.

They were both tall, though Emrys was a bit taller, and I liked the way they moved together, the way Dion kissed him greedily, his head turning into the kiss, his eyes closing. Emrys had kissed me, but I'd never seen what it looked like, that expression of intense concentration, the way his lashes swept against his cheeks. It was incredibly beautiful.

I twisted with desire, hot and strong as anything I had ever felt.

What could be more erotic than two beautiful men I adored, kissing one another?

The stab of desire was almost painful.

It was Emrys who stopped, of course. He looked at me from beneath his forelock, a sheepish expression on his face.

I can't imagine what I looked like. Not angry.

"So whose am I tonight?" he asked with some of the lightness of before, though I heard the raw tone in his voice, beneath the banter.

"Charmian's," Dion said promptly. "I've had you since you landed. So it's more than her turn. I just wanted to send you off properly."

"I see," Emrys said. He was still in his leathers, which hung loosely enough over his front not to betray anything.

"Then we'd better be going," I said.

I'm not entirely certain how we got back to the palace, or to my rooms, only that we were there and tearing at each other's clothes the moment the door closed. I sank onto my knees, taking him in my mouth as he groaned and clutched at the doorframe.

"Let me," I said. "Show me how Dion does it."

He gasped something that might have been a god's name, hard and ready in my hands.

"I'm going to have you like that," I said. "I'm going to have you as though I were a man. Mine to choose. Mine to take." One hand on him, the other caressing his buttocks, feeling him sway against me.

"Yes," he said.

"After all," I said, "I did promise to tie you up and keep you prisoner."

"You did," Emrys said breathlessly.

"I always keep my promises," I said, dragging him toward the couch instead of the bed and pushing him back on it.

"I should hate to spoil your record," Emrys said as I shoved him back. "But don't you think the bed…"

"Too wide for what I have in mind," I said, unfastening his sandals and dropping them on the floor. "And take those leathers off."

"I thought you liked them," he said, unfastening the first buckle.

"I do," I said, "but am I the master here, or you?"

He had a look of hunger on his face, as though this were something he had barely anticipated. "Definitely you, darling."

"Well, then."

In the end I was quite satisfied with my work. I thought he looked pretty, nude on his back with his hands bound to the head of the couch. I had put a firm pillow beneath his hips, raising his stiff phallus engagingly, his legs held apart by another tie that ran from one ankle to the other beneath the couch, holding them open the width of the couch.

"Very pretty," I said, running a finger down his chest from the tanned bit at the neckline across his pale belly.

Emrys moaned, arching his hips.

"Not yet, dear," I said, moistening my fingers and taking him in hand. "Not until I say."

"Sweet Aphrodite," Emrys groaned. "What did I do to deserve this?"

"Something very, very nice," I said, working my hand up and down his length, then stopping to run my fingers down the white insides of his thigh. "And if you're exceptionally good, I may even let you finish." I lifted my skirts and showed him my pubis, one finger dipping into my wetness.

"You are a goddess," he whispered.

"I'm glad you noticed," I said, and straddling him, lowered myself onto him.

AFTERWARD, we lay together panting, my head on his shoulder as he lay on his back.

"I can't believe I let you do that," he said, rubbing one wrist with the other hand.

I reached for the couch blanket with one foot, kicking it up where I could reach it and pull it over us. "You seemed to like it," I said. "You certainly begged enough...."

"I did like it," Emrys said. His green eyes fluttered shut, a look of utter satiation on his face. "I've never done anything like that before."

"Not with Dion?" I settled against him, wondering if we should move to the bed, or if it were too much trouble.

"Dion's tastes aren't so...inventive," Emrys said. "He's more of a cuddler."

I pushed one damp piece of hair back from his shoulder. "Do you like that better?"

"I like sweet and spice both," he said, his arm tightening around me. "Men and women both. A little of everything, I suppose. And you." He opened his eyes, smiling at me. "What have I let myself in for?"

"The best of both worlds," I said.

THUS BEGAN one of the happiest times of my life. I had my lover and my friend both, my daughter and my nephew, my work that I loved and my city. If ever there was a recipe for happiness it was this, to rise in the morning cool and get Demetria and Caesarion ready for their lessons, six years old and studying in earnest now. I would walk with them to the schoolroom, listening to them singing and scampering about like young birds, then leave them there smiling and go to breakfast with the Queen.

Iras, Apollodorus, and I breakfasted with her every day, going over the day's events and the briefings as we did so. Sometimes breakfast stretched on two hours when there was a great deal to do. Some days she would then retire with Apollodorus over the foreign correspondence, or with Iras over the treasury, and to such other meetings as were necessary with the exchequer, ports, or agriculture. Other days she would spend the rest of the morning in court, with those justices and advocates who sought pardon or perdition from the crown.

I would go to my office then, on an upper story facing the sea, and meet with the household staff, go over the budgets and stocking of cellars, foodstuffs, granaries, and all else required for a household of some four hundred. At other times I would meet with the Friend of Pharaoh who commanded the Queen's Bodyguard, the Master of Horse, and all of the rest. In the afternoon it was more of the same, with the end of the day given to planning whatever events were in the offing.

And then there were the building projects. All of those had to come through me as well on their way to the Queen: the progress reports, changes of plan, and bids for construction. I had initially thought this rather over my head, but as time passed I learned a great deal about different qualities of sandstone. It was an apprenticeship of a different kind, but one I enjoyed.

On a good day, I could end my work then, but at least three or four times a week I had to manage one of the dinners, banquets, or processions to which everyone was devoted. Antonius wanted to dine each night as though it were his last. This was, after all, his fabulous idyll in Egypt, and he expected the bounty of the Pharaohs. Cleopatra had never especially cared for banquets, but when at last they stepped down to smaller parties of nobles and his officers, it was less trouble. Dinner for thirty was simple. Three hundred was taxing.

Sometimes, in the evening, Demetria and I escaped the palace to Dion's apartment, eating on the balcony in the gathering night, while resined lamps gave off smoke to keep the bugs away. Sometimes Emrys was there and sometimes he wasn't, depending on his own duties, and Demetria kept up a stream of talk of her day and asked Dion to teach her about the stars.

One night, as we were coming home in the litter afterward, Demetria leaned on me, folding her arms across my belly. "Ma," she said. "Is Dion my father?"

"No, baby," I said, stroking her hair.

"That's too bad," she said, snuggling half-draped over me. "I wish he were."

"It would be nice, wouldn't it?" I said. I could not even imagine what Agrippa should make of this life.

And then there were the nights with Emrys, when he came to my room in the palace and we tumbled into scented sheets, laughing and playing like children, or thralled in passion like chains. He could give and take both, and familiarity only let us push further, trusting one another.

The only thing that marred these days was Antonius. Oh, I liked him well enough. He was pleasant and well spoken, kind to Caesarion in a grave manner, as a man who has boys of his own may be. He was not Gnaeus Pompeius in any way, except that he did not like to work.

I know Emrys grew irritated sometimes that Antonius spent so little time with the dispatches, or had so little concern for his troops encamped in Syria and Asia. A few hours, now and again, a few meetings that could be gotten through in half an afternoon — that was all there was. And he distracted the Queen.

When, for the third time, I had put off a meeting with barge owners because Antonius wanted the Queen to go with him, I complained to Iras. "Does he think Egypt governs itself? It's important she speak with barge owners. No, they're not hugely wealthy, but once a year or two she needs to see every important constituency in the kingdom. And there are only so many days in the year."

"He has had years of war," Iras said. "Let him now have a little rest. There will be enough war ahead of him."

"That is true enough, I expect," I said. The Parthians now threatened Judea, and if they began a war there, Antonius would have to go. Herod was his ally, and had stood by him when Octavian pushed. Besides, Antonius had troops in Syria. "Do you think he will go if the Parthians cross the Jordan?"

"He has to, doesn't he?" Iras said, and her eyes were level. "That is our far frontier too."

THE PARTHIANS DID, of course. They had feared Caesar. They did not fear Herod, or Antonius' men left leaderless in Antioch.

The year had turned and the harvest was upon us when Cleopatra made her best galleys ready for Antonius for him to go to Syria with all speed. I thought that we would go with him, perhaps, as they seemed happy together, but that was not to be. At the beginning of Roman February she missed her courses.

"I will take no chances," she said, as we worked out the provisioning of the ships that would go with Antonius. "Not this time." Her voice caught just a little.

"I know," I said. "It is better if you stay here. Not even a sea voyage to Antioch."

Emrys, of course, must go. We had known he would, Dion and I, but we'd had a year.

"They will come back soon," the Queen said.

"They will," I said, putting my hand over hers on the table. "They will be back before the child comes in the fall, most likely. The Parthians will not fight through the heat of summer."

The Queen raised an eyebrow at me, but did not dispute it. As once she would have, I thought. She wanted to believe me.

Antonius and Emrys sailed in March, with fair winds and the blessings of Isis Pelagia following after.

It was perhaps a month later that I sat beside the Queen while her doctor held his rolled paper to her slightly rounded belly, frowning. "You missed in February but not January?"

"Yes," she said, lying as he had told her to, her arms raised behind her head. "I'm sure I conceived in late January. I was entirely regular before that. Is something the matter?"

"You are too large," he said brusquely, and began poking and prodding again, moving the tube about with his ear to it, his brow furrowed.

I squeezed her hand, and felt her fingers shake in mine.

"What is the matter?" she asked.

He shushed her, listening.

Oh sweet Mother Isis, I prayed, please, nothing wrong. Please, nothing wrong.

At last he laid the paper down, looking grave. "There are two heartbeats," he said.

MOON AND SUN

I t was the fifth physician who said what no one else would. "Carrying twins isn't necessarily a death sentence." He was a young doctor from Philae, handsome in a sharp way, with high Nubian cheekbones and long fingers, new to the faculty at the Temple of Asclepius, where he had been teaching on the charity ward. His name was Amonis.

A collective breath ran around the room. Five specialists had been called in since that morning, each with their separate examination of my sister. Six times we'd done it over and over, the prodding and the listening, the fingers examining her closed cervix. For the Queen of Egypt to be carrying twins was nothing less than a national crisis.

"It is true," Amonis said, "that some women carrying twins die in the delivery. But the odds are not significantly worse than for a single delivery. However, the outlook for the children is graver. In my experience, twins are generally smaller and often have trouble breathing. The delivery itself is more complicated, with a higher incidence of breech births." He did not seek to evade the Queen's eyes.

I stood behind her chair. She had dressed again, and her face was calm if white. She must be Queen as well as mother.

"I will not deceive you, Gracious Queen. The prognosis for the children is not good. Often one twin is larger than the other, and that one lives while the other dies. But it is not uncommon that both babies are too small and weak, and we lose them both," Amonis said.

Cleopatra nodded gravely, as though they spoke of someone else.

The senior physician cleared his throat. "The safest course, Gracious Queen, would be to induce labor now. This early, in the fourth month, there is no chance of the fetuses surviving, but your health would be safe. Both would be small enough to pass easily. And many of the drugs I would administer have been used under medical supervision for years."

"Safely?" She raised an eyebrow.

One of the other doctors shifted in his chair, and his movement told her what she wanted to know. "Yes?" she said, turning to him.

He was the senior physician of gynecology at the Ascalepium, with thirty years' service. "No drug is entirely safe," he said sharply. "If you give a dose small enough to be safe, it may be ineffective. A larger dose of one of the stronger compounds will induce abortion, but is not recommended as late as the fourth month. There is no guarantee that we will be able to stop the hemorrhage if we begin it. I think that course is too dangerous, Gracious Queen."

"And if I carry the pregnancy?" Cleopatra's voice was level. I had never admired her more, nor envied that detachment more, that she could step back from something that so intimately concerned her.

Her own doctor's voice was gruff. "It's hard to carry twins to term. Usually a bit better than seven of the ten moons is the best that can be done. And often, most usually, the babies don't survive. You need nine moons to have a good chance, and eight is risky. When the combined weight of the twins is equal to the weight of a single infant at term, labor usually results."

"And if I carry eight moons or better?"

Amonis answered. "One child or two or none surviving. And a dangerous pregnancy for you, Gracious Queen. There are any number of possible complications that become more likely."

Cleopatra spread her hands. "Those things may happen in any normal pregnancy, Doctor. What would you tell me then?"

"You are in all other ways healthy. You are twenty-eight years old, neither too young or too old, with one normal delivery behind you. I would tell you to eat and exercise in moderation," he said. "To rest in the water in a pool to balance your humors. And to work far less than you do. I would order you to bed at the first sign of effacement."

"Then that is what I will do," she said. "We will simply take it as it comes, gentlemen. And with the assistance of Isis and Bastet, we will enrich the realm, not impoverish it."

THAT NIGHT I could not sleep. I paced outside on the terrace, half in worry, half in prayer.

I was not surprised to hear a voice behind me. "Charmian?"

It was the Queen. "Yes," I said.

She came and stood by me, looking out to sea. The wind blew her robes tight against her body, her belly too swollen for four months. "You can't sleep either?"

"No," I said.

The great light on the lighthouse turned, beams sweeping over the sea as the massive mirrors moved on their gears, calling ships home.

"What will happen to Egypt without you?" I said.

Her mouth tightened. "Is that what you think will happen, Charmian? That I will die?"

"I don't know," I said. "I care too much about this to be able to see anything besides my own fears. I simply don't know."

"Then we will take the chances, you and I," she said.

"And Antonius?"

My sister took a deep breath. "I've written to him of my pregnancy. But I won't tell him about the twins. There's too much chance of the letter being intercepted and read. And you know as well as I that if it gets out, the grain markets will crash."

"I know," I said.

"Besides, there's nothing he can do. And he will worry." She smiled, a tiny tight smile. "He'd probably run straight back here. And that's a thing he cannot afford to do."

"I wonder what Fulvia will say," I said.

Cleopatra laughed. "Probably congratulations! I think she and Marcus understand one another well."

"I see that," I said.

My sister put her arm around my waist. "We are all strange creatures, we Ptolemies. I think if Fulvia were here we might arrange everything as you have with Dion and Emrys. She asked me, you know. In Rome."

I must have looked utterly shocked, because Cleopatra laughed. "She had come up to my room to help me dress one day, a good opportunity for gossip, and to make it clear that she was closer to me than the other women. She asked me if I'd ever had a woman use her mouth on me, and volunteered to show me."

"Oh!" I said, and in my surprise blurted out the first thing that came to mind. "I suppose she taught Antonius then."

"Very well, yes." My sister laughed and embraced me. "She taught him very well."

THE NEXT THING WE HEARD of Antonius he had pushed the Parthians back over the Jordan River, and was marching through Asia toward the Hellespont, bound for Greece. Things had not gone smoothly in Judea, but he had little time to spare. His brother and Fulvia had gone to war with Octavian in Italy.

By summer Antonius was in Athens. And I knew with a certainty that his letters came less often than Emrys'. But then, Emrys and the cavalry had been left behind in Macedonia.

Hail Charmian,

I write to you from Pella, in Macedonia. You will be amused, I think, to imagine me here where Alexander grew to manhood, but this place holds no echoes of that kind for me. It is truly not much to look at, though one can see how it was once a much larger town. They say here that there was an earthquake five years ago that destroyed much, and that many of the town's citizens moved to

Thessalonika, which is not far away. There are still men here, and good grass, and we have built a good camp near the river.

I watch my horse eat where Bucephalos grazed, and wonder what it looked like then. This quiet seems more like it must have been before Alexander's time, when the Persians came here asking for fire and earth and got it. Another summer, another time ago.

You ask me what Antonius is doing, and more than that what he feels. I can't know. He is in Athens and I in Pella, even if I had his confidence, in ways I do not. They say he is furious at his brother for rising against Octavian inopportunely and getting soundly defeated. Now there must be war between them.

But at least you will have no cause to worry about me. I am doing nothing more strenuous than cavalry exercise in beautiful summer weather.

Sigismund shakes his head at me and says, "Crazy Gauls!" He bids me to tell you that if you tire of sharing me that he is looking for a good wife when his enlistment is up!

Farewell,
Emrys Aurelianus, Praefectus

The Queen made eight moons, all of the way to the week before the autumn equinox. The first part of the labor went quickly, too quickly for Amonis, who was in attendance. He kept feeling the upper part of her belly, though his face was calm. When he went out to call for more clean water to cool her face and limbs, I followed him.

"What is it?" I asked. "You can tell me, you know. I have one of my own, and I was with her through Caesarion and the miscarriage both."

He hesitated, then dropped his voice. "The first baby is fine. Its head is down and well engaged. I can feel it right behind the cervix. It's the second one that's the problem."

"What's the matter?"

Amonis took a breath. "It's transverse. Its head is right under her ribs on the left side, and its feet low down on the right. It has no room to turn with the other baby in position."

"Transverse." Transverse was worse than footling breech. Delivery feetfirst might be more dangerous for the child, but it could be done. There was simply no way a child could fit through sideways.

"I will have to try to turn it once the first one is out of the way," Amonis said. "So send a servant for purified olive oil. I'll need the slip on my hands."

I nodded and started off, movement an antidote for terror.

He caught my arm. "And say nothing to the Queen," he said. "There is nothing she can do differently, and we must deliver the first one now."

I sent for the oil, and then stood a moment in the passage before I went back in. I must compose myself before I saw her. Caesarion was sleeping. He had kissed her good night in the earliest stages, gaily told that before morning he would have a new brother or sister to keep him company. He was seven. So very young to rule Egypt alone.

I must not think that way, I thought angrily. I must not. This was not the awesome premonition of Caesar's death, but more mundane worry for my sister and her children.

I schooled my face and went in to sit with Iras at her side.

The child was born in the eleventh hour of the night, the cold hour before dawn, slithering into the hands of Amonis' assistant, who cleared its breath with his own. She choked and began to cry, a thin distressed wail.

Cleopatra was trying to push herself up on her elbows to see.

"A fine daughter, Gracious Queen," I said, holding the clean linen that her thin little body might be received in, to wrap her warm against any chill.

"The weight of a good measure of grain," the assistant said, making light of it as he checked her once more, seeing whether there was any bluish cast to her hands or feet, and that her breath came strongly. Her arms and legs flailed.

The larger twin, I thought. The strong one.

She kicked, even swaddled in the fine cloth, and the assistant handed her to me.

Amonis met Cleopatra's eyes. "Gracious Queen," he said. "The other child is transverse. I need to try to turn it. It cannot be born the way it lies."

I saw the fear cross her face, followed almost immediately by the next wave of pain. The labor did not relent, her body trying to find a way.

I held the girl to my shoulder, her soft little head cupped in my hand. "Shhh, sweet girl," I whispered. "Your aunt has you, precious. You're safe, little love."

"Just hang on tight," Iras said, taking the Queen's hand again. "Just hang on." Their eyes locked together, and I remembered how she had held me up when Demetria was born, all through that long dream of pain. "Hang on," she said.

When the contraction eased Amonis slid his entire hand inside, slickened with oil and blood, full to the wrist.

The Queen bit down on her lip, then screamed.

I saw the next contraction coming, the ripples spreading across her strained belly, clamping down on his arm.

He stilled. "Waiting," he said. "I have its head. Now I have to turn it very carefully and keep the cord out of the way. Fraternal twins. I can feel its sac intact."

My sister's voice shook. "Charmian..."

"Yes, darling," I said. I couldn't get any closer, with Iras and Amonis and the assistants.

"You'll take care of her, won't you? You'll guard my daughter?"

"I will guard her with all my strength," I said. "With all my heart, to death and beyond." I could not stop my voice from choking, though I tried. I held her to my heart instead, my tiny niece.

He turned it on the next contraction, though there was blood, so much blood. I held my niece so she should not see, not that her eyes could focus that far or that she could understand.

Amonis looked at his assistant. "Now," he said, as another contraction came. "I've got a snarl in the cord. It has to be now."

Cleopatra screamed, and he pulled his hand free in a rush of blood, intact caul coming after, tight over the second baby's face.

I clutched the first and squeezed my eyes shut in a desperate prayer. Bastet, Mother of Cats, Isis, Mother of the World...

There was a choking sound. I looked. The baby was free, limbs hanging limp, while Amonis tore the caul from its face and covered its mouth and nose together with his mouth.

Breath of life I give you..., I thought, part of the Liturgy of Isis, heard a thousand times at Bubastis and at the Serapeum.

"She's fainted!" the assistant yelled, and I saw Amonis hesitate, torn for a moment in the physician's oldest dilemma, between one patient and another.

The blood, and the Queen, her head lolling back against Iras' arm.

"Come on, damn it," Iras swore at her, Iras who never in her life raised her voice, who never lost her composure. "Come on, don't do this!"

Amonis blew, once, twice, three times, and then four. I saw a tiny fist clench, flushing pink, as the child drew a first ragged breath.

The assistant was trying to get the afterbirth, while Iras swore still, laying a cold wet cloth against the Queen's forehead. "Come on! Come back to me!"

The other infant sputtered as Amonis took his mouth away.

"Iras!" Amonis' voice cut through all. "Take the infant. Let me see to the Queen."

Awkwardly, they traded places, a servant holding the cloth for the other child. A boy, I thought, a boy and a girl, before he was wrapped and held to Iras' chest. Her tears fell on his small and bloody head.

"Your mother loves you," she whispered. "Oh, how she loves you, sweet boy."

The blood would stop or it would not.

"I think it's placental," Amonis said to the assistant, and I did not want to interrupt him to ask anything. "I don't think it's a uterine tear."

I looked at Iras. The girl was quiet in my arms now, her breath soft and even against the warmth of my skin. Iras bent her head over the baby. "I will stay with you, sweet boy," she whispered.

I walked to the window, swaying gently. It was past dawn. The sun was coming up, the first bright rays touching the sea. The seabirds were crying, turning on the currents of dawn.

Bright Helios, I thought, Ra of Egypt, Horus the Son of His Mother, oh please…

"Helios," she croaked.

I spun about. Her hair lay matted around her and her skin was pale as silk, but her eyes were open.

"His name is Helios," she said. "Helios and Selene."

"Lie still, Gracious Queen," Amonis said. "The bleeding is slowing, but it will stop better if you lie still." He looked at me. "Is the girl strong enough to nurse?"

"Maybe?" I said. Her little hands were kneading at me like a kitten, her rosebud mouth puckered.

"Put her on one nipple and see if she will clamp," Amonis said. "And you draw on the other. It makes the uterus contract more strongly. That will help stop the bleeding." He held his hand flat against Cleopatra's pubis, feeling each contraction.

I held the little girl to her left breast, popped her mouth open with a practiced motion I had forgotten I knew, clamped her jaw shut. Selene's eyes closed, long dark lashes fluttering, and she moved her jaw to suck.

"That's it, darling," I said. "That's how you do it." I bent my head to my sister's other breast and drew her nipple into my mouth, trying to find the rhythm. I suppose we forget these things when we are no longer babies, and no longer need it. Once, Iras and I had suckled from the same breasts, like twins ourselves.

It seemed a long time, but must only have been a few minutes before I raised my head.

"Let Helios try," Iras said, and I moved and positioned the pointed brown nipple for him.

He had more trouble than his sister. He was smaller and his hands and face were very thin. Selene was sucking away, more for comfort than anything as there was nothing there yet, not even the thin foremilk.

There was color in the Queen's face again, and the linens were not soaking through with blood in just a few minutes.

"I think," said Amonis, "we may have made it."

I<small>T WAS THREE WEEKS</small> before Cleopatra was strong enough to get out of bed. She nursed them around the clock this time, though there was a wet nurse too, to make sure they had enough. We did not announce the birth until a few days had passed, and the services could be ones of thanksgiving.

Selene seemed strong enough, though small, but Helios had to be held constantly against someone's chest, skin to skin. His breathing was irregular, and sometimes he stopped, as though he forgot to take a breath. Skin to skin, he would be jostled and startled, and then would draw another quickly, half-choking. It would be months yet before we were certain of him, but Selene gained weight quickly, rosy and warm.

And yet there was thanksgiving. The trumpets sounded, and fire ran down the channels in the Serapeum in celebration of the miracle of twin children for the House of Ptolemy, Alexander Helios and Cleopatra Selene, Sun and Moon, one born by night, the other by day.

A<small>NTONIUS SENT HIS BLESSINGS</small> and his wishes from Brundisium, where he besieged Octavian's allies. Word came from Greece that Fulvia had died of a fever in Athens.

"Antonius will be here soon," Cleopatra said. "He will not be long now. He will want to see the children."

"Yes," I said, but I wondered. I had a letter from Emrys too.

Hail Charmian,

Now we are in Epidauro, waiting, they say, for passage to Italy. I am not sure it will come. Antonius did not want to fight Octavian now, and since Fulvia is dead there is more chance he can come to terms. Better, of course, to end war rather than fight it.

I miss you both. Four more years. If the gods will grant I live that long....

In the new year, word came that Antonius had married Octavian's sister, Octavia.

Her husband Marcellus was dead, which was not a surprise as he had been older than Caesar, but it was very convenient all the same. Octavia and Antonius celebrated a state wedding, centerpiece of a new treaty between Octavian and Antonius. Octavian should rule in the West and Antonius in the East. The successors did not need Cleopatra.

The Queen's face was tight and grim. "He will need me," she said, "to hold what he claims. Whatever he claims."

There was anger there, real anger. She had fought her battle while he avoided his, only to win unregarded.

"He wasn't good enough for you," I said, enraged. "He was no Caesar."

"Charmian, be quiet," she said, and stalked from the room.

"The alliance is the wise thing to do," Iras said. "It would be foolish to fight Octavian now. Especially if he can get what he wants through marriage, not war."

"That does not keep me from hating him," I said.

"It should."

"Caesar would have done it."

"What she has been through for him—" I began heatedly.

Iras shook her head. "Not for him. She bore Caesarion for Caesar, and for Egypt. Selene and Helios are for herself. Can't you see that she does not need a consort? She is a goddess, complete in herself."

"She is also a woman," I said, "and if Antonius cannot regard that as well as goddess and Queen, what kind of man is he?"

"Mortal," Iras said.

THE PARTHIANS crossed the Jordan again and overran Judea. In Jerusalem, the king was killed and the royal family fled for their lives. One of the royal ladies, Alexandra, held out still against the Parthians in the desert fortress of Masada, while Prince Herod fled across the desert on a Bactrian racing dromedary to Pelousion.

He came to Alexandria, of course. Three years younger than I, he cut a handsome figure in his borrowed clothes, making his bows to the throne respectfully. He was not a pretty man, though his face had a cultured coolness to it, close-trimmed black beard and flashing eyes. He was two inches taller than the Queen; I thought they would have made an impressive couple, if things had been different.

"Gracious Queen, I beg the honor of a private audience with you," he said. "You know of my house's long friendship with the House of Ptolemy, and of my closeness to the Imperator Antonius." He did not mention, of course, how he had come with his father to rescue Caesar, when he had been besieged in Alexandria, but they both knew that.

"I do indeed consider you a friend, Prince Herod," Cleopatra said, her face unreadable beneath the heavy makeup of a court day, the double crown, and the uraeus. "And you are welcome to Alexandria and to Egypt. I am certain that you have many friends in the city. I will speak with you privately later in the week, and I will look forward to our conversation."

It became clear in the following weeks that Herod had more on his mind than troops. He was in constant attendance on the Queen, witty and charming, always at her disposal with a literary reference or a choice word. Then he moved to observing this and that small thing about her bodyguard, and how her horsemen could be better drilled.

I watched him with her, convincing her that she should learn to ride a horse, helping her astride, coaxing and laughing while he held the bridle for her. The sun glinted off his gold earrings, his beautiful white teeth. "He looks like a candidate for office," I said to Iras.

Iras smirked. "A candidate for consort. After all, if Antonius is away, what claim has he? A prince of Judea is a perfectly reasonable consort for the Queen of Egypt. Why win a throne by force when you can charm your way into a wealthier one?"

"He has a wife already," I said.

"So did Antonius."

"Who will certainly hear about it," I said.

"Perhaps that's the plan," Iras said. The Queen was laughing now, leaning on Herod's shoulder, in front of half the court. "Cleopatra certainly knows he will hear of it. If I were Antonius, I would have a whole bundle of reasons to come East, away from Rome and Octavia."

AND SO HE DID COME East, but not without Octavia and not to Alexandria.

Hail Charmian,

I am in Athens again, with Antonius, where we are planning to go against the Parthians next spring. They say that Rome must recover Judea and Syria, and that Antonius has promised Prince Herod all his support. So I suppose we will be sailing for Antioch in a few months. I do no wrong in telling you this, as all must know by now that the legions are coming in from as far as Gaul, and that Octavian has promised Antonius four of his legions to help fight the Parthians. It will be a major campaign, I am certain.

Antonius' new wife Octavia is here in Athens with us, and every night there is a play or a declamation of some kind. She is something of a scholar, it seems, and she wants to see everything Euripides ever wrote performed at Athens. Though that may be curtailed soon, as she is obviously great with child.

I miss you and Dion very much. Give Demetria my love....

She's going to kill him, I thought. When the Queen gets her hands on Antonius, there will be blood.

SHADES OF LOVE

To Emrys' surprise, Antonius did not march east that year. Instead he sent a general called Ventidius, a veteran of Caesar's army, to Syria in his stead. He remained in Athens where he presided over the Panathenaic Games and made a sacred marriage to the Goddess Athena.

Emrys, of course, did march east. While Antonius and Octavia celebrated in Athens, Emrys was in the field. I was beginning to find it hard to even be rational on the subject of Antonius.

The Queen said little about him at all. Herod went north to join Ventidius in the liberation of his kingdom, richer for a few nice presents from the Queen, but without having gotten either troops or a lover in the bargain. Instead, when the dry season came and the land was parched, we made the sacred pilgrimage again to Philae, the Queen conducting business along the way. Helios and Selene were nine months old, and deemed sturdy enough for the trip. When we returned there was both bad news and good.

Antonius was still in Athens, while his troops fought back and forth in Syria under another man. In Athens, Octavia had borne him a daughter, named Antonia, and was pregnant again four months later.

The Queen said nothing, only handed the dispatch to Iras and left the room.

Iras and I looked at each other.

"I will never forgive him for causing her this pain," I said, my hands twisting together as though I could get them about Antonius' neck.

"I don't think he much cares about your forgiveness," Iras said, frowning down at the scroll as though it were a snake in her hands.

"Probably not," I fumed.

Iras looked up at me, a rueful expression on her face. "And you ask me why I would rather have no man?"

"Not all men are as faithless as Antonius," I said. "And not all women are as wounded by it as Cleopatra." I had never begrudged Emrys Dion or anyone else, but then Emrys had not left me for another.

"But I would be," Iras said, putting the scroll in its place on the table. "And show me a man of high temper, mettle, and spirit who is not? Where should I find a faithful Dionysos?"

"I don't know," I said. Truly, it seemed to me impossible that anyone worth having would be so tame. On the other hand, I thought Antonius an exceptional ass.

WE WERE SETTLING BACK into our routines at the palace when a note came from Dion, carried by a message boy I did not know.

Charmian,
    Come as soon as you can to my apartment.
                            Dion

"What in the world?" I said to Iras.

Iras' eyebrows rose. "Maybe he's ill?"

"I shouldn't take Demetria then," I said. "Will you see her and Caesarion to bed while I see what's wrong with Dion?"

"Of course," she said, and kissed my brow. "It's probably not bad. He'll be fine."

I hurried. It wasn't like Dion to ask for things. Well, not for things that didn't involve money from the Queen for bizarre scientific experiments.

Emrys opened the door.

I drew a breath that was almost a sob, and fell into his arm. Arm, singular. The other was strapped tight against his chest in a sling, heavy wrappings beneath it.

"Where in the world did you come from? What happened?"

Dion stepped out from behind him, grinning. "He was sent by the general to buy supplies. He needed someone who spoke good Koine and had the Queen's ear."

Emrys held me about the waist with his good hand. "And who wasn't very useful right now. I broke my left arm in two places against the Parthians. My horse went down with me under her, and I can't ride or fight for months. So since I can't be any use there, and I can buy supplies without being cheated by every merchant in Alexandria, I was sent to empty the purse for grain and foodstuffs."

I leaned up and kissed him. "I'm so glad to see you."

"And I you," he said, kissing me hard and sensually, right in front of Dion. "It's been two years, and I've missed you both so much."

"We've missed you," Dion said, drawing us in and closing the door. "And with any luck your general will forget he sent you for months and months."

"Not so long as that, I expect," Emrys said, but he did not let go of me. The lines around his mouth were more deeply graven, and his fair skin scourged by sun.

"Was it bad?" I asked.

He twitched an eyebrow. "Oh yes," he said. "Yes."

In the next weeks he said little, but I pieced together what I could from the official dispatches, and from the little he would say, about a long campaign in the desert against the Parthians, the people of Syria unexpectedly hostile to the Roman forces. Herod was no help. After a year of fighting, he only held part of Galilee while Antigonus held Jerusalem and most of the rest of Judea. He had no help to give.

Emrys' body bore the marks of the struggle, flesh worn close to the bone, and the way he started up in the night, calling out to men who were dead, or shuddering in some dream. We were less lovers than family, sitting together late into the night, the three of us, talking of anything but war. Dion bore the brunt of it, as he had more hours with Emrys than I did, and I saw the shadows in his eyes when the night before had been sleepless.

We did not like to leave him alone at night, after one morning when Dion came home from the Observatory to find Emrys gone. He turned up late in the afternoon, having wandered the city looking for something, not entirely certain where he was or what he sought. That was the first time I had ever seen Dion really alarmed.

I was disturbed myself, disturbed enough to talk with the Queen's physician, who sent me to another doctor at the Temple of Asclepius. "It takes men that way, sometimes," he said. "Too much war. It's the strongest ones who bend that way, the ones who will not break. The ones who break go mad and hurt themselves or others, or sit down one day and cannot get up. The ones who bend..." He steepled his hands together, his eyes bright as though he studied something that interested him. "They bend in interesting patterns."

"That is all very well," I said. "But what may we do?"

"Time and rest," he said. "Those are the only cures. But old soldiers will tell you that many never lose the ill dreams, not after twenty years have passed. But time and rest will effect some aid if his heart is strong enough."

I came away no less disturbed. I could have told myself that without the fee and trouble.

And so we did not leave him alone at night again. I stayed with him when Dion had to be at the Observatory. Once, Emrys started up from a dream, and I was surprised to find Dion there too, curled on the other side, his body curved around Emrys who was curved around me.

"It's only us," I said, smoothing Emrys' hair back from his sweated brow.

"Oh," he said, and still half-asleep, put his arms around me while

Dion slid his arms around him from behind. I saw Dion's face, and he gave me a little shrug.

"Sleep, my darling," I said, and he did, safe between us.

IN THE MORNING, the gray light slipped in through Dion's white curtains moving in the dawn breeze, cooling and soft. I dressed quietly.

Emrys and Dion were still sleeping, the sheet drawn up around them against the morning air. Dion lay on his side, the sleeve of his oldest and softest chiton half-covering his face where he had ducked it against the back of Emrys' neck. Emrys wore no shirt, and his shoulders were pale against Dion's skin.

Seeing them curled together there, I knew we were all growing older. Emrys' fair skin showed the worst of it, pitted and scarred, his bad arm outstretched on the pillows in sleep, seamed with red lines still. They would fade to white in time, but his arm would always be stiff. He was thirty-five.

Dion, the same age, was not the swift, precocious boy he had been. There were threads of silver among his dark curls.

I raised my arms in the light. I was thirty-two, and while my skin was still good there was no denying that there was more of it. The curves of my breasts were more generous, my hips wider. Rich food had its price.

But, I thought, looking at Emrys and Dion lying side-by-side in sleep, Dion curled around Emrys' back, there was nothing in the world that I would trade for this—certainly not youth, when I had wondered if I was beautiful or if Lucan wanted me, wondered if the price of love should be everything else. This was love.

And so I dressed and went back to the palace to wake the children and begin the day.

A FEW DAYS LATER, a sunny afternoon, the Queen, the younger children, and I were playing on the broad terrace overlooking the sea. A quinquereme was putting out, her five banks of oars moving together, and the whitecaps were breaking against the harbor mole. Gulls cried on the breeze, circling where a fishing boat had just put in. Above, the vault of heaven was a clear and breathless blue.

It was not often that the Queen had a full afternoon to spend with the children, and Helios and Selene were making the most of it, tussling and falling and tugging at her with all of the enthusiasm of children who were not quite two. I rescued her from Helios' tiny hands in her hair.

Our eyes met, laughing.

"This is beautiful," I said.

"And fragile," she said.

I knew that, and none knew as well as she how all of this could be so easily shattered, the peace of the nursery, the peace of the city, half a million people sleeping in peace tonight in Alexandria. And throughout the Black Land, how many more? A hundred thousand in Memphis, seventy-five in Faynum, fifty in Thebes. And how many more? At best guess, six million people knew peace because of what we did, woke each morning to laws as fair as we could make them, to enough food and clean water, to the best medicine in the world.

"So fragile," I said.

She spread her hand against Helios' chest, where he leaned giggling against her, his brown curling hair like Antonius'. "Do the gods feel the weight of it?" she asked, her son's cheek against her own.

"They must," I said, "or They would not need us."

IT WAS SOON AFTER that Dion decided to give a dinner party. There were just six of us really, old friends of ours, and Emrys, who looked better by the day. He had put some flesh back on his bones, and no longer startled at every loud noise. We ate on the balcony in the cool of the evening, two couches of us. There was fish in an olive sauce, and everything as good as one might find anywhere in the city.

Dion arranged our couches as though Emrys were the guest of

honor, reclining on his left elbow with me reclining in front of him, while Dion sat on the end at our knees, the host taking the least comfortable spot. There was laughter and good conversation, though the other guests left early, moving on to some other party with more drinking.

"They left the good wine for us," Emrys said, leaning over me to refill our cup.

"No," said Dion, "I saved the good wine for us!" He poured into his own cup and touched it to ours. "Good friends and good wine."

"Oh yes," I said, and drank, handing the cup to Emrys.

He took it, and a sudden shadow washed across his face. "Absent friends," he said.

"Absent friends, my love," Dion said, and touched cups as though they pledged. Their eyes met, though just their fingers touched, and I felt it leap like a spark between them.

"I should go, dears," I said, starting to push up on my elbow. "It's getting late."

"Don't go just yet," Emrys said.

"Besides," Dion said, "it's your turn."

"It is?"

"It's the fourth night after the new moon except on a state dinner or the Roman kalends of the month. How can you mix up the schedule like that?"

Emrys burst out laughing. "How in the world can anyone keep a schedule like that straight?"

"I have no idea," I said, smiling. "I lost track a long time ago. I just come and go when Dion tells me to."

"Dion says stay," Dion said.

I laughed. "If you mean that, I'll go down and tell the litter bearers to go and come for me in the morning."

"They're probably drinking across the street," Dion said, "I'll go down."

He hurried off, and I leaned back against Emrys' shoulder. "He's very good to you," I said.

"I know."

"He's very good to me too," I said.

"And you are good to both of us," Emrys said, his arm tightening around my waist. "Do you know Dion's never been with a woman?"

"I didn't know it for certain, but I'm not surprised," I said. "He used to run like a startled hare whenever one got too interested. And they did, of course, when he was younger and his tastes less obvious."

"You've known him forever, haven't you?"

I shrugged. "Long enough. Let's see. Twenty-one years? And you and Dion have been on and off for ten years, almost eleven."

He laid his cheek against my hair. "It's a long time, isn't it? I only have two years left to go until my discharge."

"And then will you come home to Alexandria?" I asked.

"Yes," he said, and there was a smile in his voice. "I'll come home."

"You could raise cats like Ptolemy Soter," I said. "Or sell brass cooking pots. Or buy a share in some business belonging to some friend of Dion's who's going to make a fortune selling automatic wine coolers."

"I'll try to stay clear of the wine cooler business," he said. "And I know what happens with most of Dion's inventions." It was certainly true that some of Dion's inventions had turned out to be disastrous.

"He's a good astronomer," I said.

"He'd be one of the greatest if he weren't so easily distracted," Emrys said.

"There are so many interesting things in the world," I said. "How can he ignore any of them? Even if that means running about like an unschooled hound, barking at every scent?"

"While you are all practical concentration," Emrys said.

"I need to be," I said, my fingers closing around his wrist at my waist, feeling the pulse there. "I was fourteen when I knew what I would be—the Hand of Isis, and the Queen's hands. That's what I am."

"You are more than that," he said, and kissed me slowly and lingeringly, his hand cupping my chin sensually. I leaned back into him, reveling in the sweetness of it, the rightness, sinking into Emrys.

Dion cleared his throat. He had come back in, and sat down on the end of the couch. "Don't mind me," he said airily. "Just watching."

"Do you like that?" I said, propping up on one elbow on the yellow and blue pillows. "Do you like watching Emrys kiss someone else?"

I saw the answer quite clearly in his face, the leap of pulse at his throat.

"You do," I said, leaning forward and running my hand up Emrys' thigh, lifting his red tunic to caress corded muscle. "It's pretty, isn't it, Dion?" I lifted the tunic higher, parting his thighs and showing his manhood, which rose at my touch, smooth beneath his foreskin. "I imagine you like this very much."

Emrys made some incomprehensible noise, clutching at the pillow beside him.

"Shhh," I said. "You like to show off. Why don't you show Dion how it's done?" I took him in my hands, pleased at how quickly he responded. He did like Dion watching. Oh yes. I kept my eyes on Dion's face as I worked him with my hands.

"It would be educational," Dion said breathlessly.

"You could show him where everything goes." I lifted my skirts to my waist, one hand on Emrys, the other seeking my own center, parting the tender lips. I was slickening already. I turned the lips out, like petals, rubbing at my center. "I'm sure he'd learn something."

"No field of study too obscure," Dion said, and I could see his arousal clearly at the front of his amber-colored chiton, and I wondered how he looked different. I had never had the opportunity to closely study a circumcised man. "Never let it be said that I've neglected any concern of mankind."

"No, never," I said, slicking Emrys with my own juices, feeling the jolt of arousal in the pit of my stomach. "Come and see, Dion."

"Right here," he said, and as I lowered myself onto Emrys, Dion's arms went around me from behind. He knelt against me, his manhood hard against my back and one hand splayed across the soft flesh of my belly.

Emrys groaned.

"That's right," I said, moving on him with excruciating slowness. "Put your hand there, Dion, and feel where we're joined."

"I'm going to die," Emrys whispered. "Right this very moment."

"Just there?" Dion slid his hand between my legs, first probing at my anus, and then slipping his hand forward. "Oh, there."

I tried to rub myself against his wrist, but now the angle was all wrong and I couldn't move on Emrys at all.

Emrys swore.

"This way," I said, and pulled off, turning around to lie beside Emrys, my head against his shoulder and my skirts around my waist. "That's easier."

Which left Dion kneeling where I had been.

Emrys grinned, and reached up for him, taking him by the hand. "Come on, dearest. See what it's like." He reached down, lifting Dion's chiton and taking him in hand, shorter and thicker than Emrys, rearing more sharply upward against his belly. With his hands on Dion, he guided him into me. "Like that."

I closed my eyes, feeling Emrys' familiar hands on us both. I reached up to caress Dion's sharp hipbones, reveling in the difference, how much unlike Emrys.

"It's so big!" Dion moaned.

Emrys sounded amused. "Women are, Dion. They're made for it."

I snorted. "If you'd gotten Demetria's head out, you'd be bigger than Emrys' ass too!"

Emrys started laughing, and Dion lost the rhythm entirely.

"Can't you see I'm trying to concentrate here?" he asked plaintively. "It's not as easy as it looks."

Then I started laughing, and the three of us collapsed in a heap with Emrys on the bottom. He shrugged his way out, laughing and embracing us both. I kissed Dion, and after an instant he leaned into it. He felt different from Emrys, and it wasn't just his neatly trimmed beard. He tasted different. Fascinating. We parted and lay side-by-side, my arm beneath his shoulder on the pillows.

"You taste different," Dion said.

"I was just thinking the same thing," I said, and we grinned at each other.

"Don't you ever stop?" Emrys asked.

"Science," Dion said, and winked at me.

"How about this, then?" Emrys said, and bent his head to take Dion in his mouth. I watched them, the practiced shallow thrust as Emrys' eyes closed, his hands on Dion's hips. My own hand between my legs, I gasped out my climax before Dion did, one leg wrapped around his bare buttocks, my eyes on Emrys' face.

When he lifted his head he was smiling, but I could see the strain of arousal there too. "Now for you," I said, and drew him up to me.

It was raining. I could hear the storm coming off the sea, the winds flapping the awnings and the curtains drawn across the balcony, blowing cool through the gaps. Someone laid a blanket over us, and I curled closer. To Dion.

I opened my eyes. Dion's arm was beneath me, and I lay against his chest, cuddled under the red and brown blanket from his bed.

"It's raining," I said sleepily.

"I know. Emrys went to get the blanket."

"Oh," I said, and settled back against him on the yellow and blue pillows.

Dion took a deep breath. "Well, that was a new experience."

I canted my head to try to see his face. "Good? Bad?"

"Um…" He stared up to the awning above, as though trying to quantify the experience.

"Scientific analysis," I said. "On a scale of one to ten…"

Dion squeezed me gently. "You know I prefer men. Not that you were doing something wrong or anything. But I just…"

"Prefer men," I said, putting my hand to the smooth flesh of his shoulder. He had a much hairier chest than Emrys. "I know, Dion. It doesn't make us lovers."

"I did like watching Emrys with you," he said, letting me soothe away the tension in his shoulder, as unerotically as though he were at the bath. "I truly did."

"And I liked watching him with you," I said. "Not that I wouldn't have you if you wanted. But it's not that way between us, truly, is it? Philia, not eros."

"I know." Dion placed a kiss on the top of my head. "As though we were both wives of one man. Or I his wife, and you his erastes."

"Oddly enough," I said. "It makes more sense that way. It's your home, and you're the one who takes on the duties of a wife. And I am his male lover, with my own home and child."

"That would make us family still. Sort of."

I rolled over and embraced him. "We're family, Dion. Always."

"In a strange sort of way. But if it shows promise, then the experiment should continue. Not that you and I should…"

"No, not that you and I should be lovers," I said. "But you could watch me with Emrys sometimes if you like it."

"I do," he said. "And that time when we all three shared a bed, just to sleep. I liked that too. I shouldn't mind that sometimes."

"I did too," I said. "It was very good, actually."

He put one hand awkwardly on the middle of my back. "And you're pretty. For a woman, I mean."

"Thank you, Dion," I said, laughing.

"I do appreciate the opportunity to study," he said very seriously. "So much has been said about it that one wonders."

"Stop while you're winning," I said, and pushed the dampened hair back from his forehead.

"This couch is really small," Dion said. "The armrest is right in the middle of my back. Do you think we might try the bed?"

"We could," I said. I got up and followed him into the bedroom, trying to shake out my clothes. I should have taken the long chiton off first. It was linen, and the wrinkles wouldn't shake out.

Emrys had moved around the bolsters in Dion's bed, and held out an arm to me. "Come and get warm." Dion trundled after, carrying the blanket, which he carefully rearranged across the end of the bed on top of the sheet and other blanket, folded so it covered our feet. He'd taken off his crumpled chiton and wasn't wearing anything at all.

I gave him a sideways glance. He blushed, but climbed in with an arch look.

"Fine, then," I said, lifting mine and pulling it off over my head to drop on the floor.

Emrys' eyebrows lifted, and he drew me to him. "An absolute den of debauchery, this innocent Kelt has fallen into."

"Absolute," Dion said, hooking one leg over Emrys' knee as I curled in on the other side. "Complete."

"Yes," I said. The rain beat against the awnings, and I slept.

EMRYS STAYED three months more.

"You've got the money that your general gave you for the provisions," Dion said. "We could just take the coin and run away together with it. To Hispania, or maybe Mauretania. We'd be rich there."

Emrys shook his head, smiling. "You know I can't do that. And that's why he sent me."

"And what about me?" I asked Dion, laughing. "I have to work! I can't run away to Hispania with a couple of wanted desperadoes."

"Besides," Emrys said, beginning to pack his things. "Dion, how would you live without a great library and takeout on every corner?"

And so we said farewell again.

I HELD CAREFULLY IN MIND that it was more than Cleopatra had. Antonius was still in Athens, and his letters were all official letters, sent in the diplomatic bag.

Dion was philosophical. "He's scared to face her, Emrys said."

"He ought to be," I said. "But the more he pretends he's never heard of Cleopatra the worse it will be."

"Maybe he thinks he can just ignore it forever."

I raised an eyebrow. "Sooner or later he will need something. And then we will see Marcus Antonius again."

THE PARTING OF
THE WATERS

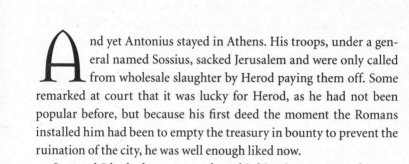

And yet Antonius stayed in Athens. His troops, under a general named Sossius, sacked Jerusalem and were only called from wholesale slaughter by Herod paying them off. Some remarked at court that it was lucky for Herod, as he had not been popular before, but because his first deed the moment the Romans installed him had been to empty the treasury in bounty to prevent the ruination of the city, he was well enough liked now.

Iras and I looked at one another, thinking it was not perhaps as lucky as all that. Inheriting a bankrupt kingdom was not so easy.

THE HARVEST CAME, grain barges toiling down the Nile to the sea. The dry season came and went, and with the Inundation, Caesarion's tenth birthday. I was surprised, standing behind him at the ceremony, how tall he had gotten, and how straight and muscled his legs. He was growing again in a spurt, and dressed in the stiffened white linen shenti of Pharaoh, he moved with dignity.

Six months younger, Demetria was nine and a half. Already her figure was changing, the straight boyish lines of childhood beginning to ripen. She had a waist, I thought one day as I helped her drape a new chiton and fasten the girdle. Soon her hips would curve, her breasts begin. Her face had more definition than before, the Ptolemy nose and Agrippa's broad forehead, a combination that didn't entirely suit a young girl.

She turned around, and her eyes were at the level of my chin, her long brown hair flowing behind her, pinned back over her ears. "What's the matter, Ma?"

"Nothing, darling," I said. "I was thinking that you're growing up."

"Of course I am," she said, with a half-amused tone that sounded oddly like Emrys. "What did you think I would do?"

I smiled, tying off the end of her girdle with the same fashionable knot the Queen used. "I don't know."

"You think I'm as small as Selene," she accused. Selene was not quite three, and she wanted to follow Demetria everywhere, only she usually created havoc when she did.

"I know you're not," I said.

Soon Caesarion would go to his own household, away from the nursery, any time now really. And then Demetria's path and his would begin to separate, Caesarion to the life of Pharaoh, and Demetria to what?

"Demetria," I said slowly, sitting down on the couch, "what do you want to do?"

"Do? You mean this afternoon?"

"Something for you, I mean. While Caesarion is having his riding lessons and learning to use a sword. When he does those things, what would you like to learn how to do?"

I expected her to say that she would like more time with the tutors, or perhaps to follow Iras in the accounts and the treasury. I would have liked it if she had said she would like to come with me and learn to do what I did, though I did not expect it.

"Oh!" Her face cleared, eyes bright. "I know exactly what I want to do! I want to go to the Temple of Isis and study with the temple singers."

I blinked. I hadn't known she had any special interest in music, beyond the songs that all children learned.

"Don't you hear it, Ma?" she asked. "The way the music is in the temple?" She hummed the beginning of one of the songs of praise, the evening liturgy. "'Star of Evening, She who made the skies, watch us, Mother, in the night....' That's what I want to do when I grow up."

"Be a singer?"

"Be a priestess," she said.

"Oh." Any desire I might have had for that life had been quashed at Bubastis, where it seemed to me that all adolescent yearning must be damped down behind endless work and ceaseless repetition of the offices. But I was not Demetria.

She was watching me, waiting, neither begging nor defiant yet. Waiting to see which she needed to be. Demetria had all of the Ptolemy calculation.

"You could study music at the temple," I said. "But it will be very difficult, and if I arrange it for you, you must promise that you will study a full year before you give it up. It's very, very hard to be a priestess. And you will have to work hard for years."

"I promise," she said. "I'll work really, really amazingly hard."

SHE DID. It gave her great pride to have something that was hers alone, not mine nor Caesarion's, or anyone else's. Anything she achieved there, she did so because of her talent and effort.

It made chaos of schedules, however. I could not leave the palace every night just before the dinner hour to go get her at the temple, and I thought her still too young to wander around town by herself. Fortunately, Dion agreed to get her four nights a week, when his lectures were done not too far from the Serapeum. She went home with Dion and had dinner, and then I came for her later. Sometimes, when I could leave early, I was there in time for dinner with them.

As Emrys had pointed out, Dion couldn't cook, but he knew every single takeout shop in town. We ate Ethiopian or Palmyran, or something less exotic, Demetria telling me everything she had learned, the rhythms of the sistrums or the flute or drum. She loved all of those things, but it was her voice that was her best instrument, a clear, high voice with surprising power for a girl her age.

"My master says I will be good in a few years," she said depreciatingly, after singing something that seemed good already to me. "I'd like to be good."

Dion nodded. "I think you will be," he said.

Demetria glowed.

And this was how Demetria came to moonlight as a performer in the Jewish theater. Dion had a cousin who had a husband that Dion sometimes did some work with, a vague recommendation that seemed to involve the chance to try a practical application for some bizarre invention of Dion's. It seemed that he was looking for a young girl to play a role in the first act of a new production, and Dion told him he ought to listen to Demetria. While I was working, and oblivious to this, Dion took her to audition. By the time I heard about it, she had the part.

"I'll die if I don't do it!" Demetria begged, falling to her knees at my feet. "I have to! I gave my word!"

"Commercial theater? You're not quite eleven years old!"

"I've sung in the temple choir in front of people!"

"That is entirely different," I said. "Singing in a choir at the Serapeum is entirely different than appearing as a paid performer in musical comedy. Women don't act in real theater, only in bawdy musical revues and comedy for dinners. And who knows what kind of unruly crowd there is!"

"You have singers with dinner at the palace all the time!"

Dion shifted from one foot to another. "My cousin's husband runs a respectable troupe. It's musical comedy, yes, but it's not low comedy."

I gave him a gimlet stare. "And you stay out of this. I have words for you later about taking her to auditions without telling me."

"I promised!" Demetria wailed, catching me around the ankles like an overdone suppliant in Euripides.

"You should at least see it," Dion said as I tried to get my feet loose.

"Come on now, Charmian. It's not bawdy. Demetria is like my own daughter. I'd let my daughter do it. My cousin's daughter would be doing it, only she can't sing half as well as Demetria."

"And she's about seventeen and old and her looks have gone," the suppliant said from the floor.

"No skimpy costumes?"

"Not on Demetria." Dion held up his hand. "My word of honor. Come and see, Charmian." He gave me a sheepish smile. "And you can see my self-propelled scenery too."

"Oh, Dion," I said.

THREE DAYS LATER I went with him. It wasn't held in a proper theater, but in one of the tiered lecture halls around town that were for rent to scholars who needed more space for large classes. It could hold about two hundred people, which would be quite a big lecture, though Dion assured me that he held lectures here himself from time to time, as his cousin's husband gave him an excellent rate on the rental.

"What do you lecture on to two hundred people?" I asked him.

"You needn't look so impressed," Dion said. "Astronomy. Empirical science. I do a series on the introduction to the scientific method that's universally enjoyed. It's recommended for new students by masters of more advanced classes, who don't want them till I'm done with them."

"You must have something of a following," I said.

"I do my best," Dion said somewhat smugly.

A sign announced the day's performance. "*Moses: A Musical Comedy in Three Acts?*" I looked at Dion skeptically.

"I promise you, Demetria's part is very respectable," Dion said. "It's only the dancing girls later on that anyone might mind. They're there to demonstrate Egyptian excess."

"I see," I said.

We took our seats, and the play began rather conventionally. A woman (and I could not tell, masked, if she were really a woman or, more reasonably, a man in a mask) lamented that her children would be born in slavery, for Pharaoh held them all captives, and had vowed to kill every child of the Jews. After a long declamation, she produced a baby doll from beneath her robes and swaddled it. "Mariamne! Mariamne!" she called.

Demetria came on, looking lovely in her simple white chiton. "Yes, Mother?"

"We will save your baby brother by hiding him in a basket in the reeds. We will set it to drift on the Nile. Better that than he die. Take this basket to the river." Putting the doll in the basket, she handed it to Demetria.

I was frowning at what seemed to me the distinctly anti-Egyptian tone of the piece, and wondering why in the world Dion had thought this was a good idea, when Demetria took the doll to her breast and began to sing.

"'Sleep, my love, on the breast of the Nile. Sleep while stars shine down on thee. Sleep, my love, on the heart of the waves. Sleep, my brother, sleep. Sleep my brother, promised one, sleep while God watches over thee.'" Her voice was clear and cool, without a single tremor or shake, a bright treble falling like water, innocence personified. She stood with one knee bent, the doll to her shoulder, her face raised as though to invisible stars. Light shone in her eyes. There was not a sound in the entire house.

She laid the basket in the painted waters and let it go, bidding farewell to the baby they must expose, the baby they could not keep. She stopped on the edge, half turned as though watching it drift away.

Somewhere in the audience, a woman took a breath almost like a sob.

And then she turned, raising her eyes to the audience, or to the invisible God. "I have to follow him," she said. "I have to!" And she ran from the stage.

I clutched Dion's hand. "She's good, Dion."

He bent his head toward me. "I told you she was. Charmian, she's exceptional. She's not but eleven years old."

There was a flourish of drums and trumpets, and with great pomp a royal procession appeared, a princess in the center, clad in pleated linen.

"Every day," she said, "I go with my maidens to bathe and play beside the river. I am Pharaoh's daughter. But what is this I hear? Is that a baby crying?"

One of the princess' handmaidens came forward with the same basket. "Here it is, Princess. It is a baby, in a basket that had drifted into the reeds. A little boy."

Pharaoh's daughter lifted the doll from the basket and held it to her, her face painted, not a mask. I could swear that was a real woman, not a man. I didn't think the Jewish theater had eunuchs on stage. "A child of the poor who could not keep him. Well, he has come to me. Do not be afraid, little one. I will care for you."

At this point Demetria sprung up, as though from among the reeds. "Gracious Lady, I know a Hebrew woman who would make a good wet nurse. She has lost her own son. Shall I go and get her?"

"Yes, do so," she said.

Demetria paused at the edge of the stage, looking toward the audience as though to take them into her confidence. "I will go find my own mother, that she may nurse her son for Pharaoh's daughter." And then she went off again.

Dion leaned to me. "That's Demetria's whole part. When Mariamne comes on again later in the play, she's grown up. Demetria only plays child Mariamne. She has that one song."

"That was lovely," I whispered. "I had no idea she could sing like that. Or act. She could do the Mysteries."

Dion looked amused, and whispered back, "These are the Mysteries, Charmian. The stories on our holiest scrolls, done before all the world, for anyone to see. That's why people mind."

"Oh," I said. I thought a few minutes, while on stage the baby, grown into a youth, seemed to be having a quarrel with Pharaoh's son, involving a lot of singing. "No wonder people mind, then. Why do you do it, Dion?"

He leaned back over. "Because truth doesn't belong to any one people, but to all of the souls in the world who seek it. And there are truths to be scattered everywhere, even in places where they will not take root for many years. Thus are we all advanced in the service of the Most High. To say this truth belongs only to the Jews is like saying that philosophy should only be studied by Greek men, or that Isis cares only for Egyptian women."

I thought a while longer. On stage, Moses had killed a soldier and was now fleeing, which seemed to involve a lot of singing, while three men dressed as archers performed in counterpoint, complete with very well executed dancing.

Dion leaned in again. "Truth makes us free, Charmian. The best we can do is to carry the banner proudly in our own time."

I squeezed his hand. "I think you are a very good man, Dion," I whispered.

It was well into the third act before I saw Dion's handiwork. As we took our seats again after the pause, he grinned at me. "You'll like this. I know you will. I thought of you when I was figuring out how to do it."

With a fanfare, the music began.

The Jews, it seemed, were fleeing Egypt, and had come at last to the edge of the sea. However, Pharaoh's chariots pursued with a heavy drumbeat and menacing trumpets. A painted backdrop of the billowing waves stood across the stage, unsupported on either end or above, rather fierce looking waves, I thought.

"'Oh, what shall we do?'" the chorus of Jews sang. "'We will be killed!'" In counterpoint, the drums and trumpets and Egyptian soldiers were all singing their parts, a big set piece of a song with all the trimmings.

Moses took his staff, topped with a serpent's head that looked rather like the uraeus, and stretched out his arms dramatically, shouting one word aloud. The drums crashed, and all of the music halted on a single note.

Slowly, with no visible mechanism at all, the backdrop of the ocean parted, each piece rolling smoothly backward with no hand upon it. There was no walk above from which they could have been pulled, since this was a lecture hall, not a theater. They did not extend to the makeshift draped wings. No hand touched them at all as the waves glided smoothly apart.

"Hurry!" grown-up Mariamne yelled. "We must cross while the waves are parted! There is not much time!"

At that the flutes began again, and the song of the Jews as they tumbled into the place between the waves, carrying children and bundles and looking fearfully behind. They passed in the middle, then broke into two lines across the back of the stage, into either wing. Last of all came Moses, his arms still outstretched, passing between the massive set pieces, each twice a man's height. The drums and trumpets began to pick up; Pharaoh's chariots were approaching. The painted waves towered over him. When he stood behind them, he once again shouted a word of command.

And again, soundlessly, and without the touch of human hands, the waves glided together once more, ending precisely together, Moses behind them, just as the music ended.

The audience broke into thunderous applause.

Dion stretched and grinned in his seat as the actors came out to take their bows. Demetria was one of the last, but her face glowed, and there was a wave of stronger applause when she came forward, for child Mariamne.

Afterward, we stood while people milled around, waiting for Demetria.

"How in the world is it done, Dion? The waves must be yours. I remember when we talked about that story."

Dion grinned wider. "On the back of each one there's a big basket of sand on a cord tied to the axle of the piece's wheels. When the sand empties out of the basket into another, the weight pulls the cord, and the scenery moves across the stage and lifts the full basket. There it sits, until the gradual emptying of the full basket into the now empty one reverses it, and the cord winds the other way. When it does, the scenery moves back. You can change the timing by varying the amount of sand, but you have to be very precise. Otherwise the waves will move before Moses tells them to. When he walks through the waves and stops behind them, he can see how much sand is left, and times the command for the waves to close to when the basket empties."

I looked at him with astonishment. "That's incredibly clever!"

"I thought so," Dion said modestly.

Demetria came hurrying up. "Well?"

I hugged her. "All right, you can keep the part! If Dion will make sure you don't have to walk home from the theater alone."

"I swear," Dion said.

Demetria threw her arms about me and Dion both. "I love you so much!"

"And I suppose we should see about voice lessons," I said. "I imagine the temple would be happy to have you as a full-time student."

THUS WHEN the play ended, just before Demetria turned twelve, she became an acolyte, spending all day, every day at the Serapeum and the Temple of Isis, arriving early for choir for the Morning Offices, and then taking lessons and lunch there. In the afternoon she had music, voice and instrumental both. In four years she would be a dedicant, if she excelled, an irrevocable commitment to temple and to Goddess. A dedicant could still marry, if she wished, but her vows were for life.

I supposed that sixteen was not too young to make that choice. I had known what my life would be when I was fourteen.

I HAD A LETTER from Emrys, written from Antioch.

> *Hail Charmian,*
> *Antonius is here with us in Syria, and they say we are going against the Parthians again next summer. I was not in Jerusalem at the beginning, as light cavalry is of no use in close street fighting,*

*but I do not want to ever see such again. I think everyone would
have been killed, had Herod not called Sossius off. I do not mind
so much facing armies in the field, but I do not like sacking cities,
and I cannot help but feel it too much. Now Herod is a very great
hero in the eyes of everyone here, as well as being a good soldier.
They call him Herod the Great without a trace of irony.*

*I am glad to hear Demetria is well and that her studies are
progressing. Does she miss the nursery and Caesarion, or is it time
for her leave that behind her so that she does not yearn for it? You
can be very proud of your daughter.*

Less than two more years…

Straight on the heels of this, Antonius' general Gaius Capito arrived
in Alexandria, with letters for the Queen and a personal plea that she
come to Syria immediately, bringing all possible supplies and ships.

He made his request as gracefully as possible, before the Queen's
entire council, clearly knowing what a position Antonius had put him
in, and appreciating it not at all. Consequently, the Queen did not tor-
ment Capito, but told him that he would have his reply in a few days,
and that he might enjoy the hospitality of the city in the meantime. He
left, looking as though he'd expected to spend the next few days in an
oubliette instead.

After he departed, the council all looked at each other, as if daring
another to speak first.

It was Apollodorus who did, who had been with her since childhood. "Gracious Queen," he began. "Herod and the Parthians…"

"Of course we must go," she said, folding her hands in her lap. "I
have not done all for the alliance, only to scrap it."

WE SAILED FOR ANTIOCH, and with thirty ships now we were quite
a great fleet. Caesarion and Iras stayed in Alexandria, but the twins
came with us. Antonius had never seen them.

This time, when we came into the harbor, we did not come like

Aphrodite of the Waves, courting. We came on a warship, and we did not sing.

Antonius recognized the difference, of course. He came to the ship immediately himself. A show of respect? I wondered. Desperation for supplies? Or did he truly want to see Cleopatra? In any event, he hurried, and he was well dressed in a harness of white leather studded with gold over a blinding purple tunic with broad golden borders, short enough to show off his handsome legs.

He made his bow to the Queen, his officers behind him, while we all stood like statues. She wore the double crown and uraeus, the snake jutting gilded from her brow, and in her pleated linen sat as still and impassive as any statue, like a carving on a wall of Isis in the Halls of Amenti.

She said one word. "Kneel."

I took a breath.

"I will not," Antonius said.

Her eyes bored into him. "Kneel to this throne, or our alliance is over."

"Cleopatra...," he began, spreading his hands.

"Kneel."

The color rose in his face. "Can't we discuss this privately?"

"The state of our alliance?" Her painted brows rose. "I think not. Now kneel as any proper suppliant. That is what you are, isn't it? Without me you will not keep what you have won."

She will break it, I thought. She is humiliating him before his officers, and surely his pride will not bear it.

Instead, Marcus Antonius sank to his knees. "There," he said. "Does that suit you now?"

"Very well," she said. "And I will give you what you want. Provisions and grain to fight the Parthians, food for your men and their horses, and a fleet to guard your back."

Bareheaded, he gave her half a smile. "In exchange for what?"

"All of the cities on the coast of Phoenicia from Ashkelon to Ptolemais Ace, and from Ptolemais Ace to Balanea, excepting the cities of

Tyre and Sidon. The province of Ituraea, between the Roman province of Syria and the Kingdom of Judea. The cities of the Decapolis in the interior of Judea, including the cities of Hippos and Gadara, and the groves of Gilead, near Jericho. Also the Nabatean coast of the Red Sea along the Gulf of Elat."

Antonius' smile faded. "You are asking for a third of our eastern territories."

"And if I do not have them, they will be overrun by the Parthians, and you will not have them either," she replied coolly.

"Half that land is already given to Herod," he said.

"How very unfortunate for him."

"Cleopatra…"

"When Herod can bring you a fleet and supplies, then no doubt it will be in your better interest to enforce his claim. Right now he brings you nothing, due to the brilliance of your General Sossius, who has managed to impoverish the nation and loot the capital of your own ally. But then," she said, pausing as if suddenly remembering something, "you weren't here, were you, Imperator? I believe you were opening the games in Athens."

Antonius' mouth opened and shut. Then he got to his feet, spun on his heels, and stalked out of the audience without another word, his officers scrambling after.

I waited until they were gone. "Gracious Queen?"

Cleopatra had not moved at all. "He will be back," she said. "He needs me more than I need him."

LORDS ·OF· THE EAST

The next day Cleopatra had an invitation to dine with Antonius at the palace of Antioch, which he had taken for his own.

"Very well," the Queen agreed, "but in two days our fleet sails for Egypt. Tell the Imperator that he must decide whether he will meet my terms, or watch his supplies sail back to Alexandria."

I wanted badly to see Emrys, who was stationed in Antioch, but did not dare to. It would be too great a test of my loyalty, with our masters opposed. I thought he must feel the same way, as he had made no attempt to see me either.

I waited while she went ashore to the dinner, and was there when she brought Antonius back to the ship for a private conversation. Of course, for the great, private conversations are rarely private. I was hanging about the back of the cabin, in case she wanted anything, and was both surprised and pleased that the bodyguard Antonius had brought was Sigismund.

We exchanged happy glances while the slaves brought wine for the Queen and Antonius. I would have gladly run and hugged him, and vice versa, but we were both on duty. He looked fit, if a bit older, and his long blond hair was now severely cut in the Roman fashion, a new scar across his cheek. He still looked like he could lift an ox, though.

We both faded into the background on our respective sides of the room as the cupbearer closed the door.

Cleopatra was all Greek today, in an Ionic chiton of pale lavender, the borders worked with violets. She sat down not on the couch, but in a hard chair, her arms resting along its armrests like a Roman legate. "Well?"

"I'm sorry." Antonius poured himself a cup of wine from the cool amphora left standing. "Is that what you wanted to hear?"

"Sorry for what?"

"For marrying Octavia. Is this jealousy?" He did not look at her, but rather into the depths of the cup. "Do you want me to tell you I don't love her, that I've never thought about anyone but you? That I didn't enjoy a moment with her and that I missed you every second?"

"Are those things true?" Cleopatra's voice was completely dispassionate, as though she spoke of someone else, long ago.

He took a quick drink of the red wine. "No."

Sigismund's eyes met mine across the room, and I could read his thought as clearly there as if he'd said it aloud: Not good.

I sincerely hoped this didn't come down to violence or kidnapping. Me against Sigismund was no contest, but he knew as well as I that I would have to try. Still, he could probably stop me with no worse than a broken arm or wrist, and he would do as little as he could.

"It seemed the wise thing to do, marrying her. It seemed the way out of a situation with Octavian, that my brother, curse him, got me into. And Octavia's not a bad sort. She's not you or Fulvia, someone I would choose, but I like her well enough. She didn't really want to get married again so soon, but she knew she had to, and that she would have to marry to improve her brother's position. She liked me better than Tiberius Nero, and she liked the idea of making peace between me and her brother." Antonius took another deep drink. "I didn't know how you'd take that."

"As the political expedience it had to be," she said. "What I do not appreciate is my letters remaining unanswered, and you sending diplomatic correspondence as though I were a mere acquaintance."

Antonius turned around, and there was something real in his eyes, something raw. "I didn't know what to say!"

Her voice shook a little, finally. "You could have said what you meant, as Caesar did."

"As Caesar did."

"Yes." Their eyes met.

"I am not your Alexander, or anything else out of a dream."

"I know," she said.

"I did love you. I do love you." He put the cup down on the table with a clatter. "What do I have to do to convince you of that?"

"Act like it."

Over their oblivious heads, Sigismund and I exchanged a glance.

"By laying vast territories at your feet as a symbol of my contrition?"

"By laying vast territories at my feet as your children's patrimony," she said. "You have not even seen them. I know perfectly well they are nothing to Roman law. Are they nothing to you as well, Antonius? I thought you a better father than that in Rome, and a better man."

"How can I ask you for that?" He turned back to the wine table again. "Cleopatra, I have nothing to say. We can't start over again. There's too much between us, and always politics in the way." He filled the cup to the rim. "If I had my way, I would come back to Alexandria with you and come to know the children, live in some reasonable way. But you know perfectly well that's never going to happen. I am going to spend my life as a series of interludes between one battlefield and another until I die, playing games I never quite understand. Octavian's a better player, Cleopatra. You last saw him years ago. You don't know."

"Then don't play against him," she said, standing up swiftly. "You have the East. Leave Rome to Octavian. Stop trying to roll dice against him to be the First Man of Rome. Do the thing that you do well. Choose territory you can hold and keep it. Forget the Senate and the people of Rome."

"Stop being Roman," he said blankly.

"Yes."

There was confusion in Sigismund's eyes, and I saw that he did not have the context I did — Ptolemy in the double crown and white warrior's shenti of Pharaoh, nothing of Macedon about him, refusing to play games of regency in Pella while the Black Land waited. It had worked before.

"Come to Alexandria," she said. "Let us build a successor kingdom in the East, you and I, to be ruled by Caesar's son and our children after us. Octavian wants the West. Let him have it! We have more than enough."

Antonius put the cup down again. "You will still have me."

She blinked, and her eyes were wet. "Maybe."

"I will swear my oath to you," he said roughly, "I will swear by any god you like that I will never again put anything before you or our children."

"Done," she said, and stepped forward into his arms.

In Sigismund's eyes I saw nothing but vast relief.

EMRYS HEARD THE GIST of the conversation from me and Sigismund both, though I did not give him all of the details. He and Sigismund had cups in hand, and I sat with them in a tavern in Antioch, a rare break from the Queen's work.

"Can the leopard change his spots?" Emrys mused. "Leopards have, but the other leopards don't like it."

Sigismund poured more wine for all three of us. "Well, you and I, Emrys, we've already changed our spots. Would anyone at home recognize us the way we are now? When we joined up we thought we'd go home in sixteen or twenty years as rich men. But in sixteen or twenty years, is there any going home? My village on the headwaters of the Rhenus wouldn't recognize me. I'd be as odd as a dragon there."

"What are you going to do when you get your discharge, Sigismund?" I asked.

"Go back to Rome," he said, taking a deep swallow. "I've a woman there, a widow with three children. She's got a tavern in the Subura she's trying to hang on to, and she could use a man about to keep the crowd civil. We've got an understanding. When I get out, we'll get married."

"That's wonderful," I said. "I wish you every happiness."

"Yes, well," he said, smiling. "Not as fancy as Emrys here, but a good future."

"A better idea than being a gladiator," Emrys said.

"Too old," Sigismund said, cracking his knuckles. "I could have done it ten years ago. But I'm thirty-six. Not as fast as I used to be. It's time to be done with campaigning. If that's the leopard changing spots, it's all to the good."

"The other leopards don't like it," I murmured.

WE WINTERED IN ANTIOCH. All was preparation for the great campaign in the spring, in which the Parthian Empire should be defeated by Antonius as decisively as it had been by Alexander. I did not have much enthusiasm for the task. I could not shake the vague feeling of foreboding, that the entire enterprise was ill conceived and badly timed.

The plan was thus: Rather than advance straight upon Parthia, as Crassus' disastrous expedition had, Antonius' forces would advance northward, through Armenia, and then come down on the heartland of Media from the west. The first city to fall should be the city of Praaspa.

Alexander could have done it. Alexander had done it. But we did not have Alexander.

FOR THE MOST PART, the winter passed pleasantly. Emrys had one more year of service—this would be his last campaign. The Queen and Antonius were all smiles, and one never saw them except together, usually with Helios and Selene in tow.

Antonius had brought his oldest child east with him, Antyllus, who I remembered as the little boy shoved on Caesarion as playmate by Fulvia in the last days of Caesar's life. Now he was twelve. He was a slim, well-mannered boy just reaching the age when it seems as if his knees and elbows were too big for the rest of him. He had the look of

Fulvia about him, and he was very gentle with the twins. I thought that he was a little shy, something of a defect in the oldest son of the First Man of Rome.

Toward spring I had a week of worry when my blood didn't come, and I wondered if Emrys and I had finally not been careful enough. I had not conceived since Demetria's difficult birth, and was not at all certain whether or not I could, but we tried to take no chances. Still, as any good physician would say, such things are always uncertain, and celibacy the only sure barrier to conception. I was, after all, only thirty-three.

After a week, it came on hard, and I breathed a sigh of relief. There were children enough in my life, with Demetria, Caesarion, and the four-year-old twins. The prospect of another pregnancy and child just now seemed daunting.

In any event, another child was on the horizon, as three weeks later the Queen missed her blood. I knew how she loved all of her children, Caesarion, Selene, and Helios alike, but I confess that my first thought was "Not again!" Her pregnancy with the twins had been so danger-ous and taxing on everyone, and very nearly tragic at the end.

Therefore, it was decided that when Antonius marched toward Armenia at the beginning of Roman May, we would return by sea to Alexandria. Antyllus would come with us, as Antonius thought him still too young for a military campaign.

Of all the times I had said farewell to Emrys, this one was the hard-est. I wept, as I had not before.

"You worry too much," he said with a smile. "I'm an old soldier and I know how to look after myself."

"I know," I said. "And I will make offerings in your name every day anyway."

"It can't hurt," he said, and kissed me good-bye.

I DID NOT HAVE TO WAIT LONG for a letter. Soon after we reached Alexandria the first one arrived.

Hail Charmian,

We are advancing with eleven legions, and as yet have met no resistance to speak of. Therefore we have stripped the countryside of provisions, and our baggage train is grown very large indeed, so we do not lack for food. However, by necessity, we move very slowly, no faster than the pace of a laden mule. This chafes the light cavalry very much! Our Armenian allies are helpful, and they have many more horsemen than we do, so you see all is well....

I wished this comforted me, but it did not. However, I had other things to think of. Caesarion had his own household now, and I had charge of the twins in the nursery, who would at the end of the fall be joined by a little brother or sister. The doctors could only hear one heartbeat, something for which I made a thank offering in the Temple of Isis.

When Cleopatra appeared at festivals or on progress with Helios and Selene, people rushed to touch her, calling that she was Isis incarnate, the fertility of the Black Land personified. And so she seemed, her two beautiful children on either side of her, with Caesarion, the Horus of Egypt, walking behind.

Summer came on, and the Inundation.

The Queen's belly swelled. The Temple of Hathor at Dendara was finished. Caesarion and Antyllus frightened everyone by sneaking out of the palace together and going about town in the middle of the night dressed as servants. Antyllus was scolded, and Caesarion lost the use of his horse for two weeks.

Iras and I laughed about it as soon as the boys were gone. "You do know," she said to Cleopatra, "they do no more than we did."

"I know," Cleopatra said, "and that is why the punishment is no worse. A Pharaoh must come to know his subjects, but a boy his age must not find it easy. If there is no challenge, there can be no triumph."

"Better that than breaking his neck horse racing," I said. Antyllus was by far the better rider, possibly because he listened to the horses instead of talking incessantly. They were well suited as friends. Caesarion was never quiet, and Antyllus never spoke, stepping neatly into the position of Companion. I wondered if that would please or displease Antonius when he returned.

If he returned.

⚜ Amenti

"Was all already lost then?" I asked. "Was it already too late?"

"It was a sacred marriage that Marcus Antonius made in Tarsus, Isis and Dionysos. You know what it means to become the avatar of a god. Perhaps Antonius understood what he did; perhaps not. It doesn't matter. For years he had been Neos Dionysos, who comes to the East bringing joy instead of swords. He had worn the god's clothes and invoked His name. It was too late to say that he had not consented to the sacrifice," Serapis said, and His eyes were grave.

Of course I knew the stories, how the Titans had ripped Dionysos apart, eating His flesh and pouring out His blood in libation on the earth. It is an old story, as old perhaps as a time when those rites were carried out literally rather than in symbol, when each year the Lord of Vines must die.

"He made the sacred marriage and wore the god's face," Isis said, as though She had read my thoughts. "No longer must a priest die each year, or a young man loving and brave, but in time of need the sacrifice must be made. And the sacrifice must be willing, for I tell you that there is nothing more blessed than to lay down one's life for others. He must have consented to the sacrifice, as Caesar did when he went down into the West."

I took a deep breath. "Did Antonius refuse the sacrifice?"

Isis nodded. "Yes. He was meant to die in Parthia. He went into the East, where his blood should have been spilled out, god to you and hero to Rome. He refused the sacrifice. When at last the time came, he was not *willing. Marcus Antonius wanted to live."*

"And that would have saved us?" I asked. "What of Octavian?"

"Should he dare touch the memory of brave Marcus Antonius, who died for Rome, hero of the Roman people?" Isis raised an eyebrow.

Mikhael shifted, the feathers of His white wings making a sound like soft wind.

"That would not have stopped him forever, of course. But it would have made things more difficult. It would have cost him time. Time was what Octavian could not afford. There is a vast difference to Romans between defeating Cleopatra, the Wicked Queen of the East who has ensnared a helpless man and turned him from his duty, and raising an army against Caesar's son. There is a vast difference between fighting a boy of seventeen and a man of twenty-seven, with children of his own and skill in arms."

I felt my eyes fill. "Ten years for Caesarion to grow up, to become Pharaoh in truth."

Isis nodded, and I saw the tears in Her eyes as well. She was His mother too, as much as I. "Ten years," She said, and Her voice was choked. "Marcus Antonius' sacrifice might have bought ten years."

"It is my fault," I said, and the tears spilled over my eyes. I thought the grief would rend me in two. "If I had somehow held Agrippa, if I had brought him to our side. I could have done it, when he was young." I clenched my hands, remembering. "Cleopatra asked me if I wanted her to write to Caesar, when I was first pregnant with Demetria. She asked if I wanted Agrippa sent back to Egypt, to a staff position. Caesar would have done it. It was little enough to ask. Agrippa was only a junior tribune then, and not yet a friend to Octavian. Caesar would have sent him back to Egypt when Caesarion was born and tactfully told him that he was sending him to guard his son, rather than because Cleopatra willed it." I tilted back my head. It was all clear, the pattern of what might have been. "He was so serious. So determined. He would have sworn his life to Caesarion, pledged Caesar that he would let nothing ill happen to his son, and having promised Caesar should have kept it all his life. He would not even have been on campaign with Octavian — they should not have been friends, had Marcus Agrippa been in Egypt instead, rather than thrown

with Octavian in Hispania. I should have asked her to write to Caesar. It is my fault." I ground my teeth against the pain.

"And why did you not ask her?" Serapis asked in His patient judge's voice.

I could not see through my tears. "Because he did not want me! He didn't write. He didn't want to. I was too proud to beg for Cleopatra to send for a man who had deserted me."

Serapis' voice did not change. "Is it true that he did not want you?"

"I don't know," I said. "He said later, in Rome, that he had thought of nothing but me. But if so, why did he not write? He said he loved me, that he had been planning our marriage for years. But he did not send me a single letter! How should I know if he remembered me or not, when he did not speak?"

"And that is a question we shall put to Marcus Agrippa, when he stands here," Serapis said, glancing at Anubis as counsel will when they consult together. "But he does not stand here, and his race has many miles yet to run."

Mikhael stirred again. "And perhaps there was more to it yet—that you would not stoop to manipulating a man that you cared for to get what should be freely given, or not had at all. If you had begged Cleopatra to have him returned to Egypt, perhaps he should have resented you even as he swore himself to Caesarion." He spread His hands, His handsome face grave. "Who is to say what the results of that should have been? He is not a simple man, and it is true that at the time he did not want to come to Egypt."

Whatever he had said later, I had always thought that was true. "He wanted to stay with Caesar."

Mikhael gave me a quick nod. "Companions' oaths."

"I respect that," I said. "I never once asked Emrys for anything he could not in conscience give. Unlike…" I stopped. I would not voice the thought that came next.

"Unlike Cleopatra?" Isis looked rueful. "She loved Antonius, and did not want him to die."

"As Caesar had," I said. "Having seen that bereavement once, I could not wish it on her again."

"Not even for the sake of all you fought for?" Serapis asked sharply. "That is the way of it. Isis is the Grain Mother. Her consorts go down into the West. That is the way of it. When Marcus Antonius refused, there were consequences."

"In the end…," I said.

Isis' face was compassionate. "In the end, it was too late."

ANTONIUS' GAMBLE

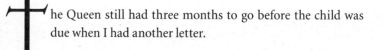

The Queen still had three months to go before the child was due when I had another letter.

Hail Charmian,

I write to you in haste, for the dispatch rider is going, and if I wish to send something I must do it now. We are besieging Praaspa. It is not going well. We have lost our baggage train to an ambush, along with hundreds of men who guarded it, and the siege equipment that we now miss sorely. The king of Armenia has pronounced the campaign hopeless and he has gone home with his horsemen. But Romans do not quit, so we go on.

We have now seen that thing I never saw before, a decimation of the troops who failed to guard the camp against a sortie. One man in ten must be executed for the failure of all, so they draw straws in each file, nine long straws and one short. The man who gets the short straw must be beaten to death by his fellows.

It was not my ala. For us it is the ceaseless work of patrol while everyone is besieged, as we are almost the only horsemen left, and there are not but three hundred of us now. I am the senior officer of them all. There are a few heavy cavalry left too, but we have no horse archers since the Armenians went.

> *And now winter comes, blowing cold and early off the steppes*
> *of the north.*
> *I love you. I love Dion. I hope that I will see you again.*
>
> *Emrys Aurelianus, Praefectus*

After that, there were no more letters. No more dispatches came to Alexandria, weeks late and brief. A silence fell that was worse than anything else.

SIX WEEKS BEFORE THE END of the year, the Queen gave birth to a son. After all my worry, this labor was both fast and normal. Amonis said that was to be expected from a fourth child who was properly positioned, and indeed it was only seven hours from the time she was brought to bed before Ptolemy Philadelphos made his appearance, as healthy a child as was ever born, on the date of the coronation of his namesake, that son of the first Ptolemy. It had been that Philadelphos who built the lighthouse, Pharos, and who decreed that our Library should collect every work ever written by man, so it seemed a good omen to name the child for him. He was, I thought, a remarkably pretty baby.

Antonius, of course, was not there. We had no word from him in weeks, nor any word at all from his expedition. In Alexandria, the days were warm and the fields green with grain. Away in the north of Parthia it was winter, and the winds scoured the uplands coming straight off the plains of Sogdiana.

Philadelphos was two weeks old when Antonius' letter came. Wordlessly, the Queen handed it to Iras, and I read it over her shoulder.

"Oh sweet Isis," I whispered. "Thirty-two thousand men." Marcus Antonius had lost thirty-two thousand men out of the sixty-six thousand who had marched against Parthia with him. "Thirty-two thousand men." The entire population of a middle-size city. "Four thousand cavalry." He had begun with less than five thousand, not counting the Armenian allies. "Oh sweet Isis."

I gulped for air, suddenly unable to breathe.

It was Cleopatra who put a chair behind me and helped me sit, handed me a cup of wine.

I blinked at her, ready to protest.

My sister gave me a tight smile. "I already know Antonius is alive. It is his signature on the letter."

Iras was frowning over the letter still. "He says he is retiring upon Berytus on the coast, and that you must hasten there with supplies, that his men are near starvation and he will have to loot the country-side of his lands or yours."

The Queen swore.

My hands shook on the cup. So few survivors from the cavalry. What were the odds that Emrys should be among them? "Sweet Isis, Epona, Mother of Horses..."

"If he loots my lands I'll... No, I won't. Because I am going to Bery-tus with supplies. We can assemble something in a week, surely."

"You are two weeks out of childbed!" Iras exploded. "You can't go dashing off to Berytus! And what about Philadelphos?"

"I have to, don't I?" Cleopatra snapped. "Philadelphos comes too. The twins and Caesarion stay here with you, Iras. Charmian, you're coming with me."

I looked up at her, surprised. It would make more sense for me to stay with the twins and Iras to go.

"You have to know," she said.

Fleets do not sail on a moment's notice. It took closer to two weeks than one before we put to sea, twenty ships filled with grain, melons, live goats and chickens, wine and oil. Philadelphos was not quite four weeks old when we sailed out of the harbor, leaving Pharos behind us, our prows pointed northward. The weather was poor, and we held our course only by dint of the strength of our five banks of oars.

My prayers were nothing but repetition, holding Philadelphos in my arms while the Queen talked with her captain. Please let him be alive, please let him be alive, please let him be alive.

I SLEPT, and in my dreams there were raging seas. A black ship struggled up and down each wave, tossed by the storm. I dreamed a gale at sea, and Dion as he had been as a youth standing by the rail, serene and clear-eyed, while a wave gathered at his back, green and crested with white foam.

I screamed aloud to him, but the wind carried away my voice, whipping my black veil around me while the wave crashed over him and took him.

I should have been swept away myself, but Marcus Agrippa steadied me against the sea, his arms around me. "The wind is fair for Egypt," he said.

"No!" I shouted, not certain what I denied. I turned in his arms, and there he stood, sure and unharmed by the tempest, older than I had last seen him. "You did not come to Egypt."

Like visions in glass, everything dissolved around us, leaving instead stones, and the courtyard of a palace with high roofs, each one painted a different bright color. "You ended here." There was the distant sound of cheers, as though somewhere nearby games were in progress. Above us, the blue sky of Persia arched, and we breathed the cool, fresh air of the mountains.

He held my forearms. His eyes were sad. "I'm sorry," he said. "I didn't mean to leave so much undone. I won't, this time."

"How can you serve Octavian?" I asked. "Marcus, you are better than this."

"I am a sword," he said, "as I was born to be. Do you ask the sword who it serves?"

"You are a man," I said, "and you may choose."

"Octavian and I, we will make Rome great," he said. "We will dress her in marble and bring her all the marvels of the world."

"At what cost?"

He let go of me then, walked a few steps away and turned, looking up at the pitched roofs, the mountains behind. His brow furrowed, as though he half-recognized it. "What is this place?"

"A reflection," I said sadly. "Ecbatana as it was when you died there three hundred years ago. A memory. A scar in the memory of the world. We all remember, we Companions. It waits for all of us, as does Babylon."

"Can you name me, then?"

I nodded, my eyes filling. "Hephaistion." Alexander's beloved general.

Marcus threw back his head, his face solemn, as though drinking in the air. The light gilded his face, his closed eyelids.

"Octavian is not your Alexander," I said, and knew in that moment what it was that held him. And how should it not? The dream of a life completed was a powerful thing, that he might finish what he had begun at Alexander's right hand, a life too soon cut short.

"I know," he said, and gave me a rueful smile. "Caesar passed out of the world before I was hardly in it, with too much age between us for him to give me a second glance, Antonius at his right hand instead of me. I was born too late, my friend. And I shall walk through this world all of my life knowing that I have missed the mark."

"And so instead you will have a Triumph on my bones," I said bitterly. "I was never very much to you, a beautiful face that caught your desire once."

He laid his hand along the side of my face. "Always more than that. You are always temptation, a beautiful thing unknowable and within reach, seeming simple and yet labyrinthine enough to lose myself in forever. Will I ever know you? I wonder."

"If you walk the labyrinth with me," I said, and blinked back tears. "You did once, long ago. Set things right, Marcus. You still can. It is within your power. Not Octavian, but Caesarion. Walk the labyrinth beneath Mount Vesuvius with Caesar's son as his faithful Companion, and come forth by day to a world made new, Egypt and Rome joined in alliance, joined in his person in sacred marriage. The power is yours to bring that future into being!"

Marcus shook his head. "You know I can't," he said.

"I know you won't."

He let go of me, stepped back as solemnly as a boy in a choir. "Will I see you again?'

"In Babylon," I said, and the word was ashes in my mouth.

WE MADE BERYTUS in bad weather, not long after the turning of the year. The Queen went ashore immediately, to the citadel where Antonius had made his headquarters, a black cloak pulled tight against the rain.

Antonius' chamber was dark. The curtains were drawn because of the wet, and there were too few lamps. When the guard announced Queen Cleopatra he stood up, swaying, like a man who has seen a spirit. Indeed, she must have seemed like one, with raindrops caught in her hair like jewels, and her face pale and white, the shadows around her eyes dark.

"Cleopatra," he said, and caught at the edge of the table to steady himself. His handsome face was worn and unshaven, and he looked ten years older, not a vigorous forty-eight, but closer to sixty.

Whatever she had meant to say died on her lips, and instead she ran to him and fell upon him, her cloak spreading like the wings of night around them. He bent his head to hers, and I saw him shake as she gathered his hands in hers.

"You may go," she said to me and the guard, and Antonius said nothing at all.

The guard shrugged at me, and we withdrew, him taking up his station by the door. My hands were shaking too.

"Do you know a praefectus of cavalry?" I asked him. "A man called Aurelianus? He was with Antonius in Parthia."

The guard shook his head slowly, and I could read the stark sympathy in his face. "I don't know anyone named that," he said. "But, Domina, you should know that almost none of the cavalry came back."

I nodded, biting my lip so that the tears would not come. "Do you know a man named Sigismund? One of the Imperator's bodyguards. He's a good friend of Aurelianus, and if anyone would know, it's him."

The guard broke into a smile, which I noticed was now missing all of his front teeth. "I do know him! He's in the hospital, two floors down on the ground floor behind the kitchens. We wouldn't be on guard duty if all the bodyguards weren't dead or in the hospital."

"I see," I said. "Down?"

"The stairs are at the end," he said, pointing.

I ran.

SIGISMUND WAS PROPPED UP on a cot at the far end, leaning over a dice game on a little table someone had pulled up. I saw him cast and for a moment wondered what seemed so different. Then I realized he was casting left-handed. His right arm ended above the elbow.

I must have made some sound, because the entire room turned and stared at me, some fifty men. At least, every man who was capable of turning and staring.

I'm not sure how I crossed the room to Sigismund, but somehow I was sitting on the end of his bed, clasping his good hand between mine while all his fellows looked on, whistling and laughing.

"What happened to him, Sigismund?" I begged. "Where is Emrys?"

"On duty down by the picket lines," Sigismund said confusedly, and I started crying.

SIGISMUND HAD BEEN ONE OF THE LAST wounded, he said, when the heavy Parthian cataphracts had pinned them against the river and punched through the tortoise of the Third Gallica Legion. He'd gone down fighting beside Antonius, who fought like a man possessed.

"A berserker in his rage," Sigismund said with satisfaction in his voice. "He'd made a mess and he was going to get us out of it or die trying. Covered me with his own shield, for all I'm his bodyguard. We'd have been dead if the light cavalry hadn't charged in among the cataphracts, stinging like bees, all three or four hundred of them we had left. They held them off until we could cross the river. And the cataphracts didn't come after us. Didn't fancy a river crossing with horses in full armor, with infantry on the other side waiting." I had brought him some beer, and he drank slowly, his left hand steady as always. "You should have seen Emrys, Charmian. He's so mild and calm that you don't expect it, when he gets that gray look of passion in his face, utterly beyond fear. Valkyries must have those eyes. As though they've seen a thousand fields."

"I know the look you mean," I said, blinking back tears.

"He wrote to you and Dion both," Sigismund said. "When we got here. But the letters must have crossed you on the way. How did you get here so fast?"

"The Queen can move when she must," I said. "And two weeks out of childbed."

"Well, the little boy will cheer Antonius," Sigismund said. "And for me, I'm well enough, all things considered. There's a bonus for my arm on top of my discharge, and as soon as the doctors say I'm fit, I'm gone. This was the last campaign for me. I'm through."

"I'm so sorry," I said.

He shrugged, and I knew the world would end before he didn't put a brave face on it. "It's my fate," he said. "I hope Mucilla will still have me. If so, look for me next time you're in Rome. A little tavern in the Subura, under the shadow of the Esquiline Hill."

"I'll look for you, Sigismund," I promised.

EMRYS CAME IN from the rain and checked.

Before he could even take off his cloak my arms were around him, saying incomprehensible things, squeezing him to make sure he was real.

He bent his head over mine, his arms around me, and I felt how thin he was, and how beneath his leathers he shivered. "I'm coming home," he said.

I stayed ashore that night, as the Queen wanted to. I had Philadelphos in the room next to the one she and Antonius had, to watch over his sleep and to rouse her when he was hungry. He nursed several times a night, and should also have to be changed at least once.

In the fourth hour of the night I sat wakeful while Philadelphos snored softly against my neck. Emrys slept in my bed. I watched him sleep, the slow rise and fall of his chest, the sweep of his lashes against his cheek. My heart was full of thanksgiving. So few of the cavalry had returned. His hands twitched in sleep, holding invisible reins.

Cleopatra opened the door, her robe loose around her. She looked exhausted, her eyes circled dark. And why should she not be, a woman with a month-old baby who has come to the end of a long journey to find that nothing is as it should be?

"Is he still asleep?"

I nodded. Philadelphos had not stirred yet.

"I'll take him," she whispered, holding out her arms. "He can come in with us, and you can lie down."

"I don't need…"

My sister bent and kissed my brow. "Tend your lover, Charmian. I'll tend my child. Get some rest."

I nodded, my eyes filling with tears. "Good night, sister," I whispered as I carefully passed her Philadelphos.

I heard the door close as I lay down beside Emrys, felt him flinch in his sleep. "There now, darling," I said, smoothing his hair where it lay on his back. "It's only me." He sighed, and I closed my eyes against him.

All in all, it was two months before we could sail for Alexandria. Antonius' troops needed time to rest and recover on our supplies, and he needed to set in motion the requirements of sending them into garrison in Antioch and Apamea. They were very much sweetened by the bonus of four hundred sesterces per man that Antonius gave them out of his own funds, especially the retirees who should have it in addition to lands in Macedon. It took Emrys all of a day to sell the deed to his future plot to some other man. It was with more than a thousand sesterces, all told, that he should come to Alexandria, more than enough to start some sort of business.

I was thankful daily that small Philadelphos was not delicate as Helios had been as a baby. Like his sister, he was strong and nursed readily, though at four months he had a bout of colic that kept everyone up at night, including Antonius, who insisted on getting up with him as though he were an ordinary man.

I came upon them at night, Antonius walking the deck of our warship as we sailed homeward, Philadelphos on his shoulder, while he talked in a low voice, pointing out the constellations we steered by. I stepped back into a shadow, not wanting to interrupt. I thought for a moment in the moonlight that Antonius was almost beautiful, now that his handsome features were worn to the bone, as though in extremity some spirit shone through that had never been apparent to me before.

I had not liked Antonius, but I could almost forgive him.

I heard a step along the deck and startled, but it was only Emrys. He had been allowed to travel with us on the flagship, because I had asked the Queen, and of course he was well known to Antonius.

Now he checked, but Antonius turned, tensing, his right hand going to where his sword should be.

"Peace," Emrys said. "It's only me, Aurelianus."

"The boy won't sleep," Antonius said, Philadelphos still curled on his left shoulder, his head beneath his father's chin. "I thought he could keep watch with me."

Emrys came along the deck and leaned on the rail beside him, looking out over our wake. "He's young to keep the watch, don't you think?"

"Could be." Antonius leaned beside him, carefully keeping Philadelphos inboard. "I remember when Antyllus was this small. It's hard to believe now. I hear he beats Caesarion at horse racing."

"And your daughters?" Emrys asked quietly.

Antonius took a deep breath. "I have to divorce Octavia, don't I?"

Emrys spread his hands but said nothing.

"I've never even seen the younger daughter," Antonius said. "Octavia writes and says I must come to Rome. I have to decide now. Rome or the East. One family or another. I can't delay anymore. I'm going to have to divorce Octavia." He looked out over the sea. "I have to divorce her to marry Cleopatra."

Emrys' brows rose, but I doubt Antonius noticed. "That marriage won't be valid under Roman law. I know surely enough that a Roman must marry a Roman citizen."

"It will be valid under Egyptian law, which is where my children are." Antonius half-turned toward the prow, the baby still beneath his chin. "Which family do I desert, which woman do I break? You sail for Alexandria yourself. Can we really leave Rome behind?"

"I was never Roman to start with," Emrys said gently. "I do not have Roman bones, lares to follow me whispering. Out of all the world I've chosen my home, but I leave no one behind me. I can walk away and say that was my last battle."

Antonius shook his head. "And I can never say that until I die. There will always be one more. I envy you, friend."

I couldn't see Emrys' face, but I could hear the compassion in his voice. "I would not take all of the wealth in Egypt in exchange for being done with war."

Antonius sighed, his arm still around Philadelphos. "And what would be the price of a normal life? Of watching my son grow into a man? I want to live, Aurelianus. I was in Parthia when I knew it, clearly as if the gods themselves had put the choice before me, to die a hero's death and have unending fame, burning like a moth too close to a fire, Icarus too close to the sun. Or to just go home. I would trade all glory, all pride, all oaths, anything—simply to go home, to my children, to marry Cleopatra."

I felt a frisson of cold run down my back, as though the bull had shied at the altar, and held my hands to avert the omen. But I knew, even then, that it was too late.

"Well," Emrys said, ducking his head, "the women of the Ptolemies are extraordinary. How can any other in the world compete?"

Antonius laid his rough cheek against Philadelphos' head, and I saw that the baby had fallen asleep. "Never, until the end of time, will there be a woman like Cleopatra."

"Probably not," Emrys agreed.

WE HAD BARELY RETURNED to Alexandria when Cleopatra set the council afire. She intended to marry Antonius. Their objections were entirely predictable. After all, the council had dealt with Antonius as long as I had.

Memnon at last cut through the debate. "I will not remonstrate further as long as we are clear on the fact that the Queen reigns with Pharaoh Ptolemy Caesarion, as she has these last years. Antonius is no Pharaoh of Egypt. His position as the Queen's official consort is entirely different."

"I believe we are clear on that," the Queen said from her end of the table. Her hair was done in ringlets, and she wore a massive collar of pearls rather than the more simple attire she usually wore for the council. "I do not suggest that the Imperator share my throne."

"What about his children?" Memnon asked pointedly.

"Princess Selene and Prince Helios and Prince Philadelphos will be granted client kingdoms outside of the Black Land," she said. "Obviously at present they are Pharaoh Ptolemy Caesarion's heirs, and should he die without children Helios would be Pharaoh, but there is no reason to think that he will not beget heirs of his body as he grows older." She looked around the table. "The marriage will not be a state affair. That I will grant you. We will marry simply and privately, when his divorce from Octavia is complete. This changes nothing in terms of our succession, and he will hold no Egyptian rank."

Glancing around the room, I saw that she had them. It would be as she wanted.

And yet I wished that it had more strings, for all I did not especially love Antonius. If he did not have Egypt, did Egypt have him?

Meanwhile, Emrys and Dion and I settled into a comfortable if unusual routine. Emrys moved into Dion's apartment, and I continued to live at the palace. Demetria lived at the palace, but spent many evenings at Dion's apartment when she finished late at the temple. Sometimes Emrys picked her up and walked her back rather than Dion, and I found myself just a little jealous of the way she told them everything, but was more reticent to me.

"It's just the way of girls," Dion assured me. "Did you tell your mother everything? She's twelve, and anyone in the world is more comfortable than her mother. Besides," he said, "she is feeling a bit fragile. Caesarion has abandoned her company for that of Antyllus."

"That was only to be expected," I said. "He's a boy. Sooner or later his best friends would be other boys. It will be several years, in the normal course of things, before he sees her again as a person. And then it will be as a young man and young woman, not as children together."

"Well, she's lost her best friend, and I think she has a hard time of it at the temple in some ways. She's talented and too smart. That's always hard. Other girls don't like that."

"I'll have a word with the Hierophant," I said hotly. "There's not supposed to be any favoritism."

Dion put his hands on my shoulders. "That's precisely what you shouldn't do. Her beautiful mother, who's not like anyone else's mother, blowing in and talking to her masters. Do you want to set her apart even more?"

"Of course she's set apart. She's a Royal Ptolemy, and the daughter of Marcus Vipsanius Agrippa. Of course she's too smart and too strange. How could she be anything else?"

Dion brushed his hand over my hair. "Someday she'll be glad of it. But not when she's twelve. Didn't you want to be normal when you were twelve?"

"No," I said. I had been at Bubastis. "All I wanted was to go home."

ANTONIUS DIVORCED OCTAVIA. If there was uproar in Rome, it was muted by the time it reached our ears. I was sorry, for I had liked her, but I had never had the impression that she felt passion for Antonius. Still, it was a strong move against her brother. I wasn't certain that was a good idea, but Cleopatra and Antonius were set upon it. Nothing should prevent their legitimate marriage and their declared intention to spend their lives as one.

Caesar, I thought, should have found some pretext to carry on two marriages at once. In fact, he had across the width of the Tiber, not the Middle Sea. But then Caesar had never loved. Or, if he had, it had never clouded his judgment. In love, as in all else, he had been reasoned and cool.

Antonius was not cool, and perhaps that is why she loved him. Wrong and hardheaded as he might be, he loved her. She came before reason. She came before ambition. She came before the gods.

Cool herself, trained to the service of Isis and the Black Land, slave to her mind and to logic above all else, passion came hard to Cleopatra. She did not love easily. With all of his flaws, she did love him and his hot head, his warm nature. And once she gave her loyalty, she never withdrew it.

THE INIMITABLES

Antonius did not go to war again until the following spring,
more than a full year later. For one thing, he needed time to
rebuild his army after the disastrous campaign. For another,
the Queen would not finance it until after the taxes came in at the end
of the harvest. Lastly, I don't think he particularly wanted to. Instead,
we spent the year peacefully, though none of us could ignore the storm
clouds on the horizon.

For my part, it was as happy a time as any I knew. When we sailed
for Philae on the Progress of Isis, Emrys and Dion both came with us,
ostensibly so that Dion could see how the astrological ceiling at the
Temple of Hathor was progressing. In actuality, it was more of a holiday, and one Emrys sorely needed.

He had come home too thin, and the slightest noise startled him.
It was weeks before he slept through the night, and I wondered if the
evil dreams would ever leave him. He had fought one campaign too
many, but at least he was whole in body, and perhaps in time his spirit
would heal as well. He had nothing he really needed to do, as there was
money enough, and he took his time inquiring into businesses in the
city. In the meantime, he walked Demetria home and helped her with
her lessons. I think he learned as much as she.

Coming into the apartment and seeing them sitting at the table,
papers spread before them and their heads together over something,
never failed to make my heart leap with gladness.

When Antonius went to war this time, for the first time, Emrys stayed behind. After they had gone without him, something in Emrys seemed to lighten and loosen, as though he finally believed that it was over. He'd tutored a friend of Dion's in Gaulish before, but now he actually taught two classes, one in Gaulish and a much smaller one in his native Brythonic, which was spoken only in Aremorica and across the straits on the island of Britain. I think he enjoyed it. Certainly Dion and I were relieved to see him going about and taking an interest in things, meeting new people as he always had before.

One day, when I had less to do than usual, but Demetria and Dion had their respective classes, we went to the Soma together. Side-by-side we paid our admission and went in, pausing just inside the doors to let our eyes adjust to the cool darkness after the bright street. There were not many people there. We walked across the marble floor, Emrys leaning back to look up at the domed ceiling and the starry skies painted there.

I went and scattered a handful of myrrh over the coals in a brazier there, intended for such offerings. The old blind woman who I bought it from took my small bronze coin with a whispered, "Bless you, Lady."

I went around the outside of the circle and came back to Emrys, who stood looking at the glass sarcophagus. I was still not used to seeing him in civilian clothes, a dark green chiton with worked borders. He seemed very tall and rawboned still. I took his arm.

Before us, beneath the epicenter of the dome, Alexander lay in his sarcophagus of glass and porphyry. The glass was thick and not entirely clear. His profile wavered when I moved, as though he slept underwater, perfect still after nearly three centuries. One could see that his hair was fair, but the details of his face blurred. Every sculptor imagined him differently, even those at first who had worked from life. Who Alexander was depended on who was looking.

I imagined Caesar would be the same. Certainly his statue in the Temple of Caesar was good enough, as such things go, but did not capture the mobile grace that animated him.

"Thinking?" I asked.

Emrys nodded. "Thinking. Wondering how they could have embalmed him like that if the embalmers weren't allowed to get to him for two days after he died."

I slid my arm through Emrys'. "I heard a doctor putting forth the theory that Alexander died of typhus. With typhus, one often lies in a coma for hours or even days before one actually dies. It's possible that he actually died hours after people thought. So it wasn't really that long."

A door in my mind began to open, and I slammed it shut, a melee around the corpse on the bed, the young eunuch's bent head as he covered him with his own body, a flash of a scene only, through the cracks of time.

Emrys nodded. He did not look away from Alexander's still countenance. "Do you wonder? Where you will go when you die?"

I shook my head, smiling. "I know where I will go. Right here. I will always return to the people I love." I laid my head against his sleeve. "And so will you, my darling. If you're ever lost, I'll find you. Again and again. That I swear to you."

He leaned down and kissed me as though I were the only real thing in the universe, kissed me in the presence of the dead. For an Egyptian, that is no strange thing.

THIS WAS ALSO the first time in several years that the Queen had gone somewhere without me. She had sailed as far as Syria with Antonius, to make her way back overland via Jerusalem and Gaza. Iras went with her, as this trip was entirely business, while all of the children had stayed in Alexandria. Cleopatra returned before the summer was at an end, and Antonius was not far behind her.

He had not really defeated the Parthians, but he had put a good face on it. Instead of storming straight back to Praaspa, he had besieged and defeated the King of Armenia, his lukewarm ally of two years ago. After a short foray into Media, he returned successfully to Syria, announcing that he was now overlord of Armenia and Media.

This announcement seemed a bit premature to me, as we did not in any sense physically hold Media, nor was the populace likely to view us as their saviors rather than unwelcome foreigners, but it was certainly better than the disastrous campaign of two years earlier.

I wondered if he would enter Alexandria as a triumphant Roman, or as the Queen's consort. Either, of course, would have tremendous political implications. He did neither.

ANTONIUS ENTERED ALEXANDRIA as Dionysos, with a procession of maenads and dancers, with flutists and drummers, with pretty boys who distributed wine to the populace. It was less a solemn Triumph than a gigantic street party in all of the quarters of the city. The temples held vast services of thanksgiving, but they were not crowded. Everyone was out in the streets celebrating instead.

Originally, he had planned to enter in a chariot drawn by leopards, but that idea was scrapped when it was pointed out that there were no trained leopards in Egypt, and the cheetahs that were meticulously trained for hunting in the desert would not draw a chariot under any conditions. The coins struck still showed the leopards, but Antonius was more prosaically drawn by four white horses. I drew a sigh of relief at that, as I had no idea how I was supposed to get the cheetahs to pull a chariot!

But it was more than a celebration, of course. It was a sacred procession. As I watched from behind one of the great columns along the front of the Temple of Serapis, I felt a chill run up my spine.

Wreathed in vine, Antonius came, bringing treasures. His onetime ally, the King of Armenia, marched as he would in a Roman Triumph, but his chains were flimsy things of gold, and he wore robes of silk. He would not bow to Cleopatra, nor acknowledge her overlordship, but instead of being garroted at the end of the procession he was sent into house arrest.

I watched the procession swing around the last corner, closer and closer to where Cleopatra waited on the steps of the temple. She was robed as Isis, of course, Isis Pelagia in blue and white, with the uraeus on her brow. Out of the corner of my eye, I thought I saw it move, and wished she had worn one of the other crowns instead.

The choirs were singing, and it came to me suddenly that more than anything it looked like a sacrificial procession. Antonius was the bull, his horns wound with flowers, brought to the altar. The feeling struck me so strongly that I reached out to squeeze Iras' hand, where she stood near. She turned, and I saw in her eyes that she had been thinking the same thing.

AFTER THAT there was a great feast at the palace, and most of the city was consumed in revelry. I was not. The next day there was to be an even greater event, and I must spend all night preparing.

The site of this should be the New Gymnasium, called that because it had been built by Auletes, rather than the Old Gymnasium, built by Ptolemy Soter. Instead of a platform for the winners of the games there were two thrones in gold leaf over cedarwood, a tall one for Cleopatra with the square lines of the throne of Isis, and a slightly smaller one for Antonius, with arms like a curial chair. On the lower level of the platform before her stood four more thrones, the largest to the Queen's right, in the block style of ancient paintings.

There was a grand procession into the Gymnasium, with representatives of all the temples of Alexandria, including the Patriarch of Alexandria, the chief rabbi of the largest synagogue. They were followed by nobles and wealthy merchants, representatives of all the cities of the Black Land, and a singing choir from the Serapeum. Demetria had her part there, among the other singers.

When everyone had reached their seats, the Queen and Antonius appeared, not carried as one might expect, but walking down cordoned aisles. Her robes were cloth of gold, and she wore the uraeus on her brow. Behind her, her cloak flowed and caught the sun. She held Philadelphos by the hand, and when he stopped, frozen at the wave of applause and shouting, she swept him onto her shoulder, waving. The crowd screamed, "Isis! Isis! Isis!"

Antonius came in behind her then, crowned with vine like Dionysos, or Serapis when his statue is dressed for the harvest. He grinned and waved as well, then put his arm around her in a charming unrehearsed gesture. Again the crowd shouted.

Caesarion followed, not dressed in the formal linens of Pharaoh, but in a chiton of rose-colored silk, like the lead in a play or the young Apollo. He was never reserved in front of a crowd, and instead of standing back, half-jogged along the cordon, grasping hands and being touched while the bodyguards tried to keep him from being crushed.

Behind him, well escorted by bodyguards, came Selene and Helios. They were six, and beautifully dressed in saffron silk, they knew how to behave at this, their first very public ceremony. Helios looked as though he wanted to run. Selene was solemn, not sporting the crowd like Caesarion. I thought, from my position to the side and above where I should make certain the program ran efficiently, that Caesarion was more like Caesar every day. I could see in him that boyish charm that people still talked about even fifty years later.

When everyone had reached the dais, and the choir had finished their long paean, almost inaudible beneath the cheers, Antonius held up his hands for silence.

He did speak well, I thought. He was used to addressing armies, and his voice carried over the crowd.

"I came to Alexandria," he said, "as a young man, when Pharaoh Ptolemy Auletes was restored to his throne. I came from Rome, and as lion meets lioness, when I saw Alexandria I was stricken." He looked over the crowd from left to right, nodding, as though to friends. "Yes, stricken. But I sailed away, and saw her no more." The crowd was silent now. Antonius took two steps to the left, as though composing his next thought. He looked out again. "And instead Rome sent Caesar." He paused, and I remembered that he had spoken Caesar's funeral oration, set the Roman mobs upon the conspirators with no weapon besides words. Antonius could speak, oh yes.

"Caesar came to Alexandria, and it was Alexandria that restored him, that blessed his endeavors and set him, like some latter-day Aeneas, on the path to victory. Alexandria." He looked to the right, then cast a glance behind him fondly. "Alexandria, and Cleopatra!"

The crowd roared. He waited until they calmed before he continued. "And of that sacred marriage was born Pharaoh Ptolemy Caesarion, Horus of Egypt. What I do today is in honor of Gaius Julius Caesar, my friend. What I do is for the honor of Rome. It has often been said that Rome is known by what she takes."

Antonius paused again, waiting as the crowd silenced. "I mean that Rome shall be known instead by what she gives!" He turned, and bowing, went on one knee before the throne of Cleopatra.

The crowd shouted, screaming themselves hoarse.

When Antonius rose, he did so to take a garland of pink roses from the hand of a servant who held it out. "Rome confirms the legitimate heir of the Divine Gaius Julius Caesar, Pharaoh Ptolemy Philometor Caesarion, as the lawful ruler of Egypt, Ally of Rome!"

He laid the wreath on Caesarion's brow, who inclined his head gravely, then embraced him.

Again, the crowd screamed.

Antonius took another thing from the servant, not a wreath this time, but a white turban adorned with a jeweled peacock feather. "His brother Alexander Helios, King of Armenia and Media!" Thankfully, Helios stayed still while he put it on his head, and I saw Antonius whisper something encouraging to him under cover of the shouting.

"His brother Ptolemy Philadelphos, Overlord of Greece and of all the northern client kings!" He put on baby Philadelphos' head a diadem in the Macedonian style. Philadelphos promptly reached up to take it off and look at it. Antonius laughed, and presented the last, a fillet of silver worked with seashells. "His sister, Cleopatra Selene, Queen of the island of Crete and of the province of Cyrenaica!" Selene inclined her head gracefully, her eyes shining. She straightened, and I saw in her something so familiar it made my heart clinch for a moment, those same eyes I had seen in my sisters' faces all these years.

Antonius turned back to the crowd, stepping down as though to kneel again. "Cleopatra, Queen of Kings!"

I thought the noise of the crowd must be audible in Rome.

IT WAS. "He has given away half of the territory for which Rome has fought!" Senators shouted. "Given away our riches to his Egyptian whore!"

Octavian wrote moderately, saying that he could not control the course of events, should Antonius continue to do such stupid things. His liaison with Queen Cleopatra was much misunderstood, and thought to be of some importance. Octavian of course was clear on the matter, and he did not let the injury to his sister and her reputation influence him. Though it was much on the minds of all Romans, of course, to see so virtuous a woman deserted.

"Fight fire with fire," Cleopatra urged. "Of course Octavian is provoked. Do not fall into his traps. You must cultivate the client kings of the East, as you once did."

SITTING AT DINNER with Dion and Emrys, I related all of this. Emrys looked grim.

"The thing everyone seems to be forgetting here is that in the field Marcus Agrippa could fight rings around Antonius. He's just whipped a few more tribes into shape over the Rhenus, and he took out the holdout Republicans in Sicily. Octavian is no general, but he has a good one."

Dion and I looked at each other. Neither of us said anything. If Antonius had been good when he served Caesar, that was gone now.

"Isn't Agrippa awfully young?" Dion asked.

Emrys shook his head. "He's twenty-nine. And he is a genius for war. May the gods help Antonius if he ever faces him in the field."

"It may not come to that," I said. "If we can win the war of words. But I fear that the war of words is already lost, drowned in Octavia's divorce."

Dion shrugged, and passed the bread. "Would Romans really go to war over that?"

Emrys' face was solemn. "You have no idea how they hate the leopard who changes his spots."

"There is no other way," I said. "Antonius cannot take Rome and the West from Octavian. That's a doomed military enterprise if ever there were one! The only solution is to become a Hellenic monarch, progenitor of Eastern kings."

"It could still work," Emrys said. "It could still work. If Antonius makes no more mistakes."

I WISHED I were more sanguine about that. I thought he drank too much, since Parthia. There is nothing wrong with drunkenness between adults, the occasional giving of oneself over to Dionysos and leaving aside dignity. I never minded it myself, when in good company.

But Antonius drank in the morning, unwatered wine before he had even eaten. Since Parthia, he drank every night, deeply and wildly. Sometimes he laid it aside for a few days and drank only sparingly with meals, but always he began again. He was never crude or abusive, nor even nasty in the way people can be when they say things they would never say sober. When he drank he laughed and joked, played games and complimented everyone about him for something at which they excelled, more affable and good-hearted than ever. He made sexual jests to the Queen in front of people until she laughed, threw his arms over the shoulders of his friends and gave them gifts, told Iras she was beautiful and clever. She was, of course, but I was surprised to see her blushing and smiling.

"We are inimitable livers," he said, his arm around the Queen's waist as a small dinner party wound down. "No one, in all the history of the world, has loved so much or lived so well as we!" He raised his cup to the heavens. "Joy!"

"Joy," I said, and raised mine as well. For once I did not work a supper, and shared a couch with Dion and Emrys instead.

The evening wore on in a warm haze, and I snuggled between the two of them, my head on Dion's breast. "Joy," I whispered. "Mother Isis, let me not forget."

THE WAR OF WORDS between Octavian and Antonius continued. Antonius, a letter from a supporter in Rome said, allegedly used a golden chamber pot. He was drunk night and day, and he played in vulgar pantomimes before the court where he wore a dress and danced with pretty boys. He was Cleopatra's concubine, and he had public sexual relations with women of the court.

Antonius threw the letter down, laughing. "So I piss in a golden pot? And they can't decide if I have a case of satyriasis or if I'm playing the catamite? Can anyone believe this trash?"

Emrys, who had accompanied me to the palace on that day, picked it up and rerolled it carefully. "Most people will not believe it. But they will listen to it. People like to hear of the excesses of their betters, and to imagine that the pleasures of Asia are so free."

"Octavian has half a dozen mistresses," Antonius said. "And what about that business of making Tiberius Nero divorce his wife while she was pregnant, so Octavian could marry her three days after the baby was born? Livia's a piece of work. They say she acts as his pimp too."

"That doesn't matter," I said. "What matters is that he maintains an attitude of respectability. Piety and gravity."

Antonius took the rolled letter from Emrys and laid it on the Queen's desk, while watchful she sat beside it. He shrugged. "Roman virtue is a joke. It's a sham. Powerful hypocrites like Octavian strutting around talking about how Greek plays are corrupting the minds of youth and how we all have to return to the Age of Saturn by exalting the farmer, when they don't mean it for a moment. They don't live that way. They eat off Attic ware and buy Greek tutors for their sons and bugger little boys if they like. A few times a year they march out in white togas to burn a goat's liver on Capitoline Hill and then go make speeches about how pure Roman blood and pure Roman culture will triumph. Marcus Antonius is at least no hypocrite."

He took Cleopatra's hand where it rested beside him on the desk. "What we build will be founded on truth, not pretense."

She looked up at him, and I saw the pride in her eyes, and the understanding between them. And in his voice I heard that same echo I had heard in Dion's "The truth will make us free, Charmian. The best we can do is carry the banner proudly in our own time."

I blinked.

"I'll stand with that," Emrys said. He looked at me. "Seven years Antonius knew about me and Dion, and seven years he looked the other way. I could have been demoted. I could have been executed, if he'd wanted to stick to it."

Antonius shrugged. "Why should I care who you bugger, Aurelianus?" he said, grinning. "As long as it's not a man in the legion. I had better things to do than worry about your chastity!"

"That's so," Emrys said, "and yet remembered all the same. I'll stand with you whatever comes."

SHADOWS ⊙ GATHERING

In summer we sailed to Philae for the Inundation, so that Cleopatra might dedicate a new part of the Temple of Isis there. Of course there were stops all up the Nile, festivals and meetings. It had become the custom for her to journey the length of the Black Land every year or two, hearing appeals, meeting local lords and clergy, and holding court again and again. No Ptolemy had done such so often since the second one, Philadelphos. Now the people were used to it again, and they crowded to see us, sometimes running along the bank as we sailed, waving. They liked knowing us. Old women in the markets of Upper Egypt commented to one another how Caesarion had grown, and how he would be a young man soon, as if he were some grandchild of theirs.

At year's end, Demetria was fourteen. I stood beside Emrys in the Serapeum while she sang her first solo in the great temple, and it brought tears to my eyes.

Emrys squeezed my elbow. "She's a wonderful young woman," he said. "You should be proud."

"I am," I said. Of all my children, she was the one I had birthed, and yet of us all she was most like Iras.

I blinked and held to his arm. I wished Dion were there too, but he did draw the line at attending offices in the Serapeum.

The Queen and Antonius were not there. They had gone to Ephesos for the winter with Iras, leaving the children with me in Alexandria.

Antonius' troops needed to be seen to, and it was a countermove against Octavian in the war of words. So far, the war was nothing but that. Antonius had offered to lay down his powers as a Triumvir of Rome if Octavian should do the same. Octavian countered, saying he would when Antonius did. Both accused the other of subverting the Republic.

In my office in Alexandria, I read the dispatches aloud to Dion, who had come to give Caesarion his lessons in Aramaic.

Dion settled back on my couch under the window. "It's not about democracy, is it? The Roman Republic is as dead as a very dead thing. It's about which model of state they will have, Antonius' or Octavian's. Will Rome join the rest of the civilized world as a pluralistic state based upon a tolerant model of Hellenistic culture, or stand apart?"

I rubbed my aching temples. "Is that really the question, Dion? Is it possible to stand apart? I don't think so. Whatever patricians decide in the Senate, whatever the much-touted virtuous farmers want, when you walk around Rome it's full of men like Emrys and Sigismund. It has a Jewish quarter, and if the Jews are persecuted more there than here, they don't go away. It has a Temple of Isis. If it's torn down, that does not tear Her from people's hearts."

Dion frowned. "Persecution's not a pretty thing, no matter how you phrase it. But no, it will take more than Rome to destroy the Jews. We just go underground like stray cats and pop up again somewhere else."

"And so will all of the rest of it," I said, putting my stylus on the table. "Compassion and freedom can't be constrained by walls of gravitas and virtus. Isis is unconquerable."

"I certainly hope so," Dion said.

Antonius and the Queen were back in Alexandria in the late summer, after trips to Samos and Athens as well. To my intense relief she wasn't pregnant again. Perhaps with the twins now seven and Philadelphos three they felt they had quite enough children. Or perhaps at thirty-seven the queen wasn't quite as fertile as she'd been. In any event, I breathed a sigh of relief.

The war of words with Octavian continued, and in its cadences I felt a certain comfort. As long as this was all, we could keep it up infinitely.

In the fall there were parties at a villa along Lake Mareotis, because Antonius, of all things, liked to fish. This irritated the Queen in a mild way when it seemed that he spent all day on the lake with his friends, leaving her to her own devices.

"You never catch anything," she said. "I don't see why it's fun to just sit in a boat and do nothing."

"I do catch things," Antonius said, his fair skin sunburned. "Come and see."

The next morning the Queen and I were rowed out on a pleasure barge with an awning to where Antonius sat, pole in hand, bareheaded. He grinned and waved.

Cleopatra leaned back on the striped cushions under the awning, a skeptical expression on her face. "All right. Let's see you catch something."

It was barely five minutes before Antonius made a huge production of having a bite on his line. He heaved and hauled, apparently fighting an enormous fish. When at last he drew it in, it was longer than his forearm, a beautiful and perfect giant. "You see?" he said, holding the fish over his head. "Antonius triumphs!"

I looked at the Queen and she looked at me. I nodded toward one of Antonius' friends who was swimming nearby, an innocent expression on his face.

Cleopatra smiled sweetly at Antonius. "I see that you have indeed caught the biggest fish in all of Lake Mareotis. Clearly I should come fishing with you more often."

The next morning we were out again, well prepared. Under the pretext of arranging the cushions, I handed the Queen's slave boy all he needed as he treaded water, holding on to the side of the boat, while Cleopatra called across the water to Antonius. "Have you caught anything yet?"

"Not yet!" he called back cheerfully. "But the day is young!"

It was only a few moments before he seemed to feel a tug on his line. "Ha!" Antonius yelled, and began to bring it in. The line twitched improbably. "It's a big one!" Antonius yelled. He pulled, and the fish flew up into the air.

Bemused, he caught it. The length of his hand, it was a nice salt fish from the Black Sea.

He looked at it stupidly while Cleopatra burst out laughing. Beside our boat, the slave boy surfaced, grinning.

After a moment Antonius started laughing too. "Maybe I do fish too much," he said, scratching his head. "They're coming already salted for me."

"Maybe you do," she said, still laughing.

AND THE WAR OF WORDS went on, Antonius' supporters in the Senate of Rome proposing the censure of Octavian, and vice versa. Every day or so we had a diplomatic packet by way of Ostia, carried by Egyptian ship. Looking out over the great harbor, I thought that Caesar would have approved. Certainly Ptolemy Soter would have. We had three hundred warships now, the greatest fleet in the Mediterranean. Antonius could command another two hundred from various allies.

I stood there at the window, thinking this, the golden sun glancing off the bright mirrors that crowned Pharos, when Iras dashed in, setting the beaded window curtain jangling. "That stupid ass!"

"What?" I spun about, wondering who she meant.

"Marcus Antonius," Iras said. She waved a scroll at me, its seals dangling. "I've just had the diplomatic packet. Octavian's read his will."

"How would Octavian get his will?"

"Because that stupid ass sent it to Rome, to the keeping of the Vestal Virgins. Apparently they're supposed to keep wills for Roman patricians."

"Why would he do that?" I asked.

"Because he's a Roman." Iras paced over to the window. "Because that's what Romans do, so he did it."

"What did it say?"

"What you might expect. He left his house in Rome to Antyllus. He left some money to his son Iullus, his younger son by Fulvia, and a dowry to his daughters. And then he left all of his properties in the East and the bulk of his money to his dear children, Alexander Helios, Cleopatra Selene, and Ptolemy Philadelphos. He also said that when he dies he wishes to be buried in his beloved Alexandria, at the side of his adored wife Queen Cleopatra."

I sat down. "Oh sweet Mother!"

"There was practically a riot in the Senate when Octavian read it aloud," Iras said. "There was a stampede to the Temple of Bellona. Octavian walked in solemn procession carrying a spear dripping blood. Rome has declared war."

BEFORE THE END of the year Antonius and the Queen sailed for Greece. It was the best place for their fleets to gather to face Octavian, and for the troops Antonius had left in garrison to merge.

In Alexandria it was almost possible to believe that nothing was happening. Caesarion had his lessons, and increasingly he took on public duties, meeting with the Patriarch, whom he addressed solemnly in Aramaic. He had asked to be taken to war, but Cleopatra had refused. He was only fifteen, she said, and should wait another year or two.

The harvest came in, the dry season began. Winter turned into spring.

Emrys fretted and followed the news feverishly. Octavian had a fleet as well, and had given it to Agrippa to command.

"Surely he's untried at sea," Dion said.

Emrys raised an eyebrow. "You don't know him," he said. "It's more than in his blood. It's in his soul."

I thought of how we had stood at Medinet Habu the last time we had gone up the Nile, while Selene and Helios played in the shadows of the great columns, looking at the carved ships, tales of a long-ago victory by Ramses over the Sea People, and felt a chill run down my spine. Yes, it would be a mistake to underestimate Agrippa at sea.

And yet nothing changed. The Inundation came with no decisive engagement reached.

The dispatches came more irregularly now. It seemed that Agrippa's fleet had bottled up Antonius' land forces in Greece, and that our fleet stood in the harbor protecting them, while Agrippa and Octavian stood out to sea, unwilling to engage on land. Our dispatches had to be carried overland and then sail from other ports, a longer and more dangerous process.

Deciphering the Queen's code, we read the dispatches aloud to the council, Iras working letter by letter.

> *Octavian cannot be drawn into a battle on land, which is greatly to our disadvantage, as on land we have both numerical superiority, and more veteran troops. Many of those men Octavian has raised recently have never seen battle. And yet Antonius cannot come to grips with them.*
>
> *We cannot stay here forever. We must at some point break out by Cape Actium. Malaria has begun in our camp from the pestilential ground, and it is not possible to just simply sit here months on end, facing Octavian but unable to bring him to battle. Many of their ships are smaller and lighter than our quinqueremes, and I do not see how they can do us much damage....*

When I told Emrys this, he threw back his head and closed his eyes. "Bigger isn't always better," he said. "You remember Agrippa's first appointment was light cavalry? Do you think he doesn't know that smaller and lighter has certain tactical advantages?"

"Why don't you say something hopeful for a change?" I snapped, my nerves as worn by worry as his. "We could just surrender and crown Agrippa now."

"Better Agrippa than Octavian," he replied.

THE NEXT DISPATCH came two weeks later.

From Taenarum, in Greece

We have fought our way free of Actium, but at some cost. We lost thirty-five ships to the enemy, from our total of two hundred and thirty, with the loss of some five thousand men. Antonius' strategy was thus, that he should engage Octavian's forces on both wings, opening the center through which our ships should pass, including the flagship and the transports, as well as the pay chests and treasury carried by several of our vessels. This strategy was successful, and in that column myself, we passed through to open sea.

However, Antonius then found himself unable to disengage from the smaller ships which pressed around him. In the close quarters he was unable to use the greater strength of our quinqueremes to ram, and the fire arrows of their smaller ships were used to great effect.

On our landward flank, a number of our ships were cut off from the main body and pressed against the coast, where they were forced to surrender. This was a significant number, perhaps a hundred of our vessels other than the ones that were destroyed in the battle.

Antonius did eventually succeed in breaking off the engagement and reaching our rendezvous at Taenarum, but our losses have been significant.

Additionally, the news has come to us that those troops left in camp in Greece have gone over to Octavian piecemeal, offered money and bonuses. Canidius went over to Octavian with five legions from Macedon, shaking hands with Agrippa on the terms that the surrendering legions would keep all of their money and goods, and be paid more besides.

We are returning to Alexandria. The ships in drydock must be finished with all haste to compensate for our losses.

Cleopatra

Caesarion, who had begun to come to the council meetings in his mother's absence, asked, "What does that mean?"

It was Iras who answered. "It means we're in trouble."

"We have ninety-some ships left," I said. "That's not nothing."

I was more troubled by the troop defections than anything else. If Antonius could not count on his legions, where were we then? We could replace ships, but we could not replace those fighting men. The leopard, I thought, and his spots.

A week later we heard more of the same. Antonius' legions in Cyrenaica had gone over to Octavian, who had promised them discharges and bonuses.

"Where will he get all this money?" I asked Iras. "He can't have enough for all he's promising."

"The same place Caesar did," Iras said ominously.

THE QUEEN ARRIVED a few weeks later. Antonius had gone instead to Paraetonium, where the remainder of the Egyptian fleet waited; the ships that had not gone to Greece but had remained instead for courier duty and to guard the coast.

Cleopatra looked grim, though she returned in the normal way with due ceremony, her ships' prows garlanded. Privately, she took Iras aside. "I need a plan," she said, "for conveying Caesarion to Upper Egypt, to Koptos or Thebes. And for sending the younger children to Philae, on the borders of Nubia."

My breath caught in my throat. Horus, sent into the wilderness.

I leaned close to her. "Is it so bad?"

Her eyes met mine. "If Antonius cannot stop the defections we will have no troops on land at all. Remember, we have had no Royal Army since Caesar."

"Perhaps it's time for volunteers," Iras said. "We can call for volunteers in the city. It will be better than nothing. There are veterans who can drill the others."

"Yes," I said through the lump in my throat. I knew exactly who that meant.

THAT NIGHT I was already dressed for bed when there was a knock on the door. I rose and opened it, surprised.

Demetria came in and sat down on my bed, her white chiton draped around her. She was tall for her age, her light brown hair flowing down her back from a single clasp, her square forehead the picture of Agrippa's at that age. "Ma, I need to talk to you."

I came and sat by her where the moonlight came in through the window.

"Does he know about me?"

"Who?"

"Marcus Agrippa," she said. Her eyes were sea blue, not dark like his.

"No." I lifted my head, remembering. "I was afraid to tell him in Rome, and we've not spoken since. Do you want him to know?"

Demetria looked out the window, down the path of the moon to the harbor. "No," she said quietly. "Not when he's done such terrible things."

"Darling, he's not a bad man," I said. "He may be our enemy, but he is a good man. I know that."

"I don't," she said, and her jaw tensed. "I see them every day at the temple, families coming to pray for husbands or brothers or sons because we have to fight this stupid war. I know Antonius doesn't want to fight it! I know he'd rather it just all went away! But we have to fight it because of Agrippa. Because he's on Octavian's side." She looked at me. "You could have made him be on our side. You could have brought him to us like the Queen has Antonius."

"I wish I could have," I said. "And maybe I could have, if I'd manipulated him better. If I'd pushed and cajoled and rewarded and tempted when he was very young. Maybe I could have." I took her hand between mine. "But I thought it was wrong then, darling. Wrong to use sex to manipulate him. We can only do what's good ourselves, and hope that it comes out for the best."

"But it's not the best in the long term," Demetria said.

"We can't know that," I said. "We may be Her hands, but we make the terrible mistake of hubris if we start thinking of ourselves as gods."

She nodded gravely. "I want to be dedicated on my birthday. I'll be sixteen, and I can do it then."

"Irrevocable vows," I said. "You will be a priestess of Isis forever."

"I know," she said. "And it's what I want. What I truly want."

I hugged her close. "Then I will wish you every joy. You know I'm so proud of you."

"There's a catch," she said, from somewhere around my earring. "I have to be manumitted. Only free girls can take the dedication."

"Oh," I said, still holding her tight, thinking how odd and strange at once it was to have her be a young woman in my arms. It was a trite thought, but it seemed such a short time ago she had been a laughing baby. "I had forgotten. I'll talk to the Queen about it tomorrow."

AND SO just after Demetria's birthday, at the winter solstice, the Queen herself and Pharaoh came to the Temple of Isis for the dedication of the new priests. I stood beside her in the vast sanctuary while three girls and two youths came forth dressed in white and knelt before the Hierophant, repeating the words of their vows with quiet voices. Demetria looked lovely in her white gown, and when the choir began to sing and the flame ran down the great channels of stone around the front, I saw her look up, the tears on her face gleaming like the oil on her forehead.

I sobbed, and it was Pharaoh himself, Ptolemy Caesarion, who put his arm around me. "She'll be fine, Mother," he whispered. Then his voice changed as though seeing something for the first time. "She's really gotten pretty, hasn't she?"

He was sixteen and a half, and she sixteen. I squeezed his arm and smiled through my tears. "She has," I whispered back.

I looked across to where Emrys and Dion stood solemnly side-by-side to receive the blessings brought by the new priests. The only time

I'll ever see Dion here, I thought with a smile. But he would do it for Demetria.

Antonius was not there, of course. He was drinking heavily, which I did not find particularly helpful. He was drunk almost every night, sitting up over the wine and falling into bed at nearly dawn.

I raged at Emrys about it one day, when I'd seen Antonius to bed first thing in the morning and then gone to Dion's. "What does he think he's doing? Is he a general or not?"

Emrys shrugged, spreading his bread with goat cheese. "He's had it, Charmian. It happens to horses sometimes. You have a good warhorse, but at some point you've had it too long. It breaks. It doesn't have the temper for fire anymore, and at the first buzzing of arrows it shies and stands shaking. Antonius is done. Just done. He can't do it anymore."

Emrys got up, and I saw what was behind him on the couch. I stood still, frozen myself.

He saw where I looked, and came and took me in his arms. "They're just leathers, Charmian. I'm drilling the volunteers."

"You're too old," I said. "Emrys, you're too old!"

"I'm forty-one," he said. "That's not as old as all that. Besides," he said, brushing my hair back. "Those are Dion's."

"Oh sweet Isis!" I clutched him. "Dion doesn't know anything! He's never held a sword in his life!"

"Neither have most of the volunteers," Emrys said. "He has to, love." He looked at me ruefully. "He's finally found the thing worth killing or dying for."

"The city," I said, raising my head. "This beautiful, horrible, bizarre and wonderful city."

"Alexandria," Emrys said. "His friends and his lovers and his students and old professors and nieces and nephews in the Jewish Quarter and the Soma and the markets and the theaters and takeout places and all of the things he has ever loved. There's a word for that. The only thing that in the end is worth killing and dying for."

"Home," I said.

To our surprise, Octavian did not come in the winter. He had problems of his own, mutinies by his troops in Italy, who wanted to be paid.

Once again, money bought us time. Ships were built on the Red Sea. Plans were laid. If Octavian took Alexandria, Caesarion should go to Upper Egypt, always the base of Cleopatra's power, unconquered and proud. There, Horus could raise another army, or wait out the turns of Roman politics. But he could not go as a child.

Thus, one morning early in the new year, when the harvest came in, Caesarion had a ceremony of his own. He and Antyllus were enrolled in the gymnasium, and Antonius made sacrifice with both of them, his son and Caesar's, as they put on the toga of manhood in the Roman way.

Egypt had a Pharaoh, and Horus was no longer a child.

It was then that news came that sent Antonius to the bottom of a wine jug. Herod had gone over to Octavian, and opened all of the ports of Judea to him in return for the cities of the coast restored to his rule.

"There is still money," said Cleopatra. "He needs it, and we have it."

When Octavian landed in Ptolemais Ace, an envoy was sent to him carrying a generous amount of cash in token of more to come, and the message that Cleopatra was willing to step down from the throne, and allow her son Ptolemy Caesarion to rule Egypt alone.

There was no reply.

Next, Antonius sent an envoy, again well armed with cash, asserting that he would be willing to retire into private life, and that large sums of money might change hands in the process.

Once again there was no reply.

"He means to have it all," I said. "He will settle for nothing less than everything."

ANTONIUS SAILED with fifty ships to cut his supply lines, but he limped back into port a month later with six. Agrippa had cut him up instead.

SIX WEEKS LATER, Agrippa took Pelousion.

The Delta lay open before him.

CAESARION SHOULD GO to Memphis," I said. "Before the Saite branch is cut."

"I do not want to go," Caesarion said. "Antyllus and I can stand and fight."

"That's not your job," the Queen said. "You must think of the dynasty."

"I must think of being a man whom men will follow," Caesarion said, and in his dark eyes I saw the unstoppable determination of the young. "How can I be Horus when I flee while my people are in danger?"

A chill ran up my back. "If you are killed in battle, what then will become of Egypt?" I demanded of him.

Caesarion met my eyes levelly. "I have brothers and a sister to come after me." There was no fear in his face. Perhaps it was that one does not believe one can die at seventeen, or perhaps it was simply that he was brave. He dropped his voice, speaking to me alone. "Charmian, Mother, I am not ambitious. How should I be, when I was born to be Pharaoh? What could I strive for that was not mine the day I was born? All of these years you have raised me to be Horus, to care for the Black Land every day of my life, to love my people and to fulfill the bargain of the Ptolemies. If my death would serve Egypt, then I am ready to die."

It was my eyes that dropped from his. "Perhaps you will go later," I murmured.

It mattered not. The Saite branch was already cut.

ⓞCTAVIAN AND AGRIPPA advanced on Alexandria. They entered the suburb of Canopus six miles away. From Pharos, their ships could be seen patrolling off our coast. The gates were shut. Antonius called all of the cavalry he had left, and such veterans as knew their way around horses.

I saw Emrys mounting up in his old leathers, an aide at Antonius' side. He disdained plate. He had never worn it, and would not start now. His helm was the one he had worn when he served Caesar.

I was beyond tears and stood silent at the rail, watching them go out to fight in the streets of Canopus, to resist every length of road to the city.

The temples thronged with frightened people, and I thought that Demetria must have her hands full. But like Emrys, she had her duty and I had mine. I went inside, and saw to dinner and the lessons for Selene and Helios, my voice as normal as possible.

At nightfall they were back.

A cavalry charge had broken Octavian's advance, and they had withdrawn to the edge of town. They would not hear our emissaries.

Emrys came in with Antonius, and I ran to him.

"Not a scratch," Emrys said, putting his arms around me. "It takes more than that to touch me, love."

"Come and eat," I said.

There were all of Antonius' favorite dishes, and I sat with Emrys and Dion, my head on Emrys' breast. Everyone smiled. The wine was the best.

When the sweets came around, Antonius lifted his glass. "To those of us who will die together," he said.

Silence fell.

And in the silence Dion lifted his cup in return. "Absent friends," he said.

I lifted my chin and drank from Dion's cup. "Absent friends," I said. "Now and forever."

IN THE NIGHT I lay pillowed against them both, our bodies entwined. I woke, for I thought I heard some strange music. When I went to the window there was nothing.

The sacrifice had not been made. Dionysos was leaving.

A COMPANY
PASSING INVISIBLE

I n the morning they went out again, all of them. The remaining
ships of our fleet sailed, and our men marched against Agrippa,
twelve thousand men against thirty thousand.

Dion looked white as he got into line with the other infantry volunteers, tradesmen and students and men who had never held a sword
in battle before. I did not hear what he said to Emrys.

Emrys stood beside his horse, and I came out and embraced him
while the Queen bid Antonius farewell with such public words as put
heart in men. "I'll see you soon," Emrys said, and crushed me against
him. I nodded. I could not say good-bye, though every fiber of my
body sang with it.

And then they were gone.

A vast hush spread over the city. In the markets stalls closed, the merchants barricading themselves in their houses as though it were darkest
night. The streets emptied. Only a few furled sails stirred in the harbor,
ships deserted along the quays. Somewhere, a dog barked fitfully.

I stood on the terrace above the sea. It was hard to believe that anything moved or breathed in the warm air.

I looked down and it was Helios who took my hand, big boy as he
was and usually past that. "Charmian, is the world ending?"

"Yes," I said, and picked him up, crushing him against me. "You
must be very brave, do you hear me? No matter what happens."

"Iras won't let anything happen to me," he said. "She promised."

"She will do her best, my love," I said. "She will do her best."

A messenger boy came clattering out, his feet loud on the stones. "The Queen wants you," he said.

She was in her room, with Philadelphos on her shoulder. "We had better move," she said.

Iras was grabbing her jewels. "There was a skirmish. We lost some men and so did they. And then Antonius' last legion went over to Octavian and the Auxiliaries too. Agrippa proclaimed an amnesty for the men of the city if they would disperse, and they did. The gates are open and Octavian is coming."

"Where are we going?" I asked, twisting around.

"To my tomb." Cleopatra slid Philadelphos on her hip. "Except for Caesarion. He's gone to the docks, trying to make it down the Mareotic Canal in disguise. He'll head for Memphis. But I can't do that with the children."

Demetria, I thought. But Demetria was halfway across the city, at the Serapeum. Even now, the Canopic Way might be in Octavian's hands. I could never get there.

"And Antonius?"

"We don't know where he is," Iras said, and I saw the Queen's face tighten. "We'll leave a message for him here, and hope he understands it."

Selene ran before us as we hurried down almost deserted corridors, echoing with our footsteps, through deserted rooms, through the dining room where no one had cleaned up last night's dinner.

Babylon, I thought. My footsteps screamed it.

Out into the hot summer afternoon, out into the park. Past the glittering fountain of Nectanebo, past the mausoleums of Auletes and Philadelphos. Past the tombs of nobles. There lay the Hipparch Lydias with his wife, winged Hermes guiding him. There lay the men and women who had built the city.

And at last Cleopatra's tomb, its great bronze doors meant to keep out robbers. It took all of our strength to bar them. We waited. I only lit one lamp, so that the oil would last. We waited in the cool dark.

I did not mean to, but I slept.

Iᴛ ᴡᴀꜱ ɴɪɢʜᴛꜰᴀʟʟ when they brought Antonius. We saw the torches and went to one of the clerestory windows that was still accessible inside from the scaffolding. Iras clambered up.

"He's on a stretcher," she called down. "He's badly hurt."

Cleopatra kicked off her shoes and climbed up, and I heard her cry out as she saw him. I stayed below, holding Selene back where she would have followed.

"Charmian, come up! We need you!" she called down, and her voice sounded panicked. I scrambled after.

Outside in the summer dusk two servants were trying to lift up a board with Antonius on it, and I heard him groan faintly as they jostled him. Iras leaned so far out I thought she would fall, her arms straining as she tried to take the weight. Somehow, with all three of us pulling and tugging, and the servants below pushing, we managed to get the board in the window.

I saw at once that it was hopeless. While Cleopatra fell sobbing on his face, covering him with kisses, Iras lifted the cloth away from where it had been pressed against his belly. Her eyes met mine. There was no recovery from a wound like this, though it might take many hours to die. Clearly it already had.

"Iras, get some wine for the Imperator," Cleopatra said, and I heard her as she bent over him again. "What happened? The battle?"

He shook his head, sweat beaded on his lip where he had bitten it in pain. "No...did it myself when I had your note...."

"My note?" She blanched. "I told you to seek me in my tomb. What did you think?"

Antonius raised his head, his lips stretched as though he tried to laugh. "What should I make of that? That you were dead, of course." He raised one bloody, shaking hand to her face. "And why should I live then?"

My eyes met Iras'. Too late.

Down below Philadelphos cried out, and I climbed down to the children. "Darlings, your father has been badly wounded. He's terribly, terribly sick."

Selene met my eyes, and she knew. And I knew that she knew. I saw it settle over her, nine years old. "We're going to die, aren't we?" she asked, her voice perfectly even.

"We're all going to die some time or other, dearest," I said. "It matters less when than how. Come and I will show you where we will be. This is, after all, your mother's tomb." We walked across the floor, away from the scaffold, away from the dying man.

Cleopatra's sarcophagus was nearby, heavy carved granite waiting for the gilded inner coffin. "Your mother will go right there someday, just like Alexander in his tomb or your grandfather in his," I said, my hand tight around Philadelphos'. "You see how it's carved with her royal cartouche here. And over here on the floor behind it are two cover stones, for me and Iras to lie behind her beneath the floor. Here's mine on the right and Iras' on the left. And your father will lie there, just beside her on the dais."

I blinked, surprised my voice was still completely normal, Selene and I carrying on this act for the boys. And Emrys and Dion? Where did they lie, even now? Would I even ever know?

"It's very pretty," Selene said. "Almost as pretty as Alexander's."

"I think so too," I said.

IN THE HOUR before dawn Antonius died. Iras closed his eyes, and she and Cleopatra carried his body down from the scaffolding and laid him out on the lid of the sarcophagus, his limbs neatly arranged, his cloak over him.

He brought himself to it in the end, I thought, the sacrifice. But it was too late, far, far too late. I could not help but pity him.

And yet, had he done it sooner we would not have been brought to this pass.

"What shall we do?" I whispered to Iras as the Queen knelt beside him. "We cannot stay here day and night with no water and a corpse. What about the children?"

She shook her head.

Octavian's men knocked on the door soon after, and the Queen went and spoke with them. I do not know what she said. I sat on the far side of the room, Helios in my lap, telling them stories.

The lamp sputtered, the oil burning low.

I didn't see the men until they jumped down from the clerestory window, three Roman soliders. In an instant one of them had a knife at Cleopatra's throat. "Nobody move!" he shouted.

I hardly could, across the room with Helios on me. They unbarred the door and we were taken.

BACK TO THE PALACE in the morning, back to the rooms we had left less than a day before, under heavy guard. The Queen's room reeked of roses, where yesterday in our haste we had knocked a vial of scent over.

"The princes and princess will return to their rooms," the officer in charge said. "One of you maidservants will accompany them."

The Queen nodded at me, and I went out with the children. Please, Mother, I thought, if it is to be done, let it be done quickly so they hardly know.

But nothing happened. We went into their rooms under heavy guard. It was little different than when Caesar had taken us all before years ago.

And my heart ached for Emrys.

"Come, children," I said. "Let's wash up and put on some clean clothes."

"Our father is dead," Helios said.

"Yes, my darling," I said, kneeling beside him. "So let's cut a lock of your hair, each one of you, to lay on his breast, and dress like a family in mourning."

"Where is Caesarion?" Selene asked. "And Antyllus?"

"I don't know," I said.

Slaves brought dinner on a tray later, and I let them eat it without waiting for me to eat first for safety. If Octavian wanted to kill them there were easier and quicker ways, and it would certainly not look natural if we all dropped dead at once.

I went over their lessons with Helios and Selene, and let Philadelphos go to bed on a pallet on the floor of Helios' room. Selene didn't want to sleep alone either, and curled up with her brothers in the whispering dark. Outside, the feet of the sentries were the only sound, passing by on their rounds.

At midnight the guard let in Iras. She looked haggard, and her usually immaculate hair was coming out of its pins. "We're trading for a while," she said. I nodded.

She caught my arm. "Antyllus is dead," she said. "He took sanctuary in the temple. Agrippa's troops dragged him from the altar and beheaded him."

"Oh my Lady Isis," I whispered. "That dear, sweet boy." Demetria. Demetria must have been there, must have seen it.

Iras squeezed my arm.

"Come," the guard said.

I went in to the Queen.

Cleopatra was white and drawn, her eyes ringed by huge shadows, but her plain blue chiton was clean, not covered as the other had been with Antonius' gore. Iras had gotten her to bathe.

I went to her and took her hands.

"You heard about Antyllus?" she asked.

I nodded.

"How are the children?"

"Fine," I said. "They've had dinner. I've kept them quiet and calm. They're upset about their father, of course."

She nodded, turning away and pacing toward the window. "Octavian won't hurt them yet. He has a plan for us." She stopped before the curtains, moving in the harbor breeze. "We're to march in his Triumph."

"Like Arsinoe." The words escaped me before I could stop them.

"All of us," Cleopatra said, her back to me. "You, me, Iras, and the children. Antonius has robbed him of the pleasure of his company."

"Octavian could never have done that," I said, fighting back the nausea that rose in me. Practical, as Emrys said. Practical to the last. "The Romans would turn on him. They would have too much sympathy for their former hero Antonius."

"And they have none for me," she said. "The Great Harlot. The wicked creature out of the East, devourer of men, the monster seducing men from virtue with Greek ideas and evil luxury. They will enjoy seeing me drooling and incontinent."

I pressed my hands to my lips. I had no prayers left.

Cleopatra smoothed her skirts down, and I saw her head lift. "I've asked Octavian if I may speak with him at his leisure. There may be something left to bargain with."

She turned and I saw the word in her eyes, though she did not voice it. We did not know where Caesarion was. If he had gotten safe to Memphis, we might have one more play. If we could buy time.

I⊤ WAS THREE LONG and tedious days before the guard came, saying that Caesar Octavian would visit the Queen in an hour.

"Thank you," she said gravely, and as the door closed turned to us. "I need my good clothes. Something modest but seemly, preferably white."

"I know the one," I said, and we prepared her. She looked like a matron in mourning, a beautiful and still not old matron of thirty-nine, but nothing like golden Isis enthroned.

Octavian was punctual. Exactly on the hour the door opened to admit him and Agrippa. Iras and I stood behind the Queen's chair, motionless.

I saw Agrippa's eyes slide to me, and his face become expressionless. After that he did not look, only kept his glance on Octavian.

"Imperator," Cleopatra said gracefully. "You have changed much since we last met. The years have given you distinction."

Octavian smiled pleasantly. "Your charm is wasted on me. In fact, this conversation is a waste of time, except that it should not be said that I have not observed the courtesies. Marcus Antonius is being embalmed and will receive a proper burial, as a Roman deserves."

Cleopatra stood, pushing off the arms of her chair like a swimmer off the side of a pool. "Then let me come straight to the point. Antonius is dead. You have Rome. You need Egypt. I will offer you the same thing I did your uncle. I can give you grain and gold, treasure and ships. Why struggle to govern Egypt when I can lay its riches at your feet? Leave me as an ally of Rome, and your task will be easy."

"I don't think so," he said mildly. "You fail to understand your place in this. This is the end. There will be no more Hellenistic kings, no more chaotic successor states with their cities and councils and half-baked democracies, no more tribes with their illiterate barbarian leaders. From one end of the Middle Sea to the other, there will be nothing but Rome." He put his hands behind his back like a schoolmaster, a trick of rhetoric. "Egypt will become a Roman province, like every other. There will be no more incestuous monarchs. Just orderly Roman rule."

The Queen gathered herself up while I glanced at Agrippa. His face was impassive, his dark hair curling across his square forehead.

"You and your children will adorn my Triumph, and then, after a suitable interval, you will meet your end." He stopped in front of Iras. "Your women will march as well. It is necessary to demonstrate the result of the unbridled rule of women, licentious and immoderate. A land ruled by a queen, with her coterie of eunuchs, hairdressers, and serving girls, comes to its inevitable end." He looked into Iras' face and chuckled. "Treasurer of Egypt. In the end, you're nothing but a cunt."

I saw something in the Queen's face harden, though her expression didn't change.

Octavian looked back to her. "Your time is over. This is the future."

"I see," she said. "And do you think the gods of all peoples besides your own so weak?"

Octavian smiled pleasantly, as though he addressed a very small child. "There are no gods. Do you think I should go on my knees to a statue of my great-uncle? It's absurd. State religion is necessary to keep order among the lower classes, and to infuse government with the correct mystique. But only weak-minded fools believe those sorts of things." He spread his hands reasonably. "Cults are for the silly, and the silly are welcome to them. But for the rest, no more weakening philosophies questioning the meaning of existence, or effete Eastern customs with their pernicious effect on Roman manhood. The rest of the world will learn where it belongs." He stopped in front of me, his eyes traveling down my neck. "Under Rome."

Cleopatra turned, and her eyes were dark, black as midnight skies, though her voice was even. "I know you. You are the enemy of life itself. You are at war with the gods."

Octavian laughed. "Then the gods are losing." He swept from the room.

Agrippa lagged behind Octavian, his scarlet cape swirling about him as he reached for my arm. "Charmian, I need to talk to you."

"I have nothing to say to you," I gasped.

He bent close, his grip urgent on my arm. "I swear to you upon my honor that I will not let the children be harmed."

"May demons eat your bones," I spat.

He took a breath, letting go, and followed after Octavian.

I sank, unheeded, to my knees. Apophis had won.

AFTER THAT we were no longer allowed to see the children. Cleopatra paced the length of her room, while Iras tried to read. Slaves brought us meals, and the guards had nothing to say.

It was several days before the door opened, and one of the guards looked in. "Domina? This man says he is one of your slaves."

"Yes, of course he is," the Queen said. I didn't even look up from the scroll I was trying to concentrate on until the door closed. It was the sound of Iras' indrawn breath that alerted me.

"Dion?"

His hair was unkempt and he wore a rough woolen chiton, his face clean shaven in the Greek fashion. I had never seen him without a beard before, not since he was a boy. It did make him look remarkably different.

I threw myself in his arms, but the Queen and Iras were already there. Dion staggered.

"How did you get here?"

"Where are the children?"

"What's happening?"

Dion squeezed all three of us tightly, and I felt him shiver.

"I got in dressed as a slave," he said. "And of course I have friends who were willing to vouch for me. Your servants are loyal, Gracious Queen." He stepped back, looking at us, his face solemn.

"Emrys?" I asked. "What about Emrys?"

The look in his eyes told me everything I needed to know. "I'm so sorry," he said, and held out his hand to me.

I closed my eyes, clinging to it, the tears seeping out the corners. "I know. I already knew." I had known. I had known when I bid him good-bye that it would be the last time I saw him, only I had thought, had hoped, these past days that it was only my own death I foresaw.

"He died in the last skirmish. The one they're calling the Battle of Alexandria. I carried him from the field myself." His voice only caught a little, as though he had repeated this a dozen times already.

"Oh, Dion."

"I carried him. I brought him home. He's in one of the rock tombs outside the Canopic Gate, my family's tomb. He's with my grandparents and my kin."

I heard the tears in his voice, but I could not open my eyes. I shook, and it was Iras' arms that were around me, her shoulder I put my head on.

Dion's voice steadied, as if speaking to Cleopatra gave him strength. "Gracious Queen, I have terrible news." I heard her breath as Dion continued: "They caught Caesarion. They caught him on the canal. Agrippa's troops cut his throat."

Iras let go of me and I wavered blindly. Cleopatra staggered, half-catching herself on the chair arm, almost falling. The noise that came from her was not even a human cry.

Dion took her hand and helped her onto the couch, the tears rolling down his face. "Gracious Queen, I thought you should know. I just thought you should know...."

"My baby..."

"Octavian said there was one Caesar too many," Dion said.

Iras clutched at his arm. "The other children?"

"They're alive. I can't get to them. I already tried. They've been taken to Agrippa's flagship. They say you sail for Rome in three days."

"On the flagship..." In the palace at least there was a chance of doing something, when they were only minutes away, but on a Roman flagship out in the harbor they might as well have been on the moon. "Philadelphos will be so frightened," I whispered. "Oh Isis, he'll be so scared!"

Cleopatra keened, and Dion held her to his breast.

"Selene will watch over her brothers," Iras said. "She'll look out for them. She's always been the strongest one." Her face twisted in pain, and her knuckles were white where she held her hands to her face. "I promised Helios I wouldn't let anything bad happen to him. I promised him..."

I put my arms around her, raised my eyes to Dion. "And Demetria?"

"She's safe at the temple," Dion said. "I saw her this morning. She's fine. She's worried and of course she's upset, but she's fine."

Cleopatra raised her head. "Agrippa doesn't know?"

I shook my head.

My sister took a breath. "Then you at least might still get out of this. Surely he will not let the mother of his child be displayed in the Triumph this way."

I shook my head again. "I will not trade Demetria's safety for my life. No." I looked at Dion. "As far as everyone is concerned, she's the daughter of the scholar Dion."

"Always and forever," Dion promised. "I'll take care of her."

"Three days," Iras said.

"Three days," Dion said. His eyes met hers, and for a moment in his shaven face I saw again the boy who had pledged himself to a princess' service. "Gracious Queen, if there were anything I could do for you, I would give my life for it."

Cleopatra sat up, and I saw it cross her like the shiver of breeze across water. "Yes, Dion. There is something you can do. One more thing."

HE CAME BACK the next morning, and though I sat stiffly while the guard decided if he should let him in, he did when Dion raised the lid of the basket. "Just figs," he said cheerfully.

With a shrug, the guard closed the door behind him.

Dion carefully put the basket on the little table beside the couch.

Cleopatra and Iras had come from the bedroom together, and now we stood like points of a triangle, staring at the basket, while the warm summer wind blew through white linen curtains.

"It's a cobra," Dion said. "The man I got it from said it ought to be good for three strikes. You die from respiratory failure in about half an hour."

Cleopatra looked at the basket, unblinking.

"Is it painful?" I asked.

"Not as these things go," Dion said. "A cobra bite is not a hard way to die."

"Thank you, Dion," Cleopatra said, and smiled at him. "I knew you would choose the best thing."

I saw his eyes fill and he ducked his chin. "Must you?"

She shook her head. "You know I must. And this you swore long ago in my coronation in Abydos, remember? When you played Set's serpent, out of the desert."

"I did," he whispered. "But I never thought..."

Cleopatra put her hand on his arm. "Even Set is not evil, and sometimes His gifts are a mercy. You have no guilt in this. I absolve you of any wrongdoing. You are my loyal man, as you have always been."

"I will never think of anything else again," Dion whispered.

I took his hand in mine. "Yes, you will," I said. "You will love Demetria and she will love you. And someday she will give you grandchildren to raise. And there will be new students, and there is still the universe in all its glory, waiting for you to understand."

"There is nothing left in it now," he said.

"If you believe that, then Apophis has won," I said. "You must build all the harder for the things that are torn down. This is a defeat, nothing more, and we must face it like soldiers. But Isis is unconquerable. Love is unconquerable."

Iras came and put her arms about him. "The world is still full, Dion," she whispered. "Live, and love, and by your love bear witness to all you have seen."

In the end, my sister and I were alike.

I laid my head against Dion's neck, as I had lain with him and Emrys. "Tell Demetria I love her very much, and I am so proud of her and the woman she has become. Tell her I love her."

I held Dion until he stopped crying, and then he went away for the last time.

Evening was coming. In an hour or so the slaves would come with our dinner.

"If it is to be done, then let's do it," Iras said.

The Queen nodded. "I'll go first."

"And we will stay to lay you out and dress you," Iras said. "So that there is nothing unseemly."

"I'll go last," I said, lifting my chin.

Cleopatra embraced me. "The one requiring the most courage, to watch your sisters die."

"I'm not afraid," I said.

THE SNAKE STRUCK ONCE, catching her in the right forearm. Iras got the lid back on the basket so it wouldn't escape, and we sat together on the couch, one on either side of her.

"Do you remember," I said, "how we climbed on the roof with Dion, and how he saved us?"

"And how we put that salted fish on Antonius' line?" She smiled at me, though her eyelids were beginning to drop. She swallowed as though it were difficult. "That was so funny."

"It really was," Iras said. "And how Auletes let us dress up in the entire treasury of Egypt?"

"I've had the best sisters in the world," she said.

"So have I," I said.

"And the best lovers. Caesar and Antonius."

"I have too," I said. "Poor Dion, left behind."

"Someone must live," Iras said, "and tell the story."

"And of course that's Dion," I said.

Cleopatra tried to swallow again, and she clutched at my hand.

"Does it hurt?" I asked.

"Dizzy," she croaked. "Just dizzy."

I could hear her breath laboring.

She grabbed at me again, her eyes half closed. "Caesarion..."

Iras drew a breath more like a sob.

"Antonius...," she whispered, almost unintelligibly. She lay on my shoulder, her chest heaving with each breath, slower and slower, until at last her eyes fixed and she was silent.

There were two of us in the room instead of three, and her absence was like nothing else.

"I have her clothes laid out," I said.

"I'll wash her," Iras said.

And we got up, making a wide path around the basket on the table. Outside, the sun had not yet quite set into the sea. "The day is done," I said. "And I will never see morning."

Iras put her arms around me. "Come, darling."

We laid her out dressed in pleated linen, with bracelets of gold and a collar that should have adorned kings, the uraeus on her brow. The embalmers would do it all again, of course, but it should be done right.

And then it was Iras who put her hand in the basket.

"Mother" was the last thing she said, and her lips moved like a child nursing as she died.

I laid her at Cleopatra's feet, and no tears dropped from my eyes. I had no more to shed.

I am the Hand of Isis, I thought, as I picked up the basket again. The Hand of the Lady of the Dead, standing before the Gates of Amenti. Gracious Isis, forgive me if I am frightened at the end! And I plunged my hand into the basket.

Perhaps it was tired, or perhaps it was already settling down for the night in the nice warm basket, but I had to poke the snake three times before it bit me. Sitting with my sisters' bodies, tormenting a snake. At last it struck, and angrily slithered out of the basket and across the floor, looking for some place better to sleep where it would not be disturbed.

"Go with Set's blessing," I said, and sat down to wait.

The doors opened and the guard looked in, a slave beside him with our dinner tray. With a crash, the slave dropped the tray. I heard him screaming down the hall.

There is nothing to be done now, I thought, and sat back in the chair. Already there were coronae around the lights, my vision blurring. Dion was right, I thought. It doesn't particularly hurt.

The door banged open again, and Marcus Agrippa came charging into the room with the guard. He looked over it in one glance, the Queen laid out on her couch, her face still and set, Iras lying at her feet with her hands folded on her breast.

He ran to me and grabbed me by the arms, dragging me to my feet. "Why?"

"You killed my baby," I said. "You killed Caesarion. You killed my baby."

"No, I swear…"

My vision was blurring, and I would have fallen if not for him holding me up. "I swear. And you will hear it, Marcus Vipsanius Agrippa. Your house will go down in blood, and you will never know peace on this earth. Waking and sleeping, it will follow you. You will rise up with blood in the morning and lie down with it at night. You will never know rest, and you will walk this earth wallowing in blood until you have made amends."

I saw him blanch, his handsome face distorted by my fading vision. I gasped for breath, but none came. My throat was closing.

"Charmian…" His voice sounded as ragged as mine, pleading.

I could no longer feel my legs.

"Was this well done by your lady?"

I strove for one more breath. "Very well," I slurred. "As befits the last of so many noble kings."

And the darkness took me.

⬥ Amenti

I bent my head before the thrones, and the tears once again choked me. *"Gracious Ones, if You have any mercy, punish me as You will. All that I have loved is lost, and I desire nothing in the world except those who are gone."* I lifted my eyes to Isis. *"At least I bid farewell to my sisters. But Emrys and Caesarion..."* I could speak no more.

I saw a look pass between Them, and Serapis nodded. Somewhere away to the side a door opened, and I heard swift feet across the floor.

"Mother?"

I flew to him, wrapping my arms around Caesarion, my face against his shoulder. He had been at last taller than me before... and now he should never have any chance, never grow anymore, never love or be the man he might have been. I closed my eyes against him, weeping, and Emrys put his arms around my back.

"Don't cry so much," Caesarion said. There was that same awkward tone he sometimes got, when something unexpected had unnerved him. "Charmian? Mother? I'm all right."

"You're dead," I said.

"Everybody dies," Emrys said, his arm around my waist. His voice sounded freer, as though something had eased in him.

"Not at seventeen," I said, and looked up at Caesarion. "Not with your whole life before you..."

His dark eyes were very grave. "I was the sacrifice. Don't you see? Isis is the Grain Mother as well as the Lady of the Sea. It's Her consort who *can make the sacrifice, but also Her son. Son of Isis, son of Venus, twice royal. Blood of the Ptolemies, blood of Rome. Don't you see? In the end, I was the only right sacrifice. The Black Land will continue under Roman rule, and Rome herself will be transformed. I had to be the sacrifice." He ducked his head, as he'd always done as a child when he expected me to scold him. "My blood for the Black Land, freely given. That's the bargain of the Ptolemies, the bargain of kings. Sometimes, like my father, you get to be very old first, but not always. I don't regret it."*

I looked up at Emrys, his green eyes on Caesarion. "And what do you say?"

He nodded, one soldier to another. "I say it was well done, my Prince. First and last, hail Ptolemy Caesar."

Emrys looked younger, the lines of the last campaign erased from his face, the gray from his hair, and turning in his arms to lay my face against his chest I could not help but feel that it was right, that he was whole.

"And Rome?" I asked.

From His throne, Serapis spoke. "There are times when a nation has come so far from all it holds dear, when the blood of innocents cries out. Only the sacrifice can heal — only the brave young man who is willing to die for all that is highest and best."

"But time grows short," Isis said. "Time is still passing, out in the world, beyond the Gates of Amenti."

I did not want to leave the circle of Emrys' arms, but I turned in them. "Do You not have to weigh my heart?"

Serapis smiled. "Daughter, We have already weighed your heart and found nothing lacking. You are not without fault, but your faults are far outweighed by your virtues. You have earned the Peace of Amenti." He looked up at the ceiling full of stars. "If you wish, you may stay here with those you love and be healed of the hurts of this life. You may walk in the forests beneath the stars of heaven with your lover and your son, greet your sisters again and those others you have loved. You may choose to be healed and in this place weep no more. I think it will be a long time before Cleopatra and Antonius come forth by day again." He glanced at Caesarion. "And Caesar, that wind through the world, must not venture forth too often in the same lands."

"Or?" I had not meant to say it, but I did.

Isis stood, and the movement of Her robes was like the movement of the sea by night. "In the world, time is still passing. They have reached Rome."

"The children." I felt my throat tighten. Helios, Philadelphos, and Selene. Even now they might be suffering. "They aren't here."

"They live still," Anubis said. "Though even We cannot say for how long."

I held Isis' eyes. "Is there a chance?"

She inclined Her head gravely. "Yes. They may live. Or they may die before you even draw your first breath in that world."

"Or they may live like Arsinoe," I said, and felt Emrys' arms tighten around me. I remembered her suffering, worse than death by far.

Isis nodded.

I asked the question, though I already knew what Her answer would be. "Can you prevent this?"

"No, but you may."

I lifted my chin, and the last tear ran down my face, the last one. "Can You send me to the children?"

"Yes," Isis said, and Her eyes were as dark and implacable as night. "I can send you now to Rome, without healing, without time. I can send you as a helpless infant, with no power or means to fight except what you carry in you. It's hardly a fair match."

Emrys' arm was tight about my waist, but I knew he would not try to stop me. He never had.

"And Iras?" I asked, though I thought I knew this too.

Isis looked at Serapis, but it was Mikhael who answered. "Iras has already gone to Rome."

I nodded, lacing my fingers with Emrys'. We were alike, my sister and I. Iras had promised Helios, and death would not keep her from her promise. I looked at Caesarion, who would not plead that I suffer for his brothers and sister. "My brave, sweet boy," I said, and smiled at him. I leaned up and kissed Emrys, warm and gentle as I had always remembered.

"Be careful, love," he whispered, and I knew that he understood me bone deep.

"Where will you be?" I asked, running my hand through his hair.

He shrugged, gave me a lopsided smile. "I'm thinking I might try Alexandria. Maybe as a girl. I'm tired of war."

"That should give Dion fits," I said, and kissed him again.

Then I released him, and stepping forward away from Caesarion and Emrys, faced the thrones. "I am ready, Gracious Ones. Send me to Rome, to the children, without the delay of healing. I will do my best."

I saw Isis smile, and then Anubis took my hands. For the second time darkness took me, and I knew no more.

ISIS INVICTA

I was born in the Subura, and the first things I remember are the narrow streets slicked with rain, and my mother trying to get in the washing hung to dry on a line between two buildings before the clothes were all soaked again. It is this I remember, a tiny apartment on the fourth floor, sleeping beside my older brother on a pallet under the window, where the night air sometimes brought in breezes from the Esquiline Hill and the scents of distant parties and dinners. My younger sister Lucilla slept with my parents, until baby came and she joined me and Lucius on the pallet. We slept like puppies entwined, and I was very happy, except that I did not like it when Lucilla wet the bed.

When I was four I tried to run away, they said, and I was gone all day while my mother and then my father, too, searched for me frantically. After nightfall I turned up, brought home by the owner of a tavern four blocks away. He said he had found me in his back alley, and that I claimed I was on my way to Alexandria.

My parents showered him with tears and thanks. I clung to him and did not want to come home. A few days later I ran away again, and was caught this time halfway to the Happy Ham, where I said I was going to see my friend. My father and I made a deal at that—I should be allowed to go to the Happy Ham, if it did not annoy the owners, Sigismund and Mucilla, overmuch, and if I would give off running anywhere else.

Running, of course, was the operative word. Going a block out of one's way to look at something didn't constitute running away, and by the time I was seven or eight I knew perfectly well that Alexandria was too far to go by myself, and that I would need a ship at least. Besides, by then the entire city of Rome was open to me. I had no lessons, and there was another child at home and still far too little money, so it seemed natural that I should work deliveries for the Happy Ham, taking people the dinners that they had ordered and bringing back the payment. Sometimes they would give me a little extra for my trouble, as I could run fast through the neighborhood with ham and fresh bread, mustard and cheese, and everything else that one might want. I never lost the money or took it for myself, though I was proud of the coppers that Sigismund paid me, as good as if I'd been his own daughter.

Once, some boys tried to take the money from me when I was coming back from a delivery, but I ran and got away from them and told Sigismund who they were. After he'd had a word with them that never happened again. He was an enormous German with a scar across his face and the stump of a right arm, but it was rumored that he'd been Caesar's own bodyguard, and that he'd once killed a man with his teeth. He looked scary enough to have done it, but I didn't think the teeth story was really true.

"How do you know it's not?" he asked with a wolfish grin as he cleaned off the bar one day, while I hung around waiting for a delivery order to be packed. "I might have."

I shrugged, kneeling on the bar stool with my elbows on the counter. "I just know it's not. But you were really a bodyguard for Caesar. That story's true."

His face sobered, and he tossed the cleaning rag in the bus pan. "It's true," he said. "And Antonius after him. But look at me alive, and both of them gone!"

"And both of them knowing their fate," I said. "They are not the ones we should mourn."

Sigismund turned around, looking at me sharply. "You're a fey little street rat, Lucia. Some god touched you in the womb, the way you say things sometimes."

I shrugged. I was a street rat, and there was nothing to be offended about in that. I put my elbows on the bar again, tracing old patterns there that some bored patron had carved with a knife. "Sometimes I feel like there's something terribly important, only I don't quite know what it is. Like I can't quite remember it." I glanced up at him from beneath my long brown hair. "Sometimes I dream strange dreams, and you're in them. Do you think the gods would help me find out?"

"Maybe," he said thoughtfully. "I'm not sure which god it would be."

Something occurred to me that I wondered about. "Sigismund, do the gods of the Germans have a place in Rome?"

His seamed face broke into a grin. "They do now," he said. "A man called Marcus Vipsanius Agrippa just built it. I'll show you."

And that was how I found the Pantheon.

After that I went there — not often. It was too far to go in the middle of the day without missing deliveries. Once in a while. When there was time.

This particular day, a patrician's slave had called suddenly, demanding the whole ham that was just coming out of the oven, glazed in honey and spices. His master had returned to Rome unlooked-for by his household, and all was shambles as there was no dinner for him, no food suitable for an important man.

Mucilla bundled the whole ham up, with suitable accompaniments, and packed it off with the slave for a fine price. She was actually singing as she sent Sigismund to get another ham down from where it hung and started mixing up more glaze. "We won't need you this afternoon, Lucia. It will be hours until this one is done."

So I took off, letting my feet and my whim guide me through the city, until at last I came to the Pantheon.

It was a new temple, younger even than I, and had been finished only three years ago. Round in form, it looked like nothing else in Rome. Inside, there was no light except what streamed down from a huge oculus in the ceiling far above the ground. In the center, where one might have expected a statue, there was nothing except a vast expanse of polished floor. All around the walls, some in niches, some standing freely, were images of the gods.

This early in the day the temple was almost deserted. A couple of elderly women were over by Adonis, and the doorkeeper was sitting on a stool under the portico, his head back against the wall, his mouth opened with snores. If his job was to keep the indigent from moving in, he would hardly notice today if half the town squatted there.

I wandered about, looking up at the bright sun streaming in. It was chilly inside. My favorite statue was two thirds of the way around.

Isis was robed in blue and white, infant Horus on Her lap. He was a very pudgy baby, and He looked out at the viewer with the smug I've-got-something-in-my-mouth-and-you-don't-know-what expression that my own little brother wore. Her face, in contrast, was serene and a little sad, Her features dignified rather than beautiful. She might have been beautiful, I thought, had She not had such a long nose.

There was someone there, and I didn't see him until I came around her, a tall man in the worn leathers of a soldier, a mud-splattered traveling cloak thrown over them. He was forty-five or so, much older than my father, with a lined, handsome face and brown hair streaked with gray.

I squeaked, and started to back away.

He turned and gestured with one arm. "Don't let me keep you away, little one. I don't bite."

"No, of course not," I said, edging back. He had startled me, that was all. There was nothing frightening about him. Of course.

He turned away from me and bent his head, lowering his eyes before Isis again. He looked so sad it was hard to be afraid.

I had a few flowers I'd picked up, ones that were dropped and trampled in the flower market, but still good enough to use. I always brought Her something. I knelt quickly, laying them at Her feet. "All hail Isis, Mother of Compassion."

"Compassion." There was so much misery in his tone that I looked up. "Do you need compassion, little one?"

"Yes," I said. "I mean, not much. I've not much to feel sorry for myself about, but the money is awfully tight and the baby's teething so nobody can sleep at night because we all live in one room, and my brother needs lessons if he's ever going to make anything of himself but a common laborer and my father says we've not sunk that low, so where's the dowry for me in that, not that I need one yet. But there are a lot of people who need compassion. Isis is the Mother of the World. She has enough for everybody." I looked at him sharply, at the deep graven lines around his mouth. "You look as though you could use some. Did someone die?"

He looked up at the statue, a curiously blank expression on his face. "Oh yes. Lots of people died."

I felt a chill run down my back. "You must be used to that, being a soldier."

"If you get used to it you are a beast, not a man." He looked at me sideways, as though weighing something, the two lines between his brows deep furrows. "Have you ever done something so horrible and so irreparable that you knew there was nothing you could ever do to fix it?"

"No," I said gently. "Mostly because I'm eight."

He cracked a smile, as I had meant for him to.

"But I think you just have to try to put it right," I said. "If you can't fix it, then you have to make amends."

He looked up, his eyes seeking the light pouring in through the oculus. "I have tried," he said. "I built this. A temple for all of the gods of humanity in the heart of Rome. A hearth where everyone is welcome. I have tried."

"And yet?"

"And yet," he said, his eyes falling again to the serene, empty ones of the statue.

"Then you must try harder," I said, putting my hand on his arm. "You must try all your life. That's the best any of us can do. Carry the banner proudly in our own time."

He looked down at me, and for the first time I thought he really saw me, eyes roving over my sharp, thin face, my long brown hair escaping from an untidy braid, my quick and restless hands. "I was asking Her forgiveness," he said, "like a boy who begs pardon with his pockets still full of stolen apples."

"Maybe you should give back the apples first," I said.

"What about the ones I ate?" The corners of his mouth moved in a hint of a smile.

"I don't think She wants those back," I said.

"Try harder?"

I nodded. "And don't do it again."

He laughed, and I thought it was quite a nice laugh, if a little rusty from disuse. "I don't think I'm likely to have the opportunity to do it again."

"I wouldn't be sure of that," I said.

He sobered, and once again his eyes searched my face. He nodded at what he saw there and something changed in the set of his mouth, something eased. "I thought at first that you were a little girl," he said, and turned to go.

"And what do you think I am now?" I called after him.

He stopped, his nailed sandals ringing on the stone floor. He turned just out of the light of the oculus, in the shadow. "I think you are the Hand of Isis."

He took his plumed helmet from under his arm and put it on, striding out into the portico while I stood beside the statue, the Mother of the World with wilted flowers at Her feet.

"You're right," I said, and in that moment all my life stretched before me. "I am."

AFTERWORD

C leopatra's children, Helios, Selene, and Philadelphos, were marched in chains in Octavian's Triumph. However, the sight of Philadelphos, barely six years old, struggling to walk in chains too heavy for him, aroused not the anger of the Roman people, but their sympathy. Instead of cheers, the soldiers guarding them earned boos. At the end of the Triumph, Octavian's sister Octavia insisted on the children being released to her care rather than prison or execution. She took them into her house and raised them with her own daughters, their half-sisters by Marcus Antonius.

Helios and Philadelphos died at some point in the next ten years. There was suspicion at the time and ever after that Octavian, now the Emperor Augustus, or his wife, Livia, had them murdered.

Selene escaped that fate. At the age of fifteen she was married to King Juba II of Numidia, who more than the daughter of Antonius wanted the last Ptolemaic princess as a bride. In her new home in Africa, Selene became a powerful queen, the mother of at least three children who lived to adulthood, and a formidable priestess and patron of Isis.

Marcus Vipsanius Agrippa became the right-hand man of the Emperor Augustus. He is known today not only for his military victories, but for building some of the most beautiful temples of the Augustan Age, including the incomparable Pantheon at Rome, dedicated to the worship of all the gods. He was married to Julia, the daughter and only child of Emperor Augustus, and through her was the grandfather of the Emperor Caligula and the great-grandfather of the Emperor Nero. However, all of his children but one died young, and most of them died by violence. It would take a far greater scope than this afterword to chronicle the murders, imprisonments, rapes, violent deaths in battle, and poisonings that afflicted his descendants. Agrippa himself died in his beloved Campania at the age of fifty-one. It has been suggested that he is the model for Virgil's hero Aeneas.

Cleopatra, Marcus Antonius, and her handmaidens were buried in Alexandria, in the tomb that had been prepared for them. Cleopatra's tomb has never been found. Perhaps even now it waits beneath the blue waters of the harbor of Alexandria.

PEOPLE, PLACES, AND THINGS

Abydos—a city in Upper Egypt known for its temples

Achillas, General—Ptolemy Theodorus' commander of the army

Adoratrice—the principal priestess of a temple, possibly the principal one of a deity

aeliopile—a curious device invented in Alexandria, essentially a steam-powered jet engine

Agrippa, Marcus Vipsanius—a Roman general born in Campania around 64 BCE. As a very young man he served with Caesar and became a good friend of Caesar's great-nephew Octavian, the future Emperor Augustus. His military contributions were indispensable to Octavian's rise to power, and his victory over Marcus Antonius at the Battle of Actium is viewed as one of history's turning points. Later he married Octavian's daughter Julia, and was the grandfather of the Emperor Caligula and the great-grandfather of the Emperor Nero. He is also known for the many temples he built, including Rome's Pantheon. He died in 12 BCE.

ala—a cavalry unit, consisting of 400 to 600 men (depending on actual strength)

Alexander the Great—King of Macedon, ruling from 336 BCE to 323 BCE. He conquered the Persian Empire, and thus gained control of Egypt, which had been occupied by the Persians. Viewed as a liberator by the Egyptians, he was crowned as Pharaoh, but did not remain in Egypt more than a few months. He was buried in a fantastic mausoleum in Alexandria, known as the Soma.

Alexander Helios—son of Cleopatra and Marcus Antonius, twin of Cleopatra Selene. He was born in 40 BCE, and died sometime before 24 BCE. It was suspected that he was poisoned.

Alexandria—a city on the Mediterranean coast of Egypt, founded by Alexander the Great. In the Hellenistic period, it was the largest city in the world, home to the greatest library of ancient times, and the seat of the Ptolemaic dynasty.

Amenti—the Egyptian name for the lands of the dead, also called the Uttermost West

Amonis—a young doctor from Philae

Antonius, Marcus—Roman general born in 83 BCE. He was Caesar's loyal supporter until his death, and afterward made common cause with Octavian and Lepidus to form the Second Triumvirate, an alliance that was strengthened by his marriage to Octavian's sister. He committed suicide in 30 BCE after losing the war with Octavian.

Antyllus, Marcus Antonius—the oldest son of Marcus Antonius and Fulvia, born in 47 BCE and executed in 30 BCE by Octavian

Aphrodite Cythera—Greek goddess of the sea and of love

Apollodorus—Cleopatra's tutor and later Major Domo

Archisomatophylax—an ennobling title given by the Hellenistic monarchs, literally "arch-bodyguard," something like a knighthood today

Aristogeiton—Athenian tyrannicide, renowned for assassinating the tyrant Hipparchus with his lover Harmodios

Arsinoe—Ptolemy Auletes' youngest daughter, Cleopatra's half-sister

Asetnefer—palace slave and former concubine of Ptolemy Auletes, originally from Elephantine in Upper Egypt, and the mother of Iras. Her name means "beauty of Isis."

Ashkelon—modern-day Migdal Ashkelon on the southern coast of Israel. In the Hellenistic period, it was alternately an Egyptian or Judean city.

augur—a priest who reads the omens by watching the flight of birds

Aurelianus, Emrys—officer in Caesar's Gaulish cavalry. He was originally from the coast of Aremorica, in what is modern-day Brittany, where his family had a sheep farm near the seashore. Ethnically, he is a Briton and his native language is Brythonic, a language closely related to modern Welsh.

automata—machines that are designed to imitate life, such as birds that flap their wings or sing, metal soldiers that move their swords or seem to march, etc. Powered ingeniously by steam, counterweights, gears, and clockwork, we would call them robots.

Babylon—ancient city in modern Iraq, once one of the principal cities of the Persian Empire, and in the late Hellenistic period one of the principal cities of the Parthians

Bastet—cat goddess, protector of children and mothers. Her sanctuary at Bubastis was one of her principal places of worship.

Berenice IV—second daughter of Ptolemy Auletes and the one who usurped his throne

Berytus—modern Beirut, on the Lebanese coast

Brutus, Marcus Junius—Roman Senator, born in 85 BCE. He was one of the leading conspirators in the plot to assassinate Caesar, and committed suicide after being defeated by Marcus Antonius at the Second Battle of Philippi in 42 BCE.

Bubastis—ancient city in the Nile Delta, sacred to Bastet

Caesar, Gaius Julius—Roman general born in 100 BCE. He expanded Roman territory throughout continental Europe, adding territories that would later become France, Switzerland, Belgium, Holland, and parts of Germany. A member of the First Triumvirate with Pompeius Magnus, their falling-out plunged Rome into civil war. He became Dictator for life after Pompeius' death, and was assassinated in 44 BCE.

Campania—Roman province south of Rome, in the area of modern-day Naples. The famous ruins of Pompeii are in Campania.

Cassius (Gaius Cassius Longinus)—Roman Senator, born 85 BCE, who was instrumental in the plot to assassinate Caesar. He was killed at the First Battle of Philippi in 42 BCE.

Charmian—daughter of Ptolemy Auletes and Phoebe the Thracian, the half-sister of Cleopatra

Cleopatra VII Philopater—The last ruling Pharaoh of Egypt, daughter of Ptolemy XII Auletes, ruling from 51 BCE to 30 BCE, she is Egypt's most legendary queen.

Cleopatra Selene—the daughter of Cleopatra and Marcus Antonius, lived 40 BCE to 6 BCE. In 25 BCE she married King Juba II of Numidia, and reigned as Queen of Numidia for the rest of her life. Her surviving children included Cleopatra, Ptolemy, and Drusilla.

couches—In the Hellenistic period, as in classical Greece and Rome, proper diners did not sit in chairs to eat, but reclined on couches something like a modern porch lounger. A dining couch had cushions and pillows, and was shared by one to three diners, who ate from a small table pulled up beside the couch.

Danuvius River—the Danube

decurion—cavalry officer in charge of a turma, about 30 men

Demetria—daughter of Charmian and Marcus Agrippa

Dion—Jewish scholar, scientist, astronomer, and magician of Alexandria, Charmian's closest friend

Dionysos—God of wine and the wild, Dionysos was originally a sacrificial agriculture god who later became the god of divine ecstasy, prophecy, sensuality, and hidden knowledge.

Epona—Keltic goddess of horses

erastes—the older of a pair of male lovers in the Hellenistic period; the lover rather than the beloved

eromenos—the younger of a pair of male lovers in the Hellenistic period; the beloved

Fulvia Flacca Bambula—Born in 77 BCE, her third husband was Marcus Antonius, whose political career she supported, even to the extent of leading an army against Octavian during the breakdown of the Second Triumvirate. Her sons by Antonius were Antyllus and Iullus, and she also had a daughter by her first marriage, Clodia. She died of illness in 40 BCE.

Gabinius, Aulus—Roman general, follower of Pompeius Magnus

Ganymede—Arsinoe's tutor and lover

Great Wife of Amon—the chief priestess of Amon in Thebes, traditionally a woman of noble or royal birth who becomes the celibate wife of the god and the administrator of all the properties of the Temples of Amon

Hermes Trismegistus—legendary sage of Alexandria, who was said to be the father of Hermetic philosophy and magic

Herod the Great—King of Judea for 34 years, he was originally an ally of Marcus Antonius who went over to Octavian's side and was rewarded lavishly. He is known to many modern readers as the King Herod in the Bible who ordered the deaths of all of the baby boys in Bethlehem in an attempt to kill the infant Jesus.

hetaira—a courtesan, literally a "companion." Hetairae were distinguished from common prostitutes by their education and refinement, and were prized for their ability to entertain in nonsexual ways with music and conversation. Some hetairae kept salons and were known for the scientists, philosophers, and political leaders who frequented their houses. Like modern geisha, hetairae were a status symbol for men in the Hellenistic period.

himation—an outer wrap worn by women in the Hellenistic period. There were many different styles, from a full-length wrap to what we might call a head scarf, and many different weights of cloth, from wool intended to keep the wearer warm to sheer fabrics that were more like veils.

Histria—the modern-day town of Istria in Romania, on the Black Sea coast

Horologers—priests who had charge of the calendar and of astronomical observations

Horus (Harpocrates)—hawk-headed god of sovereignty, son of Isis and Osiris (or Serapis)

Iras—Charmian and Cleopatra's half-sister, daughter of Ptolemy Auletes and Asetnefer

Isis—Originally an Egyptian mother goddess, by the Hellenistic period Isis had become a universal goddess of compassion with many aspects, including but not limited to the Queen of the Dead, the Mother of the World, the Queen of the Seas (Isis Pelagia), and the Goddess of Love.

Jerusalem—capital of Judea, an ancient city that was the site of the holy Temple of the Jews

Judea—the ancient kingdom of the Jews, now a Roman province covering roughly the same territory as modern-day Israel

Koine—the dialect of Greek spoken by ordinary people throughout the Successor Kingdoms during the Hellenistic period

krater—a large bowl for mixing wine, made of pottery, stone, or precious metal; a Hellenistic punchbowl

Lake Mareotis—the large, brackish lake behind Alexandria

Lucan—a student in Pneumatics at the Museum, Charmian's first lover

Lupercalia—Roman fertility festival on February 15. Some suggest that St. Valentine's Day was arranged to Christianize the Lupercalia.

Mareotic Canal—the canal between Lake Mareotis and the Nile

Maro, Publius Vergilius—Poet from the city of Neapolis in Campania, where he met Marcus Agrippa, he is better known as the poet Virgil, author of the *Aeneid*.

Memnon—the Hierophant of Serapis in Memphis, the chief priest of the God of the Dead

Memphis—Once the principal city of Egypt, in the Hellenistic period it was still a large city at the base of the Delta, near modern Cairo.

Mikhael—an angel of the Jewish god, once a warrior of Baal named Mik-el

Mount Vesuvius—an active volcano near modern Naples. Less than a century after Charmian's visit it erupted, burying the towns of Pompeii, Herculaneum, and Stabiae and killing thousands of people.

Mucilla—Sigismund's wife, a tavern keeper in the Subura

Nectanebo II—the last Pharaoh of Egypt before the Persian occupation; reigned 360 BCE–343 BCE

Nero, Tiberius—Caesar's Chief-of-Staff during his Egyptian campaign, later the father of the Roman emperor Tiberius

Octavia Thurina Minor—Caesar's great-niece, Octavian's sister. Born in 69 BCE, she was married first to a Senator, Gaius Claudius Marcellus, by whom she had two daughters and a son, Marcellus. After his death she married Marcus Antonius, by whom she had two daughters, both named Antonia. She was known as an exceptionally kind person, notably standing up to her brother and becoming guardian of Antonius' and Cleopatra's children, Selene, Helios, and Philadelphos, after they marched in Octavian's Triumph. She died in 11 BCE.

Octavian (Gaius Octavius Thurinus, Emperor Augustus)—Caesar's great-nephew. Born in 63 BCE, he ultimately became the first Roman Emperor, and is best known to history as Augustus. With Antonius and Lepidus he was a member of the Second Triumvirate, and ruled alone after Antonius' death. He died in 14 CE.

Osirion—mysterious temple in Abydos dedicated to Osiris

Osiris—Egyptian God of the Dead and Lord of the Underworld, in the Hellenistic period conflated with Serapis

Parthia—a kingdom encompassing large parts of what is now Iraq, Turkey, and Iran, sometimes in alliance with the Successor Kingdoms, sometimes in opposition

Patriarch of Alexandria—the rabbi of the chief synagogue of Alexandria

Pelousion—port city on the easternmost branch of the Nile, near modern-day Port Said. In Hellenistic times it was strongly fortified.

Pharos—the Lighthouse of Alexandria, one of the wonders of the ancient world

philhellene—"lover of Greece," a person who admires or adopts Hellenistic culture

Phoebe the Thracian—Charmian's mother, bought as a slave in Histria on the Black Sea by Ptolemy Auletes' agent because of her blond prettiness. She was originally from Vindobona, near modern-day Vienna.

Pollio, Ansinius—Roman general, born in 75 BCE. He served with Caesar in Gaul and Hispania, and then supported the Triumvirs against the Conspirators. He refused to join Octavian and Agrippa at Actium, saying that he would not fight against Antonius, a stand that ended his military career. He then took charge of many of the books that had been looted from Alexandria and with them started Rome's first public library. He also became the patron of Virgil before the Emperor Augustus did, and was a critic of the *Aeneid* as a work in progress. He died in 4 CE.

Pompeius Gnaeus—Oldest son of Pompeius Magnus, he proved to be of little worth as a general. Ultimately defeated by Caesar.

Pompeius Magnus (Pompey the Great)—Roman general who became the First Man of Rome, dominating Roman politics for a generation. Father of Gnaeus and Sextus Pompeius by his first wife, he later married Caesar's daughter, Julia. Champion of the Senate in first part of the Roman Civil Wars.

Postumus, Rabirius—Roman banker, a client of Pompeius Magnus

Pothinus—chief counselor to Ptolemy Theodorus

Praaspa—a Parthian city, now in northwest Iran

praefectus—military rank, the commander of a cavalry ala

Ptolemy Auletes (Ptolemy XII)—Cleopatra's father, who ruled Egypt from 80 BCE to 51 BCE. In their lifetimes, the Ptolemies were not known by number, but by epithet. Auletes means the "flute player," either because he was known as a young man for playing that instrument, or possibly because his round cheeks looked like a blowing flutist. The son of

Ptolemy X, he was married first to his half-sister, Tryphaena, and later to a second queen.

Ptolemy Caesarion (Ptolemy XIV) — Son of Cleopatra and Julius Caesar, he ruled as Pharaoh jointly with his mother from 44 BCE to 30 BCE.

Ptolemy Philadelphos (Ptolemy II) — Son of Ptolemy I and the second Pharaoh of the dynasty, he reigned from 285 BCE to 246 BCE. He is credited with building Pharos, the Lighthouse of Alexandria, one of the wonders of the ancient world.

Ptolemy Philadelphos — son of Cleopatra and Marcus Antonius. He was born in 36 BCE and died sometime before 20 BCE. It was suspected he was poisoned.

Ptolemy Soter (Ptolemy I, Son of Lagos) — the founder of the dynasty of the Ptolemies, ruling de facto from 323 BCE, officially from 305 BCE to 282 BCE. He was one of Alexander the Great's generals, and later became one of the greatest Pharaohs of Egypt.

Ptolemy Theodorus (Ptolemy XIII) — younger half-brother of Cleopatra, the oldest surviving son of Ptolemy Auletes

quinquereme — a galley with five banks of oars, usually a warship

Rhenus River — the Rhine

Royal Quarter — The section of Alexandria reserved for palaces and the dwellings of nobles, it also had a cemetery and its own dockyards.

Sais — city on the westernmost branch of the Nile

Saturnalia — the Roman winter solstice festival, celebrated December 17–23 with candles, gift-giving, and feasting

Sekhmet — Egyptian goddess of war, portrayed with the head of a lioness

Senate, Roman — the governing body of Rome, made up of 900 unelected wealthy and notable men who had been appointed to serve

Serapis — God of Harvest and of the Underworld, by the Hellenistic period Serapis had taken on many of the characteristics of Osiris, and is the husband of Isis.

Sheba — Charmian's cat brought back with her from Bubastis

Sigismund — German bodyguard of Caesar's, then of Marcus Antonius', originally from the area of modern Koln on the Rhine

Soma — Alexander's magnificent mausoleum in Alexandria. By the time of Cleopatra's reign, it was one of the best-known tourist destinations in the ancient world.

Spartacus—a gladiator and slave who led a slave revolt in Italy from 73 BCE to 71 BCE

spatha—the long, slightly curved sword used by cavalry Auxilliaries, longer than a gladius and intended for slashing instead of thrusting

Subura—slum neighborhood of Rome

Successor Kingdoms—Upon the death of Alexander the Great, his empire splintered into a number of Hellenistic states, called the Successor Kingdoms, of which Egypt is one.

Sulla (Lucius Cornelius Sulla Felix)—Roman dictator who lived from 138 BCE to 78 BCE, known for his ruthlessness and Machiavellian politics

Theocritus—tutor of Ptolemy Theodorus

Thoth—Egyptian God of Learning, seen as an ibis

tribune—Roman military rank given to men of good family, the lowest rank of "commissioned officer"

Triumph—a Roman civil and military procession to honor a victorious general for defeat of an enemy

Tryphaena—Ptolemy Auletes' first wife, the mother of Cleopatra; also the name of Ptolemy Auletes' oldest daughter, born in 80 BCE

turma—the smallest cavalry unit, consisting of about 30 men

uraeus—the sacred serpent of Egypt, a rearing cobra worn on the front of the crown or sometimes alone on a circlet

Vercingetorix—Gaulish tribal leader who led the most successful resistance to Rome in Gaul. He was defeated at the Battle of Alesia and executed following Caesar's Gallic Triumph.

FOR FURTHER READING

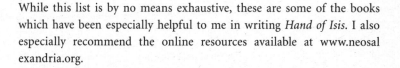

While this list is by no means exhaustive, these are some of the books which have been especially helpful to me in writing *Hand of Isis*. I also especially recommend the online resources available at www.neosal exandria.org.

Adkins, Lesley, and Roy A. Adkins. *Handbook to Life in Ancient Rome*. Oxford, UK: Oxford University Press, 1994.

Chaveau, Michel. *Egypt in the Age of Cleopatra*. Paris: Hachette, 1997.

Cullen, John T. *A Walk in Ancient Rome*. New York: Simon & Schuster, 2005.

Dando-Collins, Stephen. *Cleopatra's Kidnappers*. New York: John Wiley and Sons, 2006.

———. *Mark Antony's Heroes*. New York: John Wiley and Sons, 2007.

Goddio, Franck, et al. *Alexandria: the Submerged Royal Quarter*. London: Periplus Ltd., 1998.

Grant, Michael. *Cleopatra*. New York: Barnes and Noble Books, 1995.

———. *From Alexander to Cleopatra: The Hellenistic World*. New York: Charles Scribner's Sons, 1982.

Hughes-Hallett, Lucy. *Cleopatra: Histories, Dreams and Distortions*. London: Bloomsbury Publishing, 1990.

Kaufman, Cathy. *Cooking in Ancient Civilizations*. London: Greenwood Press, 2006.

Pollard, Justin, and Howard Reid. *The Rise and Fall of Alexandria, Birthplace of the Modern Mind*. New York: Viking, 2006.

Saunders, Nicholas J. *Alexander's Tomb*. New York: Basic Books, 2006.

Sauneron, Serge. *The Priests of Ancient Egypt*. Ithaca, NY: Cornell University Press, 2000.

Weeks, Kent R. *Valley of the Kings*. Vercelli, Italy: White Star SRL, 2001.

Witt, R. E. *Isis in the Ancient World*. Ithaca, NY: Cornell University Press, 1997.

ACKN⦿WLEDGMENTS

Hand of Isis began with a challenge. In 2005, Tanja Kinkel challenged me to write a scene for her with Gaius Julius Caesar. This was quite a tall order, but the result was the scene in which Charmian confronts Caesar on the balcony while they are all his prisoners in Alexandria, when she is trying to find out what he wants. Tanja liked the scene quite a lot, and said something on the order of "There's your next book!" Indeed it was, and I am deeply grateful to her for both the challenge and the encouragement!

There are many others without whom *Hand of Isis* would not have been written. I am especially grateful to Anne-Elisabeth Moutet, who amused me in the darkest moments with a great many crocodiles, and to Victoria Cahn, who did an amazingly fast continuity read-through when I no longer was certain what my own name was! I also would like to thank those who provided wonderful feedback and suggestions in the writing process: Lesley Arnold, Rachael Baylis, Gretchen Brinkerhoff, Katy Catlin, Mary Day, Danielle D'Onofrio, Phoebe Duncan, Claudia Gray, Mara Greengrass, Imogen Hardy, Courtney Jenkins, Nathan Jensen, Ann Kassos, Anna Kiwiel, Sharon Klug, Gretchen Lang, Wanda Lybarger, Gabrielle Lyons, Kathryn McCulley, Erin Simonich, Lena Strid, Jeff Tan, Casimira Walker-Smith, and Robert Waters.

I am also tremendously grateful to my editor, Devi Pillai, who was endlessly patient with my foibles, and my wonderful agent, Robin Rue.

I do not have words enough to express my appreciation to my partner, Amy, who managed to survive the writing of this book with grace and humor!

extras

orbit

www.orbitbooks.net

about the author

Jo Graham lives in Maryland with her family and has worked in politics for many years.

Find out more about Jo Graham and other Orbit authors by registering for the free monthly newsletter at www.orbitbooks.net

interview

What is it that interested you in this period? Why did you decide to write a book set in the court of Cleopatra?

I admit I'm kind of warped on the subject! The 1960 movie *Cleopatra* is the first grown-up movie I remember seeing—on broadcast television with all the "good" parts taken out—when I was five. I was absolutely blown away, completely entranced! I wanted to go live there, and I started playing Egypt right away with my stuffed animals and my little sister. We had a stuffed raccoon we said was Mark Antony and another who was Julius Caesar. Ptolemy was a duck. Cleopatra was a somewhat stout koala bear, for reasons I can't imagine. Octavian was a lean and hungry calico rabbit. So I've been obsessed with this period for a long time!

Even at the time, though, I remember thinking, "There are bits in the movie that aren't quite right. There are things I'd do differently. The whole scene when Cleopatra is leaving Rome isn't scary enough. And Mark Antony can't be there..." So quite some years later I had to have a stab at the story myself.

How long did it take you to write Hand of Isis?

Nine months. I really started in September 2007 and finished in June 2008, though I had begun the research about three months before that.

Do you find that real-life events are reflected in your books at all?

Not intentionally, in the sense of writing allegory. However, because my books are based on actual historical events there are often things that have remained constant or that continue to be true. For example, Marcus Antonius had a terrible time trying to conquer Parthia—and I think we can see from recent events in Iraq that it hasn't gotten any easier to control that same territory. It was a difficult thing to do two thousand years ago, and it remains a difficult thing.

Do you use any of your personal experiences in Hand of Isis?

Very much so! I worked in politics for fifteen years, principally in advocacy and event planning, and there is certainly a lot of what I learned evident in Charmian's job! One of the things I initially thought fascinating about her as a character was her job—being personal assistant to a female head of state would be an amazing job to have, and to do events that were so memorable that everyone wrote about them and that their descriptions have a fabulous Hollywood feel to them two thousand years later—Charmian is like the patron saint of event planners! And because I know how to do it, I can see all of the work and tremendous creativity that must have gone into producing those kinds of events. I have amazing respect for it.

Why did you decide on Charmian as a narrator?

I very much wanted to tell the Egyptian side of the story. All of the original sources, every single one, were written by Cleopatra's enemies. And even so she fascinates. I wanted to dig down and find her side of the story, told by a very partisan narrator, her sister.

One of your themes seems to be sacrifice. Could you elaborate on that a little?

Modern people are very uncomfortable with sacrifice. We view it as something negative most of the time. I think we've lost sight of the necessity for some people to give—not their lives, necessarily—but their time, their energy, and to give up what they want for the greater good. That's something that does come up again and again in this book. Good people cannot always do what they want, because they have responsibilities, because there are consequences.

There are going to be people who blink at Charmian having a ménage à trois with Emrys and Dion. Why did you decide to do it this way?

I think we have the misperception that our idea of the nuclear family, based on the romantic relationship between husband and wife, is in some way universal, or has always been the only way families worked. We disregard the many cultures around the world where most people live in extended families; we disregard the modern nations that practice polygamy; and we disregard the trend in the First World for more and more people to remain unmarried. We also have forgotten that in the very recent past, in the last two hundred years, we've completely changed the character of marriage from something lifelong and irreversible based on an economic contract between families to a possibly temporary romantic relationship between two people.

In Charmian's time, when most marriages were arranged for economic reasons, men were not expected to be in love with their wives and certainly not expected to be physically faithful. The Stoics were pretty much alone in saying that men should be celibate outside of marriage! Many men, like Emrys, had a wife and a lover both. The thing that's a bit unusual about it is that Dion is very much taking on the role of the wife and Charmian that of the lover!

I think it takes some putting one's head around that bisexuality is the male norm. Men are expected to like sex—with a partner of either gender. Dion is a little strange because he doesn't sleep with women at all.

Do you have a soundtrack for this book? Are there songs that inspire you?

Absolutely! I think the song that encapsulates Charmian the best is Loreena McKennitt's "Beneath a Phrygian Sky." I have listened to that song over and over again, and I hear Charmian every time.

Another song I've listened to over and over for inspiration is Elton John's "Candle in the Wind 1997," the version he did for Princess Diana. I think the adulation, fascination, and grief for Princess Diana is the closest modern analogy to what people must have felt for Cleopatra—everyone's daughter, mother, and fantasy, with crowds screaming her name as she worked the ropeline as though she were the avatar of a goddess. England's Rose, Elton John calls her. And Diana was felt around the globe. I was recently in the state motor vehicles office waiting in line, and "Candle in the Wind 1997" came on the radio. The woman behind me, an older woman who certainly wasn't English, started sniffling. I caught her eye sympathetically and she said, "She was something special, wasn't she? And she loved those boys of hers. It's a cruel thing to lose her, cruel for everybody." That's how people must have felt about Cleopatra. That's how the legend began. Like Princess Diana, Cleopatra must have touched people's hearts. Which is a difficult thing to write, but the song gave me a touchstone.

Did you have any issues unique to the time or place that made Hand of Isis *harder to write?*

I think one of my main problems, one that I struggled with constantly, was linguistic. Koine Greek is a very rich language, and often there are words for which there is no English equivalent. For example, we use the word "love" to mean a variety of things—the love of a mother for a child, the love between friends, the love between student and teacher, the love between lovers, and the love of mankind. In Koine they're all different words. For example, when Charmian is talking about how she feels about Emrys and Dion, in English the word is "love." But what she'd actually be saying is two different words: "eros" for Emrys, whom she loves as a romantic partner, and "philia" for Dion, whom she loves as a brother. It would be very clear what she meant. And I wound up tied in knots like that all of the time.

Who is your favorite character in Hand of Isis?

I love them all dearly, but I admit that Dion holds a special place in my heart. I do adore him. I felt that Ashterah got a bad deal in *Black Ships,* and so it was good to give Dion room to grow and have an interesting life. And I just had to give him credit for the self-propelled scenery! Hero of Alexandria is officially the inventor, a generation later, but I think it was really Dion!

One of the fascinating things in Hand of Isis *is the technology. How much of it is real?*

All of it! One of the amazing things about Alexandria in this period is how very modern it is. If the pace of learning and technological growth had continued, it's possible that Dion may have been right that they could have gone to the moon in a few centuries. There was a working model of a steamship, only in Egypt wood was so expensive that it was pointless to build one. The Antikythera Device was an analog computer that worked on gears and clockwork! Crude oil was already being refined into naptha, which today is best known as camp stove fuel. The aeliopile was a steam-powered jet engine. It is quite possible that if the Ptolemaic Dynasty had not fallen, and the Library and Museum had continued to be the first top-notch research facility in the world, that the year 500 CE would have seen telescopes and atmospheric flight rather than the decline of civilization into the Dark Ages.

What's next for you?

I'm going back to the founding of Alexandria next — to the death of Alexander the Great and the first years of Ptolemaic Egypt. Want to come along?

reading group guide

1. The focus of *Hand of Isis* is the relationship between Cleopatra, Iras, and Charmian. What do you think of the relationship between the sisters? All three women represent an aspect of Isis — what do you think this says about them? What does this say about the roles available to women in their society and today?

2. Do you think that Caesar's conquest of Egypt was necessary? Inevitable? Reversible? What is the best outcome that Cleopatra could have achieved?

3. Both Egypt and Rome are slave-owning societies, and Charmian is herself a slave. What are the differences between slavery in Egypt and Rome? How does it shape the states?

4. Charmian is very aware of her society's double standard about men and women's sexual behavior. Do you think there is still a double standard today? How is it the same or different than in Charmian's time?

5. Charmian is Gull reincarnate, and Agrippa is Neas reincarnate. What about these two that made them such staunch allies in *Black Ships* helps them become enemies in *Hand of Isis*?

6. Cleopatra is a woman Pharaoh — what impact does that have on her ability to deal with Rome both positively and negatively, through marriage alliances, etc.? Does it make Egypt's relations with Rome easier or harder? Would she have been more or less successful as a man?

7. At times Charmian muses on the life she would have had if she had been a man. What do you think her role would have been?

8. Charmian's relationships with her sisters are in many ways more central to her life than her relationships with men. How is this similar or different to your own experiences?

9. Faith and science are both important to several characters in the book. How do Charmian and Dion reconcile the two in their lives? Is that reconciliation harmonious? How do we deal with this issue today?

10. Is Marcus Agrippa a hero or a villain? He ends the book full of regrets. What do you see as his big mistakes?

if you enjoyed

HAND OF ISIS

look out for

STEALING FIRE

by

Jo Graham

The King was dead. Alexander lay in Babylon, in the palace of the Persian kings, upon the bed where he had died and I killed a man across his body for no reason that made any sense.

The melee had come even here, to the death chamber.

"To me! To me!" shouted Perdiccas, his head bare and his face shining with sweat. He claimed he was the heir, that Alexander had pressed his ring into his hand.

Others said it was meant for Krateros, who was not here.

And there were other claimants, of course. His body was not cold.

I took a step back, the blood running down the channels of the blade as I shifted into guard, rivulets of warmth across my knuckles. The King's legs were bare below his chiton. If he had been decently covered, the cloth had slipped in the fighting. One drop fell from my blade and glistened on a golden hair.

The young eunuch had fallen across his torso and face, shielding him with his own dead body. At least I presumed he was dead. He was still as death, his back bared to the swords about the bier.

"Push them back!" Perdiccas screamed. It seemed he was winning.

I stood, sword in hand, above the bier. No one came near. I had no reason to attack anyone.

A man went down, and Perdiccas and two others rushed the doorway. They pressed them out into the hall. I heard the dying man choking out his life, but I did not move. Who should I belong to? Perdiccas? He was well enough but had never given me a word. Krateros, who had laughed at men who married foreign women and called their sons bastard?

My master was already dead.

And so I stood above the bier, listening to my breath harsh in the close air.

Outside, the sounds of the fight were becoming distant. Perhaps Perdiccas had pushed them back to the receiving hall, or toward the bathhouse.

The lamp guttered. The fragrant oil was almost gone. Soon the stench of death would fill the room.

The young eunuch moved. I saw him breathing shallowly. Having no reason to kill him, I cleaned off my sword on the fallen cloth, stepped over the dying, and left the room.

I found Glaukos in the kitchen. He had three pots of wine before him, and an onion. The knives and food lay half prepared on the table. The servants had been preparing a meal when they were frightened away.

Glaukos looked up at me, and his eyes were red. "Come to kill me then?"

I sat down heavily on the bench. "Why should I do that, you drunkard? The world is in ruins, and you're at it again."

"You'd do best to try it," Glaukos advised. "No reason not to."

I poured a small amount into a clay cup and took a sip. It was good, strong Bactrian red, dark and rich, entirely unwatered. I expect it had been intended for the King's table.

"Elephants, he said," Glaukos said. "The King wanted elephants. I said there was no way I could get elephants. You could talk to him just like that. I said no elephants, and what was he asking me about them for, as I never had anything to do with elephants in my life. Glaukos, he said, I know you can get them for me." He refilled his cup, tears running down his face. "So elephants it was."

"I don't want to hear about your accursed elephants," I said.

"When I showed up with those four elephants on the banks of the river . . ."

"Shut up about the elephants!" I said, and knocked the cup from his hand. It broke in fragments across the floor, the red wine stain spreading.

Glaukos blinked at me. "That wasn't friendly," he said mildly. He got up with the slow, purposeful movements of a man who is already drunk, went over to a shelf on the wall, and turned, holding another cup.

I stalked out of the kitchen.

The hallway was silent. If the battle had passed this way, it was gone now. Aimlessly, I wandered the corridors. In the receiving hall, the golden ornaments were stripped from the throne, a little carved table lying on its side. I went down the corridor that led to the bathhouse.

"Halt! Who's there?" I heard a shout, and the more important sound of a bow being drawn.

I stopped. The voice was familiar. "Lydias of Miletus," I said.

"Ah." He stepped into the space between the bathhouse doors. I could see four or five men past him, some in their harness, in reasonable order. "Take your hand from your sword hilt," he directed.

I did. "Artashir," I said.

He was Companion cavalry, though he was armed with a bow. Persians learn archery very young, and I thought it wise not to doubt he could use it, when the point was aimed at my breast.

"Are you friend or foe?" he asked.

"Of whom?" I said.

Behind him the bathing pool was blue and clear. The King had spent most of his last days here.

"Of us," Artashir said, with only a slight hesitation. He was tall and angular, younger than I, with a closely trimmed beard in the Persian fashion.

"I am no enemy of yours," I said. Truth, I hardly knew the man. We had not been in the same units until after Gedrosia, and then I had not made friends.

"We are holding the bathhouse," he said.

"For whom?"

"For the King," he answered.

I laughed and even to myself sounded overwrought. "The King is dead. You will hold the bathhouse for all eternity, then."

Artashir straightened, his dark eyes suspiciously bright. "Then that is what we will do. We will wait for our orders, as Companions should."

"Wait and rot then," I said, and turned and walked away.

No arrow hit me in the back.

I could hear the battle sounds coming from the stable yard, but I had no desire to seek it out. My sword was too heavy in my hand, and the deserted palace too empty. In the anteroom to the receiving hall papers were spread, letters and dispatches, all the business of empire waiting for the King's hand. The lamps burned on in their fretted holders. In the courtyard beyond, the fountain played. I half expected it to be frozen, droplets suspended in midair. Surely the sun should not set, the droplets fall.

I wandered back to the kitchen, where Glaukos still was.

He looked up blearily from the table. "Come back, have you?"

I shrugged. "Nowhere better to go. Best to die with a friend, I suppose."

"That's the way," Glaukos said, moving over and pouring for me. Half the unwatered wine splashed out of the cup, his hands were that unsteady. "Always thought I would die with you."

I raised my cup in salute. "To death, my friend Glaukos. Death and an eternity amid the shades."

Glaukos raised his cup and looked at me over it, blinking. "You know, you've been a bit odd since Gedrosia, Lydias."

"You're calling me odd," I said. "Alexander is dead. Does it matter if I'm odd? We're going to be slaughtered in a foreign city, just like the Magi said. It's the dice. You roll enough and you lose." The wine was very, very good. It came to me that perhaps it had been meant for the King. Perhaps it was poisoned. There had been that tale about.

I looked into the dregs. Nothing to see. The flickering light made shapes on the surface, curled like an octopus in the bottom of the cup.

Glaukos touched my hand gently. "Drink up, my friend," he said.

I did. If it was poisoned, I was past caring.

I drank with him while the night came in through the windows, while the lamp sputtered and died. Silence settled over the palace. Glaukos talked on and on, making less sense. "Elephants," he whispered one last time, and lowered his head on his arms.

Poisoned, I thought. Of course.

From the far side of the room there was a rustle in the darkness. Two green eyes regarded me steadily. A great gray cat paced out of the shadows.

"Death," I whispered. I thought she spoke to me, words I didn't understand.

And night took me.

I woke to morning coming in through the window, and the loud annoying sound of Glaukos' snores. My head throbbed, and on the table were five-toed paw prints in red wine.

The King was still dead.

I was still alive.

BLACK SHIPS

Jo Graham

An extraordinary tale of a young woman who becomes an oracle — set in an age when an oracle held more power than a king

In a time of war and doubt, Gull is an oracle. Daughter of a slave taken from fallen Troy, chosen at the age of seven to be the voice of the Lady of the Dead, it is her destiny to counsel kings.

When nine black ships appear, captained by an exiled Trojan prince, Gull must decide between the life she has been destined for and the most perilous adventure — to join the remnant of her mother's people in their desperate flight. From the doomed bastions of the City of Pirates to the temples of Byblos, from the intrigues of the Egyptian court to the haunted caves beneath Mount Vesuvius, only Gull can guide Prince Aeneas on his quest, and only she can dare the gates of the Underworld itself to lead him to his destiny.

In the last shadowed days of the Age of Bronze, one woman dreams of the world beginning anew. This is her story.

"Haunting and bittersweet, lush and vivid, this extraordinary story has lived with me since I first read it." — Naomi Novik, author of *Her Majesty's Dragon*

Available wherever good books are sold

THE MAGICIAN'S APPRENTICE

Trudi Canavan

Set hundreds of years before the events of *The Magicians' Guild*, THE MAGICIAN'S APPRENTICE is the new novel set in the world of Trudi Canavan's Black Magician Trilogy.

In the remote village of Mandryn, Tessia serves as assistant to her father, the village Healer. Her mother would rather she found a husband. But her life is about to take a very unexpected turn.

When the advances of a visiting Sachakan mage get violent, Tessia unconsciously taps unknown reserves of magic to defend herself. Lord Dakon, the local magician, takes Tessia under his wing as an apprentice.

The hours are long and the work arduous, but soon an exciting new world opens up to her. There are fine clothes and servants — and, to Tessia's delight — regular trips to the great city of Imardin.

However, Tessia is about to discover that her magical gifts bring with them a great deal of responsibility. For a storm is approaching that threatens to tear her world apart.

orbit

Available wherever good books are sold